I0760866

CELIA

RUBY JEAN JENSEN

Gayle J. Foster

RUN FOR YOUR LIFE

Celia woke, twisting in terror in her bed, cold yet wet, like the swamp she could not escape.

She could smell the fetid odors of the swamp, and knew at last in inexpressible horror that it was not in the dream.

It was here, in the house somewhere. In the hall, in the room, concealed in the darkness.

She could hear something that wasn't caused by the wind. Something slid along wood, coiling along the banister rising from below, coming up the stairs. A stealthy movement. A constant movement, like a snake, a hundred snakes, writhing along an uncarpeted floor.

It was coming for her and her children.

Her bare feet silent on the polished pine floor, she whirled back to the beds where the children slept.

"Get Blair up, Jonie," she ordered. "Open the window over the porch. Climb down and run. Run as fast as you can!"

First printing: July, 1991 in the United States of America

Published by: Gayle J. Foster, Carrollton, Texas

Library of Congress Control Number: 2021905558

Cover art: SelfPubBookCovers.com/ FrinaArt

❀ Created with Vellum

PROLOGUE

To Celia, the body on the ground looked even larger in death than it had in life, huge in the thin light of the waxing moon. His arms seemed to be reaching toward her, though they hadn't moved in the long moments she had been staring down at him. All the sounds of the swamp seemed to have stopped. The frogs that had croaked in deep voices, the unseen creatures that had dimpled the dark water with soft plops, all silent now. Even the bull gator that had bellowed not far away had grown silent. There was only the ringing in her ears. The reverberations of the gunshots in her head.

I'll get you, Ceil. You kill me, I'll come back as your worst nightmare and I'll get you, and I'll get your brats. You can't kill me, Ceil. It just don't work that way. I'll get you... I'll get you, Ceil ... your worst nightmare ... me ... your worst ... nightmare.

Celia pressed both hands to her mouth to hold back her cry. Was the voice real or only part of the horror of the last two days? The memory of his threats?

She walked backward three steps and stopped again. His arms lay stretched above his head, extended toward her. His feet dropped out of sight into the black water of the swamp. His blood looked black in the moonlight, making thin rivulets into the water. Her own shadow stretched waveringly toward the creased knees of the large cypress tree.

She turned and ran, holding her nightgown up with one hand.

The house looked lonely, small, unpainted, in the expanse of unmowed grass between the edge of the swamp and the pine forest beyond. The barn in the pines was hidden, as hidden as once its contents had been.

She ran around the house and on toward the barn.

In the dark beneath the pines she found the small door on the side and went in. She could smell the dogs as if they were still here, the ghosts of all the dogs in all the small cages. There was a smell of fear and death, a horror she and the kids had never been able to clean away.

She knew where he kept the junk iron, the pieces of old pipes, rusty wrenches, anything he could use to weight the body of a dog when he threw it into the swamp. Now it was his turn.

Breathless, she felt in the dark, gathered up all she could carry, and ran back out into the ghostly silver light of the moon and stars.

She ran toward the old cypress tree, the largest tree on this north end of the Florida swamp.

When she reached the area where his body had lain she turned, whimpering beneath her breath. Where was he? Oh God, where was he? She turned again. He had risen, just as he said he would. He wasn't dead. Not Durk. He would never allow ...

She stumbled and looked down and saw the hand in the dark grass, fingers curled upward. He was still there after all.

Working feverishly, she wired the weights to his arms, to his belt, to his legs.

On her knees, her nightgown soaking up the damp that seeped through the earth from the swamp, she struggled to turn the body, to roll it toward the water.

I'll get you, Ceil ...

Tears filled her eyes and blinded her, and the trees of the swamp blurred into the dark of the still water. She was afraid of the swamp, afraid of everything. She didn't have the strength to roll his body there where he had drowned the dogs, where the swamp had become a world of countless graves.

Then he was moving. In a kind of horrible cooperation the body rolled on its own.

The dark water opened as if it opened a mouth, and then closed it softly.

Celia stood up.

She paused, then with her foot she nudged the small black handgun. The water made a soft plop as the gun disappeared.

The water turned as smooth and reflecting as a black mirror. Heavy shadows of the cypress trees floated on its surface like dead bodies. Celia stared at the water as she backed slowly away.

Something beneath the surface stirred.

CHAPTER 1

On the seventh night Celia's anxiety grew. She sensed a difference; the contrast between full moon and dark shadows was more extreme, the silence by the cypress tree more ominous.

Every night during the past week, after standing and looking into the swamp, watching for Durk to rise, Celia had gone back to the house and to the bedrooms of her sleeping children. One by one she checked on all three. Drew, so quiet always, still her baby at five. His round little face reposed in sleep was beginning to show a resemblance to his father. He was the only one of her children to have such pale blond hair and blue eyes, like Durk's. There was a squareness in his jaw, a roundness now that would strengthen to sharp bones and tight skin when he grew older. How could a father strike that small head until the child was unconscious? How could he lift that small body and throw him against the wall and turn away with no remorse, only his own strange sense of indignation, of hatred and fury that he had in some way been crossed. Because the child had fought to defend his puppy? Well, no more. It would happen no more. The bruises were fading now. But not the fear, never the fear.

She checked on Blair, who at nine had grown even more silent than Drew. He had learned it was better that way. The more silent you are, the less you are noticed. He had learned to walk as softly as a kitten when his father was around. What relief she had felt when he was born and she saw that he, like her firstborn, Jonie, had taken after her family, with their dark brown curls lying moistly on their small heads, and their dark eyes. They were like her father, and she was thankful. Yet when Drew was born, and she reached for his slippery little body and saw he was so much like Durk, it had only made her more protective of him. *God, don't let him be like Durk. God, make him gentle. Though he looks like Durk, and he can't help that, God please help his soul.* And Drew had cried for his puppy, and handled all little living creatures with such gentle care that she now wondered if God had made him too caring, too easily hurt.

But it was Jonie who had suffered most, though it was she who was clearly Durk's favorite. It was a partiality that worried Celia from the beginning. Only Jonie was asked to wait on him, to come near. "Call me Daddy," he had said to her when she cringed away, reluctant to call him anything, intense fear in her eyes. Celia saw him looking at Jonie with that smile Celia remembered when he had said the same thing to her. Celia knew the cringing within her daughter, she felt it, like a hand squeezing, pulling her skin tightly around her, pulling it in, as if she could hide within it. He had at last brought her a beautiful doll, the only gift he had ever given one of the children. The doll was eighteen inches tall, made of fine porcelain with real eyelashes and golden hair, dressed in pink antique satin and lace. It smiled beneath a pink hat with delicately fringed feathers. And Celia knew her protection of Jonie must increase.

They had no one but her. No one.

Even the law had failed them, when at last they had succeeded in running away. It was safe now, they had said, safe to go home. Back to the house on the northern edge of the swamp, the only place in the world for them. But nothing, no one, could make Durk leave them alone. He had come home in the silence of the night, like a thief sneaking into the house. But the law didn't know, and there was no way Celia could get away to let them know. Nor could she send a message. Durk had never allowed a telephone, and the house was more than a mile from the highway.

WHEN THE CHILDREN woke two days later to find their father gone, they hadn't asked where he was. It was not a question any of them would ever ask.

The nights were the bad times since then. During the day they could be together, going out to pick berries or walking to the mailbox to see if the mailman had left something. Such things as mailboxes delighted Drew. And Jonie read every catalog, every sales bill avidly.

Or they went out to look at the flowers that grew in the unmowed yard.

Some people might call them weeds, but to Celia and her children they were flowers. Drew picked a bouquet of dandelions every day and gave them to her, and they were more beautiful than the world's finest orchids.

But at night, as soon as the children were asleep, the uneasiness grew to a terrible intensity, as she felt again that same frantic urgency she had felt the night she carried the weights from the barn to his body at the edge of the swamp. Rest was not for her. She slipped out of bed, out of the dark house, and stood for long hours on the screened porch looking toward the swamp, looking toward the big bald cypress tree in the edge of the black water, seeing the grass beneath the light from the rising moon and the almost invisible path she had made between the porch and the water at the base of the tree.

Even from the porch it seemed she could see something moving beneath the water.

On the seventh night she left the porch, just as she had done every night during this past week, and went slowly along the path, her footsteps whispering in the long grass. The brightening moon cast a shadow twice her length ahead of her. The shadow of the big cypress tree became part of the swamp, a solid and impenetrable mass of darkness that left the water at its base as black and reflecting as the depths of a molten volcano. She slipped up on it silently and stopped, her bare toes feeling the dampness of the water-soaked earth beneath the grass.

The water in the swamp wasn't deep, Durk had told her. If she dared, she could wade through it for miles. But she knew he lied. He had tried to push her in, long ago, before the children came. "Try it," he'd say. "I grew up swimming in the swamp water, and I don't want a woman too chicken-shit scared to go in."

Here, near the bank of grass, the water was shoulder deep, and the ground beneath the water was soft, muddy sand. She knew, because once he had pushed her into it, and she had floundered, feeling something tangling round her legs, invisible in the dark water. He had finally put his hand down and helped her out, laughing at her screams. She knew it was deep here, shoulder deep. She had felt the slope of the watery bottom beneath her feet, and suspected there were holes hidden deep in the dark water. It should have made a safe and quiet burial place, even for a body as large as Durk's. Two hundred and forty pound? Six feet two.

Yet ... she couldn't be sure. During the day, in the light of the sun, she could tell herself, "It's okay. We're safe now." But at night she could hear the rise of the voice of the swamp everywhere but there—by the tree. Here it was silent. Where were the frogs that once had lived here? Where were the fish that used to break the surface with a soft, whispering plop?

She stood looking into the water, aware that something moved just beneath the surface, something silent and deadly, perhaps a gator, hunting ... searching for prey? Or the piranhas, swimming in schools, waiting. Or ... Durk's face, hidden by the water, his eyes open and looking at her, watching her. Durk coming back, as he had said he would, not as a man, but—

She stared, unable to step back.

The water opened, and a long, black snake-like appendage rose toward her, glistening in the moonlight with swamp slime, sliding into the grass, separating it, easing closer, its sound like the gliding of a snake, steady and almost inaudible. Then another and another, coming out of the water with only whispers of sound. But it was a sound she had heard before, in the darkest of her dreams, in the depths of nightmares. Sounds he had described to her as he held her in his arms early in their marriage. "It will come out of the swamp, Celia, at night. You must not leave the house when I'm gone. I can't protect you then. When I become this ... *thing*, I forget that once I was a man." And then he had laughed and laughed at the horror on her face, and said, "You're really a naive little thing, aren't you? You'd believe anything."

Celia stared, paralyzed in her fright, seeing it was real after all ... her nightmare ... just as he had told her it would be. It would rise above the water, like a huge aquatic spider, its dozen of legs as supple as arms, its round head bulging with eyes, and it would come after her, moving in slippery silence across the bare floors of the bedroom. After devouring her it would go after her children. Every night in her dreams she could hear the screams of her children.

Now she watched it rise above the water, one inch, five, ten, and saw the eyes reflecting the light of the moon. She heard the feelers slithering through the grass toward her. As she stood turned to stone in her fear, she felt the cold touch on her foot. In the water she saw the rise of the round, black, oily head, and the bulging eyes, staring, trapping her.

They had never left her, she knew now. Every time she had come to stand at the edge of the water, those open eyes had been watching her with the coldness and the steadiness of a reptile.

She felt the cold grasp sliding around her ankle and saw the black tentacles reaching through the weeds like a dozen black serpents, made of the black water, the swamp, the horrors of death, the terrors of her life here.

I'll get you, Ceil. I'll come back as your worst nightmare.

She felt its touch, and knew it was true.

Only then did she move. In silence, the scream of horror swollen and trapped in her throat, she struggled for her freedom. With her fingernails she pried the cold and slimy thing from her ankle, and felt its utter inhumanness, the deadliness.

Unable to scream her terror, her voice as silent as the thing that had risen from the dead, she ran, through the knee deep grass to the screened porch. Her children were in their beds, protected only by screens on windows, screens on doors.

As she paused to fasten the hook on the screen door she looked back across the expanse of moonlight.

It was coming, throwing many shadows, standing taller even than it had in her nightmares. Horrifying in the waning light of the moon, it was coming after her and her children, filling her with such fear that she moved at last without thought.

She ran through the uncarpeted house, her bare feet causing the old boards to creak. She gathered her children, Jonie first, so alone in her bedroom, then the boys. She jerked them awake without explanation. They didn't cry out, not even Drew. They had learned early to cry in silence. She felt Jonie pause. Moonlight touched the pink and white face of the doll, playing through the silk fronds of the feathers. She understood, even in her urgency. It was the only doll Jonie had ever owned. Celia reached for it and put it into Jonie's hands.

She pulled them through the kitchen at the back of the house and out to Durk's old car.

Had she really thought they could ever escape from him?

Oh God, Flint, where are you? she whispered in the silence of her mind, begging for the only creature who had ever dared defend her. But she knew where he was, his faithful body limp with death, a part of the swamp for a long time now. The chain that had killed him still strangling, holding, buried with him in the mud of the swamp.

She heard again the mocking laugh of Durk. You think your goddamned dog can save you from me, Ceil? Well, look at him now.

She pulled the car door shut, not trying to be quiet, to slip silently away so they wouldn't be heard. Her voice came startlingly loud, even to her own ears, as her hands pushed her children down.

"Get down! Stay down! Don't sit up until I tell you!"

She saw Jonie was no longer carrying the doll. It was lying on the ground in the moonlight. Jonie had dropped it. They couldn't take time to go back.

Celia pushed them down so they wouldn't see the horror that had risen from the dark water. Its shadows, thin and twining, yet enormous, stretched forward from somewhere at the back of the car and whipped across the hood as she ground the starter and pushed the accelerator to the floor.

The car roared and jerked forward, and she heard Drew's forehead strike something beneath the dash. She reached down briefly to touch him, to feel his smooth forehead for injury.

As she drove away she looked back once more. The house stood isolated, a hundred yards from the swamp, the shadow of it filled with the thing that had risen.

Then she thought she saw something else ... a fleeting glimpse of a sleek, wet body at the edge of the swamp.

And she thought she heard the rattle of Flint's chain.

JONIE LAY on the floor between the backseat and the front, feeling the swing of the car along the sandy lane that reached a mile from the house to the highway. With each jerking movement of the car her head bumped the door. On the seat above her lay Blair. In the dim light cast back from the dash, she saw his white hand gripping the edge of the seat.

She could sense her mother's fear, as tangible as ice coating her skin, as a strong odor that shocked the senses. She wanted to sit up and look, yet she stayed down. Above the seat she saw the top of her mother's head outlined by the lights on the dash. There was no sound beyond the roar of the engine as they raced along the winding, narrow road. Shadows of trees flitted by, like pages of a book being closed.

The car didn't stop at the highway but swung sharply to the right, throwing Jonie against the door. It speeded up, the transmission grinding through low to high speed before racing smoothly forward.

Jonie slowly sat up. She looked down upon her brother's face and saw the round, fearful eyes, the parted lips. He looked white as a ghost.

"It was him," he whispered. "He was coming back again, wasn't he?"

Jonie didn't answer.

She saw they were headed away from the town where they sometimes went for groceries. They were going east on the highway, and she knew only that it led to the interstate, to big cities, to the place they had gone the day Celia had dragged them to their dad's car the first time.

She still remembered her own fear that day, just over a month ago. *He*, their dad, lay sleeping on the couch. One arm and both long legs lolled off. On the floor beside his limp hand, lay an empty bottle. He was drunk, and Jonie and her brothers had moved cautiously in the house, making sure the doors didn't squeak when they went outside. The day before he had hurt Drew, and he had killed Flint, and they were afraid of him.

They had gone to play in the sand at the back of the house when they heard the door squeak. They looked up. Even now Jonie remembered the look on her mother's face, that pinched, white, half-dead mask, with only her eyes alive with something Jonie had never seen before. At that moment she was almost as afraid of her mother as of her dad.

"Come on," Celia whispered. She pulled Blair up by one arm, and reached down with her other arm and lifted Drew. Carrying him, she had gone to the car and opened the door, all the time looking over her shoulder toward the house.

Looking for Dad, Jonie knew. Always looking for Dad. She wished then, as she had wished since as far back as she could remember, that he would go away and never come back. But he was in the house, and they were getting into the car without him. She was afraid. They never went anywhere without their dad driving them. She didn't even know until that day that her mother could drive a car.

They had run away without anywhere to go. Not until they reached the highway and Celia turned the car to the right, toward the freeway, did Jonie realize what was going on.

They had driven and driven until they ran out of gas and the car sputtered to a stop at the side of the long, four-lane strip of pavement. Then they had stood in the hot sun and watched the large trucks go by, and Jonie could still feel the wind in her hair as they passed.

It was almost dark when the highway patrol car stopped.

A tall man got out of the car. He was wearing a hat that reminded her of the wide-brimmed hats men wore in old Westerns. His eyes were dark and quick, and looked from one to the other of them before he smiled. "Trouble?"

"Yes sir," Celia said, sounding as if she were talking to Durk. "We're out of gas."

"No problem," the patrolman said. "There's an exit about a mile north, and a service station down the ramp. You and the kids ride with me; we'll get you some gas.

Celia hesitated. None of them moved. Then she said, "I don't have any money."

The patrolman said nothing for a moment, then with one finger, his quick eyes taking them all in again one by one, he pushed his hat higher on his forehead. "Where you live, lady?"

Celia licked her lips and looked down at her feet. "We ... uh we ..."

A big truck roared past, and Jonie's hair whipped across her face, blinding her. She spun round with her back to the traffic. If Celia told the patrolman where they lived, Jonie didn't hear.

"Could I see your driver's license, please, ma'am?"

Celia lifted her head. "I don't have one."

There was a staring match, it seemed, in the brief silence as traffic thinned on the freeway. The patrolman looked at Celia for a long time. Jonie's heart beat heavily and slowly. She could feel it in her throat. She was afraid he was going to take them home, back to Durk. Durk would talk to him, act as if nothing was wrong, and then when the man was gone ...

Jonie trembled and hugged her arms against her chest, staring at the man, beseeching him not to send them back. "Why don't we run away?" she had asked her mother so many times in the past, but then Celia had only shaken her head. Jonie only partly understood. They could walk. They could hide in the woods where he would never find them.

The patrolman went around to the rear of the car and looked at the license plate. Then he went to the driver's door and opened it and looked in. He reached into the car and opened the glove compartment. Jonie heard it slam, a tinny sound. The man came back from the car. "Whose car is this?" he asked.

"My husband's," Celia answered, then suddenly she was talking so quickly Jonie missed part of her words. "If he finds us he'll kill us. I need help, sir, to get my children away from him. He was lying drunk when we left. I can't go back. I can't take my kids back. Please, I don't have any money, I don't have a license, but I can't go back."

The man pursed his lips and looked over their heads, squinting into the red sky where the sun had set. "Family?" he asked.

"No."

He looked at Celia again, eyes squinted. It was almost as if he doubted her word.

"None at all?"

"No, no family."

The patrolman took out a small notebook from his pocket and wrote something.

Then he began to question Celia again, but the cars were going by, and the trucks, and Jonie took both her brothers by their arms and pulled them farther away from the edge of traffic. She didn't hear what their mama told the policeman, but she saw him go to his car and talk into the radio. He stood with the door open as the night grew suddenly darker around them. When he came back she saw he wasn't angry with them after all.

"It's all right," Jonie heard him say to Celia. "We'll get you a place to stay."

For several weeks they stayed in town at a place where other women and children also lived. It was called a halfway house for battered women and children.

Jonie knew her mother had talked to a lot of people while they were in the halfway house, people who had something to do with the police, or with the people who ran the kind of houses they were living in. Shelters, some of the kids told her. They were called shelters. And one of the kids told her the shelter was built by God and his angels.

Jonie worried about her dogs, about all the dogs out in the barn in the cages. Would her dad feed them? Water them? No, he would not. Watering and feeding had been her job, and her brothers' and mother's. Then she learned that the law was taking the dogs away where they would be safe, and everything was going to be all right, because her mother was getting a divorce.

They were going home, because it was the only place they had to go. But their father was never allowed to come there anymore. So they were told.

It had seemed so strange, going home that day. Although they had been gone only about a month, the house looked different. Abandoned. Smaller. It stood in the yellowed grass like a funny square toadstool, all alone between the pines that dotted the area back toward the road, and the dark green of the cypress in the swamp.

It sounded different too. There was silence in the barn and sheds where the dogs were kept, but she had to go see for herself that all the cages were empty. Even her puppies were gone.

She stood in the still shadows of the barn and wept, her heart lonely for all the dogs and puppies that were no longer there. Although Dad had never let them stay very long, she had always grown to love each one, and she missed them. Even in her loneliness she was glad it was over. There would be no more little scared dogs, no more stolen pups ... That was what they said he did—stole them. He stole them from people's yards, from the street, from wherever he found them. He answered ads for dogs to give away free to good homes. He bought them from the pounds and from the animal shelters, and brought them here and kept them only until he sold them to the labs that needed dogs for experimentation.

They were gone, and though she missed them, she was glad.

She would never have to live with her dad again, because the lady lawyer who had come to talk to her mother had promised he would not bother them. They had a court order that he was to stay away from the house, from them.

Yet he came back and stayed for two days. Two terrible, horrible days and nights.

Then something happened. She had tried since then to remember, but each time she thought about that night she began to shake all over, and she had to stop thinking about it. It was as though something in her brain didn't want to know. It was like hundreds, thousands of nightmares all mixed up, jumbled, so there was no picture, just colors and feelings.

It was like the vague, strange light of the setting moon that was absorbed by the landscape outside the swiftly moving car, like all the unidentifiable shapes in the night.

She saw Drew's head over the front seat and heard his timid, half-whispered question. "Where are we going?"

She listened for the answer that didn't come.

Where *were* they going? she wondered too, the car lights reaching like two feeble hands into the darkness ahead of them.

Drew didn't ask again.

Beside her Blair sat up, and for the first time Jonie realized they were all wearing their nightclothes. They were running away again, taking nothing, with nowhere to go, and Jonie didn't understand. In the reddish light of the dash she saw the white shoulder straps of Celia's nightgown.

Jonie turned and looked out the rear window. Darkness swallowed the world behind them.

This time, when they ran out of gas, she prayed her mother would keep going, on and-on. They could walk. They could hide.

They could never go back.

CHAPTER 2

THE SOUND of an ax splitting wood rang through the Georgia pines, a comfort to Mel's ears. There was a special sound to a block of wood splitting. The feel of the ax against the solid grain of wood, jolting through the muscles of his back, his shoulders, his arms, released most of the tensions that had built up in him during the past week. He had spent the past eight days and some of the nights driving, carrying with him the most precious cargo in the world, a mother and her children, trying to get them to a place where they would be safe from a husband and father who wanted to hurt them, at best. Away from a judicial system that couldn't protect them.

If anyone had told him, eighteen years ago, when, at the age of twenty-one, he had joined law enforcement, that one day he would be operating on the opposite side of the law, he would have slugged them, or wanted to. Him, a lawbreaker? No. At that time it wasn't conceivable.

He had arrived home at midnight and had thrown himself across the bed still fully dressed. He hadn't awakened until almost noon. He had drifted awake to the sound of frogs in the pond, birds in the trees, and Cress scratching on the back door for attention. And for just a moment, before memories set in, he had felt a sense of peace, of coming home where everything was right and good.

After getting up, stretching, going out to see his dogs, and seeing that their automatic feeder still had plenty of dry food and the waterer was full, he stood on the back step of his house, looked at the pines that surrounded the two acres he had cleared for house, garden and pond, and gave thanks for his ten acres of privacy.

Peace. The only place on earth that held that special meaning for him.

And yet ... there were the memories. The little faces that collected like ghosts in front of his eyes when they were closed, even when he stood looking at the beauty of his ten Georgia acres, the pines, the clear water in the pond, the flowers, the grass.

He wished everyone could have as much. Especially those little kids who cowered when you looked at them, and the wives who couldn't smile, who still bore the scars of unhappy marriages, and perhaps always would.

There was the memory of his own young daughter after she had taken an overdose of drugs, the note clutched so tightly in her hand her fingers had to be pried open.

"I'm sorry, Daddy."

Her last message to him. He who had failed her after all.

And the faces of the two adults who were responsible. Her mother and her stepfather. A man he wanted to kill but could not. A man the law hadn't been able to touch.

Using an ax to split wood for his heating stove was one of the best ways to keep his mind busy, to keep from thinking about the past, about the fact that he had been unable to help his daughter.

He paused, and used a handkerchief from his hip pocket to wipe the sweat from his forehead and cheekbones. A short beard covered his chin and lower face. There were times when he wouldn't have a chance to shave for two days, three, sometimes more, and with the kind of black, rapid growth he had, the beard was the wisest way to go. Another thing about a beard and mustache was identification. Bearded men tended to look more alike. They were harder to identify.

He sat down on the chopping block, and his two dogs came up to have their ears scratched. One of them was a black and white hound mix, the other was smaller, with a touch of cocker spaniel maybe, and some beagle, maybe even German shepherd or Chihuahua, to explain its pert, pointed ears.

"Hi, guys, did you get lonely? Sorry. Elvin treat you okay? Did he come to see you while I was gone?"

Of course Elvin Cross treated them good, and he knew that sometimes when he was gone longer than he expected to be, the dogs would go over to Elvin's place and lie around while they waited. Elvin, a widower in his sixties, would walk the path that joined the two places, bringing the dogs home to be fed so they wouldn't forget where they lived.

Elvin picked up his mail twice a week and put it on his living room couch. He also kept a loose eye on his place, seeing that the feeders were full, the doors and windows locked. In fact, it wasn't really necessary here, where no one ever bothered anything, where houses were separated by several acres of pine woods or cleared, cultivated fields, where everyone minded his and her own business.

Mel scratched the perky ears of the little female dog he had picked up off the highway almost five years ago. Cress, he had named her, after Crescent, his daughter. The best he could do for Crescent now was to make sure that her namesake had a good home, a safe place.

Crescent would like that, he thought. And for just an instant he felt her presence, as if she stood near him, smiling, the way she used to, a slender little girl with dark brown eyes and a dimple in her left cheek.

Cress sat with her chin on Mel's knee and turned her eyes sideways to watch Butch, the other dog, take off after a rabbit. The rabbit had a good start.

"Don't worry, Cress, Butch never caught a rabbit in his life. He probably wouldn't know what to do if he did. He's too fat to think about eating it."

The land sloped slightly down to the edge of the water in the pond. The ducks swam toward the bank, seeing Mel at rest. He got up and went to check out their feeder. It too was automatic, like the dog feeders, letting down feed daily, ensuring they had plenty when he was gone. Even though he knew his animals were fed, he had asked Elvin if he minded checking on them anyway. Mainly to give the dogs a little human companionship during Mel's longer trips. And maybe to help Elvin keep his mind off his loneliness for Julie, his wife, who had been dead almost two years and whose absence left an emptiness even now.

Mel went around filling the feeders, and then brought the riding mower from the shed and mowed all the grass between the house and pond before going in to shower and change.

The sun was going down, its light dwindling, the shadows beneath the pines going from soft greenish grey to deep dark grey. He turned on the kitchen light and looked around to see what he could find to cook.

The freezer held a stack of prepared dinners, and he decided to heat one.

The newspapers had collected on the end of his sofa, where Elvin put the mail taken from his box at the end of the lane. He had just started looking through the mail when his phone rang.

For just a moment he stood still, listening. It rang three times, and then his answering machine came on. Mel had tensed again. His number was unlisted, and only a few people had access to it. Elvin, Mel's mother, Dorothy, who lived in Atlanta near his sister, Bess, a few close friends and relatives, and ... Norma.

He wasn't surprised to hear Norma's voice.

"Mel, I hate to do this to you, but—"

He picked up the phone.

"You knew I was here," he accused gently.

He could almost see the wan smile on her face. She was about forty, like him, and had a few wrinkles, like him. But she kept her hair pale blond, and if there was silver among the gold he had never seen it. But in her line of work, an attorney who worked in secret, in her spare time, for the Underground Railroad escape system that found places for women and children in other states, other places, she probably had plenty of grey in her hair.

"I thought you should be," she said. "I have put off calling you for the past two hours, just to give you time to unwind a little. And I'm sorry to call you again so soon, but I have a case here that I think merits immediate attention."

"Yeah, let me have it." He didn't bother to sit down.

"Her name is Celia, and she has three children. One girl, age eleven, and boys nine and five. They are scared, Mel. The worst I've seen in a long time. Maybe the worst ever. Celia feels sure there is nowhere she can go with her children that her husband won't be able to get to them. She says he will kill them all, and she believes it. I believe it too."

"The usual story about divorce and custody rights?"

"No. In this case there is no divorce yet. It's pending. But there are charges out on this man, who's out on bail now. His wife turned him in for cruelty to his children, herself, and to dogs he gathered and sold. The cruelty charge about the dogs stuck, but not the other ... yet. So she's terrified of him, even though she has a restraining order."

Mel snorted and Norma agreed. A restraining order was worth shit most of the time.

"I'm afraid she has a legitimate complaint, Mel. Can you take care of them?"

"Where to?"

"I have arranged for them to be taken to a family in northern California, via Tennessee, Kansas, and Nevada. Once there, they will be helped by an attorney friend. I'll have the names of the families that are expecting you. You've seen them before. The Archers in Kansas, the Merrows in Tennessee. The Randolphs in Nevada. And directions to the new family in California. They're all expecting you."

"Where'll I meet you?"

"At the Georgia Pines Motel, just off the highway at Belfast, the place where you picked up the Andrews children two months ago."

"Got it. You're there now?"

"Yes, I'm here. I've checked Celia and the children into a room on the ground floor. Number 210. We'll be waiting for you." There was the slightest pause, then, just before he hung up, he heard her say, "You did say you can make it, didn't you?"

He laughed without humor and hung up.

He smelled his dinner burning and hurried into the kitchen to take it out of the oven.

While he waited for it to cool enough to divide between the two dogs, he tossed jeans, shirts, socks, and underwear into his suitcase, pulling out the clothes that needed laundering and leaving them in a heap on the floor.

He thought about calling Elvin, but remembered that Elvin didn't even know he had gotten home.

He fed the dogs their special treat from the overcooked dinner. Ham, beans, macaroni and cheese. In the past year he had stopped eating meat, feeling somehow that it just wasn't right. He had become so sensitive to other creatures in the world, other animals, that eating them began to smack of a form of cannibalism. Some of the dregs of the human race he had run into the past fifteen years were far lower than the animals they "ruled." So the dogs were accustomed to getting whatever meat there might be in the TV dinners he brought home for emergencies. No more cows, pigs, lambs, or chickens would lose their lives so he could eat. Vegetarianism agreed with him. His worst problem was kicking the smoking habit. He guessed he'd always be reaching into his left shirt pocket for a cigarette that wasn't there.

His own dinner would have to wait. When a call came to pick up a woman and her kids, there just wasn't time to eat. Not until he could sit down with them someplace where it was safe.

He dressed in what he considered his uniform. Blue-jeans and knit shirt. The knit shirts didn't have to be ironed. They never wrinkled enough that the wrinkles didn't fall out when he put them on. Cowboy boots. A holster in the left boot held a Taser stun gun, while in the right boot another holster cradled a .38 Special he prayed he wouldn't have to use, but which he would if he had to.

It was a hundred miles to the motel in southern Georgia where he would meet Norma, Celia, and her three children. In his garage-barn were three automobiles. A Bronco for his own use around home, bearing a legitimate registration, and two others, with false plates, one of them a Florida license, the other New York. The Florida car, a Buick Century, was registered to an Art Cunnings, and the other, a Buick station wagon, to Steve Smith.

From his small safe he chose the identification papers of Steve Smith. When there were more than two children, he usually drove the station wagon.

He never exceeded the speed limit or drove in a way to attract attention. That was a crucial part of the Underground movement.

"I'll be there in four hours," he murmured as he switched the identification in his billfold. "Hang on."

CHAPTER 3

"Mama ..."

Drew's whisper carried across the motel room. He sat on the double bed farthest from the door, his short legs sticking straight out, his bare feet plump and pale in the light from the table between the beds. Blair sat on the other bed, his legs drawn up. Mama had uncharacteristically said nothing about Blair having his feet on the bed. Jonie, looking at the knobs on the television and wishing in silence she could turn it on, looked at their mother. Ever since the lawyer lady had left the room at sundown to call the man who was going to help them, and to get them some clothes, Mama had been going from window to window or standing at the door, listening.

"Mama ..." the whisper again, more urgent.

Celia turned her head slowly toward Drew. Jonie waited, barely breathing. Drew's round face looked rounder than usual, the way it did when he was holding back tears. His round blue eyes stared at their mother.

"I have to go to the bathroom."

To Jonie, his whisper seemed louder than a normal voice would have. Celia had cautioned them all to be quiet. Jonie stood still, waiting. She didn't know what she was supposed to do in this strange place. Be very quiet. Be still. Wait.

Celia glanced at Jonie and motioned toward the half-open door into the bathroom, then turned back to the door. She put her hand on the knob as if she were leaving, and for a moment Jonie held her breath. The room was so quiet it seemed that all of them held their breath. Then she heard what her mother had heard. Footsteps. Not light and quick like Norma's steps, but heavy, like a large man's. Like ... *his.*

They waited. Celia's hand tightened on the doorknob, and her head turned again and she looked toward the back of the room. Jonie knew she was looking at the window there, wondering how easy it would be to open it and get all of them out. But it was covered in a heavy, dark drapery, just like the window at the front.

The footsteps went by, and all of them sagged with relief. Celia said, "Take him, Jonie. Show him how to use the bathroom."

Jonie went to the bed and took Drew's hand. She loved the feel of his small hand. Though it was larger now, and had an oddly tougher feel, it was almost like it was when he was still a small baby. Having Drew born when she was already six years old, in fact, helping her mother with the birth, had been like a miracle. The baby was able to smile when Blair seemed to have already forgotten. At six months, Drew sat on the floor and smiled whenever Jonie looked at him, and when she got down beside him he laughed and tried to make sounds like the sounds she made. He made life good when they were all together without her father.

Nothing was good when he came home. Life grew silent and filled with fear. There were the haunting sounds of dogs howling or whining or screaming, almost like children. There were sounds of gunshots in the piney woods or out on the swamp where he went in his silent canoe. All her life she had been terrified of him, especially since she was three years old and he had held her hand to the stove. The scar would always be there, reaching from her palm to her wrist on her right hand. It had been a long time before she was able to hold a pencil again.

What the goddamned hell are you doing? You're not teaching a girl of mine to write! I'll teach her all she needs to know!

His fist knotted and flashed out, striking Celia on the side of her head. She fell, and seemed, oddly, to bounce several times as her hands flailed out for support. Then Jonie's hand was jerked roughly toward the heating stove and held there, and the pain seared into her forever, living with her yet at unexpected moments, reaching into her soul. Not allowed to cry, to show the weakness of tears, she screamed, and was hardly aware of the hard slaps on the side of her head.

"Donie!"

Jonie jumped, and realized she'd been standing still. She hadn't moved.

Drew was still on the bed, his left hand in hers, waiting for her to help him. But now he was clutching himself with his other hand, as if he were about to wet his pants. His face was strained and filled with fear, even though Durk wasn't around to punish him for not being able to hold his need to go so often.

Jonie picked him up and half carried him. But he was getting bigger now, and at last she let him slide to the floor. She wished he were still a baby, that he would stay a baby forever, so she could carry him, hold him, play his little games and watch his happy face. But even as a baby he had learned that when the man came into the room he should be still, be as unnoticeable as he could. He had learned. Very fast.

In the bathroom Jonie unsnapped his pajamas and slid them down. They hung around his ankles and fell off one foot when she lifted him onto the stool. His jamas were almost too small now, a one-piece suit so short the sleeves didn't reach his wrists, and legs that ended halfway down his legs. They had been among the clothes given to them when they were at the shelter.

That bag of clothes had been like a treasure chest. Jonie had found jeans for herself, a little big, but as Mama and the other ladies said, she'd grow into them. And she'd found a top she liked, but it was too small, and so Blair had gotten it. It was knit and had a tiger on the front.

Jonie walked around the small bathroom, looking at the shower behind the curtain, picking up the small bar of soap. It was wrapped in paper.

She took it to the door and held it out toward Celia.

"Mama, can I open it?"

Celia gazed at it as if her mind were a long way off.

"Mama," Jonie said, her voice carefully low. "Can I take a shower with this?"

"Later," Celia said. "Later, when we find out what we're going to do."

They had no clothes. Celia stood at the door in her nightgown, a cotton shift that had lost the color. Once the flowers had been blue, Jonie remembered. Now they were grey. Jonie remembered the day they had bought it. Sometimes Durk would take them to town. He would be in a great mood and would talk and laugh with people they saw. He would take them to the grocery store, and sometimes he'd stop at garage sales or flea markets. It was at one of those Celia had bought the nightgown. She had worn it like a dress for a long time.

"Donie."

It was Drew. Jonie loved the way he pronounced her name. There were a lot of words he couldn't pronounce correctly yet.

He had slid off the toilet and had pulled up his pajamas and was trying to snap the front, but his plump fingers fumbled. Jonie put the soap down on the long bathroom counter beneath the mirror and helped Drew.

The flush of the toilet seemed loud.

Blair slipped in silently to take Drew's place, and when Jonie led Drew out, she closed the door behind them. At home there was no bathroom. Just an old wood toilet out in the pines by the barn.

But it didn't matter. Things like that didn't matter at all.

There was a light tap on the door, and Jonie froze. She stood staring at her mother's hand on the doorknob. After a short delay there were three more taps and the feminine voice of the lawyer lady.

"It's all right, Celia. It's me, Norma."

Celia unlocked the door, her hands shaking. Jonie felt her own sag of relief. They had been waiting in the motel for so long.

Norma came in. Her hair was covered by a scarf and she was wearing tinted glasses. She was taller than Celia, so that to Jonie, her own mother for a moment looked like a teenage girl. She was so thin, so small.

Norma put a suitcase down. It bulged, it was so tightly packed. Then she reached out and pulled in another that was on little wheels. It was even larger than the first, and bulging just as roundly, as if it had been overfed. The suitcase reminded Jonie of some of the dogs that Durk had brought out to the cages in the barn. At first they looked round and overfed, but it didn't take long for them to become thin. Sometimes they wouldn't eat. Some of them wore collars with the names of their owners and with their telephone numbers, and Jonie daydreamed of being able to walk to town to a telephone, where she could call the owners to come and get their dogs, dogs that were so scared, dogs who were getting thin from not eating the dry food she and her mother and brothers put out for them.

Lots of times Jonie had cried and cried when Durk took them away again. What kind of horrors were they facing, those pets that had never known anything but the love of their owners?

Her hatred was like a knot of vomit in her throat. Her hatred sometimes was greater than her fear.

"This should keep you all well-dressed until you're settled and have a job, Celia. I tried to remember the sizes."

Norma put the smaller suitcase on the luggage rack and slipped the lock. It popped open with a small explosive sound, and colorful clothes spilled out. Right on top was a matching set of knits, pants and shirt. Girls' clothes, Jonie knew. She felt the smile, the unusual tightening of her cheeks and lips.

"How can I thank you," Celia said softly, her voice hoarse, her eyes damp. "How can I ever thank you?"

Norma touched her gently. The first time she saw Celia and her three very quiet, very intimidated children, she knew this family needed help. She had tried then, one month ago, to get them back to their home, safe from an abusive husband. She had helped her sign up for government help, and got a court order forbidding husband and father to see them. But she'd had a feeling, even then, that this would be one of those cases that would have a disastrous ending. She hadn't been surprised to hear from Celia again.

"Don't you worry," Norma said, trying to take some of the anxiety out of the woman's thin, tapered face. She didn't look as if she had ever had enough to eat. "You're going to be out of here in about two hours, and on your way west."

"Two hours?"

It was a whisper. Celia's eyes widened in dread.

"It's okay," Norma assured her. "A man named Mel, who will take very good care of you, will be here by midnight. He'll get you out of here, and you'll be traveling cross-country to the West Coast. In northern California there is a place for you and the kids. A very good place. You'll be helped there to find a place to live, and a job. There'll be new identification. You'll be able to live normal lives."

"He'll find us."

"No," Norma said firmly. "He will never find you. The last trace of you will end right here, in this motel. Your car will be picked up within the next few hours. Before daybreak it will be gone, and so will you and the children. Don't worry."

She looked at the children. Jonie stood holding the pink knit outfit clutched to her chest, staring toward her mother. All the children had lovely eyes. They were similar in expression, although Drew's were sky blue while Jonie and Blair's were a soft puppydog brown. Jonie and Blair had dark wavy hair. Drew's was almost white. The style was simple, cut straight at the back, with bangs across their foreheads. They were obviously homemade haircuts, as was not often the case with families who were running away. Many abusive fathers or mothers took pride in having a good standing in the community. People who knew them were frequently shocked to hear they were abusive to their families in the privacy of their homes. In Celia's case, the abuse had extended almost to denial, it seemed, on the man's part, as if in hiding them away from the world they ceased to exist. Norma had no doubt that he would have killed them all someday, sooner or later, making sure the world never knew about them. She prayed they would be safe now.

Norma smiled at the girl. "Why don't you go take a shower and put the new outfit on?"

Jonie's eyes glanced in a silent question at Celia, and her mother nodded yes. Jonie slipped into the bathroom and closed the door.

"All of you will need to be dressed and ready to go. These suitcases and clothes are yours. Mel will help you with them. When he gets here he will knock once, pause, and knock three more times. Then he will identify himself. Mel, that's all. You will remember that, won't you?"

So often these running families were so afraid they forgot the name, the number of knocks. One family Norma still had nightmares about had disappeared from their room before help arrived. She had never heard from them again. She prayed they had made it safely away on their own.

"Mel," she repeated. "One knock, then three. Don't open the door to anyone or anything else. There's no reason for anyone to be knocking at your door at this time of night."

Celia nodded. The two little boys were looking through the suitcase, and they had found the toys in the bottom. But there was no sound from either of them. In silence they brought out the soft little teddy bear and the two Transformers; things that turned from spacemen to automobiles. In silence they sat down on the floor. Drew held the teddy bear in both arms, folded against his chest.

"Two hours," Norma reminded Celia as she once again, and for the last time, clasped the thin, cold hand. "He'll be here in two hours, and you'll be ready to go?"

Celia nodded. "We'll be ready to go."

"Great."

Norma took a shoulder bag off her shoulder and opened it. She removed a brown leather wallet and displayed the driver's license that had been prepared with Celia's photograph.

"This is your new identification. Your new name is Cindy Beavers. We try to use names close enough to the original so it won't be too confusing. Remember, should anyone ask your name, it's Cindy. Your children are Jennifer, Ben, and David. When you reach your destination birth certificates will be waiting for you. You'll have to get used to the new names. It's important. The purse is yours. You'll find some cash in it, not much at this point. In your new town a job will be waiting. Not much, but something. A motel maid, to start. And you can go back to school. Good luck."

"Thank you," Celia whispered. "Thank you so much."

"You'll make it."

The look in Celia's eyes was doubtful, cringing. But it was a look the women often carried.

"You will," Norma said. "You'll be in good hands. No one can take better care of you than Mel. I have to go now. I have made arrangements for your car to be towed away. There's no way he could have traced you, or can trace you once you leave here. Good-bye."

She left the motel, waiting until the door closed firmly and the locks clicked into place. The long lines of the motel stretched away in a U shape, and the outdoor lights shined down on the tops of the automobiles. The car Celia had driven was still parked near the restaurant at the front of the motel, its blue paint dusty.

It stood out, somehow, even among all the other cars. Norma had a sudden bad feeling about it, and wished the tow truck would get it and take it away.

Noise from the freeway just a few hundred yards away was like a hard wind blowing, blowing. Lights of automobiles, most of them big trucks, made streaks of brightness against the night beyond. It would be two more hours before Mel could reach them, and Norma didn't feel good about it.

Two hours could seem like a lifetime to a family so frightened of being found. She didn't want to leave them alone. What did she have to go home for? No one was waiting for her. Her cats, Toby and Missy, wouldn't mind too much if she were a couple of hours late. They had it good—their own toys, a playhouse lined with carpet, an automatic waterer just in case something happened and she didn't get back at all. She always knew she ran the risk of losing her own life at the hands of a furious parent who knew she had been instrumental in separating him, or her, from their children. But her secretary knew to call her house each morning if she didn't show up at her office. If there was no answer, she was to send someone out to check.

Norma turned back, went to the motel door and tapped lightly, paused, and tapped three times more. She looked right and left along the open motel walk, but no one was in sight. She dared to call out softly again, knowing in her heart that Celia still stood by the door.

"Celia ... it's Norma."

The door opened. The pale, thin face of the young woman looked almost beautiful for just a moment with its light of relief. It reminded Norma of the faces of homeless children at Christmas when they found out something special was under the big tree at the shelter, something just for them.

"I've decided to wait with you and the children," Norma said, and stepped back into the room.

"Oh thank you, Miss Whiting. Thank you. Time passes so slow."

"Call me Norma, please. I understand about waiting, really I do. Why don't I help the boys find something to wear? As soon as Jonie finishes her shower they can get ready to go, then they can lie down and take a nap while we wait."

She went down on her knees between the two little boys and began selecting clothing for them. The jeans for a small five-year-old looked so small.

"Why don't you relax, Celia, and watch television? And when you're ready to get dressed, your things are in the bigger suitcase."

Celia looked as if she did not dare disobey Norma's suggestion, but at the same time, she was afraid of the sound. Norma understood.

Softly she added, "If you'd rather keep the room quiet, Celia, you certainly may."

Celia said, "I'd rather." Then surprisingly, she added, "He let us have one, you know. It was really for him, but when he was gone we could use it. A television. We used the PBS station for our school."

"That's interesting," Norma said. "Men like him often won't stand for television."

Blair said suddenly, "But he broke it. The last day he was home, he kicked it until it broke all over."

Celia made a soft *shhhing* sound with her lips, and instantly the boys sat still, listening.

Norma glanced up at Celia and saw that most of her pale coloring had been suddenly bleached away.

She was listening to something toward the back of the room, near the window. She moved in that direction, making no sound.

But all Norma heard was the soft sighing of the traffic on the freeway, a rising wind, and a limb, perhaps, brushing against the back of the building.

CHAPTER 4

THE THREE CHILDREN lay sleeping on the bed against the rear wall, dressed and ready to go. The small clock on the table between the beds was moving slowly through the two hours. Norma glanced at it and saw it would be another forty-five minutes.

She had thought Celia might want to talk, but Celia had said little since they sat down at the round table by the window. She shook her head at an offer of something to eat or drink and seemed unable to hold her hands still. She was listening, Norma finally realized, listening hard, not only at every movement at the front of the motel, but for something at the back.

She kept staring at the window near the foot of the bed where the children slept. It was covered with the same heavy, dark blue drapery as the front window.

"Why don't you lie down and get some sleep, Celia?"

Celia shook her head. "I can't," she whispered. She got up and went to the rear window and cautiously pulled the corner of the short drapery aside, revealing a diamond of glass and the black night beyond. "Did you hear something?" she whispered.

Norma listened. She had learned early that these women could detect danger where no one else could. They were so attuned, so sensitive to everything that moved.

She heard the distant but fading moan of traffic, then someone slammed a car door, and voices, male and female, called out to one another with no regard for the sleepers behind motel doors. They sounded as if they were bringing their party to the Georgia Pines. A motel door thudded dully as it shut, and the voices dimmed and receded, swallowed by the distant roar of traffic.

Celia was still looking into the night at the back of the motel.

Norma joined her at the window. In the distance the lights on the freeway curved away to the west and faded. Right behind the window something tall and sturdy stood, like a black pillar.

"A tree," Norma said. "Trees. Pines. That's where the motel gets its name. So many trees."

Celia dropped the curtain back into place. She had showered after the children were through and was now dressed in cotton jeans and a long-sleeved plaid shirt. Norma noticed that of all the clothing in the suitcase, Celia had picked the dullest colors.

Norma hadn't been able to forget the car. It was registered to Durk Nolan, and she didn't want the police, or anyone, taking an interest in it. The tow truck operator was scheduled to pick it up by midnight. From here he would take it to a garage in town that would repaint it and give it a new serial number, after which it would be sold to help with the expense of buying Celia a car when she reached her destination. Norma wouldn't know until tomorrow morning exactly what time the car had been removed. The sooner it was out of the parking lot, the safer they would be.

Josh Rivers, owner of the new, one-truck Rivers Trucking Line, sat at the counter of the truck stop just off the freeway, his rig loaded with lettuce and parked headed north. He had to have the lettuce in Baltimore in another twelve hours, and that didn't leave him much damn time to have a snack. He had ordered two doughnuts and a big mug of black coffee, and had eaten the doughnuts in four bites. The coffee was going to take a little longer.

He gazed across the counter at the mirror behind the rows of mugs that carried the names of truckers who stopped in regularly. Right now the row of mugs looked like a mouth of half-missing teeth, and behind him in the booths sat the truckers with the missing mugs. Their conversation circled his head like bees, so that he didn't hear any of it well enough to zero in on one thing. So far, he didn't have a mug of his own. In his days of driving for Hones Truck Lines he had come through pretty often, but nowadays, with his own truck, bought just two months ago, he was able to go in any direction. Wherever he could pick up a load.

The trucker beside him asked, "Going north?"

"Right," Josh said. "Baltimore. Lettuce."

"I drive a transport, loaded with Chevies. Work for Butler, down in Tallahassee."

"You're almost there."

"Yeah. Then I get a couple of days off. You driving your own rig?"

Josh nodded. "A couple months now."

"You're on your way."

"I hope so. Both me and my wife worked hard and saved hard for a long time to get started on our own." Josh swallowed his coffee. He didn't have sipping time. As he got off the stool he clapped the other driver on the shoulder.

"See you around," he said.

"Right. Good luck."

Josh went out into the night. The gravel in the wide parking lot shifted under his feet. Traffic along the freeway was dying down. It was mostly trucks now. He turned left around the end of the building.

Lights on tall poles shined down on a couple of dozen parked trucks, but his own, sitting out in the middle beneath a light, stood out, its red paint shiny and new, recently washed and polished. He, Sandra, and their six-year-old son, Jamie, had spent yesterday afternoon cleaning it up, polishing it, getting it ready for the trip.

Josh paused to light another cigarette, looking at the cherry red paint of the bulging top. Beautiful. Jamie had wanted to ride along, and Josh had promised him he could. The very next trip that wasn't so long. The next trip where he knew what he would be hauling back. As soon as Jamie's mama could get off from her waitress job to join them.

It was Josh's dream that by next year Sandra wouldn't have to work away from home at all. Then, in the summertime, she and their son could travel along.

He went closer to his truck, paused again, took two long drags off the cigarette and dropped it to the gravel. With the toe of his boot he ground it out until all the sparks were gone. He hadn't started smoking in his truck yet. Didn't want to stink it up. Not smoking in the truck would help him stop smoking, maybe, which Sandra had been begging him to do.

Josh grinned on one side of his mouth with the memory of his first cigarette. He was twelve years old when he and his sister swiped a couple of their mother's cigarettes and went out behind the shed in the rear of the yard. It lingered in his mind as one of the most daring and exciting things he had ever done. They had sat and giggled and coughed and choked, and then Lindy had turned a number of shades of green and gotten sick. She never smoked again. But Josh kept swiping a smoke now and then until he was able to buy his own.

Not until he had swung himself up to sit in the truck did he realize his door had been standing a couple of inches open.

He sat still, alert. Then he turned on the dome light. His maps were still there, his log book, everything he carried with him. Even the change in the plastic cup holder Sandra had put in the cab. Behind him, the sleeping compartment was partly closed and dark. He reached back but felt nothing but the blanket, still tucked in smooth, the way his wife had fixed it. At last he shrugged and turned the switch. The engine came to life, almost as quiet as a car. He pulled it into low gear and headed toward the freeway.

Some guy must have been admiring his truck. Opened the door and looked in, and then didn't quite shut the door. That was okay. Josh was proud of his big red rig. He could see himself gleaming down the highways.

He turned on the radio and positioned himself comfortably. Sometime in the darkest hours of the morning he might pull off at a rest stop and sleep an hour or so. Or he might just have another cup of coffee, a piece of pie, or even eggs and toast. Not exactly dieting material. Already his belly bulged against the steering wheel. He tried to keep an eye on it, because he didn't want Sandra adding his weight to her list of improvements.

The night passed outside his window. He entered a thick forest, their spiked tops outlined like lace against a lighter sky. Stars blinked through the cold, dark distance. At times the forest fell away and was replaced by low roofs of houses or fields of vegetables or fruit trees. As he drove north into Georgia the wind blew through the window, mild turning to cool, cool turning to chilly.

He rolled up the window.

The music on the radio changed to rock. He reached down and flipped the dial for a country station and found none. Too damned much rock these days, and not the good old rock and roll that had some *real* rhythm.

He turned the radio off.

The cab seemed insulated from the world, all sounds beyond muted. A truck on the southbound lane gave him a short muted honk of greeting, and Josh returned it. Traffic had thinned. The road curved ahead in darkness, coming again to a forest along the roadside.

Silence descended. There was only the soft engine sound. Josh yawned loudly. And then, as he leaned back to relax against the plastic seat, he heard a sound in the compartment behind him.

The bedclothes moved. Blanket against sheet. Soft, rustling.

Josh held his breath, his hands hard on the wheel. *Don't jerk the wheel.* That was one of the first lessons a training truck driver learned. Whatever it is—a wreck in front of you, an animal crossing the road, even a human—don't jerk the wheel sharply in either direction. Slow down immediately, turn carefully in whatever direction you have to go to avoid the problem.

But there was no problem in the road. The problem was behind him.

He remembered finding the door open. Why hadn't he turned on the light in the sleeping compartment and given it a look?

Evidently he had company. Someone was back there.

Josh tried to relax. A hitchhiker. Relax, he told himself. Only a hitchhiker. The guy must have gone to sleep and turned over, causing the rustling sound of the covers.

At least he didn't snore.

Josh drove on, both hands tense on the wheel, listening.

His strange cargo must not breathe either, because if he did, Josh couldn't hear him.

Or her.

Her?

No way.

"Hey, back there," Josh said aloud. "Hitchin' a little ride?"

He waited.

There was no answer, and at last a strange, chilly sensation began somewhere on Josh's spine and curled upward onto the back of his neck.

He looked for a place to pull over, but the side of the road was edged by a railing, indicating a drop in the land just off the shoulder that wasn't visible in the night.

His passenger, maybe, was a heavy sleeper. Josh leaned forward. The seat beneath him shifted, making a sound as he reached for the CB mike. He clicked it on.

Behind him the rustling sound began again, a strange, continuous movement, as if whoever was there was sliding toward him, crawling, keeping the blanket moving against the sheet on the mattress. The crawling among the hairs on Josh's neck kept pace with the crawling in the sleeping compartment.

"Long John calling, Long John. Anybody out there?"

The CB radio cackled distantly like an old witch out to get him.

"Come in, wherever you are. Mayday, mayday."

Whoever it was in the compartment was getting closer to him. Beneath the static in the CB Josh could hear the subtle but steady sound of bedding rustling, of movement within it or across it. Maybe the guy was getting up.

Josh looked over his shoulder. The blackness in the compartment seemed to be moving. Josh frowned, squinting against the darkness there. At first it was like looking into a barrel of black snakes. He could see only the movements, the shadows; he could see something rising, filling the opening behind him.

"Hey!" he shouted, fear causing his voice to rise several pitches, anger making it bellow. "If you want a goddamned ride, just say so, but say something. Who the hell are you?"

A horn blared in front of him and he whirled back to face the road and saw he was about to mow down the railing on the right side. A truck coming from the other direction passed by, a whirr of lights and horn.

Josh dropped the mike and gripped the steering wheel with both hands.

He felt the touch of something cold and wet on the back of his neck, but he wasn't sure if it was real or only the awful fear that pulled at him. Then it was encircling his neck, the fingers like ice, like several snakes, tightening, choking all life from him.

He was heading toward the railing, toward the fall down the bank into God knew what. A river, maybe.

Serves you damn well right. Try gettin' out of that, he thought as his own hands struggled to pull from his neck the tightening bands that encased it. *The truck goes into a river, we both go.*

He thought of the pythons his neighbor kept. Snakes that choked the life from their victims. He thought of the baby in Houston he had read about once that was killed in its crib by its father's pet python. But these were fingers around his neck, hard, cold, wet fingers. The hands of a man whose face he couldn't see, whose motives were lost in the blackness of the night.

Whoever he was, they were going over together.

And then he was crashing through the railing and down, down ...

• • •

"Good God!"

Wayne Johnson had been watching the truck in the northbound lane of the freeway since the first moment he spotted it after rounding the long curve. Something was wrong with its driver, he saw in that first good look. The truck was wavering back and forth across the road, and finally it headed straight for the railing. In his rearview mirror he saw it swerve sharply to the right, go over the side, and disappear into the darkness below the road.

He craned his neck, slowing his truck, looking for a place to pull over. Meantime he shouted into his mike, "Need help out here on seventy-five, about one mile south of the turnoff down to ... to ..."

He couldn't remember the name of the town, but he had just stopped at a restaurant called ...

"The Georgia Pines Motel! A truck off the road. Help."

Shit. He hadn't been driving long enough to know how to use the damned CB, or what to say when he did use it. "Mayday" he tried, again. "A trucker in trouble."

He spotted a crossover between the lanes and pulled into it, left his truck running, and almost fell out. Behind him the CB crackled with an answering voice, but he didn't go back. Down the road came the lights of another truck, and he positioned himself safely to one side of the road and began waving his arms.

The big truck slowed, and Wayne ran to the cab.

"A truck just went off over the hill there. Call for help, will you?"

Wayne turned and went running through the broken railing and down through the weeds and brush on the sloping hillside. Below, on its side, lay the big red truck, motor still running, lights blazing helplessly into the darkness.

As Wayne stumbled down the slope he thought he saw something moving away, just at the edge of the light beams. A man running? The driver?

"Hey!" he yelled. "You okay?"

But whoever, or whatever, it was going away from the truck, heading northward into the night.

An animal, Wayne decided, frightened by the fall of the truck into its domain.

He reached the truck. The wheels were still spinning. The engine purred. The lights burned.

Wayne climbed up and looked down into the cab.

A mam lay crumpled against the door on the downhill side, a dark pile of silence in the dimness of the cab.

Wayne pulled the door open, struggling to heave it up and back where it would not fall forward and crush him. He called out, trying to get an answer. But the man against the other door lay still, his head twisted back and down in a strange way that didn't look right. As Wayne's eyes adjusted to the dim light in the cab, he could see the open eyes of the man staring upward at the ceiling, or at the stars beyond the ceiling. There was something dark at the corner of his mouth, working slowly down onto his neck like a river growing.

Nothing about the position of the bleeding, staring man seemed warranted by the position of the cab. The truck hadn't rolled over, it had only rolled onto its side.

"Hey, down there!" a voice from the road above called. "Anybody in there?"

Wayne started to reach down for the man and decided against it. Better let him be until help came. He looked like his neck might be broken.

"Yeah!" Wayne yelled back. "The driver. I guess the driver."

On the highway above he heard a siren, still in the distance. Wayne reached for the dome light switch and turned it on.

The man lying wide-eyed against the door, crumpled like a big rag doll, was dead. And he looked as if he had seen hell itself in that last moment before death.

CHAPTER 5

A CAR DOOR closed somewhere outside in the motel parking lot, and Celia was up again, nervously alert. Norma rose too, her back beginning to feel stiff from sitting so long in the chair at the round table. The footsteps sounded positive and sure of the direction, as if the man knew where he was going. Norma moved toward the door, listening. It could be Mel. Yet there was something about the steps that didn't sound like Mel. A heavy dread filled her.

Norma checked her watch. It was still fifteen minutes until midnight. She touched Celia reassuringly as she passed by. The three children had been sleeping, though restlessly, for the past hour and a half, but Celia only looked more and more tired as the minutes dragged by.

The footsteps came straight to the door and then seemed to hesitate. Norma waited. Celia was holding her breath, Norma noticed, and then realized she too was holding her breath.

Yet the footsteps did not seem particularly to disturb Celia, as Norma thought they would. Most runaway women feared the step of any man. Celia was merely waiting, listening.

The steps moved hesitantly on past the door.

"It wasn't Mel," Norma whispered, then in a normal but soft voice she added, "I didn't think the footsteps sounded just like his. After a time, you get to know a person's steps."

"I know," Celia said.

Norma went back to the table. Her water glass was empty. She took both glasses and filled them with ice she had brought from the ice machine in one of the breezeways, and then filled them with water in the bathroom. She brought them back to the table. Celia was still sitting there, her hands clasped in front of her on the black formica table top.

"Drink some water," Norma said, placing the glass near her hands.

As if Celia hadn't heard, she said, "He'll get here before the man does. Before Mel."

"He? Your husband?"

"Yes. He knows where we are. He's following."

Norma stared at Celia. Light from above played softly on the young woman's high cheekbones. She had full lips, and the lower one protruded and curved softly downward, making a shadow beneath it, just as her lashes made shadows on her cheeks. Such a pretty girl. Hardly more than a girl, at twenty-eight.

"How can he know where you are? Did he see you leave home?"

"Yes," Celia whispered.

This was the first Norma had heard of that. Initially, Celia had told her only that they had to get away, that her husband had come home after all, defying the court order. She was shaking with fear and had driven half the night to reach Norma. She had kept looking over her shoulder, as they all did.

Because Norma had dealt with this family a month ago, she knew the danger was real. Durk Nolan was a man in his forties, years older than his petite wife, a huge man with massive shoulders and a muscular build—unkempt, contemptuous, cruel. He seemed, in some way, less human than most of the other people she dealt with. She had seen his contempt for the law, for all authority. She had seen the way he looked at Celia. There was no love there. Indeed, the man looked as if love were a foreign word to him, except perhaps to use as a tool to get what he wanted. Later, when she saw him in court, she saw a large but clean-shaven man wearing not a suit with a tie, as she had expected, but a neat shirt and cords, a man who tried to look accepting of the judge's words when he was fined two thousand dollars for cruelty to animals.

But he had recognized Norma, and the look he had given her when he left the courtroom sent cold dread into her soul.

"If he followed, what was he driving?" Norma asked. "You had the car. His pickup was seized to pay his fine."

Celia bit the edge of her lower lip. "He wasn't driving."

"Then how could he have followed you? You're miles from home."

Celia glanced down and said nothing.

Norma felt oddly disturbed and unsure of herself. She remembered their telephone conversation that morning. She had asked then if Durk was following. In these situations, it was vital that she learn if the spouse had any knowledge of the actions of the escaping family.

There had been a long silence. So long Norma wondered if they had been disconnected.

Finally Celia had said, "I don't think so."

"Then go to the Georgia Pines Motel, just off Seventy-five at Belfast. Wait for me in the restaurant. I'll be there within the hour. Have something to eat. I'll pick up the check when I get there."

"We can't go into a restaurant," Celia whispered into the phone. "We're in our nightclothes. We didn't bring anything."

"Then wait in the car."

"He'll find us." The cry was desperate.

"Then drive around the town and meet me there in thirty minutes. At the motel. Don't worry. I'll take care of you."

She had arrived at the motel ahead of them. Three minutes later the old, dusty sedan showed up. As soon as Norma made sure they were all right, she rented the motel room. Then she left to make arrangements for the trip west, get the clothes, and call Mel.

For a few moments Celia pressed her lips tightly together, and her soft brown eyes stared into Norma's. Then, as if she had made a decision about something, she leaned forward over the table and whispered, "You don't understand. Durk isn't like other people ... He can do things other people can't do. He's out there. He knows where we are. He's following. He knows where we're going. He'll always follow." She sat back. "Until he finds us."

She whispered the last few words so softly Norma barely heard them. But Norma could plainly see her terror. A terror so many battered women shared.

There were more footsteps outside the motel room. Norma went to the door, her hand resting on the knob. Celia backed up until her legs were against the first bed.

He knows. He's not like other people.

What do you mean? Norma wanted to ask, but there wasn't time now. This time the footsteps sounded like Mel's. He had learned to walk with a softness that was almost Indian, bringing out, perhaps, a bit of his distant ancestry.

"It's Mel," Norma whispered.

The footsteps stopped at the door, then came the one knock, not loud.

Norma waited, holding her breath with Celia for the three knocks. They came, one after the other. And then the deep voice.

"Mel here."

Norma opened the door. She could have hugged and kissed him. His square-jawed, almost ugly face was downright beautiful in the slant of the motel light. His beard was well-trimmed but longer than she had ever seen it before. There were narrow streaks of white etching the black hair on each side of his chin. His sideburns held sprinkles of white. He wasn't quite forty years old, but there was old, old sorrow in his eyes. He had told her once that his daughter had killed herself when she was only thirteen. He hadn't been able to help Crescent, he said, even though he was in law enforcement. After her death he had quit his job and more or less dropped out of society. Beneath the exterior of the personality she revealed to him in their work together, Norma felt the love she could have given him. It would be so easy. If ever they had time together. Maybe someday.

She had never been so glad to see him as she was now.

"Mel," she cried softly, and put her hand on his arm. She felt the warmth of him, the solid muscle. His shirtsleeve was rolled up partway, revealing a good heavy growth of black hair on his arms.

Strangely, she thought of Durk Nolan. He had been wearing a short-sleeved shirt the first time she saw him, open down the front, and there had been no visible hair. He was as smooth-skinned and hairless as a ... snake. Or an eel.

"Mel," Norma said, as soon as she had closed the door behind him. "This is Celia. Jonie, Blair, and Drew." She pointed toward each child in turn.

All of them appeared to be sleeping soundly. Then she noticed that Jonie's eyes had opened just a slit, and that she was watching. Checking Mel out, Norma thought, making sure it wasn't her father. Jonie sat up rubbing her eyes.

"Steve," Mel said. "I'm carrying an ID with the name Steve on it, Celia, so if we're stopped by police and you have to use my name, remember it's Steve." He looked at Norma. "You've got IDs ready?"

"Yes. Cindy, Jennifer, Ben, and David. The birth certificates will be waiting with Rodney in Alturas in California."

She slipped a piece of paper into his hand with the names of the families and the locations where they would be stopping for much-needed rest as they crossed the country, all in a special little code they had worked out together. None of them was a stranger to him. He had stopped there before. They were all a special part of the Underground Railroad.

"Alturas. Up in the high country, huh?" Mel slipped the paper into his shirt pocket and picked up the two suitcases on the luggage rack. "Is this all?"

"Yes. It's time to go, Celia. You're on your way."

Mel said, "Let the boys sleep. I'll carry them out. I'm driving the station wagon. Celia, I'll be calling you by your new name only if we run into authorities, such as highway patrol. It's easier to travel together that way."

Jonie was up, following Mel out the door. Norma saw Mel's station wagon in the driveway just beyond the parking spaces for the cars. It was idling softly.

He had the back window and tailgate open, and he slid the suitcases in. Working quickly, he put them to one side and covered them. Then he hurried back into the motel and picked up Drew and carried him out and laid him on a blanket between the suitcases.

Blair struggled up out of bed and followed him. Mel helped him into the back of the station wagon, then closed the back window and the tailgate and locked them.

Jonie had climbed into the backseat, but Celia hesitated, looking at Norma.

Norma went to her, hugging her closely for the first and last time. She felt hot tears in her eyes.

"Take care. Call me if you need me. But don't be afraid."

Mel came up behind Celia, and with his hand on her elbow helped her into the car and closed the door. He turned for just an instant toward Norma and looked into her eyes, and then he was gone, hurrying around the car and into the driver's seat.

As the automobile spun away Norma stared after it. She saw a small, pale face staring out the window. Light flashed on Drew's silver-blond hair, and then he disappeared. A terrible feeling turned her hopes dark.

She told herself it would be all right. She was just extra tired.

She watched the taillights as the car moved toward the office of the motel and around and to the right. It disappeared. In a few minutes it would become part of the dwindling traffic on the freeway, headed northwest through Georgia.

The first stop would be in Tennessee, at the home of the Merrows. Many families had stopped there on their way to their new homes, but Norma had met the Merrows only by telephone.

Norma sighed. She always felt so alone and lonely when Mel, or one of the many other drivers, pulled away with their people. So alone.

She returned to the motel room, straightened the bedspreads, and made sure the key was in plain sight on the dresser. Then she turned out the light and pulled the door shut behind her.

She walked briskly down the walk past draped windows and closed doors. Most of the rooms were dark now. She passed the office, where lights still burned, but no one was in sight beyond the wide windows. She saw potted plants, a leather sofa, two overstuffed chairs, a small television, and a counter beyond with maps and picture postcards.

As she crossed the parking lot by the restaurant, she noticed the dusty old sedan was gone.

It was the first good feeling she'd had all day, other than the few moments of being near Mel. The car Celia had driven from her isolated home on the edge of a Florida swamp had at last been picked up and taken away, sometime during the hours they were waiting for Mel.

It was going to be okay. Celia and the kids were safe. There would be no record of them from here on. Only a few people would know what had happened to Celia Nolan and her children.

She unlocked her car, got in, and pushed the lock button. Then she sat still, staring at the blaze of truck lights on the freeway above.

She could go home now and rest, sleep. She would get up tomorrow morning and go to her office and handle the real estate case in which an elderly mother was buying a house her daughter owned. A quick claim deed was all they wanted. It would be simple and easy.

But she couldn't get her mind off Celia and those scared, subdued kids. Even in his sleep Drew had held tight to his new teddy bear.

Durk isn't like other people. He can do things other people can't do ...

CHAPTER 6

AT A TIME like this Mel needed eyes all around his head. He had to watch the road ahead, the side roads, and the road behind. It helped if the children were quiet, as these were, and the woman silent. As most certainly Celia was.

When he first arrived at the motel he had seen a man with a bucket going into one of the breezeways. Mel assumed he was one of the overnight customers. He kept an eye on him nevertheless, and was relieved when he disappeared. When they left the motel the same man was standing in the opening of the breezeway watching, and Mel caught a glimpse of light reflecting on a ring of keys at the man's belt. The proprietor. He was curious, no doubt about it. But curiosity wouldn't kill them.

There was no one else in sight, except Norma.

He had watched her for just a moment in the rearview mirror. She had looked so forlorn standing there in the driveway, her hands in the pockets of her linen jacket. As the car turned right around the end of the motel, he heard Celia draw a long breath, a sigh. Of relief? He didn't ask and she didn't offer. He was glad. He needed all his senses at this moment. For watching.

They had passed the motel restaurant down at the end of the building. A few cars were parked in front of it, and a couple of big trucks in the gravel lot beyond. Through the windows in front he saw two couples sitting in booths at the windows, and four men at the counter. None of them was looking outside.

He drove past, watching the street behind in the rearview mirror. No cars, no pedestrians.

He found the street leading to the on-ramp. Houses down the block were darkened. The street lamps shone down on bare sidewalks, green hedges, and one lone cat wandering down the middle of the narrow street.

The night air was growing cool. He rolled up his window. The on-ramp led off from the tangle of streets and upward onto the interstate northward. On the other side of the viaduct, the on-ramp to the southbound lane was empty.

The brown station wagon was the only automobile, Mel thought at first, and they were safe. But then a car started on a side street below the on-ramp. Its lights came on, shining southward. It moved quickly away from its parking place and turned right.

Mel watched it in the rearview mirror as he continued on up to the highway above. The car was following.

The speed limit was fifty-five, and within seconds the speedometer needle had reached the limit. Sharp wind whistled through unseen cracks around the windows, fine as the strings of a violin. He speeded, adding another five miles an hour, something he didn't ordinarily do, but few patrolmen would stop him at that speed. He had to see if the car was following them or just happened to pull out at the same time they did.

The car behind dropped back just a little.

Ahead of the station wagon were two trucks, one behind the other, observing the speed limit precisely. Mel passed them, taking a chance the car behind was not an unmarked highway patrol car.

The trucks took up the view in the mirror now, and the car was lost somewhere behind.

A sign indicated an exit, the last of three exits to this small town.

Mel said, "We're going to take a little detour." His voice was low and soft and as casual as he could make it. He didn't want to alarm Celia or Jonie, who was still awake, up and watching the road alertly.

Below the highway, just off the exit, were the lights of a service station and another motel.

Mel slowed the car and pulled into the exit lane.

THE PROPRIETOR of the Georgia Pines Motel stood watching the whole rigamarole, as he thought of it. The woman who had rented the room, paying in advance, had stood and watched the man in the station wagon take the woman and three kids and leave. She had stood there for quite a while, then she had gone back into the motel. Sanders figured she would stay there the rest of the night.

But before he reached the door to the office she was out again, into the car, and was gone.

He had seen her before, two or three months ago. Something of the same thing had happened then. There'd been a woman and two kids, both of the kids pretty small. And, come to think of it, the same man had come and picked them up.

What was going on?

It didn't matter. He'd been managing motels for thirty years, and in that time he had seen some odd things. Mostly body builders, as he called them, or belly blenders. BBs. In and out. Usually a man and woman, but sometimes it was hard to tell.

He went to the room the woman had left and found the door unlocked. He turned on the lights. The room didn't look as if it had been occupied at all. He checked the bathroom and found the towels had been used. He gathered them up, folding wet washcloths and bath towels into the terrycloth mat. He checked the beds and saw the sheets hadn't been used. Or if they had, they had been carefully smoothed again.

The key was on the dresser. He picked it up.

People frequently checked in for a few hours and left again. But they never had kids.

The thing about the little kids bothered him. If the woman, who had signed in as ...

He couldn't remember.

He went back into his office and opened the register. Molly Brown. Who the hell was she kidding?

Molly Brown?

Still, he hadn't given it a thought at the time, even though she had looked familiar.

Number of people? One.

She had sneaked in the woman and kids. Not that it mattered. She had paid her forty dollars in advance, and she was already gone at half past twelve.

The door opened. A man who looked to be in his fifties came in. He was dressed casually, shirt open at the neck, a light-colored, lightweight jacket over slightly darker trousers. But he looked rich. What was he doing here?

"Got a room?"

The sign outside blinked no vacancy, because Sanders hadn't had a chance to change it yet. This time of year the rooms filled up early, and would for the rest of the summer.

"Just so happens," Sanders said, "I do. For one?"

"Two."

The man signed the register as Alan Smith and Mrs. Smith. Why didn't these BBs ever think up some original name, like Beezleblubber? Make it a little more interesting for a bored motel proprietor.

Sanders looked out the window as the guy was writing down his license number and saw he was driving a BMW.

Uh-huh.

He'd like to get a look at the girl, but she was hidden in the shadows. Two to one she was in her early twenties. Young enough to be the old guy's daughter, or maybe even granddaughter. Some guys in their fifties had grown granddaughters.

Well, Sanders wasn't out to judge. But he knew when he got home and told his wife she'd snort about it.

What did it matter? The only reason he told his wife these things was to bait her.

Wonder what she'd say about the woman who called herself Molly Brown?

"Hey, Mr. Smith," Sanders said as the middle-aged man started to leave. "Would you mind taking towels along with you? Save me a trip, and you an interruption, later."

The man smiled slightly beneath his mustache. "Well, we don't want that, do we?"

His voice was what Sanders would have called silky, but his wife probably would have said it was cultured.

Sanders gathered up a stack of clean towels from the room behind his office and handed them over the counter to Mr. Smith.

He stood behind the counter and watched the man leave. He looked almost comical carrying the stack of white towels. It was probably the first time he had ever carried towels, Sanders thought, and turned away with a grin.

• • •

MEL PARKED at a shadowed area just around the corner from the motel offices at the third exit and got out of the car. He could see the large eyes of the young woman as she silently watched his every move. She was puzzled and afraid, but she would be more afraid if he told her they had been followed by a car. At least, it had seemed that way, and this was the only way he could be sure they hadn't. They were lucky there had been another exit a mile farther down the road.

He walked around behind the station wagon and stood still, watching.

There was less activity at this motel. Though it was a larger motel, with two floors, there was no restaurant, no club, not even a place to buy a soft drink, except for machines on the walkways. Down the street toward town he had seen a convenience store, but the front parking area was brightly lighted, and it would have been the worst place they could have gone.

In the shadows at the end of the long motel he waited, watching the exit from the freeway down which they had come. But it remained dark.

Long minutes passed. On the freeway, still elevated above the town on a bank of soil that was planted with some kind of wavy grass, two more trucks went by, and four cars. The car that had driven onto the highway behind them had gone on sometime after he had parked.

Mel returned to the station wagon, locked his door, and started the engine.

"Sorry for the delay," he said softly to Celia.

Behind him Jonie moved, as if settling down from a strained nervousness. The two little boys were out of sight in the bed Mel had made in the rear of the station wagon. Asleep, he hoped. Certainly very still and quiet.

Celia said nothing. She didn't ask what the delay was for.

Mel said, "I had to make sure we weren't being followed."

Still she said nothing.

"Why don't you lean the seat back and get some rest?" Mel encouraged as he pulled the car back onto the on-ramp and headed north. "We're going to be driving for several hours. There's a lever down on the right side of the seat. Pull it up and you can lower the seat different degrees."

He heard her draw a long breath, and the seat moved a couple of notches down. She lay with her face toward the window, and Mel noticed she had left the seat high enough so that she could see out ...

CINDY. My name is Cindy. My children are Jennifer, Ben and David.

How could she remember? Not Jonie, but Jenny. Not Blair and Drew, but Ben and David, or Davie. Always. After they reached their new home in northern California.

She tried to picture northern California. All she knew of it was what she had learned in studying with the kids, and on the travel shows. Mountains, she knew. Mount Shasta, for one, a white-capped peak that rose above the rest of the mountains. A river called the Sacramento, with a big dam. Tall trees. Snow in the winter? Not like southern California, with the ocean breezes and the sunshine and orange groves and people. People, people, people. And now smog.

She remembered her daddy talking of that. Once there had been orange groves, but now there were people.

Cindy is my name.

Cindy.

Her identity had changed before. Only not so rapidly then. Not so desperately. Once her name was Cecelia, and she was part of a small, loving family.

Her first memory dawned like a thin silver moon in her distant past.

She was three years old. Her mother and father had just brought home a new baby brother. Snow was falling outside that day, and she had waited impatiently to be dressed in her snowsuit so she could go out and play. Daddy was going to help her build a snowman. She looked at the tiny baby in her mother's arms and asked, "Can he go?" They had told her she was going to have someone to play with.

They laughed, both Mama and Daddy, and Daddy picked her up and set her on his shoulder. "Next year," he said. "We'll put Teddy in his own snowsuit and you in yours, and me and Mama in ours and we'll all go out and build a snowman."

Only next year Daddy was no longer there. Sometime during the year there had been a funeral. Cecelia had stood beside her mother with no one to hold her hand any more. She smelled the flowers and another odor she could never identify but that had always meant death to her, and she shivered in the coldness of losing the man she loved best in the world.

"Where's Daddy?" she had asked, later, unable to believe that he was in that white casket. "Mama, where's my daddy?"

Her mother hadn't answered. She sat with the baby in her arms, clinging to him even when he cried, and stared off into the distance.

Sometime during the next few years the climate had changed. They had moved, although she couldn't remember the move. She only noticed that in place of snow in the winter there was warmth and rain. And her name had changed too. Nobody ever called her Cecelia after her daddy died. Now it became Celia. Teddy called her Celia because he couldn't pronounce her full name, and her mother seemed lost in another world, and never called her anything.

Names changed over the years. People changed.

Celia lay in the car seat with her face toward the window. Occasionally, in the distance, she saw the light of a house, a farm, or something she couldn't identify. Sometimes she saw the outline of a small town against the horizon, and sometimes trees, black and mysterious with the distance, the lack of light.

Her eyes closed. The hum of the car and the slight sway was comforting. For a moment she could believe she was three years old again and was being rocked to sleep by her daddy.

She slept, drawn into the comfort of blackness.

And then she realized she was not sleeping. She was looking into the night outside the car window, and he was there. The reaching arms, the writhing tentacles, the huge horror of him, shadows thrown forward onto the hood of the car as he, as *it*, kept pace with the swiftly moving car. Couldn't Mel see? Couldn't the man see the danger there, the movement, the silence, the swiftness, the awful size of the thing that was not octopus, not spider, but something of its own making—with eyes that bulged from the round, wet, black head; black eyes that bulged like malignant growths and glistened in the night just outside the window. Eyes without lids, eyes that never closed. Couldn't Mel see those eyes? Couldn't he see the movements of the long tentacles closing in on the car?

A snakelike feeler edged down onto the windshield, feeling for entry, or taking the first grip on the car. Another stretched down on the window next to Mel—black, slimy, tightening. It was slowing the car. Couldn't Mel see that the car was being pulled back, ground to a halt? She had to get her children out and try to get away. Out the back—*the back*—but the back was covered by the writhing black body as it wrapped itself around the car.

She heard a sound, a groaning, a strangling. One of the arms was reaching into her window, through the glass as if it weren't there. It was touching her—cold, wet, slimy—something made of the mud in the swamp and the evil that had been Durk.

Something had grasped her left arm and was squeezing, tightly, so that she was being torn apart.

"Celia? *Celia!*"

"Mom?"

She woke, starting upward to a blessed freedom.

She sat up in the seat and looked around. Outside in the dark trunks of black trees swept past. Not the body of the thing from the swamp, not the arms, the legs of that thing, but trees. Limbs in the passing swiftness of night. Trees. Not Durk.

She leaned back, her eyes closed. She felt cold now, and shivered.

"You going to be all right?" the man asked.

"Yes, thank you."

Jonie said, "Bad dreams. Nightmares. Mama has nightmares sometimes."

Celia sat up. "Yes, I'm sorry. I didn't even know I was asleep." Stay awake, she told herself. Watch carefully, for all of us. They don't know what's out there. No one does but me. Stay awake, to be sure what you see is real.

The night quieted. The hum of the tires on the pavement soothed Celia. They were leaving. They were far away from home. Like Norma had said, they were safe now. She had to believe that.

Yet he was out there, somewhere in the dark night. Celia sat looking into the darkness and tried to separate shadow from shadow and identify each correctly. Trees, limbs of trees, rocks, the falling and rising of land, darkened houses, with the windows glaring at them as they passed, reflecting the car lights and seeming to watch them with burning eyes. They were all moving so fast that every tree, every limb, even the bulky outlines of dark buildings, became what she had seen rise from the swamp.

CHAPTER 7

THE ONLY LIGHT in the motel room came from the television. It was situated halfway along the wall at the foot of the beds, between the entry door at the front and the bathroom door where Andy was taking his shower. The bathroom door was almost closed, edged by a crack of light.

The movie on the television was showing a stripper on a stage above cheering men. Shadowy musicians played rhythm and blues slowly and seductively.

Alene stood with her hands on her hips watching for a few minutes, a smile on her face. She was still fully dressed. The urge to join the stripper became overwhelming.

"Bullshit," she muttered. "I can do better than that."

She started unbuttoning her blouse, doing her little dance in the limited space between the two beds. "Hey, Andy, come and watch," she called.

The shower sprayed, on and on. Beating down on his head, probably, she thought to herself as she gave in to the sound of the music and the excitement of the strip. She whirled her blouse into a far corner of the room, and then did the same with her skirt. The pantyhose required a more difficult maneuver, and by the time she struggled the last toe off, she fell laughing into the lamp table.

She paused to take a drink straight from the bottle of Jack Daniels that Andy Daniels—Andrew Daniels, at his office—had pulled from the paper bag and left on the lamp table. Daniels for Daniels. Alene giggled.

With the pantyhose out of her way, she made a somewhat awkward leap into the middle of the bed nearest the back wall and continued her strip. Bra, slowly, slowly. She didn't have much to go yet, just a strip of panties.

Why hadn't she ever thought of stripping before? Ever since she was fourteen and had found she had a model's figure, she'd been trying to get jobs modeling or acting or anything that took advantage of her looks. She had even tried to get a job in the movies. She would have liked that very much, and she used all the money her absentee dad had sent her for graduation and took a bus to Hollywood. She didn't have money to fly and eat too. So she rode the bus, with kids bawling behind her and people talking in languages she couldn't understand. The bus had stopped every ten minutes, it seemed, and it had taken her days to get from Florida to California.

Becoming a movie star turned out to be a joke. Although she wandered the streets of Hollywood for a long, long week, with the rain ruining her hair every time and the smog burning her eyes, the only people who had discovered her were the pimps. If she had wanted to be a stupid, streetwalkin' whore, she yelled at the last one to approach her, she'd have stayed in Miami. "Well!" he huffed, and backed away, and that made up her mind. She used the rest of her money for a good meal and a raincoat, and then she hit the road and hitchhiked back home.

And here she was getting ready to spend the rest of the night with her boss.

At least he was rich, even if he was married. But the rumor was he'd been married about four times, and that had given Alene an idea. She was out to be his fifth wife, if she could swing it.

As soon as they had entered the motel he'd kissed her. Then he put her away from him as if he were afraid of her.

"Do you mind if I shower?" he'd asked. "I'd like to get out of these clothes."

She shrugged, puzzled. She'd been in a few motels before, and she'd never had a man who wanted to shower first.

"Sure. Whatever you want."

Alone, standing on the firm mattress of the bed, she undulated her body to "In the Heat of the Night," unfastened her bra, but kept it hugged against her.

She was one of the cocktail waitresses at the nightclub Andy Daniels owned. What would happen, she wondered, if she suggested that he start a stripping act, and let her be the star?

"Hey, Danny boy, come and watch!"

The sound of the shower was like rain beyond the walls, dulled by distance. What was the matter with him? Was he afraid to come out? It seemed like he'd been showering for thirty minutes. Did she make him nervous? If so, good. That was a very good sign.

She eased the bra off her high, small breasts and twirled it around and around the way the stripper on television was doing, and then let it go.

It struck the window at the back of the room. She heard the snap of it against the glass, and for the first time she noticed the drapery did not fully cover the window. A night breeze was entering, cooling the air in the room. Something, or someone, was holding the curtain back, staring in through the open window.

She squealed softly and folded her arms across her chest.

Somebody was watching her from the window.

She stared, seeing something, something that somehow seemed to have no definite form. It moved, and she stared open-mouthed, unable to voice a sound.

The movement at the window seemed a part of the black night beyond. The light of the television, coned forward and enveloping her, made the corners of the room dark and featureless. She stared into the darkness of the window, and stood chilled and unmoving in the middle of the bed.

"W-who's there?"

Her voice was barely a squeak. She wanted to scream for Andy, but the shower was still running like a mountain waterfall beyond the bathroom door.

A thought came to her. Andrew! He had crawled out the bathroom window and come to the back window of the motel and was playing a joke on her.

But she couldn't laugh.

Maybe it wasn't a joke. Maybe he was a weirdo and had brought her here to murder her. She hadn't known him a long time, after all. Most of the six months she had worked in his club she had known him only as the boss. But no, she knew him well enough to know it couldn't be him. He was still in the shower. She heard him cough, a short sound beneath the running water.

She was afraid. She had been afraid before, but not like this. A strange tightness was coming over her body, paralyzing her like an animal that froze when it sensed death near. She tried to think. If it wasn't Andy, was it the motel manager? He had stared hard toward her through the window of the office, trying to get a look at her, as if he knew she and Andy weren't married. None of his damned business, but maybe it had brought out something crazy in him.

"Who's there?" she asked in a steadier voice, sinking to her knees on the bed, her arms still folded across her breasts.

Something was crawling through the window. In the darkness there she saw movement ... movements, it seemed, of something black against the darkness—indistinguishable features, shadows within shadows. She began to have a feeling it wasn't human. The cold fear, that had begun when she first noticed the drapery was back and the window partly open, turned now to naked terror.

The door was across the room behind her. She saw it in her mind, it too shrouded by darkness, but she couldn't move toward it.

Her bra lay on the floor at the base of the wall beneath the window. A pale, ghostly bit of material in the dark corner. She saw it move, lifted by the moving darkness.

Shadow separated from shadow and developed form.

The figure became a man as it emerged from the shadows and moved into the cone of light cast by the television. He was large, incredibly huge for a mere man. Like a dark apparition he loomed between her and the bright face of the television.

He brought with him a sickening smell of decay.

The scream she struggled to bring out, an instinctive call for help, died as she stared at him. The bra was in his hands, and in the dim and flickering light he seemed to be tightening it, twisting it. She saw arms, long and snakelike, more than two, a writhing movement as fluid as if he swam.

The light was playing tricks on her.

Suddenly the sound of water in the bathroom died away. Andy was coming. Andy ...

She was moving, her body unfrozen at last, as she made a frantic dash for the bathroom door.

The bra, now a taut string, stopped her. It circled her neck and jerked her back and down into the darkness at the foot of the bed.

Her fingers dug at it, but it was embedded so deeply in her flesh she could only feel the indentation it made.

• • •

THE SHOWER HADN'T HELPED. He'd tried hot water and then cold. Still, he was as nervous as a nineteenth-century bridegroom. Beautiful Alene. Like Alice, of *Alice in Wonderland.* He had thought of her as a lovely young girl, with her long blond hair and her wide, innocent blue eyes, ever since she had come to him asking for a job. He had wanted to put her in his office as secretary, or at least as a receptionist, but she didn't know how to type and didn't seem interested in the money she'd make as a receptionist. So he had hired her as a cocktail waitress.

She was trying to make enough money to go to acting school, she'd said.

He toweled most of the moisture off his body and then wrapped the towel around him. He looked for a robe, but there was none. What did he expect in a forty-dollar room, rented past midnight?

He was falling in love with a girl young enough to be his daughter and then some. When he was around Alene, when he looked at her, he felt seventeen years old again.

He had a notion to put his clothes on, go out there, get down on one knee, and propose marriage to her. Instead of what he'd had planned earlier.

His wife wouldn't care, not if she got her share of the money. He'd learned that money was what most young, beautiful women were after. And all his wives had been young and beautiful. Some of them had developed real brains, too, shrewd as hell. It was as if when beauty faded, brains compensated.

The room beyond the door seemed unusually quiet. The television was turned low. He pushed the door open slowly.

Light from the television shone like a distant moon on the pathway between the two beds. And in that splay of light she lay, her body pale and twisted, naked except for brief, pink panties that at first glance were invisible.

He stepped forward, staring as the bathroom door swung back and the brighter light outlined the still body on the floor.

"Alene? *Alene!*"

He knelt beside her and saw the pink strip of lacy material twisted so tightly around her neck it seemed a part of her. He saw the horrible contortion of her features, the protruding tongue, the open, bulging eyes.

He picked her up and ran with her, holding her even as he fumblingly unlocked the door. And then, screaming for help, he ran down the walk toward the office.

• • •

"What in the mother of God is going on?" Detective Pearson of the County Sheriff's office asked no one in particular as he moved among the lawmen from the county and the small town's police force. "A strangling two hours ago a mile away in a wrecked truck, and now here."

Andrew Daniels, whose driver's license claimed he was fifty-seven years old, and who had checked in under the fictitious name of Smith, was the most logical suspect in the death of the girl. The motel proprietor had given him a robe to put on, and he now sat in the well-lighted office, right in front of the window, his head down. On the floor, her lovely body now draped with a sheet, lay the girl. Daniels had carried her to the office, for some damned reason. Instead of using the motel room phone, he had picked her up and run down the walk with her, both of them naked except for the girl's panties.

Pearson had examined the room where the crime occurred. There was no doubt the killer had entered by the back window. He was, Pearson felt certain, the same dude who had killed the trucker.

He thought of his wife and two kids at home alone, and wished he could go be with them. A madman, who evidently had hitched a ride with the trucker and then killed him for some unknown reason, had then hit this motel, and now a twenty-one-year-old girl lay dead. Why her, and not the man?

"I was in the shower," Daniels said when Pearson went back to question him. "I didn't hear a thing."

It was going to be a hard night, Pearson thought. They'd have to talk to everyone in the motel, find out if anybody saw or heard anything.

Andrew Daniels owned a club in Tallahassee, it seemed.

"Why did you come all the way up here?" one of the other detectives asked. "Tallahassee has all the motels you could use."

Andrew Daniels, so colorless he looked sick, lifted his head, swallowed, and said, "It wasn't ... it wasn't like that, really. It started out just as a ride, a night off for both of us. We had dinner at a place, a seafood place, I don't remember the name. And we just drove. Coming in here was a ... sort of an accident." He shook his head. "Nobody knew we were here. Nobody."

The motel proprietor watched and listened. He thought of the women and children who had been in the room earlier, and who had been picked up by the man in the brown station wagon, but he didn't say anything.

Molly Brown? There was no way to trace her anyway. The address would be wrong, just as the name probably was.

Maybe the killer had gotten the wrong girl.

Maybe he was a psycho who didn't care who he got.

Maybe he was outside, or in one of the rooms now pretending to be asleep.

The police would learn about Molly Brown, that she had checked in about eleven o'clock in the morning and had left again, because he had rented the room to Daniels around twelve-thirty. Sooner or later they were bound to ask for that register so they could check the people who were in the motel.

Pearson came toward the desk.

"We'd like to see—"

"I know," Sanders said, pushing the register toward the sheriff's detective.

Pearson's finger ran down the list of names and stopped at the room number where the girl had been killed. He looked up.

"You rented this room twice today?"

Sanders shrugged. "Not uncommon," he said. "When one leaves, I just clean it up and rent it out again."

Pearson nodded and looked again at the register. He was interested only in the people who hadn't checked out yet, not the ones who were now gone.

Sanders drew a long breath. Whoever they were, wherever they were going, they were safe.

It was the kids, he thought to himself. It was the kids he cared about.

CHAPTER 8

AT DAYBREAK, with the sun a rosy suggestion on the eastern horizon, Mel pulled into a rest stop and parked. The lot was empty. The brick exterior building that contained the restrooms looked cold and deserted. Behind the building pine trees grew tall, the grass beneath them carefully mowed and tended. A forest of deciduous trees—oak, maple, dogwood, all now fully leafed—rose with the hills of north Georgia. They had passed through the myriad freeways of Atlanta during the late hours of the night, and the state line of Tennessee was only a couple of hours away.

He had driven faster than he usually did. Reaching a sixty-five-mile-an-hour limit on the interstate, he'd stretched it a bit. With the exception of a few big trucks that were traveling at the same rate of speed as he, there had been little traffic after one A.M. Something about the car that he had lost back at the beginning of the trip had made him nervous, itching to hurry away with this woman and her three helpless kids.

They were all still asleep, the boys sprawled over the makeshift bed in the rear of the station wagon, the girl lying neatly on the back seat with her legs drawn up, knees together; and their mother in the reclining seat, her face still facing the window. Through the night he'd heard all of them moaning in nightmare at various times.

He got out of the car and stretched. He hadn't gotten sleepy all night. Most of the time he didn't, on those nights when he had to hurry out of one state into another. But he was glad to see that Celia and her children were sleeping soundly.

Children usually could.

Celia sat up suddenly, blinking.

She gazed at him a moment as if she didn't recognize him.

"Good morning," he said. "Rest stop."

"Where are we?"

"About halfway between Atlanta and the Tennessee border. We'll be out of the state in a couple of hours. There are restrooms here, if you need them. We probably won't find another rest stop for a hundred miles. But I'd let the kids sleep, if I were you. We'll stop to eat when we see a restaurant."

He walked across the pavement toward the broad bands of highway that stretched through the rolling countryside. The highway had been cut into the hill on the other side, and the exposed layers of limestone looked ghostly pale in the early dawn light. Birds, by the millions, it seemed, were singing in the trees all around.

He watched an eighteen wheeler roll down the hill on his left and roar past, going north. Another one, slowing, pulled into the rest stop entry road. A couple of cars went by in the southbound lane.

He couldn't forget the car that had followed them a ways last night. Yet he knew it had been a false alarm. A coincidence. Just something to rattle him.

Pictures of home entered his mind. His two dogs would probably be in a position to watch the lane, as they always were when he came home. The ducks would probably be pulling their heads out from under their wings and waddling over to the feeder. Sometime later in the day his neighbor, Elvin, would come over and check on the dogs and ducks, walking through the path in the pines that joined their places. Elvin had told him that the dogs often followed him home and sat around awhile, then disappeared back down the path.

Someday, Mel thought now, he'd stay home with them. He'd walk that path with them, if Elvin was still alive.

He caught himself reaching into his shirt pocket for a cigarette. He was nervous, he realized, far more so than he usually was on these trips. His fingers touched the note Norma had given him instead of the fantasy pack of cigarettes he'd been searching for.

He unfolded the note and read it as he crossed the pavement back toward the walk to the restrooms.

First stop, the Merrows in Tennessee. He'd been there several times before. They were a family of three, the parents in their late thirties or early forties and one daughter about fifteen. Nice people. A little farm, twenty or thirty acres, a hobby, not a livelihood. Fred had his own real estate business in town.

Second stop, the Archers in Kansas. Their farm was about two thousand acres, and it definitely was a working farm, the livelihood of the Archers, and a damned good one. The Archers were not among the farmers in financial trouble. They grew wheat, mostly, and the rolling plains on which it grew were beautiful. He had seen it when it was growing green, and he had seen it when it was ripe and ready to be harvested. Fields of gold, he had thought then. They were scheduled to stay two days there.

The next lengthy stop was in Nevada, at the Randolph's. They had a ranch in the mountain foothills with horses to ride. A real western setup. Three days rest there. The kids would love it. At least, most of the kids he had taken there did.

In between, they'd be stopping in motels.

He began tearing the paper into small bits. When he came to a trash can he dropped it in. If he were stopped by police, who often were after him on behalf of the aggrieved parent, or by private investigators, the people on the note would be in trouble. This time, if the police were after him, he wasn't aware of it and apparently neither was Norma.

He had only the father and husband to watch out for, so far. He realized he didn't even know what the man looked like, what his name was, or what kind of car he might be driving. The trip had started so fast he hadn't had time to learn anything. If Norma was worried that a woman and her kids were in danger, then they were. That was all that mattered to him.

When he entered the breezeway to the bathrooms he saw that Celia had brought her kids with her. Of course she would have. A nervous mother on the run hardly ever even went to the bathroom without taking her child, or children, with her. He had seen a family of six squeeze into one small restroom at a service station because the mother didn't trust anybody. The last he had heard of that family, they were settled happily in a southern Texas town and beginning to trust again. Norma always kept in touch with her families for as long as necessary. His conversations with Norma always centered on those families.

"Would you mind ... ?" Celia asked.

Mel understood, even though she didn't finish her sentence. "Sure. Come on, guys."

They were good-looking kids, all three of them. Jonie was almost as tall as her mother. He guessed her to be eleven or twelve. Like his Crescent, she was developing early, with small breasts pushing against her blouse. The sight of that early development on a young girl chilled him now. They were in such danger of being molested by those crazy bastards that liked little girls and would do that sort of thing. It was as if they figured the girl was still too young to know what was being done to her.

The two little boys went with him into the men's room. The littler one looked up at him for a long moment before extending his hand to be held. With his other arm he hugged a small teddy bear.

Mel looked down at the older boy and saw a wistfulness on his face that made Mel's heart feel as if it had suddenly been squeezed dry. He reached out, and Blair hurried close, his small hand feeling as callused as a ditchdigger's. This boy had done some hard work.

A trucker was washing his hands at the long row of sinks. Mel nodded good morning to him.

"Nice day," the trucker said. "Good weather to be traveling."

"Yes, sure is."

Mel guided Drew into a stall and then stood outside the door. Blair hesitated until Mel opened the adjoining stall door for him. They were quiet children, deeply unsure of themselves. They had hardly said a word. Of course, they'd been sleeping most of the time. They'd probably wake up with a bang later on. He hoped they would.

"Traveling?" the trucker asked.

"Yes."

"Summer vacation?"

"That's it," Mel said.

"Going anyplace in particular?"

"No."

Drew came out of his stall, and then Blair. Mel took both boys to the sinks and waited until they washed their hands and faces.

"A couple of nice boys you got there."

"Yeah, thanks."

"I get all the traveling I want," the trucker said. "When I get a vacation, all I do is sit in a chair in the front room watching TV, or out in the backyard watching birds and kids and dogs and cats. Anything but traveling.

My wife, she'd like to get in the car and drive over to the coast or somewhere. But she doesn't ride this truck twenty-four hours a day."

"Right," Mel said, adding, "Good talking to you," as he went out the door with Drew's hand small and firm in his.

He would have to leave them in the care of their mother before he could go back into the restrooms for his own toilet. Even though the trucker was probably on the up and up, he was more talkative than most, asking more questions, and Mel hadn't felt safe leaving the kids unguarded even for a minute.

There was no one in the breezeway.

They waited.

Birds sang, and a couple of squirrels ran across the grass behind the restrooms. As if playing tag, one chased the other up a pine tree. Both boys watched, but neither one said anything.

Mel felt a tug on his hand—once, twice. He looked down. Drew's small, round face was looking seriously up into his.

"Can I have a drink?" Drew whispered. Mel had to lean down to hear.

"Sure, sure."

Mel picked him up and held him over the water fountain. Blair stood close, watching carefully. When Mel set Drew down he asked Blair, "Can you reach it?"

Blair nodded, and showed that he could. Water dripped off his chin.

The ladies' restroom door opened and Celia came out, with Jonie close behind.

"Here's your boys," Mel said. "You can walk around in the grass at the rear of the building if you want to, for a few minutes."

Celia nodded, and motioned her boys close. They went out the back of the breezeway just as the trucker came out of the restroom.

He waved. "Good luck on your vacation."

"Thanks. Same to you," Mel added, when he saw the man wasn't going to pause to ask any more questions. He waited, watching, until the man disappeared along the walk toward the front.

Paranoid, he chided himself as he went back into the restroom. Getting so paranoid he even suspected a lonely trucker of being part of the network out to stop people like him and Norma.

Cold water on his face felt good. He dried it off with his handkerchief. No paper towels in this place, only the kind of drier that blew warm air. Practically worthless so far as he was concerned.

He went back outside and found Celia and her three kids with their backs to the wall on the eastern side of the building. The sun had broken free from the horizon and was sending weak rays through the trees. Not enough to warm the building wall yet.

"Ready to go?"

Celia jumped. Jonie too, it seemed to him, jerked sharply around.

"In the car we've got some of those so-called healthy snacks. What are they called? Can't think of the name. I always carry a couple of boxes along."

He got no answer. Most kids knew the names of things like that.

Drew ran to catch up with him. Mel felt the small hand reaching for his. On impulse Mel swung the little boy up into his arms, and caught a fleeting glimpse of a smile, not quite certain. Mel carried him, getting pleasure he hadn't felt in a long time from the warm weight of the child in his arms. Just before he set him down into the rear of the station wagon, he gave him a close hug. A child of five was still a baby, he thought, as he released Drew.

Blair was waiting beside him.

Celia said, "Why don't you get in the door, Blair? You can climb over the seat."

Blair said nothing, and Mel understood what he wanted. He too wanted to be picked up and hugged, briefly. Mel lifted him.

"Going in the back is more fun, eh, guy?"

Blair nodded.

Mel hugged him, and felt the yielding lean, the pressure of the boy's cheek against his. Mel felt a burning behind his eyes. He couldn't start loving these kids. In a few days he'd be leaving them more than two thousand miles away and would never see them again.

The two little boys settled down with their backs against the backseat, and Mel opened the box of snacks.

"Granola bars, that's what they are. Made out of oatmeal and raisins and stuff like that. Sounds like plain old cookies to me, doesn't it to you, boys?"

They both nodded.

Mel handed them the opened box, and got two others and took them to Jonie and Celia.

He settled in and fastened his seatbelt. "There are drinks in the ice chest in the back," he told Celia. "We'll stop within the hour for breakfast. As soon as we find a place that looks good."

He wanted to ask her some questions about her husband, the man they were running from. But he would like to do the asking when the kids weren't listening.

But if he waited, he would probably get no chance. He could see she was one of the mothers who kept her kids close. He glanced back. Jonie was opening the two boxes of granola bars. The boys took their box, settled down, and started eating. Celia sat with her box he had given her in her hands, unopened. She stared down the road ahead.

"I need to ask you a few questions," he said in a low voice, "just in case we run into trouble along the way—"

She looked sharply at him. "Trouble?"

"I mean, there likely won't be any. I'm not expecting any. But I need to know of your husband's possible contacts, his description, that sort of thing."

He saw her chin tremble, pucker, smooth again. Her teeth clamped onto her lower lip. She shook her head. "Do you have a picture of him?" Mel asked.

She shook her head.

He saw she couldn't talk about him. Her color had changed, bleached faintly. Her hands, on the box of granola bars, became nervous and agitated. Her fingers picked at the paper, and her hands trembled so hard she had to put the box aside and intertwine her fingers tightly to hold them still. She turned her face away and stared out the other window.

Mel reached over and touched the back of her hand briefly. "It's all right. Forget it."

He could ask Norma when he contacted her from the Merrows. No problem. Ordinarily he wouldn't need to know. Only once had he run into trouble, and that was before he had picked up the woman and her child. A man with a knife had confronted him. At first he'd thought it was a plain robbery attempt, and then, with the man's first words, "Okay, where is she?" he knew it wasn't robbery. The guy was young, no more them twenty-two. But he had looked sixteen. It hadn't taken Mel thirty seconds to take the knife away from the guy, who then sat down and started bawling like a kid. But if he had known the guy's description ahead of time, he might have been more prepared. After that, he liked knowing what the man looked like.

In the case of the young kid, who had a drug habit as well as a habit of pulling a knife, there had been no trip to safety. The young wife had decided to stand by him while he went into drug rehab. Mel had never heard any more about them, so he guessed they had made it.

In the case of Celia and her children, about all he knew was what he saw. Fear. Extreme fear. And within him was a strange sense of danger, more than he had ever felt, as if the shadow of the man loomed over them.

JONIE SAT with her back against the right door so she could see back down the road behind them. Her dad was a fast driver. A lot faster than Mel. He could be driving any one of the cars or pickups on the road behind them. There were more and more cars and pickups now, as the day grew brighter and longer.

He liked pickups better. He would be driving the kind with a gun rack on the back window, and he would have his rifles and his shotgun there. The police didn't know it, but he even had an assault rifle. The kind that could spew out bullets like a machine gun. With one swipe of the barrel, one pull of the trigger, he could kill them all. He had shown it to Jonie the last day he was home, on one of those days when he wasn't supposed to be there.

He had said to her, "Come here, girl," and motioned to her to follow him out the back door. She didn't want to go, but she was afraid not to. Especially when her mother confronted him.

"Where are you taking her?" Celia demanded. She had stood in front of him, between Jonie and him, even though she was trembling.

Durk stared down at Celia, a slow smile coming on his lips, the kind of smile that could turn into a sneer so rapidly. Jonie pushed between Celia and Durk.

"It's okay, Mama," she said.

The sneer came. "She's got more sense than you do," Durk said to Celia.

They went out of the house and across the barren back yard to the barn. It was big and still now, all the cages empty. At first, in the still twilight of the barn, Jonie had been afraid Durk was going to punish her because of the dogs, for him having been turned in to the law. But instead he picked up something that had been leaning against the wall. It was another gun. He had so many one more didn't matter. He knew she hated them. He laughed when she drew back.

"See this?" he said.

It looked shorter but more threatening than his shotgun or his rifles, but she said nothing.

"It's called an assault rifle. It can shoot down an army." He raised it to his shoulder, sighted at a group of cages on the other side of the barn and pulled the trigger. The shots rang harshly in her ears, and she cried out and threw her hands up against her head. The cages on the other side bounced as if they were in pain.

He was laughing again, looking down at her with a glitter in his eyes. "See what I can do to that judge that said I can't come back to my own house? See what I can do to your mama, and your brothers? To you, too, if you don't—"

At that moment the door burst open and Celia ran into the barn, her face so white Jonie was afraid she was dying.

"What the goddamned hell are you doing?" Celia cried, her face taking on color as she yelled. Then to Jonie's astonishment she snatched the assault rifle out of Durk's hands. "Don't you *ever*—I mean ever—do anything like that again!"

For just a moment Jonie thought she was going to pull the trigger and do to Durk what he had done to the dog cages, but instead she threw the shiny new rifle into the dirt of the barn floor. It bounced, spun once, and dug into the soft silt.

At first Durk had seemed stunned into inaction, then his fist knotted. Jonie moaned, and her eyes closed instinctively so that she didn't see the blow. She heard her mother fall. When she opened her eyes, Celia was on the ground beside the rifle, blood oozing from the corner of her mouth. Durk picked up the rifle, kicked Celia hard, and walked out the barn door. It slammed so hard behind him the walls shook, and the rusty old cages rattled faintly, as if the ghosts of dogs were still there, trembling.

As Jonie was helping Celia up, dusting some of the fine, silty dirt off her, she heard Blair scream out.

"Oh, God!" Celia cried softly, that awful sound of helpless misery in her voice, a sound made up of tears unshed and prayers unspoken.

Jonie blinked back from the memory. That day wasn't the last time she had seen her dad. She remembered, vaguely, seeing him once more. In the night. But she didn't want to remember.

So she watched for a pickup, especially, with guns in the rack. She sat with her legs up in the seat, the seatbelt twisted and loosened around her before she dared slip it off, and watched all the other automobiles on the long, broad highway. Especially she watched the pickups. With gun racks.

In the back, within reach of her left arm, sat Drew and Blair. Blair had curled up with his chin resting on the ice chest. He liked to watch scenery go by. Blair was always tied to the television set whenever a travel show came on.

Drew was playing with a little Transformer toy from the suitcase Norma had given them.

Sometimes she almost forgot to watch for pickups. The scenery was changing. The hills rose green as green could be on both sides of the wide highway, and sometimes now they drove for miles without seeing a house. They were in the mountains of Tennessee.

She had heard Mel say it wouldn't be long before they reached the Merrows, where they would be staying for a couple of days.

Then they were going on, and they would have a new home and new names, and Durk ... would never be able to find them.

Jonie frowned, a memory struggling against her will to remember. She squirmed in the seat and forced herself to think of really nice things. Of being just like everyone else. Of going to school and having friends. She'd read about friends and had seen shows on TV about friends, but she'd never had a real girlfriend in her life. Or a boyfriend.

Was it possible that she could go to school and be like everyone else?

That faraway place in Alturas, California, didn't seem at all real. It was like a dream only half dreamed.

Jonie knew, suddenly and with cold dread, they would never get there.

CHAPTER 9

THE ALARM CLOCK BLURPED IRRITATINGLY, on and on. The grey Persian cat, Missy, meowed, stretched, and rose from her spot on the pillow, went over to Norma, and sniffed her face.

Norma struggled up, Missy's tickling whiskers against her face more of a wake-up than the alarm clock. Somehow she adjusted to alarms, no matter what they were. She reached over and turned off the clock, then she sat in the bed with Missy in her arms. Toby, a long, slim alley cat, stretched up from where he had slept at the foot of the bed and came for his morning loving.

Norma sat slumped, feeling drugged. When life went smoothly, she went to bed with the chickens, more or less. When the sun went down, she was ready to sleep. When it came up, she was usually ready to rise. These late nights were hard on her.

"Gotta move, babies. You can go back to sleep."

Missy followed her to the bathroom door and sat grooming herself while Norma went through her own grooming processes.

She dressed in a blue suit, the jacket unlined and cool, the blouse white and open at the throat, the skirt with an inset of pleats low in the back. She wore her skirts on the longish side, believing the length slenderized her legs. She had stopped wearing high heels when she was still in her twenties, and now wore neat little pumps whose one-and-a-half-inch heels were made to look higher.

More awake now, she went to the kitchen, poured a cup of hot coffee that had so conveniently turned itself on at six o'clock, and then went out onto the back patio to drink it.

Birds were already taking a dip in the birdbath. The roses were blooming beautifully, and the vines growing on the privacy fence made her small backyard look like a jungle in some faraway land. She loved it.

She wondered at times what Mel's ten acres were like. He had a pond, she knew, and a lot of privacy. The swampland to the south of his acreage was not likely to be built on, so his privacy was assured. When they were together, if they weren't talking business, they were talking homes and pets.

She had bought her own small two-bedroom house the second year of her law practice, over ten years ago. Then she had struggled to make her payments on the house and on the government loan for her education.

When she'd gotten both paid off, instead of putting money back for herself, for her own future, she had gone into the Underground Railroad to help children in abusive families. Children and women, sometimes men, who she couldn't help in the courtroom. Her idealism had been shattered in a hurry.

Growing up in a small town in Florida, she had never known of child abuse. It came as a shock to her. Something she would never forget.

That first child was four years old and had one arm in a cast. One of his small legs had grown crooked from three breaks that hadn't been treated. His face was bruised, with big purplish spots on his cheekbone and beneath his eye. He held his head sideways.

She took him away from his two parents, who sat on a bench in the hallway, into the privacy of her office. The social worker had asked her to talk to him, to see if he would open up to her. She and the doctors who had seen him felt he was a victim of abuse, but they couldn't get him to talk.

"Hi," Norma said to the child, who stared up at her without trust. "What's your name?"

For a long pause he said nothing, then he murmured, "Tommy."

"Tommy, how did you get hurt?"

He said nothing.

"Tommy, what should I say? How did you hurt yourself?"

"I fell."

She knew from the reports that he lived in a house at the edge of town. The only stairs were on the porch. Three steps down. The family was not poor. Both the parents worked, earned money to buy what they wanted, had good health insurance. But the child had not been taken to a doctor until he was in the first grade. He had shown up after a two-day absence with a broken arm, and the school had taken him to the doctor.

"He has brittle bone disease," the parents were on record as saying. But there were no medical facts to back it up.

"Where did you fall?" Norma asked.

His eyes searched the room, or searched for an answer. "I fell off the ... I fell at the playground."

He wouldn't change his story. Yet he hadn't fallen on the school playground, and there was no park near his home. When Norma took him back out to his parents she saw his mother smooth his hair back from his forehead and kiss him. She saw his father pick him up and hug him, and heard him ask, "You okay, Tommy lad?"

How could anyone suspect such loving parents of child abuse? Norma wondered. The social worker and the doctors were all wet. There was love here, obviously.

Tommy had watched Norma as his father carried him out. There was an expression in his eyes Norma didn't understand.

Later, when she heard of his death, she thought she understood that look. Desperation. *Keep me,* that look had begged. *Keep me away from my mother and father.*

The parents had eventually ended up being charged with murder. But it was too late.

Norma had never known before of the deception some people were capable of. She had never known that a parent can kiss his child one moment and torture him the next.

It was her most extreme failure.

She had gone to Tommy's funeral. The casket was bluish grey with silver handles, very elaborate, and the parents were there, weeping, wailing.

Norma didn't understand. Not then, not now.

She was now thirty-nine years old, and although she had dated several men she liked, and a couple she might have married, her work had occupied her so completely that she'd had no room for a family of her own.

Except for her cats.

In the patio door at the back of her small family room, which was really an extension of her kitchen and dining room, there was a small door through which her cats could come and go as they pleased. Sometimes when she came home she found them in lawn chairs on the patio. But usually they were at the front window in the living room, watching for her.

She loved them dearly.

"Why on earth don't you get married?" her sister, Dee, asked, too often.

"Yes," her mother agreed every time there was a family dinner. "You're going to be alone in your later years, Norma. That worries me."

"It's okay," she tried to assure them. They knew a bit about her work, her real work, the Underground. They knew she didn't make any money from it, and that she put a large part of the money she earned from her law practice into it. And that too worried them.

"You'd better watch out," her dad said almost every time she told them of a case. "You'd better be careful. One of those people might come after you."

So she had stopped telling them. They often asked, "Are you still helping out with that Underground thing?"

She couldn't lie, but she could be brief. "Yes." That was enough. Then she learned to shade the truth—a lot. "A little. Occasionally. Nothing to worry about."

She said good-bye to her cats. "See you later, Missy, Toby. Try to miss me a little, okay? I'll bring you a nice treat." Missy didn't like fish at all. Wouldn't touch any cat food that had fish in it. But Toby thought it was the most fantastic thing in the world. Oddly, Missy liked candy. So occasionally Norma brought home a chocolate bar, which she shared with Missy.

Tonight would be a chocolate bar night. A kind of celebration. She felt so good about Celia and the kids and the new future awaiting them.

Norma arrived at her office a little late. In the outer office sat the two secretary-receptionists who worked for the three attorneys who made up the Collier law firm.

"A guy's been trying to get you all morning," Laura said. She was a pretty blond in her mid-twenties. At home, Norma knew, she had a much-loved two-year-old son. Her husband was a construction worker and had built their house himself. They were trying to get it paid for. As soon as that happened, Laura was going to quit work and have another baby or two or more. They both wanted a big family.

Norma's feeling of having things under control instantly fled.

Nadine, the other secretary, a middle-aged woman who had worked for David Collier from the time he first opened his own office twenty-five years ago, said, "As soon as I opened the door I heard the telephone ringing. I didn't know if you wanted your home phone number given to him."

"Who?" Norma asked. Not Mel. No, it couldn't be. He knew her private number.

"He wouldn't give his name."

"You have a court appointment at ten, remember. And a client coming in at 9:30."

"Yes, I remember."

"And what about the meeting at the mayor's about the dinner for that club thing?"

"Could you get me out of that?"

"I don't know how."

"Think of something."

"That's at three o'clock," Nadine called after her. Norma went on into her office, took off her jacket and hung it up, and went to her desk. The phone rang. She picked it up before she sat down.

"Sorry to call you here, but I lost that private number." She knew his voice immediately. Johnny Rains had towed away and worked over many cars, pickups, and vans for her.

"It happens. I'll give it to you again. Everything okay?"

"No. I went over to that motel you told me about to get that car about two o'clock this morning. Couldn't get there before that. And it was gone."

"Gone?" It took a thought to realize the significance of what he had said. *"Oh, Lord. Gone?!"*

"Gone."

"How could that be?" She was talking to herself, thinking of the many miles Celia and the children had driven to get to the motel, and the distance her husband would have to have walked from their home to get to another car. Could the husband have found the motel so soon?

"Somebody took it. It might have been stolen."

"Yes. Oh." That wasn't what she'd been thinking about, but it was possible, and that was far better than having Durk Nolan somehow reach it and take it himself. Theft was far more probable. She prayed it was so.

"Another thing," Johnny said.

Norma listened carefully, alert to something in his voice she couldn't yet identify.

"There was a murder in the motel. I think in the same room you might have rented, because they said a woman had checked out of the room and a couple checked in after her. The woman was strangled."

Norma frowned hard at the wall. She didn't realize she had not answered until he was talking again.

"And that's not all. Less than a mile from that motel, a trucker had a wreck. Another trucker saw it and called the police. They found the trucker strangled. Just like the woman in the motel. Except the woman had been strangled with her own bra, and the man with bare hands." Norma stared at the wall, bombarded by images as broken as a scattered jigsaw puzzle. Celia, her kids, Durk in the courtroom, Celia, Mel. A trucker, dead; a woman, dead.

"There was police there when I got there," Johnny said. "It wasn't the man with the woman who strangled her. Whoever it was came in through the back window of the motel room. Whoever it was that killed the trucker must have stowed away in his truck. He had a new truck with a sleeper compartment. It was messed up some, they said. And had some stuff from a pond or swamp in it. And there was some of the same stuff on the window. So they know it was the same man."

Norma listened. She put her palm against her forehead and pulled a map of the United States out of a drawer she unlocked with her other hand. There were several routes marked on it in red ink. The map, like the duplicate she kept at home in a drawer in her small den, showed the routes of the Underground Railroad system, even into Canada. One route even went down into Mexico. Mexico had been more difficult to get into for many reasons, most of them having to do with the economy.

"They just about picked me up," Johnny was saying. "Wanted to know what I was doing there with a tow truck. I told 'em I was just passing through. But I think I'm on their shit list for awhile." He paused. "I had to let you know."

"Johnny, thank you. I don't know what to say. I guess we've always been luckier than we thought."

"Kind of looks that way. The thing is, the car was gone when I got there. And two people were murdered before that, real close. Kind of ties in, don't you think?"

"It sounds that way."

She sat in her chair staring at the wall for long minutes after Johnny's call.

She picked up a ballpoint pen and began tapping it against the desk blotter. She should tell the police about Durk Nolan, but if she told, they'd want to know how she knew. Then they'd probably bring Celia back for questioning. They'd certainly start looking for her. They'd get Mel, they'd find out one of the major arteries of the Underground escape system. A lot of families would be in danger of losing their newfound security.

She didn't blame the law enforcement people. They did what they had to do. They tried. Even the judges, some of whom she would gladly have sent to a secluded island for the rest of their lives, did what they could on what they had to go on. She knew how difficult it was to judge who was right and who was wrong when the child was afraid to tell the truth and the parents, or, as was usually the case, the parent, was so careful to cover up his or her abuse. Often, not even the other parent knew until it was too late.

She understood the law and its helplessness so much of the time in unraveling the truth.

She bent over the map. They'd have to do the best they could.

How could he have known what motel Celia would be in? How could he have followed at all? If he had ridden in a truck as a stowaway, he couldn't have known. Yet he had found the car. He had—he must have—killed the woman in the motel, perhaps thinking it was Celia.

Norma didn't understand how he had managed to follow as far as he had. She rolled the pen between her fingers and stared out the window. Trees and blue skies blurred into one blotch of color. Somehow, Durk Nolan had followed his family. Celia had said there was only one car. But there must have been another—nearby, available to him. He had seen the direction she took. Yet that didn't explain the truck, or stowing away on it, or the killing of the driver.

Maybe Durk had simply known Celia would try to contact Norma. It wouldn't have been difficult to find out where she lived.

But that too made no sense. He had not come here. He had followed Celia directly to the motel. Not only to the motel but to the room she had been in earlier in the night.

Norma suddenly felt as if she had been blindfolded, as if a curtain lay between her and a truth she would never know. She had never felt so confused, so undecided about which way to turn.

She checked her watch. She should leave for court soon.

Mel and Celia and the kids were on the road. There would be no way she could reach him until evening.

But she had to talk to Mel. It was the only thing she could think to do.

CHAPTER 10

HE HAD TURNED off the interstate about fifty miles north of Nashville and had found the two-lane highway that led through the town of Clarksville. At a small cafe he settled Celia and the kids in a booth and told them to order whatever they wanted. He returned to a telephone in the entryway and called the Merrows' real estate number. He asked to speak to Alice or Fred, and for a few moments listened to music tinkling over the line.

"Fred Merrow speaking."

"Mel Barton. Norma said you would be expecting us?" Fred Merrow's voice lost its professional ring and softened. "Say, you made good time. We weren't expecting you until evening. Go right on out. Robin's home and looking for you. Alice and I will be in at the usual time. You must have made it without any problems?"

"No problems," Mel said. "We've traveled straight through the night and day. We're all a little strung out."

"Go rest. We'll be home by six o'clock."

Mel went back to the booth where the kids had ordered milk shakes. Celia started to get up. Mel motioned to her to remain seated.

"It's all right. We're only four miles from our destination. Let the kids finish their milk shakes."

Celia said in a low voice, "Hurry. Don't dawdle, Blair." Blair bent over his straw and sucked noisily. Celia frowned at him.

Mel said, "We'll be staying with the Merrows two nights and one day, if you have no objections."

Celia looked down at the table and said nothing. Jonie's bright eyes watched him for more information.

"You'll like it there," Mel said. "All kids do. There's a girl, Robin, fifteen or sixteen. And there are animals and ponds, one of them for swimming. And plenty of room and privacy. They have a big house, and they're very hospitable. For one thing, they leave you alone, if that's what you want."

He saw Celia look out the window. And then Jonie, too, was staring out the window toward the gas pumps at the convenience store next door. Jonie's look of eager interest, of a smile just beneath the surface, changed and hardened. She squinted, staring at the pickup.

Mel tried to see the driver beyond the glare of late afternoon sunlight on the windshield. All he could see was a rack in the rear window, and the lineup of several black-barreled rifles or shotguns.

He looked at the little boys, but their backs were to the pickup at the gas pumps, and they were just finishing their shakes.

Celia stood up.

"Are you ready?" Mel asked. She was still staring at the pickup.

Then a man got out. He was built like a barn, with broad shoulders. He looked almost as wide as he was tall. A dark beard covered his face. Mel could almost feel the sag of relief in Celia and Jonie.

The man they were running from, Mel surmised, was nothing like the man who had driven the pickup. The pickup itself, the guns, were part of the faceless person who was somewhere behind them, but the man was different. He reminded himself again to ask Norma for a description.

Celia had her boys up with a motion of her hand. Jonie helped by pulling Drew along in front in a protective gesture, as if putting herself between him and danger. He hugged his teddy bear against his chest with one plump arm.

They left the cafe, where the waitress was laughing with a couple of guys down at the end of the counter, and went out to the station wagon. It was beginning to look a bit dusty. A bit long in the tooth, too. And no wonder, Mel thought as he settled in beneath the steering wheel and looked at the odometer. Close to a hundred thousand miles. Good for another twenty before any work would have to be done on it, though, he hoped.

They drove out of town and into a tunnel of trees. Hills rose on each side. The road was narrow, blacktopped, and almost private. They met no cars.

"There are only four families that use this road," he told Celia. "The Merrows live at the end. Two more families live on this next little road to the left and just about an eighth of a mile from the end of the lane another turns off to the right. They're some people called Scott. They are the original owners of it all. Fred Merrow bought his twenty acres from them, and had the house and ponds built."

Jonie, just over his shoulder, asked, "How do you build a pond?"

Mel almost jumped. It was the first question Jonie had asked him.

"A bulldozer digs a shallow, wide hole in the ground, the way it's done when a swimming pool is made. Then the natural rainfall fills the hole. If it has a proper clay bottom. In some parts of the country building a pond is impossible. Not enough rainfall, or not the right consistency of earth. Here, one of the ponds has a stream of water feeding into and out of it. Robin will show it all to you."

"Who's Robin?" Blair asked.

"Robin is the Merrows' daughter. She'll be waiting for us."

They turned right, past broad, decorative brick corner posts, and the land opened up into a small valley. In the middle, on a knoll, stood a white two-story house with broad porches and a sloping green lawn. Behind the house were several sheds and barns, red with white fences. Tall trees shaded the house and many of the sheds. Behind Mel Jonie gasped. He understood. It was a breathtaking sight, this entry to the home of the Merrows. He never failed to marvel at their generosity of opening their home to the total strangers he and other drivers so often brought here for a one- or two-night stay. They never asked questions, they just opened their hearts.

Robin, slender, wearing blue jeans and a tucked-in blouse, came down the steps of the house. Her long, dark hair curled over her shoulders. She had grown a little, it seemed to Mel, since he'd last seen her a few months ago.

Robin, with two golden retrievers running at her side, went around the house, following the driveway. She waved at the kids in the car, and hesitantly, bashfully, they returned the greeting.

Mel drove into the open garage door that Robin motioned toward. There the station wagon would be out of sight of any visitors.

In the musty twilight of the garage they got out of the car. Robin, smiling at each of the kids, moved in to help carry suitcases.

"You're tired, I know," she said. "I'm Robin, and I guess you're Jonie? And Blair and Drew. And Mrs.... ?"

"Celia, just call me Celia."

"Hi, Mel," Robin said. "Are you dead?"

"Just about. I think you've added another inch to yourself since last February, haven't you?"

Robin laughed. "Which direction?"

They went up the back steps and onto a long screened porch and from there through a large country kitchen with a round oak table near wide windows at one end. From the kitchen they entered a hallway leading to a back stairs that led up between two walls.

In the upper hall, Robin opened the door to the small bedroom at the rear where Mel always stayed when he was here.

"Take a nap, sir. You remember where the shower is. We'll call you when it's time to eat."

With the door closed behind him, and the footsteps of Celia and the kids going into rooms next door and across the hall, Mel collapsed across the bed. Fortunately, he had gotten a bit sleepy only a couple of times, in the middle of the afternoon, as the pavement took on the aspect of a hypnotizer's pendulum. But he had blinked his eyes a few times, reminded himself he had only another hundred miles to drive, and coaxed himself into wakefulness.

A shower, he thought, would feel good. He'd get up and ...

Sleep overwhelmed him like a gun butt on the back of his head.

ROBIN SHOWED Celia and Jonie to one small bedroom where the twin beds each hugged against opposite walls and there was barely room between for a nightstand.

"My mom and dad," she explained, apologizing for the sizes of the bedrooms, "took an ordinary bedroom and made it into two when they started uh ... taking in guests so often. You know, like ... ?" Sometimes she almost got her foot in her mouth. Mouth and foot disease, her dad called it. When she got that problem, she cured it simply by stopping talking.

Celia stood like a wraith in the slant of late afternoon sun. Jonie seemed a bit more substantial, even though she was smaller than her mother. She was standing in the sunless area between the beds. Robin had already left the two boys in the room across the hall, where there was a big, hefty box of toys. In that room, which was as large as these two bedrooms put together, there were two trundle beds.

Robin touched Jonie's hand. "If we don't hurry, the sun will be down before I can show you around. Want to come out with me? Mrs... . Celia, you can come too, if you want. If you'd rather stay in, the bathroom is just next door, and I promise to take care of your children."

Celia nodded. "Thank you." Then, as Robin guided Jonie out the door, she asked, "Where are you going?"

"Just out to see the animals," Robin said. "Is that all right?"

Celia hesitated, and Robin felt obliged to reassure her.

"We're way out in the sticks, Miss Celia. Nobody ever comes here without special invitation and special directions! And I promise you I'll watch very carefully over Jonie and the boys."

Celia nodded.

At the doorway to the boys' room, Robin saw Blair and Drew standing by the open toy box. They simply looked without touching. She suddenly felt more than her usual sympathy. She was flooded by sadness. These kids, even Jonie, seemed so much more timid and unsure of themselves than any of the others.

"Come on," she coaxed. "Let's get some fresh air. Besides, it's time I'm doing the animal feeding. Come and help me."

They followed her down the back stairs and out into the backyard. She kept up a stream of conversation, pausing often to allow one of them to join in, to ask a question, make a comment. But they stayed in a close little group around her and said nothing. Sunshine glinted on Drew's pale, straight hair. It looked bleached, it was so blond. Jonie and Blair's had reddish highlights in the sun. So pretty, with their soft waves.

She told them about the beautiful thoroughbred horse, Quicksilver, who had broken a leg during a race. The owner, who had a lot of horses, had been going to put her to sleep.

"But my dad, who was at the race that day, him and Mom, made arrangements to buy her. So here she is. And her leg is okay, you see. Our veterinarian put a metal splint in it and kept her off it until it healed."

She opened the gate into the barnyard and closed it behind the children. "You see, she has a baby. I've named her Silver Star, after her mother, and because of the white star on her face. Isn't she darling?"

They looked over the stall at the mare and the baby filly that was still wobbly on her twiggy legs.

"Would you like to pet her?" Robin asked Drew.

At first he pulled back his hands into knots behind his back, but when Jonie put one hand gingerly through the boards of the stall and the baby horse reached toward it, Drew also put his hand out.

Robin fed Quicksilver a mixture of grains, and when she was finished, and the stall gate was closed behind her, she saw that Jonie was looking around. Looking over her shoulder, looking toward the shadowed hill behind the barn, where trees created a dark world even in the afternoon. Robin was stunned by the look of dread and fear on the girl's face.

"Come on," she said, with an effort at enthusiasm she was losing. She had thought the kids would enjoy helping her feed the animals. Most kids did. But these kids were different.

A low whisper came from Drew. "Where's Mama?" Robin looked back at the house. Celia was outlined in the second-floor window, like a painting within a frame. A red glow from the sun reflected off the window pane and lightened the window in a strange, bloodlike way that brought cold goosebumps to Robin's arms. Even as she watched, the sun lowered and the window pane turned a metallic grey, like an ocean surface.

"Your mother's okay," Robin said. "She's resting. She said you could go with me to feed the animals. Let's feed the pigs now. Do you know they all have names, and they all come when they're called? Pigs are very smart. My pigs are named Berta, Sadly, and Gwen. Real girl names." Blair asked, "Why are all your animals girls?"

Robin laughed at the question. Blair liked the dogs, she saw. He had his hand on Buster's head, and Buster was eating up the attention, gazing up at Blair with rapture on his face.

"The boys are all out on pasture," Robin explained. "The girls are in the barnyard and stalls to have babies."

"Oh."

"Tomorrow we can walk out to the pasture and see the others, if you want. We have cows there, and horses, and pigs and goats and sheep and—"

Jonie was staring toward something so intently that Robin turned and stared too. She saw the mirror-like surface of the big pond behind the barn.

"That's the main pond. Would you like to go see it?" She led the way around the barn and down to the edge of the pond. White geese and dark green mallard ducks on the far side began swimming toward them. Robin wished she'd brought their grain, but she'd have to go back to the barn after it.

Jonie seemed mesmerized by the water, staring with a frown toward it.

"At home we have a swamp," Blair said. "It's got trees growing in it. Doesn't your pond have any trees?"

"Only on the other side," Robin said. "Trees in the water would die. The kind of trees we have here."

"I don't want to stay here," Drew whimpered. He stood several feet back on the bank. "I want my mama."

Jonie hurried back to Drew. His face crumpled, but there were no tears. Jonie bent over Drew, whispering words Robin made no effort to hear.

Blair said to Robin, "He ... our ... father ... used to drown our dogs in the swamp, before the judge made him stop."

Robin stared horrified into Blair's face. But she had been coached by her parents to make no comments concerning anything a child might tell her about an abusive parent. She touched Blair reassuringly on the shoulder, and with him, followed Jonie and Drew back to the house.

She would have to go alone to finish doing her chores. She had hoped to have company to walk along the pond edge, to scatter grain to the ducks and geese, all those things most kids enjoyed.

She wondered where Blair, Jonie, and Drew were from. Someplace where there were swamps, in which trees grew. Far south, surely. The trees must be cypress. She had seen them on trips to other places. Trees with knees, they were called. Worlds so far away from her own, it seemed.

But what was it about her pond that scared them so much? It was clear, from the spring that fed it, and the grass was mowed right down to the edge on the sides toward the barn and pasture. It was a beautiful pond, and she loved it.

A KNOCK on the door woke Mel. He sat up quickly, blood rushing away from his head and making the world spin for a moment. The room was almost dark, as if someone had pulled a blind. But the window was still uncovered, he saw. Beyond it the night was gathering. The knock came again.

Mel stood up and used his fingers to comb his hair back. "Yeah. Come in."

The door opened and Fred Merrow looked through. He had a round, firm, ruddy face, the kind of skin that would never wrinkle. Bright bluish-grey eyes crinkled at Mel.

"Sorry to wake you. How're you doing?"

"Better now." Mel shook hands with Fred.

"Dinner isn't quite ready. The reason I got you up is because Norma's on the phone. Something's come up that's got her worried. You can take the call on the phone in the hall up here if you want, or downstairs."

"I'll take it up here. And then if there's time, I'll shower."

"Take all the time you want. We'll wait dinner. I think Robin's been stuffing the kids ever since you got here, anyway. She usually does."

Mel and Fred went into the wide front hall of the second floor, where Mel stopped at the telephone. Fred went down the front stairs and through the door to the den. When Mel picked up the phone, he heard Fred hang up the other extension.

"Norma?"

"Mel, how are you?"

"Okay. We're all okay. How about you?"

"I'm fine, just worried. Something happened at the motel last night not long after you left. The room where we stayed was rented out again to a couple from Tallahassee, and someone broke into the room through the back window and murdered the woman. Strangled her."

Mel frowned, staring at the wall, at the mahogany banister that surrounded the balcony and edged the sturdy stairway that descended into the hall below, but he saw the motel room with the draped window at the back.

"Also," Norma said, "they think the same man killed a trucker not far away. He was strangled too."

"You think the killer is Celia's husband?"

"Could be, yes. Celia's car was gone. The tow truck driver who always picks up the cars for me said the car was gone when he got there. We have to assume the killer took the car, and I'm afraid the killer might be Durk Nolan and that he's following you."

Mel thought of the car he had managed to get away from last night. "What kind of car was it?"

"An older car, an Oldsmobile, I think. Maybe '77 or '78. Blue. Four-door."

The car that had followed them last night was newer than that. Mel hadn't seen it close enough to determine the make, but it had the bubble shape of a small Ford, and he thought it might have been white or grey.

"Light blue, dark blue?"

"Medium. I know that's not much help," Norma said, her voice seeming to fade away. It returned. "I had to call and tell you, just in case he has somehow managed to follow you on to the Merrows."

"No, I don't think that's possible. The kids have been watching out the back of the station wagon all day. Celia was always turning and looking back. If any of them had seen anything like their car, they would have said so. No one car stayed close to us."

He heard Norma draw a deep breath. "Good. Of course, he might have ditched that car and gotten another. So you wouldn't be looking for the blue Olds."

"Then he would have lost our trail if he'd taken time out to steal a new car and ditch the old. What time was the strangling at the motel?"

"At 1:15. Between 1:10 and 1:20, so they figure 1:15. The man had been taking a shower, a long one, presumably, and he found his girlfriend when he came out. He carried her down to the office, and the police were called at 1:25. They—the couple—checked into the room about fifteen minutes after we left."

"I saw a guy watching us. I thought he was the proprietor. He must have seen us leave."

"He did. I found out today that he had seen you and Celia and the kids leave and had checked the room after I left and found the key. So he just rented it again."

"The police know all of that?"

"No. My information comes from another source. He, the motel guy, whose name is Sanders, by the way, didn't mention to the police that he'd seen you, Celia, or the kids. I gave the name of Molly Brown. If the police saw it, they didn't seem to think it was important."

"Good."

"I just wanted you to know and be on the lookout."

"And this husband of Celia's. What does he look like?"

"Durk Nolan, age forty-four, six feet two, two hundred and forty pounds. He has long thinning blond hair and a very high forehead. His eyes are pale and very piercing, cruel. He makes me think of a snake. But of course I saw him only in court, and I was definitely prejudiced. I hadn't heard much story from Celia, and nothing at all from the kids; they just wouldn't talk. But I could see they were all terrified. And anyone who is cruel to animals you know will have even less feeling for humans. This is a deadly one."

"But only you and I know the complete route, right?"

"Right. And no one knows where you're stopping over except the people you'll be staying with."

"But they don't know where we stopped the night before or where we're going next, or where our final destination is, right? Where is your information filed? Does anyone else have access to it?"

"It's on my computer in my office at home. And there's a map showing all our routes in my desk. No one that I know of has access to either. No one has broken into my house. No one in the Underground business even knows my home address. They have my phone number, unlisted, just as you do."

"Then it doesn't seem likely that Nolan could have followed us. He might have assumed we'd take the interstate north. But he wouldn't know exactly where we would exit or where we would switch to a different route. Maybe the murders are just a terrible coincidence."

"Mel," Norma said after a moment, "be careful anyway."

"Believe me, I will," Mel reassured her, and quietly hung up the phone.

CHAPTER 11

"Da- Da-"

Blair couldn't say it. He choked on something that clogged his throat, something that felt like the dog vomit in the cage before him.

Call me Daddy, you dumb little bastard. Can't you even talk?

The voice roared in his ears so that he couldn't tell if it went on and on or it was just an echo. All the dogs in the cages around him in the big, dim barn were howling and whining, and the hand on the back of Blair's neck was crushing the life out of him just like the hand in his stomach crushed, tightening with each echo of the shout.

I told you to clean them goddamnedfuckin'cages, and you ain't got a lick of work done in the past hour. See the puke there? Clean it up! And whenever I come by, you call me Daddy! Or you call me sir!

The hand on the back of Blair's neck shoved, and his face was plunged into the vomit of the cringing new dog. Blair couldn't breathe. He couldn't ... breathe ...

BLAIR TURNED IN HIS BED, struggling against the memory.

He wasn't there anymore, in the big barn that sent back sounds from the rafters. He wasn't there pulling the wheelbarrow from cage to cage, digging into the manure and vomit with his small shovel. He wasn't seeing dogs that hung their heads because they had been forced to go into their cages, or die because they couldn't.

He didn't have to live with a man he couldn't call daddy. Or even sir.

The room was dark, but he wasn't afraid. He could see the long, pale light of the window across the room, and he could hear Drew move now and then. Drew thrashed in his bed like an animal held against its will. Like he was trying to get away too.

Laughter ... he could hear it in his mind. Laughter when something wanted to get away and couldn't. It was like an evil chuckle that sent icy knives through his whole body.

He turned again and faced the wall and the door to the hall. Mel was across the hall in one of those rooms, he thought, or maybe he was right across the wall, right at the head of his bed.

He thought of the station wagon and the way the back of Mel's head looked. The dark brown hair and the funny cap Mel wore sometimes with the little brim sticking out to shade his eyes. He wore sunglasses, too, and a beard.

But the color of his hair, it was like his own, almost. It was like father and son. When Blair sat behind the seat looking forward he watched people in cars passing by, and sometimes when they looked toward him he felt something he'd never felt before. It was like being lifted, way up, by God's hand. Up above anything that could ever hurt anymore. Up into the clouds and the blue sky, and feeling that singing inside, that beautiful singing that had no words but was just a feeling.

He felt that way because he knew the people looking at them thought Mel was his daddy.

"See how much that little boy looks like his daddy, did you notice?" The lady in the passing car would be saying to her husband.

My daddy.

"My daddy."

Blair's voice whispered into the room, again and again.

"My daddy."

His mama was going to marry Mel, and together they would live in the high country, wherever that was. He could see the cabin on the mountain-side, and it looked just like the cabin Heidi from the storybook lived in. There would be goats and sheep and flowers growing. And cheese and bread. And the dogs would be happy and free.

Mama would bake cookies and pack them in a basket, and Mel would hold Blair's hand on his left side, and Drew's on his right, and they would walk down the mountainside and ...

Sometimes they would keep riding in the station wagon, going on and on, with the trees flashing by.

And sometimes Daddy would hold him on his lap, at bedtime maybe, and press his hand against his face, the way the daddy did in the storybook Blair had left back there.

Today Mel—*Daddy*—had held Blair's hand. Together they had walked to the bathrooms at the rest stop. And later Daddy had put his hand on Blair's head.

Once, as they rode along, Daddy told them a story about when he was young. He had lived where they had a pasture that was big enough to keep a pony, he had said, and he got to ride his pony. There was a path around the pasture, and flowers bloomed along the path, and the pony, whose name was Princess, liked to stop and eat the flowers.

"What color were the flowers?" Blair asked.

"Yellow," Daddy said. "Little yellow daisies." Then he laughed. "I used to think that was where chiggers lived, because every time I walked through the yellow daisies I got chiggers."

"But Princess ate them."

"She didn't care if I called them chigger flowers."

Yellow flowers. Tiny little yellow flowers. Jonie had picked a bouquet of yellow flowers on a day that he didn't want to remember. The picture came into his mind and wouldn't go away, and he could feel the heat of the sun as he followed Jonie. Then *he* was there, stepping out from the shadows of the pine trees beside the barn.

He took Jonie's wrist in his big hand, and his eyes were narrowed like a window shade with a rip at the top that looked out upon the faraway blue sky, and he smiled at her in a way that made Blair feel scared.

Those for me? You picked your daddy a pretty bunch of posies? Well, for that I'll give you a kiss.

Jonie tried to pull back, but he was stronger, a lot stronger. He pulled her to him and his arm hid the back of her head from Blair's eyes. Then he put his face down slowly, those slitted eyes staring at Jonie's face, and he kissed her. The kiss lasted a long time, the way the kisses on some of the television shows Mama wouldn't let them watch if she caught them in time. It lasted and lasted, and he heard Jonie trying to cry. It was like the cry was coming from a long way off. Blair could feel it in his stomach, and his stomach began to hurt.

Suddenly he was running through the hot sunshine. He crossed the field with the tiny yellow flowers and ran into the house. Mama was washing dishes at the table, her hands in the soapy suds in the dishpan, and Drew sat on the floor playing with his puppy.

Mama looked at him. He couldn't talk, his stomach and chest hurt so much. But he didn't have to.

Mama ran out the door, her hands coated with suds. She knew. Without him telling, she knew.

A long time later Mama and Jonie came into the house, and he had driven away in his pickup. It had roared and spun its wheels, and sand flew and made a curtain behind as the pickup disappeared.

Ever after that Jonie had turned pale when *he* came home, when he reached for her and held her wrist. She had stopped laughing, or even talking, when he was around.

But it was all different now. Now they were going to be living a new life, with their real daddy.

Tomorrow they would drive on the wide, long highways again, with Daddy at the wheel. Daddy looking into the rearview mirror to see that everything was all right.

To make sure he wasn't following.

Once today Daddy had looked over his shoulder, back down the highway, and then he had winked at Blair and smiled and said, "It's okay, guy."

Blair felt like his grin had spread all over his body as he lay in his bed and grinned at the ceiling.

They were going away—he, Mama, Jonie, and Drew. They were going away with their new daddy, their *real* daddy.

"My daddy." It sounded so good in the silence of the room. "My real daddy," he lowered his whisper until it was almost just a movement of his lips. "My real daddy has come and got us and is taking us away, and we're going to live in the high country and be happy ever after. And that's the honest-to-God truth."

Blair turned and pulled the blanket up over his head. Drew coughed, a muffled sound, as Blair drifted away on his dreams.

He knew it was okay now, because Daddy had said so.

He had come to rescue them. Finally. At last.

Blair slept, and dreamed of high country, with the top of the mountains lost in fluffy white clouds. His daddy Mel walked at his side.

• • •

DREW TURNED IN HIS BED, flinging his arms out, tossing his head. Sweat coated the back of his neck and dampened the hair around his ears. He moaned softly.

In the bed across the room Blair turned over, wrapping himself in his blanket, lost in sleep.

Drew tried to run, to get out of bed and run away. He wanted to run and run until he found a place where nothing would ever hurt him.

The window was open, and the curtains swayed. He could see them, see through them, the way he could see through ghosts.

"There's a ghost in my room!" he had once screamed to his mama, but instead, he had come and had slapped him for yelling in the night like that and waking him up. He had pushed Drew's face down into the pillow and held it until Drew couldn't breathe, and his voice was mean and shallow behind Drew's head.

"You won't be seeing any ghosts now, will you, huh? Will you?"

And when he had let go, Drew hadn't dared move. He sucked in a long, cool breath of air and lay still, and the ghost went back into the darkness, afraid too.

Tonight he wasn't going to cry for his mama, even though he knew he wasn't here. Tonight the ghosts whispered at the window by the foot of his bed and came into the room and went out again, like pale, white mist-like birds.

What scared him more was the water. He could see it glistening under the light of the stars and the thin moon that came through the trees. He could see the surface of the water, as still as the mirror above the dresser. He could see the dark shadows of the trees in the water.

He could see his dog Laddie, there, floating in the black water. *He* had put Laddie there, because Drew had spilled his glass of milk at the breakfast table. He had punished Drew by throwing his dog into the water.

Drew stared, his eyes straining in the dark. Laddie was gone.

It wasn't the swamp he was looking at, it was the pond. He wasn't at home in his room, he was in a strange house where the window was high off the ground.

He stared at the water. It reflected the light of the sky, too, like the swamp. Something moved there, beneath the surface. He couldn't see it yet, but he knew it was there.

Helpless, he clung to the window frame, a cool wind blowing into his face. Then the wind stopped. The trees stopped moving, the curtains stopped moving. The world stood still.

Drew watched the water.

The surface opened, and a round, shiny black head rose. The many eyes stared black and bulging toward Drew at the window. Then a long snakelike arm rose, feeling for the edge of the pond, then another, and another, and finally so many arm-leg things that Drew could not count them. They seemed to tangle in the pale light of the moon and stars as the horror rose from the pond and stood tall and huge at the edge on its dozens of legs.

Drew heard the horse crying in the barn, its whinny blending with the cackle of chickens, the grunting of pigs. A dog howled.

The thing was coming toward the house, standing tall on its legs, reaching forward with its arm-legs, staring up at Drew with its hundreds of eyes. He knelt by the window and watched it, unable to cry out, to call Mel to help him shut the window.

He saw it go past the barnyard, past the animals, and come to the house. And he knew it was at the wall.

Then he could hear it crawling up the wall toward the window. It pulled itself up the wall, a sound that was like the whispering movement of water in the swamp around the creases of the cypress knees. A black, long, snakelike arm reached into the window, through the screen, and then another and another, and Drew felt the cold, deadly touch of it on his cheek. He felt it sliding around his neck, pulling him out of the window toward the invisible mouth that was ready to devour him.

The scream came out of him like a bubble bursting.

CHAPTER 12

CELIA WAS out of her bed and on her feet before she was consciously aware of hearing Drew scream. It was the most terrifying, terrified sound she had ever heard. In all her years of hearing one or another of her children cry out in the night, this was the worst.

MEL HIT THE FLOOR RUNNING. He wasn't sure who was screaming, but he knew where it was. Across the hall. In the boys' room.

The hallway seemed crowded with people in nightdress. He saw Alice and Fred, pajamas and pink nightgown; he saw Jonie, running toward the other door, and Robin.

When he reached the door to the boys' room he saw Celia down on her knees with Drew in her arms. She was rocking him back and forth, both of them on the floor. Drew's arms were tight around her neck, and he was telling her something in a mumbling, half cry.

"It comed out of the pond, Mommie, it was big and black, with a round head and lots of eyes that hated me, and it had long, long legs that looked like black snakes, but it walked on them and it stood tall, so tall, and it climbed up the side of the house and was reaching in to get me."

"Oh my God!"

Someone behind Mel turned on the light. It was a sudden shock to find the room brightly and suddenly illuminated. At the window the curtains danced in the wind, fluttering. Mel looked for something, anything, that would explain Drew's nightmare.

"It was only a dream," he started to explain.

But Celia was rising with Drew in her arms and desperation in her eyes. She looked directly at Mel.

"We've got to get out of here, now. *We've got to leave.*"

THEY TRIED TO DISSUADE HER. Alice put her arms around Celia's shoulder and said, "He'll go back to sleep, Celia. Maybe you'd be more comfortable taking him into your bed."

"It's almost daybreak," Celia said, feeling an urgency to hurry and leave that she could not explain to any of them. She didn't expect them to understand.

Fred made a half laughing sound. He stood in the doorway behind Alice, his hands in the pockets of his plaid bathroom. "Daybreak on Saturday around here doesn't mean anything except pull the blanket over your head. We never get up and around on Saturdays until about ten o'clock."

"I do," Robin said, her voice seeming to float from nowhere. Celia didn't see her in the room. Jonie too was gone now, out into the hall or maybe into the other bedroom getting dressed and ready to go. Celia hoped she was.

"Well, yeah," said Fred. "Robin's our early bird. That's why we called her Robin. She came with the rising of the sun."

He laughed again. He was often laughing, but it seemed to Celia there was a quality in his laughter that was a bit forced. He reminded her of herself on those days in the past when she had tried so hard to be happy for the sake of the kids.

"We have to go," she said. "You've been so nice. But we really have to go."

She looked up at Mel. He was still standing in the room, near the doorway Fred and Alice blocked. He was watching her steadily. When she tried to close the suitcase, he came and helped her, and then took it by the handle.

She wished she could tell them. Her little boy might have had a nightmare, but he had described to her the very thing that had risen from the swamp. The thing that Durk had become.

Celia looked from the window. Dawn was breaking in the east, and a misty grey light seeped down upon the open area behind the house. She stared at the surface of the pond. It was like a mirror laid into the ground. It had a solid look, except for the slow crinkles that moved across it from one bank to the other. There was nothing on it, not even a water bug that she could see.

But she knew. It might be there, just below the surface, watching her. Drew had seen it, somehow, in his sleep. And that made it ever more real, more dangerous. They had to run.

ALICE FELT A STRANGE LET-DOWN, a disappointment, as she watched them leave. She had looked forward to having them stay the weekend. Tomorrow they would have gone to church, and afterward they would have had a picnic. The food for the picnic was already in the refrigerator. She and Robin had shopped for it Thursday evening, as soon as Norma had called and asked if Mel could bring a family of four for a couple of days.

They had made such great plans, she, Robin, and even Fred. As soon as Fred heard there were a couple of boys, he had planned to take them horseback riding. Most boys, and girls, too, loved riding. Also, there was the go-cart out in the garage, just waiting for a couple of little boys to take it a few noisy whirls around the trails Fred had made.

She hadn't even had a chance to dress before they left. With Fred and Robin she stood on the back walk and watched the station wagon back out of the garage, turn, and leave, going around the house and down the lane.

Blair waved at Robin. Then Drew lifted his hand. Jonie waved. When they were almost gone, Celia looked back and watched them until she was out of sight.

The awful let-down feeling reached from Alice's throat to her stomach. It was a feeling she had tried to get away from. In all the years since she had found Fred and together they had worked to build a future that was happy and safe, she had been running from that feeling.

Maybe Celia was running from some kind of feeling too, maybe more than she was running from a husband.

When Fred put his arm around her shoulder, and Robin looked at her, Alice forced a smile to her face. But Robin kept staring at her, and Alice knew that old look was in her eyes.

"Mama, why are you sad?" Robin used to say. The first time, Robin was only three years old, and Alice hadn't been aware Robin even knew the meaning of the word *sad*.

"But I'm not sad, dear," she said. "I'm very happy. I have you, I have your daddy, why would I be sad?"

Yes, why was she sad? Why could she not get away from her past?

"But your eyes are sad," Robin had said.

Alice had never been able to get the expression of sadness out of her eyes so that Robin didn't detect it. She could put a smile on her face, make her voice light and chattery, she could talk all day to whoever would listen about local news, national or world news, or even clothes and food, but she couldn't change that awful, deep-down feeling and the film it had left over her eyes.

She hugged Robin. "Looks like we're going to have to change our plans this Saturday, eh, chickie?"

"Looks that way, Mom. Of course, we could still go shopping."

"Sure, we'll do that. Are you coming back in?"

"No." Robin looked off across the neat grassy area between the back of the house and the outbuildings and barn. "I think I'll just go feed the animals. I heard Quicksilver kicking her stall."

"Feed the animals in your pajamas?" Alice asked, and then noticed Robin was already dressed in jeans and sweater.

Robin grinned at her. "Wake up, Mom."

Fred opened the screen door to go back onto the porch but then paused. "Why don't you let Quicksilver and the young one out into a pasture today? It's supposed to be a warm day, up in the seventies."

"All right. They'd like that."

Robin went toward the barn, the two dogs bouncing along happily, one on each side of her. One of the four cats that lived in the barn area came meowing toward them.

Fred asked, "Coming back to bed?" He yawned without covering it with his hand. "Too early to be up on Saturday morning."

"I don't think so. I think I'll have coffee instead."

She heard him go through the kitchen, and even heard his footsteps on the back stairs. She waited, listening, and heard the squeak on the fourth from the bottom step. Then the sounds of him were gone.

Robin had disappeared into the barn, the dogs and cat with her. Alice sat down on the step, her chin in her hands. Around her birds sang, their voices coming from the trees, the bird houses, the air. Happy, cheerful sounds.

But it was as if she were surrounded by a cocoon of sorrow. Like a web it had woven itself around her and it remained, sticky and not to be removed.

She remembered another time she had sat like this, when she was three years old. In the house behind her, her baby brother Dean cried on and on, a weak sound that was growing weaker. She had tried to feed him, but there was no milk left in the house. She had fed him water in the dirty bottle she had tried to clean the curdled milk out of, and he had spit it up. She had taken his dirty diaper off, but there was no other to put on him, so she had just wrapped him in the blanket.

When was Mama coming home?

She had no daddy that she knew of. Daddies came and went, laughing with her mother, and she never knew which was hers and which was Dean's. Every daddy who came to the house she hoped would stay, but they never stayed long.

She was scared and hungry.

She went back into the house. The screen hung off the door at the corner, and a strange cat was on the kitchen table eating the crust of bread she had left there for later. She stared at the cat, and it stopped eating and stared at her. It was long and skinny. Its ribs stuck out through its fur, and its eyes were filled with the same feeling she had inside her.

She started to scare it away. The crust of bread was the last in the bread wrapper. The wrapper lay empty on the other side of the cat, brown and limp. But the cat was hungry too.

She walked around the table, giving the cat plenty of room so it could finish eating. It watched her. At the doorway she looked back and the cat had gone back to eating. There was nothing left but crumbs, but the cat was picking them up from the bare tabletop, one by one, in a very dainty manner.

Alice went to the bedroom. Dean lay still, no longer crying. He had put his fist into his mouth and was sucking hard on it. He looked so little. Like the cat, his ribs stuck out. He had kicked the blanket down, and his toes looked blue and cold.

She shivered in the cold room even though she was wearing her sweater.

She picked up the baby. When she did, he took his fist from his mouth and turned his face toward her, his mouth open. She pulled the blanket around him, enclosing his arms. His mouth and eyes closed, and he leaned his head against her chest. But he was cold.

She carried him back outside. In the kitchen the cat had turned over the catsup bottle on the table and was licking the rim of the empty bottle.

Alice went to the back step and sat down, the baby in her lap, her arms holding him close. He was only a little bit bigger than her doll.

The doll had been given to her at Christmas by people who came to the door with a basket of food and fruit.

They had remade it, the lady said. And a real Santa Claus gave it to her. He had a white beard and a red coat, and he was lovely. She wondered where his reindeer and sleigh were. And she saw his helpers weren't little, like real elves, but were big. And he too was big, not like an elf. Elves were small, weren't they? She had asked her mother, and the daddy who sat in the kitchen where Santa Claus and his helpers couldn't see him.

Her mother didn't answer. She just wanted to get rid of Santa Claus, get the door shut, and go back to the daddy in the kitchen.

Alice had to stay in the bedroom, but she didn't mind. She had the new doll. The only doll she'd ever had in all her life. And on the bed was Dean, himself like a doll, so little, and so new. He was only two weeks old then. She had already learned to diaper him and give him his bottle.

When she heard the door shut and knew her mother was gone for the night, she didn't feel quite so alone. Not as alone as she had before Dean was born. Before Santa came bringing the doll and food.

For a whole week they ate. There was even canned milk in the basket, and Alice poured it into the bottle for Dean. Sometimes it made him sick. But still he drank.

She sat with him in the warm pool of sunlight on the back porch. He lay still in her arms. He hadn't tried to pull his fist out from beneath the blanket so he could suck on it.

Alice watched the driveway for her mother's car. She had been gone for so long Alice no longer remembered when she left.

The sun grew warmer, but the baby got colder and colder. Finally Alice looked down at his little face, so thin, so pinched and pale.

His eyes were open, staring up.

But they stared without moving, just like her doll's, only the doll's eyes were brighter and shinier.

The baby felt stiff and cold, like her doll.

Something was wrong with Dean. Her baby brother. The only person in the whole world who stayed with her.

Alice got up and started walking. She went around the house and out onto the sidewalk, where her mother had told her never to go.

Cars went by on the street, but she didn't try to stop any of them.

She walked down the sidewalk and past the warehouse, to the street she would have to cross to go on to the grocery store. There Mr. Coddle would give her a piece of candy. He would tell her what to do about Dean.

Dean, so cold in her arms.

She began to run, to cry. She'd had a kitten once that got run over, and it had turned cold and stiff, and its eyes had looked strange and shallow and never moved again.

A woman on the sidewalk stopped her. She looked at Alice, crying, and the baby in her arms. And then the woman was pulling Alice along with her and screaming for help. Cars began stopping. People gathered. And Dean was pulled by force from her arms ...

Alice sat on the step with her chin in her hands, staring off across the green pasture behind the barn. There, rising with the dawn, were three cows with baby calves.

Somewhere in the barn was Robin, who had never in her life known what deprivation was. She had been introduced to child abuse when she was about ten years old but only by meeting children who were victims of it. Alice had met Fred in the orphanage in which they both grew up, and after they had worked hard and managed to buy this place, they admitted to each other that the emptiness was still there. So they had opened their home to people who needed help.

Alice had been in therapy, and she understood where her feelings of sadness came from. At age three, she had tried to take care of her baby brother, but he had died of starvation in her arms. He was only six weeks old. She had done all she knew to do then.

But the guilt was there. Why hadn't she gone for help before he grew cold in her arms?

She had kept waiting for a mother who didn't care. A mother so involved with drugs and men that she hadn't given a thought to the children she left behind.

Her mother's name was Cyndia. Cyndia Clark. After Dean's death, Cyndia had been charged with manslaughter, but the lawyer who had defended her made the excuse that Cyndia was badly abused as a child and had never learned to love. She went free.

A bitter anger stirred in Alice every time she thought of Cyndia. Childhood mistreatment was no excuse for letting an infant starve. Dean had been Alice's warmth. Her only source of love. And he had died in her arms.

Oh, God, if only she had gone for milk. If only ...

So the sadness was there, and she knew where it came from. She didn't hear about her mother again until she was grown and decided to try to find out what had happened to her. She was horrified to learn Cyndia had married three more times and had five children from those marriages. Four of the children were living with their fathers. Only one child remained with Cyndia. A girl, fifteen years younger than Alice. At times Alice wondered about her, but she didn't even know her name.

Alice felt the tightness of her lips and forced them to relax. She was trying to get over the bitterness. Someday it might be gone.

She felt better when she was at work, her mind busy with the customers, the real estate deals. Life was filled with busyness.

Still, never a day passed that she didn't think about Dean, that she didn't suffer for that poor, tiny, helpless infant who had no nourishment beyond his fist.

She went back into the house. It was so quiet. She and Fred had talked about adopting a houseful of kids. They had talked, with Robin, about taking in foster children.

She had tried for years to get pregnant again, but it seemed as though nature gave her one chance, and only one.

Robin. An angel on earth. She thanked God daily for Robin.

They had given up the idea of foster children when they heard about the Underground Railroad for abused families. Fred had brought the information to her and left it up to her. They fixed up the extra bedrooms and put in another bath, small but complete. Slowly the network had unveiled itself to them, revealing itself as active all over the United States. Like the webs of a garden spider it reached out, but not as a trap, as a safe pathway to freedom.

Fred, too, had been an abused child. His mother hadn't run away, but there'd been a stepfather who had hated Fred and beat him daily. When Fred ran away at fourteen, he finally wound up at the orphanage. By the time they both left, at age eighteen, they were planning to be married.

It was good being together. But she could never tell him—that man who was her father, mother, lover—that even in his arms she felt sad and lonely and afraid.

In the kitchen she put on a pot of coffee. She opened the refrigerator and looked at the food she'd planned to cook for breakfast. She sighed and closed the door.

Coffee was all she wanted.

She heard footsteps above. They stopped, started, stopped. She began listening.

Fred was up.

And yet ... the steps were overhead, in the spare bedrooms. And there was something about them that didn't sound like Fred walking.

A board squeaked. The board in the hall outside the extra bath. What was Fred doing there if he had gone back to bed? Alice stood listening, coldness rising on her arms and up her neck to her cheeks. There was a long silence as she waited.

The silence was broken by a scuffling sound in the front of the house.

She heard a strangled cry, and then another, and something that sounded like a body falling.

"Fred," she screamed, and went running to the back stairs.

She jerked open the stairway door and looked up. The stairwell was almost dark. It looked long and steep, rising to a door that closed off the upper hall.

But the door there stood half open, and as she started running up the stairs, a black shadow filled the opening.

CHAPTER 13

"FRED? WHAT'S WRONG?"

He didn't answer. He stood in the shadowed doorway, in the hall that was still dim with night. The rising sun had not touched this part of the house.

She had paused halfway up the stairs, and now she started up the stairs again.

"Fred, I heard ... I thought I heard ... footsteps, someone falling, someone ..."

At last she realized that the figure standing like a sheet of ice between her and the top of the stairs was not Fred. This man was much larger than Fred. His shoulders almost filled the doorway, and his head was barely an inch from the top.

She could see none of his features. He seemed made of a black substance left over from night. A sudden fear gripped her, holding her still for just a moment as she stared in silence up at him.

"Who are you? Where's Fred?"

Her voice was high-pitched with hysteria.

He took one slow, deliberate step down toward her, but didn't speak.

Robin.

My God, I have to keep Robin away!

She whirled and almost fell as she ran down the stairs. Her motions seemed made of nightmares, of slow movements, of heavy limbs and quicksand surfaces. The hall below was a beacon of welcome, of lighter worlds, of a door to safety. She had to reach Robin and get her away from whoever it was that had invaded their home.

She felt the touch on her throat. A cold grip tightened, choking off her scream, jerking her back, pulling her up the stairs with a strength that seemed inhuman.

She couldn't breathe. Her fingers lifted toward her throat, fluttered in the air, and fell.

Robin ... run ... !

THE PIGS GRUNTED CONTENTEDLY at the trough, eating a mixture of mash, water, and grain. They had small eyes, soft dark brown like most animals, like Robin herself. The one she had named Gertie looked up at her as appreciatively as a dog, chomping with her mouth open. Robin smiled. That was one advantage to being an animal, she thought, no one expected you to close your mouth when you chewed something good. She could remember her mother telling her, years ago, "Robin, close your mouth when you eat."

Robin bent and rubbed Gertie's side. The pig immediately flopped over onto the ground, her eyes closed in *ecstasy* as Robin scratched her. The food would probably be eaten by the other pigs before Gertie got back to it, but the petting was more important.

Robin left the pigpen while there was still some grain in the trough for Gertie, and climbed over the fence.

She sat for a few minutes on the upturned bucket in which she had carried the pigs' feed and looked off across the pasture and pond toward the trees. She had already turned Quicksilver and her baby out, and the young horse, looking so cute on her long legs, as if she were a toddler trying out an awkward arrangement of stilts, was gamboling around her mother. The mother grazed, head down to the grass, but the three-day-old filly didn't know what to do with the grass. She ran, fell, got up and ran again.

The scenery was so beautiful. The green hill rose beyond the green pasture, and the pond, a reflection of colors, was beginning to pick up the blue of the sky. On the pond, swimming, ducking their heads beneath the water, were the ducks, the geese. A strange water bird, some kind of crane with a long neck and a small body, had settled on the far side of the pond and seemed to be contemplating the other fowl. Robin watched it for a few minutes before she got up and went to rinse the feed bucket.

She wished the kids were still here. Blair would have enjoyed this, she felt sure, if he had stayed long enough to loosen up. And perhaps Jonie and Drew wouldn't have been so afraid either, if they could have stayed at least one day.

She hadn't even had a chance to wish them a safe journey this morning. She had been so surprised at the sudden departure, before it was fully dawn, she had stood like a dunce watching them go.

Where were they going? They had come from a place where cypress trees grew in a swamp. Were they going where snowfalls were heavy and the nights long?

She looked around at the safe haven of her home, at her own valley, and felt the happy lilt of being here. She wanted to share her feelings.

With the two golden retrievers at her side, she ran toward the house. As she entered the back porch she called out, "Mom? Dad?"

The dogs stopped on the wide step outside the screen door, and Robin crossed the screened porch to the kitchen.

She stopped. The house was quiet and filled with the lingering twilight of night. It felt oddly chilled, and empty. She had a feeling she shouldn't move or make a sound. But that was silly.

"Mom?"

They must have gone back to bed.

She turned on the kitchen light, then looked in the refrigerator. But they always held a big, hot breakfast on Saturday morning. And this morning Mama had planned to have a bunch of stuff, including blueberry muffins, which Robin loved.

She closed the refrigerator.

The house was so quiet.

Then, somewhere above, she heard a footstep. And then the odd little creak in the floor that meant that someone was passing along the hall near the guest bathroom.

Mama must be up there cleaning, doing up the rooms, taking off used sheets, bringing down bath towels and washcloths.

Robin went into the small hall leading to the back stairs.

"Mom?" she called out, and her voice seemed to echo from somewhere above, something she had never noticed before.

The hallway was dark, the door at the top of the stairs open, the hallway there unlighted. Tunnels of darkness. Why would Mom be gathering up used sheets and towels in the dark?

She noticed, then, something on the stairway. A dark shadow among dark shadows, where there should have been only steps.

Staring at it, at something that must have been dropped, Robin turned on the light.

Her mother lay head down on the stairs as if she had fallen. Her head was twisted backward and sideways, and her eyes stared down toward Robin.

"Mother!" Robin screamed, and went down on her knees, pulling herself the few steps upward toward her mother. *"Mom!"*

She lifted her head toward the top of the stairs and screamed out, "Daddy! Dad! Mom has fallen! Help me!"

Above, in the silence left by her voice, she heard the creak of the board outside the guest bathroom. But there was no answer to her cry.

She lifted her mother's head and then saw the contortion of her face, the bulging eyes, the protruding tongue. Blood trailed like dark red threads from her nose, her mouth. Slow streams that had started and now stopped.

Robin's mind shattered, pieces of it garnering strange episodes from normal life, tossing them about like puzzles in the wind. She saw herself at school. Her best friends Shelly and Gina walked with her across the grass toward the football field. She saw herself again with Tod at the junior-senior prom, she in her first formal, he in his tux. She felt the kiss in the dark outside when he pushed her up against somebody's car and she got dirt on her dress. She felt the giggles she had felt then, as she only half-heartedly pushed him away. And she felt her daddy's arms as she cuddled on his lap in the den in front of TV as they used to do when she was five, six, seven. Every evening, the three of them, with the dogs allowed to come in too and stretch out on the floor.

And then she saw a funeral that hadn't come to pass yet, with her mother ... and the flowers.

And she saw a stranger in the hall above. Someone who walked stealthily and who had stepped on a creaky board he hadn't known was there. Or perhaps he didn't care.

She wanted to go up and find her dad. They had to help her mother.

She looked up at the doorway above and saw the shadow of someone moving closer, coming to the door, pushing it farther open. The light on the white door changed as the door opened and the dark form moved nearer.

Instinct came to her rescue. With all thoughts abated, she moved backward rapidly, turning and running, slamming the door at the foot of the stairs.

She ran across the kitchen and out the door and across the screened porch and out into the grass. The dogs got up and ran with her as she crossed the lawn and went around the pasture fence to the woods.

Through the woods, a quarter of a mile away, Jim and Ellen Scott lived. They were in their sixties, almost always at home working in their flower and vegetable gardens.

It was the only place she knew to go.

She ran, tears beginning to blind her. Mucous running from her nose dampened the corners of her mouth. She was aware of the dogs beginning to cast worried glances up at her as they tried to keep by her side. She pushed tree branches out of the way and kept running.

JIM HOED ONIONS. He still planted them in beds, just like his grandfather had. A neat little bed of soil built up, with the onions going crossways. Ellen's people had planted them in long rows across the garden, like any other vegetable, like tomatoes or beans or peas. But a really proper onion bed was built up and the onions planted crossways.

There wasn't a weed in his garden. He paused and leaned on his hoe. The garden took only half as much space as it did in the beginning of their marriage, when the babies were coming and there were mouths to feed. Now, with half as much garden, they had vegetables running out of everything at harvest time. They gave vegetables to all the kids, who didn't seem to know what to do with them.

"*Can* the damn things," he'd told Connie and Sheila last summer when they had looked with dismay at the crates of tomatoes. "Your mother used to spend eight, nine hours a day canning."

Sheila looked at him with pity. Or was it contempt? At the best it was impatience. "Dad, no one cans anymore."

"Well, if they did, they'd be fewer hungry people in the world!"

"Canning factories do the canning."

Humph. He could snort the sound through his nose and make his feelings known without saying a word.

Nobody appreciated anything. Especially the kids. If the women nowadays would stay home and raise their children instead of getting jobs so they could earn more money, and if they would either raise vegetables or buy them from a farmer and can or freeze them, they wouldn't have all the problems they had. There was nothing any better for the soul, or the muscles, than hoeing in a good garden. Nothing like seeing those little green sprouts growing.

Now, as he stood in the first light of morning looking in satisfaction at his garden, his old dog got up and barked toward the woods.

Jim stood looking in the direction the dog was going, slowly, arthritically. *Bark, bark.*

"What's there, old boy?" Jim asked. The dog gave his tail one wag and stood still, staring toward the woods.

They came into view, dodging trees, running. A girl and two dogs.

In that first sighting, Jim was seeing again his own Sheila coming through the trees, happy and laughing ... Yet there was something wrong with the picture. She wasn't laughing, she was crying. And it wasn't Sheila, it was Robin, the girl who lived next door.

He took a hesitant step toward her, stopped, and put down his hoe. Carefully, with the sharp point downward. He laid it down without looking at it. He was aware of Ellen coming out of the house, and her call, "Jim? What's wrong?"

Then he saw Robin fall just as she reached the grass of the lawn. The dogs stopped with her, one of them licking her face. Jim hurried, breaking into a run.

She was rising, lifting herself from the ground when he reached her. Ellen was suddenly at his side, her arms around the girl. Jim could see Robin was terrified. He saw the streaks of tears on her face, scratches on her skin, bits of green leaves and a thin twig caught in her hair.

In breathless sobs she told them, "Mama ... she's dead. I think, I think, Daddy—"

Ellen cried out a series of questions. "Dead? Why? How? When did it happen?"

But Jim was thinking about the family, such a happy family. Was Robin saying that her father killed her mother?

"Who did it?" Ellen persisted, holding the girl, wiping her face with her ruffled apron hem.

"Someone ..." the girl sobbed. "Someone's in the house. I don't know who it is."

Jim was going after his car as fast as he could. But he heard about the third person with relief. Not Fred. Fred hadn't killed Alice. Thank God. It would be too much for the girl to have to bear.

"Call for help," he said over his shoulder. "Get us the police and ambulance. Get somebody. I'm going over there."

"Jim, don't go! Get the police first!"

He got into his pickup and spun it around and down the long driveway to the road. He turned right without slowing and pushed the accelerator to the floor. When he came to the brick corner posts that marked the entrance to the Merrow place, he had to slam his brakes on to make the turn, and even then the rear of the pickup slid sideways and nudged the bricks on one of the posts.

The pickup straightened and roared down the lane and into the open. The white house sitting like a queen on her knoll was touched with sunlight and looked as peaceful as a Grandma Moses painting. Nothing and no one stirred around the house. He could see the horse grazing in a small, fenced pasture beyond the barn, and he saw the glisten of sunlight on the pond, and the ducks and geese swimming around like always.

He pulled the pickup onto the grass in front of the house, turned it off, jumped out, and ran to the front door.

It was unlocked as he expected it would be. No one in these parts ever locked a door.

The interior of the house was still and shadowed. He stood still, listened, and heard only silence within. Somewhere outside the birds sang. He heard the songs of a wren and a cardinal close to the house.

Where was her mother? He hadn't waited to ask.

He crossed the foyer and began climbing the stairs, hearing nothing but his own sounds. His steps on the carpeted stairs, muffled. His breath, as harsh and rasping as if he had been running too.

In the hallway above he paused. The carpet of the stairway stretched down the hall. A bedroom door stood partway open.

"Fred!"

His call struck the silence and shattered it. Without using his voice again he began to look.

Fred was in the bedroom, on the floor at the side of the bed. And looking at him, Jim knew for certain he was not the one who had killed Alice. He lay twisted, as if every bone in his body had been broken. His neck had dark marks, and his face was pushed down into the carpet of the floor.

Jim, kneeling, started to straighten him, turn his face around. He slipped one hand under the dead man's cheek, and then remembered. *Don't touch.* The police wouldn't want him to touch Fred or anything else in the room or house.

He got up and started looking for Alice.

He found her on the back stairs, and he turned away, leaving her as he had left Fred.

The house was large, with six bedrooms on the second floor and at least as many rooms down below. He searched it all, opening every door, looking into every closet, careful to use his handkerchief so he wouldn't mess up any fingerprints.

When he heard the sirens he went out onto the back porch and around to the front to wait. There was no sign of the killer, how he had come, or how he had left.

But whoever he was, he was no longer in the house.

Jim Scott had never felt so tired as he felt now as he watched the police car and the fire department rescue truck spin off the driveway and onto the grass to park by his pickup.

CHAPTER 14

SHE WAS the most beautiful girl Mel had ever seen. Her hair was long and glossy dark brown, with highlights of red, and hung in natural curls past her shoulders. Her skin was as smooth as satin, or velvet, and contrasted like day against night with her hair. When she smiled at him, he was lost. That little voice somewhere in the back of his mind that sounded suspiciously like his mother's and that was saying over and over, "Look beyond the beauty, Mel. What's she really like? All sparkling dark eyes, pink lips, dark hair, white skin and perfection? Don't you believe it, pal. Look beyond the beauty," was as lost as he was.

He was a rookie cop in the state police, patrolling a stretch of highway between Atlanta, Georgia and the state line of Florida, and she was skimming the surface of the earth in a green Corvette, doing eighty miles an hour in a fifty-five mile zone.

He loved his feeling of power over her, and yet he was trembling in his boots as he wrote out her ticket.

Name? Kyla Johnston. Address? Telephone number? A suburb of Atlanta, a good neighborhood. And the damned car wasn't even hers. She shrugged a very attractive shoulder. Her driver's license, which she'd had for the four years since she turned sixteen, lay warm in his hand.

"He said I could drive it," she said. "My brother. I didn't steal it or anything like that." She smiled up at him, and he saw the dimples. Lord, what else did she have going for her? He tried to get a good look at her figure, and saw she was wearing shorts. The leg that lay casually sideways, the foot still on the accelerator, but loosely, was as perfect as her face.

"It's going to cost you, you know."

"Well, I had to try it out. You don't buy something without trying it out, do you?"

He almost got lost again in the suggestiveness of the question. She smiled up at him, giving him a good straight look at her lovely eyes. The pupils were so large he suspected she might have been puffing on a joint recently, but he didn't try to pursue that one. Most of all he wanted to know her better.

No, *hell* no, he knew all he needed to know. He wanted *her*, despite the little voice practically doing handstands to get his attention, yelling at him to forget the beauty and take a good look at the girl beneath the surface ...

The image of Kyla blurred, the highway uncoiled before him, another highway, another year, another age. The image grew more distant as he stared into the past.

He and Kyla were married two months to the day after he stopped her for speeding. Her folks gave her a big wedding, her mother complaining it was much too soon to prepare for it properly. But he put up with it because it was what she wanted. And she had come down the aisle on her father's arm like an angel. The most beautiful vision he had ever seen.

Until Crescent.

Crescent was born two years later, a carbon copy of her mother, only with his slower reaction to the world, his quieter acceptance. By that time the differences between him and Kyla were obvious. His mother had been right, little voice and all. She hadn't come right out and said she felt it was a poor match, but Mel had sensed it in her. Sensed it, perhaps, in himself.

There was a difference in background, for one thing. Kyla had never had to work. She'd had everything handed to her. She had grown up having a good time and had expected it to continue. Her friends were mostly well above middle-class. Some of them had real money, the kind that was passed down from several generations ago. College had never created a money problem for any of her friends. Fun was a necessity of life for Kyla.

Mel hadn't minded. He wanted her to be happy. But he also wanted her to be a mother to their child, to stay home with her. He knew his work kept him away too much. He began to know when he observed with a growing sense of helplessness the way Kyla was growing away from him.

"I'm lonely, Mel," she'd said that terrible night so many years ago. "You just aren't around enough."

"Kyla, baby, I have a job. I have to work. You have Crescent to keep you company when I'm gone. And your family and friends."

She wouldn't look at him. Her lovely eyes, so much like Crescent's, looked at the floor, at her hands, at everything but him.

So then he knew.

There was another man.

Well, he rationalized through the sharp pain, as sharp as a punk's switchblade, Kyla had been only twenty when he married her. She was practically a baby. Wasn't it natural she'd be attracted to someone else sometime? They only had to work it through.

He had asked for and gotten a different job in the state police department. He spent more time at his desk now, closer to home, making sure he was home every evening and weekend, so far as it was possible. The work was still in the traffic department, though less interesting, but it didn't matter. In the years of their marriage he had been moved from patrol to drug work, and he had found it very challenging. He was still an investigator, but doing more of the desk work.

He wondered about the other guy. Was she still seeing him? She seemed so distant. Whenever he looked at her she was staring off into the wild blue yonder.

The knife kept twisting in him, the punk growing larger and more threatening, his switchblade sharper.

Then she was gone.

God, just like that your home is gone, your child is gone, your wife ...

Walking into his house that February evening and hearing the silence was like walking into a prison without walls. Even though he knew he was physically free to go anywhere he could afford to go, the walls were around him, sealing him in with loneliness.

"Kyla?" he called into the small house. It was their first home, a two-bedroom ranch. They had planned to move soon to a larger one. At least, *he* had planned it that way, talking to her, telling her how good life would be, in a sense trying to buy her love, he realized, but he didn't care. Whatever it took to keep her. To keep Crescent.

Where was his little angel, coming as fast as she could to jump into his arms, yelling, "Daddy! Daddy! Mama, Daddy is home!"

That was the worst part, he realized through the anger that began to roil within him as he walked through the house. The worst was that she had taken Crescent.

He found the note on the pillow, as if to mock him. It told him briefly she couldn't stand it anymore. Goodbye.

The other man's name was Harley Wardell, Mel learned. He was tall and handsome and reckless, the ladies' man type, and Mel could see in Kyla's eyes that she was crazier about him them she'd ever been about anybody in her life, including Mel and Crescent. He came with her to the house to pick up some things she wanted, as if Mel were too dangerous for Kyla to face alone.

As Mel watched them going into the bedroom he had shared with her, Harley's hand touching her back, her shoulder, her arm, intimately, the way Mel used to touch her, Mel grew angry enough to turn to the violence they must have expected. And then suddenly something happened inside him and he was looking at Kyla through new eyes. Though it still hurt, something had snapped. All that mattered now was that he not lose Crescent.

He leaned against the wall and folded his sums across his chest. "Where's Crescent?" he asked.

"She's with my mother."

He stood in the hallway, making them go around him. "I'm coming after her this weekend," he said. "Have her ready to come home on Friday evening at 6:30."

"Mel, I don't think it's good for her to come back right now."

"And I think it is. She can stay with me for the weekend, and I'll bring her back to you Sunday night."

Kyla didn't look at him, but her guy gave him a hard, hot stare, and Mel had a glimpse of the future.

It hurt, at first, not to have Kyla's love. But they had been lovers seven years ago, so maybe you couldn't expect such young love to last. And maybe most of the love had been on his part, not Kyla's. But it hurt like an open wound, unhealing, not to have his little dark-eyed, dark-haired daughter to come home to.

He had tried to get custody, but Kyla fought him, and in a way he was glad. It showed that she loved their daughter after all. So when custody was shared, he certainly had no objection. Kyla was Crescent's mother. She was a good mother, or so he thought then ...

He blinked, his thoughts transferring from that world to this. The highway rolled in a long curve to the left, where it had been cut out of the low hill, and streaks of stone and soil lay revealed in tones of brown, black and white.

Beside him Celia reclined slightly in the seat, her face turned away from him toward the window. He wondered if she were asleep. The kids in the back were quiet, as they always were. No scuffling, no arguing from boredom.

It was still early, the sunlight slanting across the road as thinly as a sinking sun.

Lost in his reverie of the past, time had become dreamlike. It seemed they should have gone a lot farther than they actually had.

He looked at the gas gauge. One quarter.

He had planned to fill the car today in Clarksville before hitting the freeway again, but they had come through town before anything was open.

Ahead of them was an exit, and in a small valley off the freeway, where a strip of black state road angled off into the hills, was a restaurant, a motel, and a convenience store with rows of gas pumps covered with a flat roof.

"We need gas," Mel said, his voice husky with disuse. He cleared his throat. "The kids probably need a bathroom. And you can have breakfast here."

Celia sat up, looking ahead, then looking back at her kids. Mel caught a glimpse of her face and saw the anxious, scared look was still there.

The boy's nightmare had scared her more than it had the boy. He wished suddenly he could erase the fear and bring on a smile. He had no idea what her smile was like. Did her lips turn up at the corners, or was her smile straight? He had seen a few smiles in which one corner of the lips turned down. More like a smirk.

He heard the stirring of the kids in the back as he pulled onto the exit and guided the car slowly to a stop at the stop sign.

There was no traffic on the highway below the interstate. Too early, he supposed.

He pulled out onto the two-lane blacktop strip and across it to the collection of buildings.

It was a self-serve station, as most of them were these days. He edged the car up beside one and turned off the engine. The roofed area under which they sat had four rows of pumps, but he was the only customer.

He got out and opened the back door. The boys climbed over the seat and crawled out behind Jonie. Before he could get around to the other side, Celia was already out. She looked at him in a silent question.

"Go on to the restaurant and get something to eat, I'll be over as soon as I get the gas in the car." He started to give her some money and she shook her head.

"Norma gave me money, thanks."

They went out into the sunlight, crossing the pavement to the restaurant. Mel watched them go. No matter where they were, they tended to stick together in a little group. The boys didn't run on ahead or lag behind.

Mel put the nozzle into the gas tank opening and turned it on. He checked the tires and the oil, then stood watching the freeway, listening to the sounds of birds, and of the passing trucks. A few cars were beginning to show up, some of them with suitcases strapped into racks on top of the cars. A couple of motor homes went by, and a few smaller campers.

The gas pump switched off. Mel capped the tank, closed the lid on the porthole, and went toward the office pulling bills out of his billfold.

The attendant, a woman, sat on a high stool behind the counter. Behind her the radio spilled out the news. At first Mel didn't pay any attention, then it dawned on him the guy was reporting a double murder near Clarksville.

He caught a name. *Merrows.*

"And now," said the newsman, "the weather. Lovely spring weather surrounds us now and lets us know what we wait for all winter long. The temperature will be—"

"Did you hear what they said about the murders in Clarksville?" he asked the attendant.

Her lips pressed together, the corners turned down. She looked bored and sleepy, as if she had partied too long last night.

"Even here in the sticks it's not safe," she said. "You move to a place where you think you won't hear crap like that, and you hear it anyway. Is that all, mister?"

For a moment he didn't understand, then he saw she was handing him his change.

"Oh. Yeah." He turned away, feeling into his pocket for change. He turned back to the counter. The young woman was already engrossed in the paperback romance novel she'd been reading.

She lifted her head and blinked at him.

Music had replaced the weather report on the radio.

"Would you mind giving me some extra change?" He laid out a five-dollar bill.

"Sure. No problem."

He gathered up the quarters, exchanged a couple of them for dimes and nickels and went outside. He looked for a telephone and saw one at the other side of the building, away from the restaurant, toward the motel.

He dropped in a coin and gave the operator the Merrows' phone number.

It was answered on the fourth ring, after a short delay, a strange male voice said in Mel's ear, "Hello."

Not, "The Merrows' residence".

"Could I speak to Mr. or Mrs. Merrows, please?" Mel said.

There came the slight delay again while Mel's stomach slowly turned to ice.

"Who's calling?"

"I've decided to buy some real estate they were showing me, if I can make a few changes in the deal. Could I talk to one of them, please?"

"Sorry. What is your name?"

In the background Mel heard voices, all of them male. They were distant, muffled, as if the guy on the other end held his hand over the phone when he wasn't talking.

Mel hung up the phone.

He called information and got the number of Jim and Ellen Scott, the neighbors of the Merrows, the people Fred said he had bought his land from and with whom they often visited.

After only two rings a woman answered the phone.

Another hello, but there was something in her voice that made Mel know he'd reached Ellen Scott. He had to confirm it.

"I'd like to speak to Jim or Ellen Scott, please."

"Yes, this is Ellen Scott."

"I'm a friend, an acquaintance, of the Merrows. I tried to reach them and couldn't. Could you tell me if there's been trouble at their house?"

"Oh, Lord," she cried softly. "Both of them, Fred and Alice, were murdered early this morning. Their daughter, Robin, came running to us, her face scratched, crying. The only reason she's alive now, I reckon, is because she was out doing her chores. When she went into the house she found her mother on the stairway, dead. And she came running over here. Jim drove over to their place and found both of them dead. Strangled to death. Fred was on the floor beside the bed in the master bedroom, in his pajamas. And Alice was on the back stairs."

There was a brief silence on the phone that Mel didn't have the presence of mind to fill. In his eyes the scene of the double murders became more clear than the scene at the motel.

Ellen's voice continued. "We figured the killer, whoever he was, had gone into the upstairs, and maybe Fred surprised him there. And then on his way out he, the killer, met Alice on the stairs. That's the way the police have it figured maybe. Or, I think they think Fred had an enemy, and he—"

"Excuse me," Mel said. "Robin's there with you?"

"No, not now. Her aunt came and got her."

"I guess the killer hasn't been caught?"

"Not that I know of. They don't even have any suspects. It's terrible. If it was robbery, how did the robber manage to find that place? It's back at the end of the road. He must have known where he was going."

Mel listened until his three minutes were up and then let Ellen go. Her speculations were only speculations.

Mel looked at his watch. Norma might be on her way to work now. He had to talk to her.

He counted his change. He thought of reversing the charges, then decided they wouldn't want that kind of record on her phone bill. He would have to say what he had to say in three minutes.

Her phone rang and rang, and just as Mel was about to hang up, Norma answered.

Her voice sounded breathless.

"Norma—"

"Mel!" she cried. "I was on my way out and heard the phone. Are you at the Merrows'?"

"No, we left just before daybreak—"

"Left! But ... so soon?"

"Norma, listen. We have to change the route. He must be following. I don't know how, but he is. The Merrows, not Robin, thank God, were murdered this morning not long after we left, evidently. I just happened to hear it on a radio where I stopped for gas, and I called their neighbor. They were strangled, just like the others. The only thing we can do is change the route."

"Dear God," she said under her breath. Then, speaking swiftly and clearly, she said, "All right, I'll send you north to Nebraska, then, to the farm of Cora and Lorne Mendel. I'll call them and tell them you're coming. When you get there, go straight west to Wyoming, to the Cooper's ranch. You were there last year and the year before, do you remember the place?"

"Yes." He made mental notes. The Mendels in Nebraska and the Coopers in Wyoming. The Mendels were a childless couple in their sixties, as energetic and alive as most people years younger.

The Cooper ranch was run by an elderly man and his son, who was no longer young himself. They were a couple of old cowboys, as Mel thought of them. Friendly, eager to help, never nosy. They were carbon copies of each other—wiry, thin, short, agile. He had never gone there when they didn't act as if he and the family he brought were long-lost relatives.

Nebraska and Wyoming. No one knew where they were going, except him, Norma, the Mendels, and the Coopers. This time there was no chance they'd be followed. He'd get Celia and her kids to California if it killed him.

"I'll call them tonight, Mel," Norma said. Then, "I don't understand how he followed you. He had to be close behind. That's the only way he could have come to the Merrow's."

"I know."

He didn't tell her the Merrow home was at the end of a private lane that was probably a quarter of a mile long. Where had the car been parked? They must have passed right by it on their way out. Maybe it was pulled into the darkness of the trees. Maybe the guy was walking through the woods to the house, or hiding there, when he drove out. Nothing made sense. Why bother the Merrows? Why kill them? It was as if the guy killed everyone who was trying to help Celia and the kids, or otherwise got in his way.

"Be extra careful, Norma."

"Oh Mel, you're the one—"

"Your three minutes are up," the operator said.

"I have to go, Norma."

He hung up the phone and went back around the convenience store to his car. When he got in he sat for a minute looking around.

The guy couldn't have followed them this time. He was in the Merrow house when they were already on the road.

Mel had planned to drive over to the restaurant and park, but before he started his car Celia and the kids came back in their close group, serious faces all watching him. Celia was carrying a paper bag and the kids had foam cups with lids and straws.

They stopped. Celia said, "We'll wait while you have breakfast. We'll wait in the car."

"You didn't eat?"

"We have our breakfast here." She hesitated, and he saw the anxiety on her face, as if she knew what lay behind them. "I have enough for you, too, if you don't mind. And coffee."

He felt relief. He wasn't hungry anyway, at this hour. Like Celia, he wanted to be on the road.

"Coffee will be enough. Ready kids?"

They nodded in unison, serious faces turned toward him, beginning to trust him, it seemed. He felt a warmth he hadn't felt in a long time, as if he were surrounded by family.

He closed the doors behind them as they settled in the car, and made himself push the feeling away.

He would get them to California and leave them, and never see them again. He would get them there safely. That was all he was here for.

CHAPTER 15

NORMA'S HAND trembled as she punched out the number of the local police. A female voice answered. Norma lowered hers to barely higher than a whisper, just loud enough for the policewoman to hear.

"About the murders ... of the girl in the motel ... and the trucker ..."

"Could you speak up please?"

Behind the voice on the phone Norma could hear phones ringing and the dispatcher's voice droning on and on. She raised her voice slightly.

"The murders ... the strangulations ..."

"Yes. Who's calling please?"

"Look for Durk Nolan. *Durk Nolan.* He has a record in Florida."

"Who is this? What is your name?"

"Durk Nolan. He might have done the killing. Florida." Norma hung up before her call could be traced.

She sat back in her chair, shaking all over. She clasped her hands tightly together. He had to be stopped, that was all. She had not only Celia and her children to think about but the people he had already killed. And now there was no question in her mind. Somehow he had followed them.

She got up and went to the bookshelves and pulled out the container that held the fifty maps of the United States. She pulled out the Florida map and checked to make sure she remembered the county where Celia's home was.

She went back to the phone and sat a minute thinking. If she called information for the number of the county sheriff's department, could it be traced to her phone? She wasn't sure.

She unlocked the drawer that held information about the most recent families she had helped into the Underground Railroad. She pulled out Celia's file, looked through it, and found the number of the county sheriff.

But it was long distance. If the police associated her with Celia's disappearance, the call would be on her telephone bill.

She tapped her fingers together and frowned at the wall, then she dialed Wade Turner. He was a retired policeman who occasionally helped out in the Underground Railroad, and she knew she could trust him.

He answered the phone on the seventh ring, just as she was about to lose hope.

"Wade, this is Norma. I'm sorry to disturb you, but I need your help."

There was a hesitation that lasted long enough for her to wonder if he knew who she was. They hadn't worked together for almost a year. She also wondered if he might not be well, and was getting ready to ask when he spoke.

"Norma. Yeah, Norma. Whatever I can do. What do you need?"

"You've heard about the murders, the strangulations of the girl at the motel and the trucker out on the freeway?"

"Yeah. What?"

"I think I know who may be doing it. There was another couple, a man and wife up in Tennessee who were helping a family, who were killed in the same manner last night."

"What do you want me to do?"

"Inform the county police down near the coast where the family lived. Tell them to look for Durk Nolan."

"Okay, wait, got my pen. Durk Nolan, right?"

"Right. I thought you might be able to get that information to them without letting them know where the information came from."

"Yes, I can, don't worry. Everything going all right with you? Personally, I mean?"

"Fine, thanks. And you?"

"Been fishing some, that sort of thing. But I'd rather be at work, and I'm glad you called. Give me the rest of it, and I'll wander down close enough to give them a call from a pay phone."

She gave him the number of the county sheriff's department where Celia had gotten a court order for her husband to stay away. A court order that hadn't worked.

CELIA

• • •

Celia reclined her seat a couple of inches and lay back with her head on the headrest, her face toward the window. The kids were reflected in the glass, small faces like ghosts, through which she could see the trees beyond, a moving wall of green.

She closed her eyes, listening to the hum of the engine and the singing of the tires on the pavement. *Hurry, hurry.*

She wanted to ask him why he drove right on the speed limit instead of a few miles above it the way most of the other cars seemed to, but she was not yet that comfortable with him. The first night they were on the road he had driven faster part of the time, and now, as daylight seemed to concentrate on their car, as the sunshine followed them like an arrow pointing their way, saying to all the world, *there, there they are,* he drove so slowly.

She tried to relax. She had told the kids back at the restaurant to drink very little so they wouldn't have to stop for a bathroom. And she had asked the waitress to fill their cups with ice.

"If you get thirsty," she whispered to them as she handed them their cups of Coke or Sprite, "Suck on an ice cube. We don't want to stop any more often than we have to."

"Why, Mama?" Blair asked before she put her hand over his mouth. "We're a long, long ways from home."

"Shhh."

Shhh. She didn't have to repeat her warning. They were so still now she thought they might be asleep.

She closed her eyes.

Durk's face came before her, smiling, his ice-blue eyes looking at her the way they had the first time they met. In the beginning she had read into them something that didn't exist. Something she needed so badly in her life.

She was scared, that night twelve years ago, more scared than she had ever been before. At least at home with her family she hadn't been scared, and she thought about going back as she clutched the brown paper sack that held all her belongings closely against her stomach. She couldn't spend another night trying to find a place to hide.

The park was getting dark. Lights on tall poles were beginning to come on, signaled in some way by the darkness. But their pale lights only made the shadows behind the shrubs darker.

The night before she had slept on the cold cement floor of the ladies' room in the park. The night before that she had spent her last penny for a room in a cheap rooming house, where it seemed no one was trying to sleep but her.

She had thought it would be easy. When she walked out of her house three days ago she had thought all she had to do was get a room, get a job, and take care of herself. She knew two girls from her class at school who had gone to work at McDonald's the day after school ended.

"Mom, can I get a job at McDonald's this summer?" she had asked the day after school was out for the summer.

Her mother sat on the sofa—sprawled, actually, with one of those everlasting beer cans in one hand and a cigarette in the other. Always, the cigarette was about to drop an inch long worm of ashes.

Celia hated the way they lived. After her mother had married Tim, a fat-bellied beer drinker who went around the house in his jockeys and nothing else, their lives had deteriorated rapidly. First of all, there were several stepbrothers and stepsisters who were just like their dad, and then Celia's mother had started turning out more babies. Three in three years. Celia loved the babies. When they were small their presence made up for some of the things she hated. Now they were no longer babies, and they didn't need her so much.

She hated the end of school each year, when she'd have to stay home and do the laundry and the dishes and try to keep clean sheets on the beds. It was more than she could bear, she decided when she turned sixteen. She had one more year of school and then she could move away, but this year, if her mother would let her work at McDonald's, she could even help support the family.

It was so embarrassing to go through the checkout line at the supermarket with her mother and wait until she paid for their food with food stamps. Her pride shriveled each time, and it seemed the clerks looked at them with disgust.

"I could help pay for groceries, Mom."

Her mother took a drink of beer, mashed the can flat in the middle, and said, "Bring me another beer, Ceil." Celia stood a moment waiting for her mother to answer her request for permission to get a job. She waited a moment too long.

"I said get me another beer, goddammit. Don't you have your ears on today?"

Something inside Celia burst. Her mother had never hit her in all her life, the way she did some of the younger children. But she couldn't remember when her mother had spoken tenderly to her. Kids ran through the house screaming and fighting, some of them laughing. Doors slammed.

"I'm not getting you another beer," Celia said, spacing her words carefully, speaking distinctly even though she spoke through her teeth. With her body bent slightly forward and her fists clinched at her side, she said, as her mother turned her head slowly and glared at her. "Not now, not *ever, Mother!*"

She watched her mother's face turn a deep red. The woman got up off the couch and yelled, all the time staring at Celia, "Tim! Tim, did you hear what she said? This little bitch can't stand up here and tell me ..." She suddenly jerked her hand out and pointed a finger toward the door. "Get out!" she screamed. "Out!"

Tim came out of the bedroom in his shorts. He hadn't shaved in a day or two, or showered, either. He rubbed his belly with one hand and yawned widely. A line of reddish hair reached from his navel to his chest. Celia looked at him with revulsion. Sometimes he pretended to get a job, and maybe he did, for he'd be gone during the day for a few days, a few weeks, and then he'd start complaining about his back. Celia's mother would give him long massages, and tell him he didn't have to work if he didn't want to.

The place they lived in was a dump, and Celia had never asked a friend to come home with her. She was suddenly, almost violently, sick of it all.

"What the hell is going on?" Tim asked, yawning.

"All right," Celia yelled back at her mother. "I'll get out!"

She ran to the bedroom she shared with whoever of the stepsisters happened to be home and started grabbing up her clothes. She had a couple of skirts, two pairs of jeans, some ragged underwear, and two pullovers. She stuffed them all into a paper bag she got out of a kitchen drawer.

As she left the house her mother called after her, "And don't ever come back!"

The door slammed.

At first she felt euphoric being on her own. The world was hers. The fresh air smelled great, and she was filled with energy. She planned as she walked. She would get a job, get a room, save her money, and in the fall she would go back to school and finish her last year of high school. Then she would work again, and save, and go to college.

In her purse was twenty-one dollars she had earned helping a teacher at school. She had never told her mother about the money, earned a couple of dollars at a time. No one in the family knew she had it.

Two nights in the dirty little rooming house had cost twenty dollars.

The third night she slept in the ladies' room at the park. She had walked and walked during the day, across town, to the other side of the world, it seemed, but no place did she see a "Help Wanted" sign. She had not tried to get a job at the McDonald's close to home because she knew some of her family would spot her there.

And something told her it would have done no good anyway. The jobs were already filled by teenagers who had put in applications before school was out. They hadn't waited.

She walked the paths of the park in the deepening night, aware of the light going from the sky. Aware too of the awful fear that was settling in her empty stomach.

She didn't want to go home. Would her mother even let her in the door? Her brother left last year. He was only fourteen years old, and her mother still hadn't tried to get him to come home. If she knew where he was now, she thought, she'd go to him. He stayed with friends here or there, he had told her when she ran into him at the mall once, but he hadn't told her the names of the friends. He acted as if he hardly knew her anymore.

She didn't have friends to go to. She'd never made a close friend in her life.

She met a man with a dog and she stopped, amused for a moment at the sight. The man was hurrying to keep up with the dog.

She went on, past young couples with arms intertwined, past an elderly couple on a bench. But most of the people were going toward the parking areas, toward their cars, going home.

Celia found a bench and sat down. The light on the pole shined through the nearby trees, so the light was patchy. She chose a shadowed area at the end of the bench and tried to shrink into it. Nightbirds sang in the distance, one of them an owl with a chilling, vibrating cry that sounded as if it didn't belong in this world.

"Hey, sweet lady"

The voice startled her. She jumped, stifled a cry, and stood up. The guy was grinning at her from behind the bench. He was young, maybe no older than she, but looked like he had taken steroids. His muscles bulged and shone as if oiled in the dim light from the pole. He was wearing an undershirt that was purple or black. Behind him stood several more young guys, all oily looking and swaying slightly on wide-spread feet. They were all staring at her, but only two or three of them grinned. The rest were deadly serious.

She started to walk away, but the greaseball in the purple shirt was suddenly beside her, and his hand closed on her arm. The others moved in a half moon around her, leaving only one side open, the side toward the parking lot, where a few cars were still parked.

"Hey, wait, Babe. We don't bite hard ... most of the time."

Others laughed.

"Please," she said. "I have to go. My ... my dad is waiting for me."

"Oh yeah, where?"

"There! There," she said triumphantly, pointing at a man who stood leaning against a shiny red pickup out in the parking lot. Even from the distance she could see the handsome outlines of his face, his hair that absorbed the light in a pale golden halo, and his smoothly tanned skin. There was even something about him that reminded him of her own daddy. He was tall, broad in the shoulders, and had his arms folded across his chest.

"Oh yeah? I don't believe you."

She hurried across the grass toward the tall blond man. Her heart was pounding so hard it smothered her. What would she do when she reached the man?

She looked back and saw the gang was following her, the grin still on the leader's face. He was about ten feet away, waiting for her to prove to him she had a protector.

She glimpsed something in the hands of one of the gang members who stood further back. He was tugging it between his hands, and the light caught it and glinted as he moved from shadow to shadow beneath the trees. She blinked, disbelieving. Handcuffs? Handcuffs like the police used when they came for the man next door who was into drugs? She knew they were meant for her. There would be plenty of hands to cover her mouth to smother her screams.

She ran toward the blond man, crying out loudly enough for all of the gang to hear.

"Here I am, Daddy. Sorry I'm late."

She ran past the blond man still leaning against the pickup fender, opened the door, and pulled herself up and in, slamming the door behind her.

"Let's go, Daddy, I'm going to be late at the ... the gym."

The blond man turned toward her. Even in the spotty light in the parking lot, with the shadows of tree limbs moving around them, she could see the light blue of his eyes and the amused expression there.

Her heart was in her throat. What if he turned out to be part of the gang? The father figure, more or less? What if they were into white slavery?

What if ... what if ...

Then he was straightening and turning to face the gang of young men who stood scattered in the heavy shadows of the park.

At that moment a police cruiser came into the parking lot, moving slowly. It went down past the red brick restrooms, came on slowly around the curved end of the lot, and came by right behind the pickup and out toward the street again.

When Celia looked back to see what effect the police cruiser had had on the gang, they were gone. Blended into the darknesses of the park as if they had never been there at all.

She saw the blond man coming to get in the pickup. She opened her door and slid out.

The man smiled at her through the two open doors as he stooped slightly, one foot up ready to get in.

"So now, my little daughter, where do you think you're going? You'll be late at the gym."

She shrugged, her eyes caught and held by his.

"I think you'd better get in and tell me what you're doing out here running from a gang of perverts with a brown sack in your hands."

He sat in the pickup seat and put his hands on the steering wheel. He looked straight ahead, and she saw his profile etched against the darkness beyond. His nose was straight, a bit sharp at the end. His forehead slanted back, and she saw his hairline was receding. He was old enough to be her father after all, and more perhaps. And something about that evaluation made her feel safe.

Slowly she got back into the pickup, though she left her door standing open. She watched him, but he didn't look at her for a long while. Then his face turned. The smile was gone, but she read concern and gentleness. She thought she read those qualities. She needed desperately to read those qualities in his eyes the color of a northern sky.

She began to tell him. Her daddy died when she was three, and her brother ran away two years ago, and her mother told her three days ago to leave and never come back. She was out of money and didn't have a job and didn't know what to do.

He reached across her and pulled the door shut. His arm barely brushed hers, hugged around her paper sack of clothes. Most of them used now and needing washing.

"I'll get you a room. And I know a woman who owns a small restaurant. She'll give you a job. Think you can wait tables?"

"Oh, yes. Oh, yes," she breathed. "How can I ever thank you?"

"My name is Durk Nolan," he said, smiling at her as the pickup moved toward the street. "What's yours?"

"Celia. Just ... Celia."

CHAPTER 16

"I LIKED it when you called me Daddy," Durk said as once again they sat in a park, a different park. His big hand closed warmly over hers. She felt lost in him, protected by him, and she read love in his eyes.

She had known him a month now. He had kept his word, rented a small room for her where she could lock the door against the world, even against him. He had taken her to the restaurant and conferred in private with the round little woman who owned it, and Celia was given a job. She earned fifty dollars a week, plus her tips.

The tips didn't amount to much. If she got a quarter she was delighted. The cafe was small, with booths against one wall and a six-foot strip of worn linoleum between them and the counter with the stools. Prints hung on the wall, dusty and wrinkled, most of them pretty pictures from an old calendar that someone, perhaps Leona, the owner, had framed.

She was happy there. And Durk came in almost every day and ate—breakfast, lunch, sometimes supper. He tipped her a dollar every time. But from him she didn't consider them tips, the way she did her quarters. She saved them beneath her mattress. Someday she was going to buy him a nice gift with those dollars.

It was three weeks before he came by her room on her day off and asked her if she'd like to drive around. When he brought her home on that first day, he kissed her lightly on the lips. He didn't touch her. He just leaned down and kissed her.

She had read about thrills, but she had never felt one before.

For a whole week afterward she watched the door of the cafe and listened for his knock on the door of her room. But he didn't show up.

She asked Leona, "Where do you think Durk is?" She tried to be casual, not to let her feelings show. "Why has he stopped coming in?"

Leona shrugged a plump shoulder. She always wore scoop-necked blouses that showed the tops of her full breasts and the crease between. Pale freckles dotted her skin.

"Who knows? Men like him, they come and go."

"I thought you knew him real well," Celia said, surprised.

"Naw. He's been here a few times."

"But..." She was thinking about the night he brought her here and cornered Leona in the back hallway that led to the kitchen and bathrooms and on to Leona's own private living quarters. "But didn't he talk you into giving me a job?"

Leona laughed shortly. "Honey, he paid me your first week's wages. I'd only seen the man a couple of times before that. I didn't even know his name."

Celia stood stunned, feeling somehow deflated, used, humiliated in ways she didn't understand.

Leona patted her arm. "Don't worry, honey. Your job is safe. I never had a girl in here who could take over the way you have. Nor clean the way you do. You're even a pretty damned good cook."

Celia didn't bother to tell her she'd been cooking and cleaning for the family since she was seven years old.

"But the man," Leona said. "He's too old for you anyway. You're lucky if he don't show up again."

For two days Celia felt lonely and sad. She saw her small room becoming a prison, and she did a lot of window shopping in her spare time. Yet she hurried home nonetheless in case Durk showed up at her room.

He didn't come to the restaurant again, but he was waiting for her one evening when she walked home from work. She saw the red pickup when she was still a block away and started to run. When she reached it, he had the door open.

He wasn't smiling. Without speaking he started the engine and started driving.

"How would you like to marry me, Celia?"

"Wh- what?" Even in her dreams she hadn't dreamed that.

"Well, why not? You're alone and so am I. I have a house in a very private place. You could sunbathe without a stitch on and not have to worry. I make good money. I deal in laboratory equipment, so I'm on the road a lot. But I'd sure like to have you waiting at home for me. I'll keep you supplied with books so you can read while I'm gone, and there's a TV if you like that."

"Durk ..." She leaned against him, put her face against his shoulder so he wouldn't see her tears. "Yes, anything you want."

"I liked it," he said softly, "when you called me Daddy."

"Daddy," she whispered. But it didn't feel right on her lips or in her heart. She wouldn't have married her daddy. That would have meant sleeping in the same bed with him.

He turned the pickup at the next block and started back toward her room.

"Go in and get your clothes. Leave the key with the landlady."

"How about my job, Durk? Leona is counting on me now."

He took hold of her chin. "Not Durk. Daddy. *Daddy. It does something to me*. See?"

He took her hand and put it on his crotch. She felt a huge, hard thing there that was like a coiled snake. She could feel it pulsing, stirring, enclosed tightly within his jeans. He had massive thighs, massive shoulders, and she was aware for the first time of his strength, his power over her. She gasped, her hand feeling the heat within the crotch of his tight jeans. She stared into his eyes, mesmerized by their icy blue. The eyes came closer, closer. His lips touched hers, as lightly as butterfly wings.

"Daddy," he whispered. *"Call me Daddy."*

CLARK THURMAN, sergeant in the county sheriff's department, drove out the highway toward the almost invisible turnoff to the place where Durk Nolan had lived before the court ordered him to stay away from his wife and children.

"Keep an eye out for the road, will you?" he said to the deputy, Davis Olson, who rode with him. "You'll see a small mailbox, and that's about all. The road is just a sandy lane in the trees."

"Which side?"

"Left side. I was out here a couple of times, and the road was hard to find both times."

"He the guy who had the dogs?"

"Christ, yes. You wouldn't have believed the conditions those animals were living under. Cages so small some of them couldn't turn around. No matter how big the dog, all the cages were the same size. The wife, Celia, and the kids tried to keep them clean, fed, and comfortable, but it was impossible. They had let some of the bigger dogs out, and they just huddled back in the corners of the barn."

"Where are they now?"

"Humane society. Probably some of them went back to their owners. Others put to sleep. What're you going to do with an overpopulation of dogs or cats? Lots of new homes found, though. People always come forward to help in cases like that. Some people."

'Well," the deputy said, "the test labs. Wasn't that where they were going?"

"*Shit.* Some improvement."

They didn't talk for awhile. Olson pointed, and Clark Thurman saw the mailbox.

"That it?" Olson asked. "No name. About to fall forward on its face. Funny the mail carrier didn't make them fix it up."

"They probably didn't get much mail anyway. So what did it matter to the carrier if it fell on its lid?"

The car moved along the sandy lane almost silently. Pine trees, as thick as they could grow, made a forest on each side of the lane, at times almost swallowing it.

"What made them think it was Durk Nolan doing the killings up in Georgia and in Tennessee, you suppose?" Olson asked as he looked off through the trees, where shade was a perpetual entity, dark and endless.

"An anonymous tip."

"Barking up the wrong tree, if you ask me," Clark muttered just as the mile-long lane ended and he drove out into the sunlight.

The lane continued on in a long curve toward a small five-room house that had a screened porch across the front. There was not a single tree close to the house. Only the long, brown grass waving in the gentle breeze that came in from the Gulf.

On his left, half hidden by the pines that surrounded it, was the big old barn. Its double doors stood open now, and the dark interior looked haunted. The lane curved past it and on toward the house. A weed-strewn lane veered off it toward the double doors of the barn and disappeared there.

The place looked deserted. No car stood at the back porch. There was no pickup parked near the barn. Not this time.

He stopped the car and got out. The other door slammed just as Clark walked up to the back door. Something pink lay in the grass. He looked down at it. Once it had been a beautiful doll, about eighteen inches tall, with real hair and eyelashes. It wore a pink satin dress and a matching hat with feathers that were now torn and scattered in the flattened grass. Something had crushed it.

Olson stopped at Clark's side. "Run over by a car," he said. "The little girl lost her doll. What a shame. It must have cost a lot of money, too, the way it looks."

Clark stooped and lifted its arm, then let it fall again. The arms were still intact, but the head and legs were broken to bits. The porcelain exterior had shattered like crushed eggshell. It would fall to pieces if he tried to pick it up.

"Not a car," Clark said, puzzled at the condition of the doll. "There aren't any tracks on it. It looks more as if it was squeezed hard by something."

He spent a moment longer looking at it, then climbed the steps to the back door.

The door was unlocked, and he went in after his knock was unanswered, calling out, "Celia? Clark Thurman here. Sheriff's department."

He knew no one was there. He could feel it. But he walked through the five rooms looking, his shoes loud on the bare wood floors.

The bedrooms were small and dim, their blinds pulled. In the boys' room both narrow beds were mussed, covers thrown back. And in the room that must have been Jonie's the bed was also unmade. The only bed that hadn't been slept in since it was made up was in the other bedroom. A double bed with sagging springs, it was neatly spread with a chenille cover.

He went out the front door and stood a moment looking at the dark cypress trees. It was down there, Celia had told him, where Durk threw the dogs he hadn't been able to sell. She hadn't been able to stop him.

There was a thin, threadlike path going straight from the screen door of the porch to a huge cypress tree at least two hundred yards away. Between the house and the trees hot sunshine turned the grass more yellow by the moment.

Clark adjusted his hat to shade his eyes and went down the path toward the cypress trees and the swamp. He didn't know how far the swamp reached before it gave way to the Gulf and the ocean waves, but there was a feeling of great distance, of miles of dark water.

The big cypress tree stood out just slightly from all the other trees of the swamp. They angled back from it in a V, and then curved and came forward again, so that the small unpainted house whose boards had turned a peeling silver grey was in a kind of circle made by the cypress trees of the swamp and the pine trees of the woods.

He had never felt such isolation.

He looked back at the house. There was no sign of the deputy. He was probably searching the barn.

Clark went forward. When he was within ten feet of the black, still water around the base of the cypress tree he stopped. Something large had lain on the grass near the edge of the water, crushing it. Part of the grass was beginning to rise again.

A dark spot near the water caught Clark's attention. He went forward, squatted, and took out his knife.

The dark substance had soaked into the ground about a quarter of an inch. Ants were working busily at one edge of it. Whatever it was seemed to attract the ants, and Clark had a hunch it was blood. The last hard rain had been a little over a week ago, so the blood had been spilled since then. The crushed area suggested the body that had lain here was much larger than the average large dog.

He stood up and moved around it and looked down into the water. At first he saw nothing but the dark, reflecting surface, then an object a few inches below, caught on a projecting root, slowly became visible.

He stooped, reached into the water, and took careful hold of it, recognizing the cold, round barrel of a handgun. He pulled it up dripping dark water. A .357 Magnum revolver. He checked and saw it was empty. It hadn't been in the water long. There was no rust, no algae, no collection of any form. He laid it on the grass and began looking around for a stick or something that would give him an idea of the depth of the water, or of the possibility of something else being in there with the gun. There was nothing but grass.

He stood looking from the dark round spot where, he knew without analysis, something's blood had soaked into the grass, to the revolver, to the water.

Celia and her kids were gone. The whole place had a weird, deserted look, even though clothing and furniture had been left in the house. He had a hunch that someone had died here recently, and this time not a dog.

The blood was fresh, a week old at the most. It had to be that recent, or it would have been washed forever into the soil.

Had Durk Nolan killed his wife and kids and dumped them here? Maybe, but he wouldn't have left his gun behind. A man who loved his guns as Durk Nolan did would not have dropped the gun into the water with the bodies.

Had Celia killed her husband and then split?

If Clark could be sure that Celia had killed her husband and dumped his body here, where she said he had put the dogs, he'd go quietly away and say nothing. But it might be the blood of Celia or the kids.

He picked up the gun by the barrel and went back toward the house. Before he was halfway there the deputy came out.

"Go radio for assistance. We need to test a few things. I'm going into the water to see what I can find." He handed the gun to the deputy. "Careful with this. Might be a murder weapon. I don't think it's been in the water long."

Clark turned back toward the water, walking faster. When he reached the edge of the swamp he stripped down to nothing and slipped in. The water felt warm, and thick as soup. He felt as if he were sinking into a thin form of quicksand, and couldn't help his sudden urge to crawl out before it was too late. With effort he pushed inward instead.

He felt down with his toes—down, down. It was a hell of a lot deeper than he had thought it would be. His head was under water before his toes touched bottom. At first he felt only sand, then his toes touched something hard and root-like. He nudged and felt it move. He jerked back instinctively, then he pulled his head down deeper into the water and opened his eyes.

It was a dim and murky world. Small fish swam away, and a mud turtle moved swiftly and disappeared into the murkiness of black tree roots and growing water plants. He had little more than half his arm length in visibility, but it was enough to see the shredded clothing, the clean bones of something that once had been human.

He moved over it, looking, and saw the rusty iron weights with which it had been sunk. He moved on, toward the skull. It lay amidst what seemed to be a bone yard. The floor of the swamp was littered with bone, only slightly lighter in color than the roots of the big cypress tree.

He came up for air, gasping. He blinked water away from his eyes, feeling a stinging under his lids, as if some of the almost invisible debris that floated in the water had lodged there.

The police cruiser was out of sight behind the house. His partner was nowhere to be seen. There was only the house in the center of its barren setting, the tall pines that circled it, and the edge of the barn visible in the pines beyond the house. The silence was broken only by bird song, and not too far distant, the sudden roar of something in the swamp that was probably an alligator. He couldn't be sure. He had heard so few of them in his town-bred life.

He pulled in a lungful of air and ducked again to examine the skeleton more carefully.

By the looks of the clothes—a man's jeans, a man's shirt that might once have been white, grey, or blue—the dead person hadn't been in the water a long time. The clothes were pulled apart, torn, chewed, shredded, just enough for whatever it was that ate the flesh off the body to get to that flesh.

Clark crawled forward, cringing from the touch of bone beneath his hands, yet unable to find a place that wasn't littered with it. Something large and dark moved to his right, and he stared toward it, hoping it wasn't an alligator. Then it disappeared into the darkness of tree roots.

He edged forward along the floor of the swamp, trying to get an idea of the size of the man.

Six feet, at least, maybe more.

The skull had fine hair waving from patches, but it was impossible to be sure of the original color. Each strand seemed to be coated with something. Tiny bugs, perhaps. Each strand was like a worm, undulating in the water from the few patches of flesh left on the man's skin.

There was also a series of holes in the skull, three that he saw, that his finger fit into. About the right size for a .357 revolver bullet to have made.

Whatever it was that ate the flesh off the guy caused him no pain, because he was dead when he was tied with weights and put into the water.

Clark came up again, crawled out, and stood for a moment naked in the drying sun. Then he began to dress.

He had a regret. He not only wished he had come alone, he wished he hadn't told Olson to get help out here.

The man in the water was Durk Nolan. Without a doubt in his mind, Clark felt it was Nolan. The size was about right.

Celia, somehow, must have managed to shoot him, and then she, maybe with the help of her kids, pushed him into the water after tying weights to him so he wouldn’t float away and possibly be found by someone.

If he had known ahead of time what he was doing, Clark would have said nothing. Let her go. Let her old man disappear. Let her and the kids live in peace.

But it was too late. Already, on the trail cut through the trees, two county sheriff's cars were approaching.

CHAPTER 17

NORMA ENTERED the restaurant where Wade Turner was waiting for her. His message to meet him had been on her answering machine, with the time of 5:15. He had been waiting close to an hour. If she couldn't meet him, the message said, call him at Baker's Cafe.

Baker's Cafe catered to a blue-collar crowd. The front room was the busiest, with booths and windows and a long counter curving into a U. The back room had tables with cloths and no windows. There were two tables of diners across the room from Wade. He sat at the table in the farthest corner, his back against the wall, his chair angled sideways to the table, one leg up and the ankle resting on the other knee. He was the only person in that part of the room.

Norma smiled as she went toward him, but a tremor of nervousness clutched her stomach.

He stood up as she approached. She put out her hand.

"I wasn't expecting to hear from you so soon, Wade. I was delayed at the office today, or I would have been here sooner. Sorry."

"It's okay. I wasn't doing anything else anyway. You're looking good, Norma. It's been awhile." He pulled out the chair opposite to his, so that she would be against the wall too, facing the empty tables nearby.

He looked older than when she had last seen him, several pounds thinner, his hair with more grey, his eyes more tired, more disillusioned, perhaps. Norma sat down, and Wade turned his chair to face the table, resting his elbows on each side of his coffee cup.

A waitress came through the door pulling her little pad and pencil out of her apron pocket.

"It's a bit early for me, but you go ahead, Wade." In truth, she preferred eating at home with a tray on her lap in front of the television, with her cats at her feet.

He shook his head and pushed his cup nearer the waitress. "Just fill me up again, if you don't mind."

"A Coke for me," Norma said.

After the waitress brought their orders Wade Turner edged his chair away from the table again so he could watch the door.

"It's not Durk Nolan doing the killing," he said. He spoke slowly and casually, as if he were talking about the weather.

"Not Durk Nolan! But it has to be! Nothing else makes sense."

"Nolan's dead, Norma. He's been dead for some time now."

She opened her mouth, and then closed it. She felt all her preconceived thoughts shattering. He might as well have shown her a broken mirror and told her it was in fine shape.

Turner had blue eyes. He rarely blinked. He had a way of staring directly into his subject's eyes that kept them still and waiting. Norma was reminded that he had been a detective in the police force, and he had probably broken down many a lie just by staring down his suspects.

"I went down there and hung around," Wade said. "I told them I'd gotten a strong tip from an anonymous source that Nolan might be the murderer wanted in Georgia and Tennessee. They sent a couple of men out to the house Durk's family lives in to check on Durk, to see if Celia had seen him. I was there when the call came in. No one, nothing was around the place. Celia and her kids were gone. But they found a man's body in the swamp, right near the house. There's even a path from the back door to the spot where the body was. I should say his bones, since his flesh had been eaten away."

She couldn't take her eyes from his, though his face seemed now to be shimmering behind the broken mirror, or beneath murky swamp water.

"Eaten?" she whispered. "Eaten by *what*?" Horrors she didn't want to hear whispered in the back of her mind.

"Who knows? Fish, crawdads, worms, gators. That swamp connects eventually to the Gulf, and all kinds of these little, and not so little, fish come into these waters."

"How can they be sure it's Durk if ... ?"

"It's not an absolutely positive ID, but as near as you can get without proof like DNA blueprinting or dental records and that sort of thing. Everything fits. I drove out to the house to see for myself. Most desolate place I ever saw. The sheriff's department people were there and the state police forensic bunch. They had brought up some dog bones and this skeleton. There was some flesh left here and there, mostly on the backside, enough to prove the man was white. There wasn't anything else much left but skeleton, some bits of scalp, light blond hair. Teeth had never been taken care of. The guy must have been afraid of dentists. No records that could be found. A lot of these ... bums never have any dental work done. He was six-feet-two, large-boned, and what clothes were left, shredded blue jeans and a blue work shirt, could have been right out of Nolan's closet." His chair creaked as he shifted his position. "They eventually decided it was Nolan, and I agree. Everything fits."

He had moved to sit sideways in his chair, but she couldn't move at all. She stared back at him, her mind a muddle of confusion.

He motioned with his hands, palms up, and then cupped them loosely on each side of the coffee mug.

"Somebody shot him, at least three times, right through the head. Then they tied pieces of rusted iron to him and rolled him into the swamp. A .357 revolver was found, caught on a root just under the edge of the water."

"How long has he been dead?" she heard herself asking, as if somewhere in her mind she had accepted the fact that Durk Nolan was dead and that Celia might have lied to her. Something was definitely not as black and white as she had thought it was.

"The flesh on his back indicated perhaps two weeks at the most."

"Two weeks," she repeated in disbelief. Then Celia must have known. Wade Turner misinterpreted her brief shake of the head, and began explaining.

"You get a school of fish after a body, and it doesn't last long. Of course they're looking for his wife, Celia, to question her about this shooting. She and her three kids are missing."

"Celia is my client," Norma said in a very low voice, leaning across the table toward Wade. "She came to me two days ago. She was so scared she could hardly talk. Durk Nolan, ordered by the court to stay away from her and the kids, had come back. She ran away again, taking the kids, his car. But he was alive then, and she was terrified that he was following them.

Since then, four people have been killed—all connected in some way with Celia. Who could it be but Durk Nolan?"

It was his turn to stare a moment. The tip of his tongue nudged the inside of his cheek, poking it out as if a wad of chewing tobacco were hidden there.

"I think you might have been lied to."

"But why?" she cried, a question that came from deep within her. Even though she was beginning to doubt her client's word, she didn't want anyone else to know that. No one but Mel.

Turner shrugged. The lump in his cheek moved and disappeared. "I figured you had something to do with the disappearance of the woman and kids. They're all alive then, obviously."

"Yes."

"They were beginning to search the swamp within several miles reach of the house to make sure the wife and kids' bodies weren't there too."

Norma looked down. "And very obviously I can't disclose their whereabouts, or even that I know they're alive, because I'm not at all sure that Nolan isn't the one who's following them." She raised her eyes again, more poised now, once again at least outwardly sure of her position. "Since there was no positive identification of the body, I have to assume that it was Durk Nolan Celia was running from. It had to be, Wade. You didn't see her. The girl was terrified. You can't fake terror like that."

"Sorry, but everything about the body says it is in fact Nolan. The location, the color of his hair, the size. That's about all they have to go on, but it fits. Several molars were missing. Front teeth intact. But, as I said, no dental records on Durk Nolan have been found. No Social Security number, nothing. And of course fingerprints are gone, thanks to whatever ate him. But there are a few hair strands, and what's there is the correct color. The size of the man, the location, everything fits. They have no doubt at all but that Durk Nolan was shot and his body dumped into the very spot where he dumped all those dogs. Dog bones litter that area of the swamp over an area a hundred feet long, but most of them are at the exact spot where the man's skeleton was found. They brought up the intact skeleton of a Doberman with black fur from beneath the body of the man. Most of it had been eaten too, but there was enough left to show its color and breed. It hasn't been dead a long time, maybe a month, six weeks."

Flint. Norma remembered Celia telling her, at the shelter where Norma first met Celia and the children, "He killed my dog, Flint. He had given him to me when he was a puppy, and then just days ago he killed him. I'm terrified he'll kill my children, too."

So that at least fit Celia's story. She didn't tell Wade. He was saying, "They have no blood sample taken from him when he was alive, no records they can find, so examination of the bones won't help. I think you can be sure it's Nolan. Whoever did the killings, the stranglings, wasn't Nolan."

Norma took a sip of her Coke and felt the pleasant sizzle on her tongue. She tried to think.

"Surely all those murders weren't just a coincidence!" She gave him a brief account of the stranglings, carefully leaving out specifics. She didn't mention Mel's name.

Wade turned his stare toward his coffee and was quiet a moment.

"I can see where you thought it was probably her husband. Did Nolan have a brother or someone who might be out for revenge?"

That someone might be acting on Durk Nolan's behalf hadn't occurred to Norma. It made her feel only more confused.

"Celia said he had no family that she knew of. She said Durk would never even talk about a family." She hesitated, wondering if she should go on.

"Yeah? I'm waiting."

"Well, it was just that I had my doubts about Celia for awhile. She said Durk told her that he had no *human* family. He was part of the swamp, and that if she ever tried to get away, he would rise out of the swamp and get her. I think she really believed he was some kind of monster made up of the deepest, most frightening characteristics of the swamp world."

There was a brief silence, then Wade asked, "How old is Celia?"

"Twenty-eight. She has a daughter eleven. She's been married to Durk since she was sixteen. As soon as he married her, she said, he took her to his house at the edge of the swamp. It was isolated, a mile to the highway, several miles to another house. She was kept there like a prisoner. She had her three babies at home, no doctor, not even a midwife. Her children were never sent to school. Durk rarely even took Celia and the kids to town. He did allow them to have books and a television, and that was their only contact with the world."

"Good God. And no one ever turned him in?"

"Evidently not."

"The people who go around every few years checking on school children, seeing that they're sent to school, where were they?"

"I guess the family was so isolated nobody knew they were there. At least Celia did her best to educate them. All three children can read, and read well. She taught the two oldest all she knew about math, which goes up to algebra. The youngest, who's five, can count to one hundred, which I suppose is about average for a five-year-old."

"But anyway, you got the idea Celia is a little ... paranoid, believing her husband's bull about the swamp? You think she really believed it?"

Norma looked down. "She was so bullied for so long, and so frightened, not only of her husband, but of the place she lived, of the swamp in particular, that she believed anything he told her. He had her believing that he was watching her even when he was gone. That while he was away looking for dogs to sell to laboratories, he was still watching her. He even had her believing that he could turn into some kind of swamp monster. Interestingly enough, when she spoke to the psychiatrist, she didn't admit the monster part."

"Then that proves something, doesn't it? When she talked to you, she was like a child who sees monsters under her bed, or, in this case, in the swamp. But when she talked to the doctor, she realized it wasn't true and simply didn't mention it."

"Evidently."

"Then what she's running from now is her fear, isn't it? The man wasn't capable of all he claimed. She probably killed him herself. As for the stranglings ..." He hesitated, then said, "Odd coincidences do occur, as we both know. The woman at the motel was with a married man. The trucker? He picked up the wrong hitchhiker. The couple up in Tennessee, well, they've been in this Underground Railroad for several years. It could be someone who found out about that, or it might be someone who had a grudge that has nothing to do with anything but plain old revenge. Or it could be they just surprised a burglar."

He could have talked all night on that subject and she wouldn't have been convinced. It seemed to her that it was too much a coincidence. The trail of death was clearly following Celia.

"Well," he said at the last, "I'll leave it up to you how to handle this thing about Celia. The law wants to talk to her. She's in no danger at home anymore, it seems. But as far as I'm concerned, I don't know a thing about her."

"Thank you, Wade. For everything."

They separated. Wade told her he'd keep an eye on what was

happening with the identification of the skeleton, and if anything different came up he'd let her know.

By the time Norma reached home and had sat a few minutes in her car in the garage, staring into the gloom of the darkened interior, she was more perplexed than ever.

Something was wrong. She felt it in her own bones, as if they were at this very moment being savaged by sharp-toothed but invisible little swamp creatures. Terribly, inexplicably wrong.

She had to talk to Celia. She had questions to ask her.

Norma got out of her car, locked it just in case someone managed to open the locked garage door, and went into the house.

The cats came meowing to meet her, swiping their bodies along her ankles as she walked through the hallway to her office. She bent to pet them, greet them, tell them they were good girls.

In the office she turned on the desk light and sat leaning back in her chair, listening to the soft hum of the lamp.

She got the Nebraska map out and located the nearest airport to the Mendel farm, then she made a reservation for a flight out to Omaha, Nebraska. The earliest she could go was in two hours, which would put her in Omaha about 1:30 in the morning. It would be almost two o'clock before she could get a car and get out of town.

She unlocked the drawer and pulled out the address book with the phone numbers of the people she called caretakers. She turned to the M's and found Cora and Lorne Mendel's number.

Cora answered. Her voice was soft, gentle, and sounded as if she were in the next room.

"Cora, this is Norma. Mel hasn't arrived there yet, has he?"

"No, he hasn't, Norma. I wasn't expecting them until late tonight, perhaps even tomorrow."

"Yes, I know. They'll probably stay somewhere in a motel tonight. It's really too far for them to have gotten there this soon, I should have known that. But I'm coming out, and if by some chance he gets there before I do, tell him to wait, Cora. I'm flying out to your place tonight, arriving on the 1:30 flight to Omaha. I need very much to talk to Mel and Celia."

"Is there a problem?"

"Yes. Something very strange has come up. A body found near her home has been identified as Durk Nolan, Celia's husband. And I definitely need some answers I can't get over the telephone. So if you don't mind, I'll have to disturb you in the wee hours of the morning. I'm sorry."

Cora left a brief silence on the line. "He's dead? You just found out?"

"Yes. Something very strange is happening. And I need to talk to them."

"Do you want us to meet you at the airport?"

"No. I'll rent a car and drive out. I should be at your house by ... you're about thirty miles from the Omaha airport, aren't you?"

"Yes, thirty-six miles the shortest way. You have the map, don't you?"

"Yes, I do. If all goes well, and the flight is on time, I should get to your place by three o'clock tonight. I'm sorry to put you to this trouble, but I really have to talk to Celia and Mel. A telephone conversation just wouldn't be good enough."

"Is there any other message you'd like me to give Mel if he drives in tonight?"

"No, just tell him to wait for me. I have to talk to Celia. Don't say anything to her until I get there."

"All right. We'll be looking for you."

Cora hung up the phone and stood with her arms crossed over her stomach, gazing at the cornfields across the road from the deep yard at the front of the house. This kind of thing had never happened before. She had been talking on the phone to Norma for several years now, but she had never seen her and had never expected to.

She went back through the house to the kitchen. Wind sang and whistled around the eaves of the house, a musical variety of notes. But today they weren't the soothing sounds she was used to hearing.

She looked at her watch. Almost time to start supper.

CHAPTER 18

Cora Mendel's kitchen was called, in modern decorating magazines, a country kitchen. It was large, a center of family activity from the cabinets and cooking area at one end to the black iron heating stove at the other. There was an arrangement of three comfortable chairs near the heating stove, which was situated on a low platform of red bricks, with bricks on the wall behind it and a black stovepipe rising straight up through the ceiling.

The chairs were recliners, two of which Cora and Lorne favored and the third for whoever happened to drop by. A soft, three-cushion floral sofa was against the wall. In front of it a candy bowl and stacks of magazines sat on a coffee table. Against another wall was a white wood entertainment center, which housed a television, stereo, and speakers, with cabinets below where the collection of records was kept. Elvis was there, on plastic 45s, and Brook Benton, a favorite of Cora's, as well as older artists on the larger, fragile 75s—Duke Ellington, Glen Miller, Les Brown, Harry James, Woody Herman. In the privacy of her bedroom Cora had stripped to the intoxicating music of "Night Train" when she was twelve, and had fancied herself a beautiful, abandoned, wild woman in a big wild city. At thirteen she had learned to jitterbug to "Tuxedo Junction." Dancing had become her big thing during her teenage years. She would trade sleep for dancing any night, and it was in a nightspot close to Lincoln where she met Lorne. She was seventeen. Two months later, a few days past her eighteenth birthday, Lorne whispered in her ear, "Marry me." They stood in each other's arms outside the same nightspot in which they had met, and with the strains of Glen Miller playing in her ears, she had whispered "Yes." They got into the car and searched until they found a justice of the peace, and before dawn came they were husband and wife.

It all seemed so long ago. Nothing changed much around the farm or the house in the gathering years. Only the entertainment center had been added, made to her specifications at a local cabinet shop. Lorne had frowned and sworn over the cost, but Cora had learned early in her marriage that if she wanted to survive, she had to ignore his ill temper and his stubbornness.

Cora didn't know what time Mel and Celia would arrive or how long they would stay. Lorne wouldn't be eating supper until it was too dark to work in the fields, and there was a chance Mel would drive in by then. She had prepared extra food just in case. If they didn't come tonight, the food could be put into the freezer to be brought out when it was needed.

A large standing rib roast had been cooking in the oven since mid-afternoon, and its aroma now filled the kitchen. Mel, she knew, didn't eat meat, but he loved her home-baked bread and scalloped potatoes and corn. He was one of her favorite fly-by-nights, as she thought of them. There was a gentleness about him that appealed to her, and she liked thinking that her son, had he lived, would have been like Mel.

She wasn't even sure the baby was a boy, the miscarriage had occurred so early in her pregnancy. There were times she thought of the baby as a girl. Her dreams of the baby during her brief pregnancy showed her a baby girl sitting on a grassy hillside with the blue sky in the background. A baby girl about nine months old, smiling at her, her perfect head crowned, haloed, by golden ringlets. Every night during the pregnancy she dreamed the same dream, the same baby, with no variations.

Then, only two months after she'd been told she was going to be a mother, the pains and the blood came. She was alone in the big farmhouse with her pain and her fear. She eased down onto the bed and lay very still, her hands pressed against her abdomen as if that would stop the loss of her baby. And then she had prayed.

When Lorne came in from the field he took her to the hospital.

She shouldn't think of those days, she reminded herself. That was when she had known once and for all that life would never give her what she wanted.

She went out the kitchen door and onto the porch. She could see the horizon over a sea of green corn. The corn looked more like tall leaves of iris. Gravel roads, straight as stretched string, marked the boundaries of farms, separating farm from farm. In the distance she saw the houses, barns, and silos of other farms, but they were just tiny images swallowed up by the endless green of cornfields.

Distant tractors hummed in the air like the summer drone of bumblebees on the flower blossoms. Two tractors now working in the fields belonged to Lorne, one driven by him, one by his hired man, Mark Townsend. They would be coming toward the house soon. Shadows were lengthening, the sun gone. The air was growing chilly.

She went down the steps. The backyard seemed empty without Blue Bonnet, her Australian shepherd dog. The dog liked to follow the tractor when there was nothing else to do, and Cora missed her.

She walked down past the henhouse, where her twenty hens and six roosters were settling down on their roosts for the night. Two of the hens, surrounded by baby chicks nestling beneath their feathers, were still outside. Cora roused them and shooed them gently toward the door of the henhouse. The hens were fluffed up with motherhood, their feathers extended, making them look twice as big as when they weren't mothering a brood of baby chicks. The chicks tagged closely at their mothers' sides, little fluffy balls of yellow. But this time Cora was not cheered by them.

Even after all these years the pain was often as sharp as the day she came home from the hospital, the words of the doctor still reverberating through her heart and her head. "You'll never be able to have a baby," he had said as he removed the bandages from her stomach. "We had to remove your Fallopian tubes to save your life. When the fetus died, it caused an infection that filled your tubes. It had been dead quite some time. It was completely decayed. We couldn't even identify its sex. And the infection was on the verge of spreading through your body. We had to save your life."

Knowing she had lost the baby and had undergone emergency surgery was hard enough, but hearing those words from the doctor was like hearing a messenger from God saying, "You are hereby sentenced to isolation for eternity. In coldness and loneliness you will live forever more. You will never be a complete person, you will never have a child, never be allowed to be a mother."

Later, when she visited the doctor for her first checkup after surgery, her grief still raw and open, the doctor told her, "We'll get you a baby, Cora. Very often young girls who have to give up their babies come here. I know you'd make a good mother. I can see your potential for giving love to a child. We'll get you one, three, as many as you feel you can give a home to. And they will be lucky children."

She went home to Lorne with hope in her heart, but Lorne looked over her head, as he had been doing since the second week of their marriage. He saw only his cornfields, it seemed to Cora, or perhaps he saw the family he had really wanted, the mistress who wouldn't divorce her husband for him, the child they'd had together. He shook his head. No. No adoption.

She would never have known why, probably, if she hadn't seen the pictures. Cleaning in his office, she had opened a drawer filled with snapshots of a little child, from infancy to the age of two or three. In many he was in the arms of a dark-haired woman, and in one Lorne looked down at him with love. The resemblance was overwhelming evidence. The child was Lorne's. There was the oval face, the reddish hair, the same straight nose and the dimple in the chin.

"Lorne ..." she said to him when he came in for dinner, showing him three of the most recent pictures, dated the very month of their wedding. In all of them he was holding the child and looking down at him adoringly, and in one the woman stood with her hand on his shoulder. A gesture of possessiveness. "Is this why you don't want to adopt? Because you already have a child? Why didn't you tell me? Who are they?"

She watched his face turn pale. He snatched the pictures from her hand. She saw his eyes take on a sudden cold anger that frightened and shocked her.

"Don't you ever bother my things again," he said, and spun away from her, going down the hall and into his office. The door slammed.

It was her first terrifying sense of aloneness. It would return again in full force every time she tried to reach Lorne and found him staring over her head out the window, looking at his fields, his barns, everything but her.

Pride kept her with him, she realized finally as the years drifted by. She was too proud to let her family know what a horrible mistake she had made.

When he refused to adopt a baby, she packed her clothes. But she didn't leave. She was four miles from town, with no car of her own and no money to call a taxi. Lorne handled all the money. Their home was an inheritance from Lorne's grandfather, and it was the kind of home she had dreamed of, a large, old, solid farmhouse, white, with big trees in a big yard. A long driveway between rows of cedars. White chicken house, where the hens had the freedom of the back yard. Red barns and tall silos.

Once she wept on her mother's shoulder when her mother wanted to know why she wasn't happy. Maybe she had expected to be told, "Go. Find happiness somewhere else." But her mother had said instead, "What would you do without him, Cora? You've got more than most women do. You've got security, you've got a man who can buy you what you need. Where would you go? What would you do? We don't have the money to help you. And a woman on her own out there doesn't stand much of a chance. Everybody makes mistakes. I can't believe he didn't love you when he asked you to marry him."

Maybe that was what she wanted to hear. Something to keep her there, to keep her hoping. So she had gone home and stayed, but hardly a day passed as the years went by that she didn't look at the horizon and wish she had the guts to take her suitcase and walk that four miles to town and try to find another life.

Time had slipped by, her days filled with the gardening in which she lost herself, days babying her flowers, her animals, and especially her dog and cat, both raised from infancy.

She had joined clubs, the humane society and a few women's clubs. Then she had started as a volunteer at the hospital in the children's department.

It was there she saw her first abused child. The little guy was four years old and sat with big, sad eyes in his crib, stripped to his waist, his body healing from cigarette burns. She knew she couldn't take him home with her. The mother was trying to get him back. She was in therapy, and she had turned in her boyfriend for the torture of the child. He was in jail. But the young mother, Anne, was scared to death, Cora saw the first time she met her.

"I don't know what to do," she whispered to Cora. "He said he'd kill us when he gets out, and I'm afraid. I knew he'd never let me get by with turning him in."

A social worker finally told Cora that she was connected to an Underground Railroad for desperate people who needed to protect children when the law couldn't. Anne and her little son disappeared into the Underground, and after thinking about it, Cora approached Lorne.

"We have all these rooms," she told him, careful not to sound too eager, too desperate. "Those people need help. I understand that occasionally we would be opening up our home for a family in a stopover on their way to a secret place, a new identity ..."

She began to realize, after talking for five minutes, that Lorne was listening. She felt as if she were not hearing him correctly when he said, "I think that's a great idea, Cora. I think it would be just what you need."

What you need ...

In all the years of their marriage he had never indicated that he was aware of her needs.

She was not so much touched as surprised. She felt an odd distance from him now, after forty-two years of living in the same house and eating at the same table. Forty-two years of listening to his farm talk, when he felt like talking to her at all. He had hardly seemed to notice when she had moved into a bedroom of her own after she had lost the baby. They had existed in a kind of cold harmony. He came to her bedroom for sex, leaving her unsatisfied as her feelings for him slowly dried up. When he whispered in her ear that he loved her more than anything on earth she scarcely heard it. Love, she thought in silence, is showing it day by day. It didn't even matter when she learned he had burned the pictures in the drawer. But it was too late.

"Go ahead and do what you have to do," he said that day, a day that changed her life and gave her something more than her flowers, her dog and cat, her hens, and her thinking spot under the tree by the irrigation ditch where she could look at the distant horizon.

Now she hummed as she made her way back to the kitchen. She would go upstairs and prepare the bedroom that Mel or the other drivers who came through always used. It was at the back of the house and had a view of the big barn with the cottonwood trees beyond. Then she would prepare the boys' room and the girls' room. There were twin beds in the girls' room with trundle beds beneath. In the boys' room were bunkbeds. The largest family that had come through consisted of a mother and five children. Relatives of her husband had been trying to take her children away, with the permission of the court, and she was running. Cora knew only that the Underground was helping her. That was all she needed to know.

Norma had told her there were three children. Jonie was eleven, the two boys, Blair and Drew, were younger. That was all she knew.

"You'll be comfortable here," she said aloud as she entered the house and went up the single stairway, her cat trotting along at her ankles. "Comfortable and safe, eh, Ginger?"

She bent to caress the long, red fur of the cat. A warm gentle happiness surrounded her.

They wouldn't know it, but Celia and her children would be her family for the brief time they stayed with her. They would be her daughter and her grandchildren.

CHAPTER 19

"WHY DON'T YOU DRIVE FASTER?" Celia asked, keeping her voice low so the kids wouldn't hear. Jonie had scooted down into the seat and had been still so long Celia knew she was sleeping. In the back, the boys had begun to talk, to argue over the coloring books Norma had included with the new clothes. Drew wasn't coloring within the lines well enough to suit Blair. They weren't listening to her, that was all that mattered.

She felt Mel's eyes on her, and she glanced sideways at him, but then turned her eyes back toward the road. The scenery had changed some after they crossed the Mississippi River. The land was still rolling, but they were beginning to see cornfields stretching on and on from one low rolling hill to another. Trees grew in the gulleys, dark green and thick leafed, and she wished she could take her kids and go hide among them where they would never be found again.

"I would like to," Mel said. "But if I exceeded the speed limit we might get stopped by the highway patrol. I started out in my career as a highway patrolman, and I know a speeding car comes under a lot of scrutiny. On the other hand, one that's going too slow is suspect, too. They're often transporting drugs. So the speed limit is the safest."

"I didn't know you were a policeman," she said, surprised.

"I'm not. Not now."

She looked at him again, at his profile against the window in the slant of the setting sun. He was thirty-five or forty, she guessed, younger than

Durk. His beard hid the curve of his chin, his mustache camouflaged the shape of his upper lip. She could see his lips weren't full, but they were wide. He had dark eyebrows and deep-set, very intense eyes, especially now, as he squinted against the sunlight even though the visor was down.

"Did you quit?"

"I took an early retirement."

She felt more curiosity about him at this minute than she had felt in a long time. In the past few days she'd met more people than she had in all her years of marriage to Durk, but she hadn't had room for curiosity about any of them. Until now.

"Do you spend a lot of time doing this?" she asked him.

He smiled slightly. The corner of his lip toward her turned up. "Quite a lot."

"Do you get paid? I mean ... is it a job or something? I don't know very much about how it's organized except I know a lot of people are involved."

"No, I don't get paid. It's all volunteer. Of course, my expenses are reimbursed if the organization can afford it. The only money the organization has is donated, and it's used mostly for the resettlement of the families who need it."

"Like me and my children."

"Like you and your children."

Celia looked down the long highway. It could have been the highway in Florida or Georgia or Tennessee, except this one was in Missouri. The only changes were the hills bordering the long, curving highway. Sometimes smaller, sometimes larger, at times they flattened out and became cultivated fields filled with fruit trees or long rows of vegetables, as they were in Florida. The hills almost seemed to move in front of them, like the waves on the sea, rising, falling, undulating. The movement of the earth from the car window was hypnotizing, as if the car stood still and the earth moved.

In the back of the station wagon Drew said, "But I did. I did it just like you said, Blair."

"No, you didn't. You made it purple, not green. Whoever saw a purple tree?"

"I did."

"Where!?"

"On Sesame Street, that's where. They had a purple tree!"

"Well, don't you know that wasn't a real tree? It was just a pretend tree."

"That's what my tree is too, a pretend tree."

Celia looked back in time to see Blair shrug. Both boys sat bending over their coloring books. The array of rainbow crayons were scattered between them. Drew carefully selected another crayon, and Blair concentrated on coloring his own picture.

Jonie was asleep on her back, her knees drawn up and pressed tightly together, one hand lying on her stomach, the other hanging down out of sight. Her face, turned sideways toward the back of the seat, her cheek pressed against the cushion Mel had given her, looked at this moment almost as young as Drew's. Her lips were relaxed, parted just a little. Her lashes lay long and dark on her cheeks.

Celia looked down the road. The sun had sunk beyond the next hill and the highway looked shadowed. Ahead of them was a blue car she hadn't noticed before, and she watched it closely as they came upon it, watched it until she saw it was newer than Durk's car and had a dark red license plate. Missouri.

She drew a long sigh and leaned her head back. Norma had said her car—*his* car—would be towed away. The paint would be changed to another color and it would be resold.

Why was she watching for Durk's car? He couldn't be in it, following them. Durk, the man, was dead.

She thought of Mel, driving such long hours, treating them with genuine care and concern. She believed it was genuine, that it was characteristic of this man to treat people well, no matter who they were.

"You must be away from home a lot," she said.

"Sometimes."

"Do you have a family? I mean, a wife and kids?"

She sensed the depth of his hesitation and wished she hadn't asked. It was none of her business.

But then he said, "Not anymore."

She wanted to ask what happened, but she couldn't invade his privacy. It wasn't like her to be that nosy. She didn't know how to act around people anymore, she thought, suddenly angry at herself. She had allowed Durk to keep her isolated far too long. And worse, she had allowed him to isolate her children. Her fear had paralyzed her, kept her chained to old ways for far too long. Instead of going for help she had stayed and tried to make things right. She could hear in her heart the howling of the dogs. She would always hear that sound, every time she closed her eyes. The way she had heard it the first time Durk took her home.

The green trees outside her window blurred, and she closed her eyes, her face away from the driver whose hands held the steering wheel with firm control.

DURK HAD DRIVEN with one hand that day he took her home. The other hand held her close to him. His arm hugged her around the shoulders, and the hand clasped her arm. He kept looking down at her, telling her how beautiful she was.

"A doll," he said, "You're a doll, a living doll, Celia. Do you know that?"

Her lips felt as if they would never stop smiling. No one had ever called her beautiful before. She knew it wasn't really true, but she hoped Durk would go on telling her so. He used his left hand to pull the turning signal on, and he slowed the pickup as three cars came around the curve in front of them.

"We're almost there, doll. Home."

She looked to her left and saw more of what was on the right—a deep green wall of trees unbroken by any kind of building.

They had been married by a justice of the peace just a few hours ago. After their private little wedding he had taken her to a restaurant to eat, then, he told her, they were going home.

The pickup turned left into a narrow lane that wove like a dark thread through the trees. Darkness fell with the turning, and touches of moonlight spotted the road ahead. Still using his left hand, Durk leaned against her and reached for the light switch. The bright beams destroyed the patches of moonlight on the narrow trail.

For the first time doubts assailed her. The tires were silent on the sand, and the lights swung as the road curved and outlined the trunks of hundreds, perhaps thousands, of tall, slender pine trees. Celia felt closed in beneath the roof of green needles.

Suddenly the trees were gone, and the lights shined out over a wide area of grass. He stopped the pickup and turned off both lights and engine. He rolled down the window.

She heard frogs peeping and croaking, and intermittently there came a distant bellow. Chills rasped over her body, and Durk hugged her to him, laughing.

"What's the matter?"

She shook her head. "Nothing." Then, "What's that noise?"

"Frogs. Birds. Whippoorwills. Mockingbirds. And gators. But that was probably a bullfrog you're talking about. See," he pointed to the left. "There's the house."

Moonlight shined down on a square grey house, reflecting a yellowish glow from the window panes. It was like a huge, squat creature with grey scales had crawled out of the swamp and was watching them approach.

She told him that, and he replied, "There are a lot of scary creatures out here watching you, Celia."

He removed his arms from her and started the engine again. The pickup moved slowly in a broad curve toward the back of the house.

She stared at his profile. His voice had sounded strangely threatening.

She wanted to laugh, to say something bright and funny, but the words lodged in her throat.

He parked in the shadows right behind the house. "Stay here a minute."

He got out and went into the house. The lights came on, shining out the door onto the steps at the back of the house, and onto the grass, green and long and uncut. In the moonlight she saw the long, circling row of trees beyond. The house was surrounded by trees in a broad oval, dark and private. There were no other houses visible.

And then she heard the howling. It penetrated her soul, sinking into the most primitive parts of her brain and arousing fear and another feeling buried for a moment under the ancient fear.

It began with one animal, little more than a whimper that seemed to come from just behind the pickup bed. Then another joined it, and another, until a symphony of howls shattered the evening.

She clutched the door handle and clung hard.

She noticed the barn, almost buried in the dark shadows of the trees, its front touched by the silvering moonlight. The cries were coming from that barn.

The howling softened, almost died away, and then rose again, led by one voice. And with it came the buried feeling, rising above the fear. Sorrow. As distant and as deep as the beginning of life itself.

Durk strode out of the house, something long and black in his hands. He raised it and fired.

The sound reverberated in the air, followed by a startled silence. The howling had stopped along with the singing of the frogs and the birds he had called whippoorwills.

"Sons of bitches," he said, and leaned the gun against the house.

He came around the pickup to her door, opened it and lifted her out, his arm going under her knees. She stiffened.

"Relax," he said. "I have to carry you over the threshold, don't I?"

She lay stiffly in his arms and looked at the dark barrel of the gun as they went past it and into the house. She had never seen a real gun before, and she had an instinctive fear of it.

"Durk, that howling ..."

"Daddy," he said. "What did I tell you?"

He carried her through a kitchen that looked as barren and grey as the exterior of the house, and into a hall and then into a bedroom. There was no blind on the window. He laid her on the bed.

"The, the howling," she pleaded. "What was it? Wolves, dogs?"

"Forget it," he said, undoing his belt and stripping off pants, shirt, undershirt, and shorts.

He stood naked before her, his eyes roaming her body, and she felt hot tears beneath her eyelids. She resisted a strong urge to roll off the bed and crawl beneath it.

When the howling started again, low and mournful, rising to a cry of anguish, she closed her eyes and wept with them.

The next day she learned what caused the howling. The barn was filled with caged dogs, the cages in double and triple stacks. She stood in the doorway and stared in disbelief, every instinct in her body revolting against what she saw.

"Turn them loose!" she shouted at him. In the daylight she saw him as she had never seen him before. The night was still with her, a night of pain and loneliness. *What am I doing here?* she asked herself a thousand times during the night. Only now, looking at the dogs that cowered as Durk came by their cages, did the pain of the night recede under this new sickness, this pain in the soul, this feeling of pain for other creatures. She ran after Durk.

"I said, turn them loose! What are they here for? Why are you keeping that big dog in that little cage? Turn them loose!"

She grabbed his arm as he opened a cage and the dog shrank back, terrified.

He turned, his eyes icy, that cold northern blue she had admired. He raised his hand and brought it down on her cheek—hard, flat, a slap that knocked her sideways.

A dog in a cage behind her growled and leaped against the door, and Durk swung to it, an almost animal sound in his throat. He jerked open the door and slapped a muzzle on the dog. He dragged it out of the cage, his hands around its throat.

"This!" he shouted at her, as the dog struggled in his hands, snapping helplessly at the air, the muzzle leaving it room to open its mouth no more than an inch. "This is what happens when you don't mind your own business, girlie. Just take a look! You're dead. You hear? You're dead!"

She screamed and tried to fight him, to keep him from strangling the dog. He allowed her to beat on him, to tear his shirt, his hands tight at the dog's throat. She saw the pleasure on his face, the silent laughter as the dog struggled, its eyes glazing. Between her own screams she heard the whines of dogs and the rattle of cages as some sought the farthest corner, others tried to burst through the doors. And at last, when the dog lay limp in the soft dirt of the barn floor, she dropped beside it on her knees, her face down and covered by her hands, cowed by her own helplessness.

He left her for a long time, it seemed, and she remained there, weeping helplessly. Then she felt a pull on her arm.

He lifted her with one hand and pulled her along on one side, the dog on the other.

"You've got some lessons to learn, girl, and now's the right time. These dogs are my business, and none of yours except to go out and clean their cages and water and feed them, see? And when something around here needs to be got rid of this is what happens. Now I want you to watch closely to make sure this doesn't happen to you, understand?"

He pulled her with him to the edge of the tall trees south of the house. Long before they reached the edge of the grass she saw the glisten of dark water.

They came to a stop beneath the overhanging branches of the largest of the cypress trees. The water pooled between the grass and the tree, dark and deep. She stood back from it, looking into the forest that grew in the water, seeing plants growing there, creating a deceptive floor of green.

She felt sick, as if all reality had been stripped away, leaving her in a world of horror.

Durk stooped, removed the muzzle from the dog's head, and threw the limp body into the water. At first it floated, the long fur growing wetter, heavier.

Then suddenly something tugged at it, drawing it down. It almost disappeared, then bobbed up again. She stared at it in dumb horror. It was dead now, no longer feeling the fear and the terror. But she would never forget that it had tried to protect her from Durk. It had lunged toward him, held back by the metal bars of the cage.

She looked back at the little road that led to freedom. Then she looked at the barn. How many dogs were there, needing help?

If at night she could slip away ...

"Listen, doll," Durk said, in the tone of voice of yesterday, of the weeks before he married her. His hand felt hot on her shoulder as he pulled her to him. "Don't even think of that."

"What?" she said numbly.

"Of running away. You see ..." He took her chin in his hand and forced her face back toward the swamp. The dog was gone, swallowed by the black water as if by a mouth.

"You see," he said. "Eyes. Everywhere there. Look, you'll see them. Be quiet a minute."

His arm on her shoulders held her, and his hand squeezed her chin so that she couldn't look away from the dark, still water among the trees.

The eyes appeared in the water against the creased roots of the trees, in the deceptive green growth farther out in the swamp, in the darkness and the wet. She knew what they were.

"Frogs," she muttered, determined not to let him scare her.

"Some of them, yes, but—"

The eyes disappeared the moment she spoke, blinking away into the dark water. She felt her breath grow shallow and her heart pound. She wanted more than anything to turn and run and keep on running. It didn't matter where she went, so long as she could get away.

"But the others," he said. "They're there. You wanted to know where my folks are. I'll tell you. They're here. Out there, if ever I had any. Even when I'm gone, and I'm gone a lot, I'll be there, too. In the water, watching. Always watching you. That is the only thing in the world you can ever depend on. I'll be watching you."

His hand squeezed harder and harder on her chin. She felt her mouth distort. She felt the pain, but it was only physical, nothing at all like the inner pain she felt, the sorrow, the fear. The growing fear.

"I'll tell you," he whispered near her ear. "I can turn into a creature you can never get away from. There's this huge, round, black head, with eyes all around. Those are the eyes you see out there. They're mine. Have you ever seen a large spider? An octopus? With long arms and legs, dozens of them, six feet, seven feet long? Have you ever seen something that big stand up on those legs? And they can wrap around your body like snakes, slither around you, and crush you slowly, like this."

His hand slid from her chin to her throat and slowly tightened. She didn't fight him, she merely turned her eyes and looked up into his. She stared unblinking as his hand tightened. He could kill her as he had killed the dog. And perhaps he would.

Then he smiled, and his hand moved back to her cheeks and chin, forcing her lips into a pout. And he kissed her.

Then he led her back to the house.

CELIA STARED out the window of Mel's station wagon, seeing the grey house, seeing the barn.

She had learned to take care of the dogs the best she could, and one day, on one of those days when Durk treated her as if he really loved her, on one of those days he brought her a puppy. He came into the house with the little trembling creature in his hands and put it into her arms. It was black, slick-haired, and would have a pointed muzzle when it grew up. Its ears were soft and floppy, as soft as velvet.

She held it against her swollen belly, where her first child kicked within, and looked up at Durk.

"It's for you," he said. "It's a Doberman pup, and you can do with him what you want. He'll keep you company when I'm away from home."

She stared at Durk, disbelieving, and he said, "Well, feed it, for Christ's sake. I took it from its mother and it needs food."

There were times when she could almost smile at Durk, and this was one of those times.

Every day she expected him to take her puppy away, but he didn't. The little pup grew up following behind her as she went about her chores. She named him Flint because of his color.

Flint seemed to have an instinctive distrust of Durk, and when those dark eyes stared at the man, Celia put her hand down on the dog's head and drew him back, afraid for him.

Flint stood by her as her babies were born, and allowed them to tug on his ears and tail when they became toddlers. His black coat gleamed, and he had a long, wolf-like lope as he went ahead of her to the barn when she went out to feed and water the dogs.

As Durk had said, he was gone a lot, and it was those absences that made life bearable.

He had shown kindness, she told herself, in giving her the puppy, in allowing her to keep the dog. While hundreds of others passed through the cages in the barn, Flint stayed.

As Drew grew up, from a baby to a toddler to a little boy, Flint watched over him carefully. It was as if he had decided Drew needed special protection.

Drew loved the puppies in the barn, and Celia had a bad feeling about it. She tried to keep him away from them, but he kept slipping into the barn, Flint at his side, and from the cage of puppies he finally took one.

Celia closed her eyes tightly. She could still hear Drew's scream when Durk learned what he had done.

She ran out of the house that day, only a few weeks ago, and around to the front, following the sound of Drew's breathless scream. He was down by the swamp, and Durk was there, looking into the water.

Flint, oddly, was not with Drew. He stood stiff and still halfway down the path between the house and the cypress tree.

Through Drew's screams came words almost indistinguishable, liquid with tears.

"My puppy! Bring me back my puppy!"

Celia knew without seeing. Durk had taken the puppy from Drew and thrown it into the swamp. As she hesitated, the fear and horror that always lay just beneath the surface coming upward like vomit into her throat, Durk reached back and grabbed Drew by the back of his shirt and with long strides started off toward the house.

Terror held Celia fast. She was aware that Blair and Jonie had come out onto the screened porch and were standing as still as she, as still as Flint.

Don't, a voice deep within her said, *Don't*. As if the dog could hear her silent thought, her command, she repeated, *Don't. Don't move.*

Flint didn't move as Durk passed him, Drew screaming in his arms, helplessly flailing.

Just before Durk reached her as she went to take Drew from him, he looked at her. With that light of contempt in his eyes that she knew signaled danger, he stopped, lifted the little boy high over his head, and, as Drew's scream choked off in terror, threw the child.

The small body hurtled past Celia, struck the side of the house and fell, limp and still.

Celia knelt briefly at his side, and then with her hands shaped into claws, with her mother's instinct gone mad, she went after Durk.

Flint leaped, a growl deep in his throat, his eyes fired with hatred. Before Durk could strike Celia the dog was on him, his teeth sunk deep into Durk's shoulder.

Durk threw him off and whirled like a fighter, on his toes, and swung a fist at the dog as he leaped again.

The blow caught the dog on the side of the head and knocked him back. Staggering, he rose and leaped again, and Durk's hands caught him by the throat.

Holding him away, the dog's legs jerking, Durk slowly strangled him. Celia fought for him, hearing her own strangled cries rising from her throat.

Then came the silence. Flint lay on the ground at her feet, his red tongue protruding from his mouth, his eyes open and staring.

Moaning, aware that her nose was bleeding and her face cut from the repeated blows of Durk's fist, she crawled over to Drew and lifted him into her arms.

CHAPTER 20

CELIA STARED out at the landscape. They were on the outskirts of a city, but she saw superimposed on the outlines of buildings against the horizon the bodies of Flint and of Drew.

Drew had come alive in her arms. She sat on the grass with him cradled against her and wiped the blood from his nose and held his bruised head against her breast. He was going to be all right. She would make him all right again. But her dog was dead.

Durk fastened a chain around the neck of the dog and dragged him to the grassy verge of the swamp, into the shade of the cypress tree. Then he tied weights to Flint's body with thin, sharp wire. She stood by, knowing the kids were silent on the porch, watching as Durk used his booted foot to kick Flint into the swamp.

After Durk left, going off in his pickup, Celia stood by the water, looking down into its darkness. Flint was gone. She could no longer see him there, his black body sinking into the murky depths.

She raised her eyes, looking into the depths of the swamp, and was aware of the other eyes watching her. She could smell death, and she saw within the dark water the swarming of something, mud stirring up from the floor. The water moved sluggishly, like a thick soup boiling, but didn't reveal what it hid. Odors came from within the swamp, odors of rich blossoms mingling with decay, and she thought of hell, the mixture of attractive and deadly blossoms, and of pain and dying that never ended.

She looked at the pine forest as she went into the barn to take care of the dogs in the cages and felt that Durk was there, just as she had felt he was in the swamp. Watching her. She prayed he would not come back. But that afternoon he drove in with more dogs and parked his pickup down by the barn.

It was that very night she took her kids and left the first time. After Durk fell asleep she felt in the pockets of the jeans he had dropped on the floor at the side of the bed and found the keys to the used car he had bought a few weeks earlier. They got away, and it was always a wonder to her that they succeeded. It seemed too good to be true.

For one month they knew freedom. She had thought they were safe. The law was on her side. But no law had power over Durk.

Now she was running away again, but she felt no freedom, only fear. She knew his powers now. She alone.

Celia felt the station wagon slow and heard a signal light begin to click. She sat up. Mel was driving off the highway toward the lights of gas pumps, convenience stores, motels, and even a small grassy park with a children's playground.

"It's getting late. This looks like a good place, okay?" Mel asked.

One small voice said, "Yes." But Celia saw the heads of the other two nodding solemnly, as if Mel, too, though he was facing away from them, had eyes that could see in all directions at once. She understood. It was that feeling of always being watched.

"Mama," Jonie said as Mel pulled the station wagon into the gas station, "could we eat our supper in the park?"

Mel said, "I think that's a great idea. A picnic."

Celia said nothing. She was torn between wanting to go on, to keep driving deep into the night, and seeing that Mel got proper rest.

"If your mother has no objections, you can pick a table. I'll go get the food," Mel said, getting out of the car. He unlocked the rest of the doors.

"Mama?" Jonie pleaded.

"Yes," Celia answered.

"Do you like pizza?" Mel asked.

The three children were quiet, and Celia answered for them.

"They've never eaten any."

"Then we'll all give it a try and see if you like it. Go on out to the park and I'll bring the pizza over as soon as I get the car taken care of.

They walked across the paved parking lot and a quiet street that passed between the motel and the playground. A low stone wall with gate openings surrounded the park, closing in the swings and slides and picnic tables. Tall trees sheltered the tables. Lights in the park burned steadily. Insects fluttered around them. The shadowed areas beneath the trees looked cool, but the air was pleasantly warm.

The boys ran to the swings, and Celia went to a picnic bench and sat down with her back to the table. She crossed her arms at her waist with hands clasped on elbows and watched Jonie wandering about, going to a fountain to drink, then over to the restrooms, where she disappeared from sight.

Celia felt a tug of apprehension and stood up. Maybe someday, when they were settled again, one of her kids could get out of her sight without her feeling that terrible chill. But now, after a slight hesitation, she followed Jonie. They had all been riding a long time without going to the bathroom, she reminded herself.

"Drew," she called. "Blair".

Drew jumped off the swing immediately and then stumbled and fell on his plump knees. He squatted, his face screwed up as he examined his scrapes. Celia started toward him.

Blair had not gotten down. "What?" he yelled, swinging higher.

She bent over Drew and brushed gravel and sand from his scratched knees. "You're going to have scabs growing on your scabs," she said, smiling at him. He hopped around, limping, and Blair again yelled, "What!"

"Get down! Come to the bathrooms with us."

Lately Blair was exercising an independence that both pleased and worried her. During their month in the shelter he seemed to have learned he didn't have to be afraid all the time. "We'll go to the restrooms now; you can play later."

"Ahh," Blair complained, but he jumped off the swing and followed.

Ahead of her Drew limped along for awhile before he forgot his latest wounds and began to run. He had a duck-like wobble, left over from his toddler days, that she adored.

She stood outside while the boys went into the men's room, waiting, guarding. When Jonie came out of the ladies' room, she told her, "Stay here, wait for the boys. I'll be back in a minute."

Celia looked around before she went into the restroom, but of course they would be safe here, in a park so brightly lighted.

The restroom had several booths, and a cold, hard cement floor, unpainted. A half-dozen washbasins hung on the wall opposite the booths.

It reminded her of the restroom in the park in Tallahassee, the park where she had met Durk.

She went into the farthermost compartment, as she had done in the restroom in Tallahassee so long ago, when she was sixteen and had nowhere to sleep except on the cement floor in the corner compartment. Several times during that long night someone had pulled on the door, but finding it locked, had moved on to another toilet.

She washed her face and hands and dried them on a paper towel that felt soothingly rough. Then she hurried out.

Jonie was holding Drew up to the highest of the water fountains, while Blair had the water in the lower fountain turned on full blast and seemed more to be bathing his face in it than drinking.

Celia said, "Blair. You've wasted enough water, haven't you?"

He took a last long gulp and straightened, water dripping from his chin. Jonie put Drew down, and the boys went running across the park toward the swings. Blair had a long, lanky start on Drew, and left him behind.

Another family had come into the park, and three children about the ages of Blair and Drew were heading toward the slides and the swings. But the voices of those children filled the air like birds in the trees, joyous and happy and free.

Celia sat down on the same bench where she had sat before, near enough to the swing set and slides to be able to watch her children. She saw Blair and Drew standing back now, close enough to each other to touch, watching the newcomers. Jonie was strolling idly, bending to pick something small and yellow. A dandelion.

Celia watched the other people who had arrived at the park while she was in the restroom. A man and woman with two children took a picnic basket from their car over to a table near the stone wall. Voices drifted to her, murmurs in the distance, the eager young voices of the children, the traffic on the streets and highways, the sounds of the nearby city. Kansas City, Missouri, Mel had said as they approached.

Celia looked for the station wagon, and saw it had been moved over to the restaurant.

She thought again of the shelter, and of the mam who had mowed the yard there, changed the light bulbs when they burned out, and swept the long hallways. He also helped women and children move in and out if they had luggage, boxes, or bags.

She had been there two weeks before he spoke to her. He had smiled often, every time she saw him, but she hadn't heard his voice.

Then one day she met him in the hall.

"Hi," she said. "Do you know where my kids are?"

"Sure. They're in the backyard, in the sandbox."

"Jonie too?"

"Well, no, not Jonie."

He ran his fingers through his long hair. It was almost white, although she didn't think it was grey. It seemed more like very light blond hair, like Durk's, only it had streaks of deeper brown. His face was young, the skin pulled tight over strong bones. He was a big man too, as tall as Durk, though so thin he verged on bony, and he stooped, his shoulders rounded as if he had carried heavy loads before his bones were strong enough to stand the burden.

His eyes were like his lips, always smiling.

"Where is she?" Celia cried, feeling that awful knotting in her stomach.

"Oh, it's okay," he said quickly but mildly. "She's in the main room watching a television show with a couple of the other girls."

Celia sagged with relief and turned back toward her room.

It was a small room, furnished with two beds and a chest of drawers. The main room, as the handyman had called it, was where all the people in the shelter went to watch TV or play games or just talk. Off the main room was the dining room, and behind that the kitchen. Today was Celia's turn to help with the cooking. She pulled the door shut and then went down the hall toward the kitchen.

"Celia."

She stopped, startled, her heart jumping into her throat for a moment, even though his voice sounded nothing at all like Durk's.

He was still standing in the hall where she had first seen him, with the push broom handle resting against his chest. His eyes had a serious look. The crinkles were still at the corners, but the smile was gone.

"You know my name," she said, surprised. They had hardly spoken to each other.

"Your daughter, Jonie, told me. I asked. My name is ..." He hesitated, then said, "Kent."

She smiled and nodded, thinking to herself it probably wasn't his real name, and then she went on to the kitchen to help with the cooking.

They began to talk after that, she and Kent, just little things, like the weather or the show that had been on TV last night or what new family was coming in to take the place of the one that had left.

It was two weeks before she grew curious enough about him to ask why he was here, doing these odd jobs. Where was his family? Where was he from? She wondered if he was an outcast from his family, as she had been. Why was he here?

"Just passing through," he said, and changed the subject. She still wondered, but she didn't ask. She understood his reluctance to talk about the past.

She often thought she would like to fly away into the sunset with her kids and never look back, never think back.

But she had found the thinking back a larger and more important part of her than the present.

Sitting in the park now, she watched Drew and Blair tentatively approach the noisy children and begin to mingle with them, to claim swings of their own and begin to swing. Jonie went to Drew and pulled his swing high into the air over her head before she let it go.

Celia held herself tight, keeping herself from crying out at Jonie, *You'll make him fall!* But Drew didn't fall. He clung to the chains of the swing with tough little hands, and Celia saw a wide smile on his face, dimpling the cheeks and putting a little ray of joy in her heart. Beside him Blair pumped hard and got his swing to soaring as high, almost, as Drew's.

Mel drove the station wagon slowly around and over to the stone wall, and the boys jumped off their swings and ran to meet him. Jonie went too, to stand at the opened car door while Mel handed something out to her. He gave capped Styrofoam cups to the boys, then from the car he brought a couple of large, flat boxes.

Celia stood up, and using the paper towel she had brought from the restroom, brushed from the table the leaves and twigs that had fallen from the sheltering tree.

"I think we've got some hungry kids here," Mel said, and Celia turned, putting out her hands for the boxes.

THIS WAS FUN! Jonie could feel a smile at the corners of her lips and on the corners of her heart. It was just like being a real family with a wonderful dad.

A delicious aroma rose from the boxes as her mom opened them. She recognized the smell of cheese, tomatoes, and spices, as well as fresh-baked bread.

"I've got the forks and knives," Drew said, and placed a napkin-wrapped package on the table.

"I don't know why they'd want to give us forks," Mel said. "We eat pizza with our hands, don't we, guys?"

The boys nodded, as did Jonie, even though they didn't know anything about it.

"You eat pizza with your hands, of course," Blair agreed, looking up at Mel with a light on his face Jonie had never seen before. Blair always managed to sit right next to Mel and gaze at him with that special look.

It made Jonie feel sorry for Blair. Didn't he know that Mel was only helping them get away? That in a few days Mel would be leaving them somewhere out west, and they'd never see him again?

Drew was still Mama's baby, and that was good. He wouldn't be so disappointed when Mel left them. He was beginning to leave his teddy bear in the car now and then, she had noticed. And to her that meant he was getting more secure. Jonie felt more secure too. She could even watch a blue car like her dad's and not be so scared.

Like the one that was turning off the highway and coming slowly down toward the convenience store. It was passing the convenience store now and coming on toward the motel. The driver was going to spend the night in the motel, as they were.

Jonie held her half-eaten piece of pizza at the edge of her open mouth and stared at the car.

It looked exactly like the car they had run away in. Long and blue, with a dent in the right fender.

The car slowly passed the overhang at the front of the motel office and drove toward the park.

She could see now that it held only the driver, and he was staring toward the park ...

A long, shuddering chill passed through Jonie. She could feel her dad's hands slowly crushing the life out of her. She stared, unable to move.

The car eased nearer, and rolled beneath one of the tall lights at the edge of the park.

She saw the thin, set mouth, the narrow slit of his cruel eyes. She saw the light touch his hair and wash it of all color, so that it looked iced over, as she was ... She saw him, as clearly as if she were still back in the house by the swamp and he was walking across the room to hurt her.

A sound came from her throat. The pizza fell from her hand. She lifted herself from the bench. She tried to tell them, to warn her mom that he had found them. Her voice wouldn't work, except for the gargle of sound that she couldn't shape into words.

She knew they were all staring at her, but none of them was looking toward the street. Then the blue car suddenly speeded up and disappeared behind the dark row of trees at the end of the park. Jonie's formless cry became a rush of words.

"Oh, God! Oh, God, no!"

Mel rushed around the end of the table and took her in his arms.

"Him ... *him* ...", Jonie wept, shaking all over, her hands clinging to the front of Mel's shirt. "It was him, it was Dad. I saw him. The car, he was driving the car, our blue car. He went that way. He saw us. He looked straight at me."

Celia clutched Jonie's arms, shaking her as if trying to wake her from a nightmare.

"No, Jonie, no," she kept saying. "No, Jonie, it's okay. It wasn't him, it couldn't have been him."

"He's coming after us! He won't let us get away!"

"No, Jonie, no," Celia cried.

Somehow Jonie had shifted from Mel's embrace to her mom's. Celia was still trying to shake her and hug her at the same time. They rocked back and forth as Jonie clutched Celia's shoulders. Why couldn't she convince her mother? *He* was coming after them, and he was going to kill them all.

"He's going to kill us—"

"No! Jonie, it's impossible. It was not Durk!"

How could her mom say it was impossible? She had seen him, as clearly as she saw Mel, Celia, Blair, and Drew. Drew had begun to cry, and Blair was staring down toward the end of the park, where the blue car had driven out of sight. People from the other tables were staring at them.

Mel asked, "The blue Oldsmobile, Jonie?"

"Yes! It went that way."

"It can't be," Celia said, hugging her hard. "Don't you remember? Norma was having the car towed away. Remember?"

Mel began to gather things up from the table. Blair helped him, working quickly and in silence. Throwing away paper cups, plastic forks and knives, gathering up napkins, Blair worked at cleaning off the table.

"Get in the car, kids," Mel said quietly but with a deep urgency. "We've leaving. It's only two hundred miles on to the farm. We can get there by midnight if we start now. Come on, boys. To the car."

Seeing that her brothers and mother were safely within reach, Jonie hurried to the sanctuary of Mel's station wagon. She glanced back once as they drove away, but she didn't see the blue car.

It was there, she knew now. Somehow he had gotten the car again, and he would never let them get away.

CHAPTER 21

MEL WORKED QUICKLY at the rear of the station wagon. He unrolled the foam mattress and spread it out and unfolded a blanket and smoothed it over. There were three more blankets. He tossed two of them over into the backseat where Jonie was getting in.

"One's for you," he said. "One for your mom. The nights are colder up where we're going this time of year."

Jonie pushed one of the folded blankets into the front seat. Celia had reached the car and had opened her door. The two boys waited, one on each side of Mel. He arranged their blankets and pillows, then lifted them into the rear of the station wagon and pulled the hatch down and locked it.

A car was going by slowly, coming from the direction Jonie had said she saw the Olds go. He kept his eye on it as he hurried around to the driver's seat. But the car was white and filled with a family and so many kids some of them probably belonged to neighbors. The driver was looking for a parking spot at the park. As Mel started his car and pulled away from the low stone fence, the other car drifted into a spot farther on down.

Mel made a U-turn and went back toward the freeway, but instead of driving up onto it, he took the underpass and then a street to the right. No one said anything, no one asked why he was driving into a residential section. They all were quiet again, as quiet as they had been that first night when he had picked them up at midnight. Celia pulled up the folded blanket and hugged it against her stomach.

Mel looked in the rearview mirror and saw the outlines of Blair and Drew's heads. He increased the speed of the car, keeping an eye behind and to each side.

How the hell had that bastard managed to follow them? Though it seemed Celia doubted that possibility, Mel could not take a chance that Jonie had been wrong. He hoped to God she was wrong. But if by some chance she wasn't, then they had to lose him.

Mel knew the area well enough to know their best bet was to stay on the interstates. Narrower roads were also more time consuming, and more dangerous. Once they got to the farm they'd surely be safe. He hadn't thought he was being careless when he drove into Tennessee, but at the time he had thought Celia's car had been picked up by the tow truck. Celia, of course, still thought so.

He had to talk to Celia. But he'd wait until the kids went to sleep.

"Lie down, boys," he said. "Try to sleep. You, too, Jonie."

In the mirror he saw the heads disappear as the kids obeyed. There was a tug at his heartstrings as he thought of these kids, subjected all their lives to an abusive father. How could a man make his kids so scared of him? At that moment he had the urge to backtrack to the motel, make sure Celia and the kids were safe inside, and then go out to wait for the bastard who had made them into scared little rabbits. Just once he'd like to meet him.

But he had to get the kids safely away first.

The clock on the dash ticked off ten minutes as Mel drove the streets on the south side of the interstate. No cars followed, and none he met were blue 1976 Oldsmobiles.

He headed for the interstate. The streets were getting narrower, more crowded. He drove through a business section as narrow and dark as a tunnel, the buildings rising on each side, all traffic temporarily left behind. Then he turned right onto a through street, crossed a bridge over the Missouri River, and followed the signs toward the interstate north. They would drive straight north now until they reached Iowa, and continue on north along the river to Omaha. At that point the way was as well-known to him as the country roads to his own place in southern Georgia. Nebraska country roads, as straight as a yardstick, separated one section of land from another, and cornfields as far as the eye could see were bordered occasionally by a row of trees. It could get monotonous if one missed its beauty. Every state, whether it grew corn or oranges or cactus, was pretty country. Each state was, in its own way, beautiful.

But there were times, increasingly now, that he wished he could stay home with his dogs. He wished the world would grow gentler, parents kinder to their children. He wished all the hurt would go away. Instead it seemed to be increasing. The drugs, more rampant every day, were making people crazy. People who were basically good changed completely under drugs, including alcohol, which most people didn't even think of as being a drug. He wondered if Celia's husband used drugs. There were so many things he needed to know, as well as so many things he needed for Celia to know.

He reached the access street to the interstate and pulled into the traffic. From below the cars and trucks that traveled the wide highway looked like streaks of light, nothing more. Among them they were glaring orbs of light, reaching into the station wagon from behind.

The city fell behind, and the road reached straight north with only a slight curve here and there. Mel, watching behind for the lights of a patrol car, increased his speed, passing other automobiles, changing lanes frequently, always watching behind for the headlights of a car that appeared to be doing the same thing.

He located a truck that was driving seventy-five in the sixty-five speed limit zone and moved in behind it. An eighteen wheeler, it was great protection. When it slowed, he slowed, and a couple of minutes later they passed a patrol car sitting in the grassy area between the north and south lanes. About a mile past it the truck speeded up again, and Mel kept close enough behind it that no other car could move in and separate them.

The kids had been quiet a long time. With the sway of the car and the silence and the dark, with only the headlights of other cars sweeping through the station wagon above their heads, they surely had fallen asleep. Riding in a moving car at night was as sleep inducing as being rocked in someone's loving arms.

Mel looked at Celia. She was still hugging the blanket against her chest, her face straight ahead though there was nothing to look at but the rear end of the truck.

"Celia," Mel said softly, hoping the kids wouldn't hear him.

Celia's face turned, and he saw the pale triangle of it, the narrow chin, the silky dark hair curling down on her wide forehead. Her eyes were dark, like her kids' eyes. In the dim interior of the car, with the glare of lights from other cars now dropping away as the night deepened, those dark eyes looked like holes in her face.

He felt like reaching over and putting his hand over hers, but he gripped the steering wheel instead.

"Norma gave me a description of your husband and of the car. I wasn't going to tell you, but I think now I should. I called Norma early this morning, when we stopped for gas and breakfast, and she told me your car disappeared before the tow truck operator got to it."

The dark holes in her face seemed to grow even larger and deeper.

"Disappeared?" she whispered. "Stolen?"

"It was gone. It's possible, entirely possible, that your husband followed you, took the car, and is now still following us, or trying to. I don't think he's behind us right now. If we're lucky, we lost him in Kansas City."

A car approached from behind, overtaking them, driving at least eighty miles an hour. In its lights Mel saw Celia's face clearly. Her mouth had opened and she was staring at him hard, her eyes steady and unblinking. Beyond her the lights of a small town sparkled in the distance like brilliant stars in the sky, the horizon a black line far away.

Mel watched the other car through the rearview mirror and saw it was hanging right behind them. It made him uneasy, and he wished he dared speed up and pass the truck and see if he could get away from it. But he couldn't take a chance on being stopped by a patrol car.

After driving a quarter of a mile behind Mel and the truck, the car behind speeded up suddenly and went on around, and Mel saw it was a low, black job, a Corvette, possibly.

The traffic behind was spotty now, and falling back as the truck passed a line of cars. Mel stayed behind him as if the truck were connected to the front of the station wagon.

When he looked at Celia again she was facing the truck.

"I wonder who really took it," she said. "Some kid, maybe. Stole it. Broke in and hotwired it. I gave the key to Norma. I don't know what she did with it."

"You seem pretty sure it wasn't Durk."

She sighed deeply and swallowed, and for a moment Mel had a feeling she was going to tell him something. Then she turned her head away from him, toward the distant small towns and the dark horizon.

The truck angled into the right lane again and settled down to a steady pace of seventy-five miles an hour.

"There's something else you should know," he said. "There were a couple of murders back in Georgia. One was a trucker near the motel where I picked you up, and the other a young woman in the motel room you vacated. She was killed by someone who got into the rear window of the motel not long after the room was rented out again. And then—"

"Murders?!" Celia's face was toward him again.

She sounded confused, as if the connection between her husband, the stolen car, and the murders still did not occur to her.

"Yes," Mel said. "And while I was in paying for the gas this morning, in Kentucky, I heard on the radio that the people we stayed with last night were both murdered early this morning, apparently not long after we left there."

"The ... the Merrows?"

She whispered the question, shock in her voice.

He nodded. The truck was slowing to sixty-five, and Mel noticed a truck in the southbound lane blinking its lights on, off, on. There was another patrol car ahead. It used to make him mad as hell the way motorists, even the drivers of Volkswagens, would warn speeders that he was waiting to nab them. He had wished then he could drive an unmarked car. He slowed behind the truck, dropping back to an acceptable distance, and held the car at a steady sixty-five. Now, on the other side of the fence, he appreciated the warnings.

"All of them?" Celia asked, still whispering. "All three of them?"

"No, thank God. Robin was outside doing her chores. She went back to the house and found her mother dead, strangled, on the back stairs. She ran to the neighbor's house and—"

"Oh my God!"

Celia clamped both hands over her mouth and stared at him, her eyes almost invisible in the darkness of the car, the dash light soft and only highlighting her hair and the direction of her look.

"Oh, Lord! Oh, I'm so sorry," she said, her voice breaking from a whisper to a low cry. "I didn't think, I didn't know, it was only me—mainly me—I thought ... Not even the kids, I hoped. I prayed."

Mel wished he could pull over and try to comfort her, but he had to keep driving. He reached out and touched her on the shoulder. He could feel her trembling, and some of the awful fear reached him.

"Celia?"

"I thought it was me he wanted to kill. Just me. I mean, I know he'd ...

he'll kill my kids too, just to get even with me. But I didn't think he'd ever kill anyone else. Why would he kill the others?"

"We assume he's after everyone that gets in his way. He probably hitch-hiked a ride with the trucker. We don't know how he came exactly to the motel where you were staying. The truck went off the road less than a mile from the motel. He somehow found out what room you were in, but by the time he broke in the other woman was there and you were gone. He killed her out of fury, probably. Then he took the car and headed north, just as we did."

She was still staring at him. She lowered her hands slowly, but she didn't answer. When he saw she was not going to say anything, Mel went on.

"So he knew your general direction, somehow." Celia was listening, watching him. Her eyes seemed to be getting larger, while the rest of her face sank into the movement of lights and shadows.

"At the Merrow's farm in Tennessee he must have parked the car in the woods there off the road. And again he got to the house too late. He killed both Fred and Alice. But Robin escaped by being outside. When I heard about it, I called Norma. She told me about the car being missing. So now at least we know he's behind us. She said she'd get the police to check on him, so they'll be looking for him, and maybe they'll get him."

He didn't add what he was thinking. That the police would be looking in Tennessee and Georgia, but would they look in Missouri? How much information would Norma give them?

Should he pull off the interstate at the next exit and find a police station and put Celia and her kids into police custody?

"When we get to the farm," he said, "I'll call Norma and find out what's going on. It might be a lot better for you and the kids if we turn you in to the police and—"

"No! *Oh no, no, no!* Please, promise me you won't do that. Promise me, *please!"*

He heard the tears in her voice and didn't understand.

"But Celia," he said, "they'll protect you. I know they were unable to help you when you ran away the first time, but they did the best they could. This time there's a possible series of murders against him, and they have something to work on. I don't mean to trivialize abuse. It's terrible and it's real, but there isn't much they can do in a month's time. But in this case, they can sock the bastard in jail right away."

"You don't understand," Celia cried, and seemed to shrink in her seat, lowering herself as if to hide, leaning closer to the door, bringing the blanket higher in her arms. "You just don't understand."

"I want to protect you and the kids."

"If you really mean that, then just keep going. Please! Promise me you won't take us to the police. Promise me. If you don't want to be involved anymore, then just drop us off at a bus station and we'll make out okay. But we can't go to the police."

He drove in silence for awhile. He tried to understand Celia's feelings. After all, she had gone to the police once for help, but they hadn't been able to keep Durk from coming back. Then he thought about Crescent. Even he, a police officer, had failed to protect her. There were some things, many things, that were beyond the law's control.

"You can just leave us off in the next town," Celia said quietly.

"No! I'll take you on. Don't worry. Try to sleep. I won't leave you and the kids." This time he would depend on no one else to protect these children, this woman.

He heard her sigh. She unfolded the blanket and pulled it over her arms, and he reached down and set the thermostat higher.

The darkness sang with the sound of tires on pavement, the growl of the trucks, the whistle of wind through a tiny opening somewhere in the car.

CHAPTER 22

Jonie listened, lying still in the seat, the blanket pulled over her.

For awhile she had sat up and watched the other cars on the road, but all she had seen was their lights. Behind those lights she imagined the blue Oldsmobile that she had seen in the driveway between the park and the motel. Behind every set of lights that Oldsmobile drove, and its driver could see her, see her chin on the seat, watching, even though the interior of the station wagon was dark. He could see her.

The sway of the car was lulling, but her hands continued to clench the blanket beneath her chin.

It didn't seem real that those nice people where they had stayed most of last night could be dead now. The man, Fred, had offered her a second brownie at the supper table last night. He was such a nice person she knew he wouldn't have gotten mad even if Drew accidentally spilled his milk or Blair had been sick at the table the way he so often had at home when Dad was there. He was one of those dream-like fathers who kissed and hugged his daughter in a good way, not a bad, and who had never whipped her.

Durk had started touching her in a bad way when she was still so young she didn't understand what he was doing. The first time it happened she was so glad at first, and so pleased that he was hugging her and kissing her and sitting down in the living room with her on his lap. She didn't remember her dad ever holding her before in all her life.

They were alone in the room. Mama was in the kitchen, and the boys with her, Drew still so little he had to be carried around.

"Come here," Durk said to Jonie, and at first she thought she might have done something wrong and he was going to whip her or slap her face.

"I said come here," he repeated. He smiled and held out one hand.

The smile didn't reassure her. Lots of times he smiled just before he struck. But she went to him, because not going would have brought his fury onto all of them.

He picked her up and hugged her, and then he kissed her on the lips and hugged her harder. His hand cupped her bottom, and then he lifted her skirt and began rearranging her panties, looking down into them.

It was then that she began to feel uncomfortable. The first flush of pleasure that had come with the caresses turned back to the fear she had always felt around him, and now was tinged red with shame. But she was afraid to move, to try to push his hand away when he put his fingers between her legs and spread them apart.

She heard a scream behind her, and then she was falling as Durk stood up. She struck the floor and rolled, kicked, she thought, because there was a sharp pain in her side. She glimpsed her mother coming at Durk with her right hand made into a claw, her left arm holding the baby.

Jonie saw her mother's face contorted and white, her dark eyes like fire. She stooped and laid the baby on the floor. He was crying now, and he turned onto his stomach and lifted himself to his hands and knees, balancing there, screaming, as afraid as Jonie.

Celia lunged at Durk, and he struck her. She fell back against the wall, blood running from her nose and mouth, but she got up again and went after him. This time he kicked her. She fell and lay quiet.

Swearing, Durk left the house. Above the baby's cries Jonie heard his pickup start. She stood immobilized with fear in the middle of the room until her mother came to and sat up, the blood clotting yet still oozing threadlike from her nose. She put out her arms, and Jonie ran into them.

Later Celia told her about bad touching. And she told Jonie that she should always stay close to her.

Durk was gone for a long time, and Jonie hoped he wouldn't come back. But finally he did. After that, though, Celia kept all three of them close to her when Durk was around. But there were times when she had to go take care of the dogs, and even though she and her brothers stayed together and Mama was not far away, sometimes Durk caught her and touched her. It seemed to amuse him that she ran from him. In the back of her mind she could hear his laughter following her through the open rafters of the barn.

As she grew older Jonie wondered why they didn't leave. They never even went to town unless Durk took them. But couldn't they just walk away, go live in the woods? She didn't even know her mom could drive until that first night they ran away, and that was little more than a month ago.

In the shelter she met a lot of nice people. She met girls who were like friends for awhile, until they left to go home again. They exchanged addresses, but she never heard from them. One was named Cammie, she remembered, a girl with blond hair cut straight across at the bottom. Another was named Deborah, but she kept more to herself. The way Jonie herself did at first.

And there was the nice handyman, Kent, who seemed to pay special attention to her and her brothers. It was, she suspected, because he liked their mother. Jonie didn't know if she could trust him, yet he was gentle and quiet and never bothered anyone.

One day he had asked her about her dad, and if her mother was getting a divorce.

"Yes, I think so," Jonie said. "We're getting a court order, too. So we can go home and he can never go there anymore. All the dogs have been taken away because he was charged with cruelty and fined a lot of money."

"When are you going home?" The smile that was always on his face disappeared, and he looked oddly sad. He had stopped clipping the hedge and waited for her answer.

"Pretty soon. I don't know when."

She looked around at the backyard of the shelter. It was surrounded by a green hedge, and had lots of trees at the back, magnolia, and oak, and near them was the playground with the swings and sandbox. Drew was playing in the sandbox with two other little boys, and Blair was swinging. The house was big and white, with a blue roof. Mama had called it a haven, not a shelter. To Jonie it sounded like she said "heaven."

"I like it here," Jonie said. "But Mama said since we've got a place to go we have to make room for other families that need a haven."

"You have a smart mama. She's pretty, too."

"Is she?" Jonie hadn't really thought about that. "I guess she is."

"Where is your home? Where you're going back to?" Jonie told him, describing the countryside, the town where they went to buy groceries sometimes, the road out to the house, the mailbox that was leaning forward so that when they did get mail, junk mail, sometimes it fell out on the ground.

"Is it all right if I come out sometime?"

"Yes, sure. But I guess maybe you'd better ask Mama."

"Why can't I surprise her?"

Jonie shrugged. "I guess that would be okay."

They had been home only a couple of days when Kent came. She saw the car from the bedroom where she was making beds. It glided slowly out of the pines toward their house. It scared her, seeing it creeping so quietly toward them. She thought it might be Durk in a new car.

She ran, terror in her throat, to the kitchen where her mother was cleaning up after breakfast.

"Mama! There's a car coming!"

Celia's face turned pale. Together they went to the back door. Celia opened it barely a crack. They peered out and watched the car move at a man's walking pace slowly along the sandy trail between the house and the forest of pines.

They recognized him at the same time. A great sense of relief flooded Jonie as Celia flung wide the door and cried, "It's Kent! I can't believe it! How'd he know where we live?"

It was the first time they'd ever had a visitor, and it was like a miracle. Someone cared enough to come and see them.

Celia was smiling, her face flushing as Jonie looked at her.

"One of the boys must have told him," Celia speculated. "Or ... or ... you?"

"I thought it was okay. You don't mind, do you?"

Celia didn't answer, but she didn't have to. She ran down the steps and into the backyard. The car came to a stop.

Kent walked into the house and sat down as if he were an old friend. Jonie and the boys sat on the floor listening. Celia asked about the people at the shelter, and he told them, talking in his easy way, the same way he worked. Slow and easy, smiling, reminding Jonie of some of the dogs she had taken care of in the barn, dogs that wanted to please, to do nothing that would get them hurt.

Kent stayed for supper, and after supper he helped with the dishes. Mama even laughed a couple of times before dark came and Kent said he had to go.

"No, don't go," Mama said. "It's a long ways back to Tallahassee. A couple of hours."

"I'm not going back to the shelter," Kent said. "I quit my job."

"Then where are you going?"

He shrugged, smiling. "I usually never know. I just go."

"Then stay awhile. The boys can double up in one bed, and you can have the other."

He didn't leave, not then. Jonie and the boys went on to bed, with the boys both sleeping in Blair's bed, Drew with his pillow down at the foot of the bed. Jonie drifted to sleep to the distant murmuring of Mama and Kent's voices, his soft and deep, hers light and airy.

She woke later to the sound of another voice, and fear kept her pinned to the bed. Durk's voice. A few short, clipped words that she couldn't understand. She lay still, more afraid than she'd ever been in her life. He wasn't supposed to come back, but he was here. She listened to heavy footsteps on the board floors, Durk's and Kent's. They went through the kitchen and out the back door.

Where was Mama?

Silence filled the house after the door closed. She listened hard for a car to start, but all she could hear was the frogs in the swamp, the nightbirds, and from far off the bellow of a bull gator. She listened so hard her ears began to buzz deep in her head, and when she heard the *pop pop pop* she thought at first it was only in her head.

But at the same instant as the popping sound the frogs in the swamp nearest the house, by the big cypress, abruptly grew still.

Before, when Durk was home, those silences meant he had gone down to fish or to take his boat out into the swamp, or that he had dragged a dog down there to be thrown into the water. Now she didn't know what it meant, because all the dogs were gone.

She wanted to get up and run, but she lay still.

Then she heard a deep sobbing somewhere in the house.

A few minutes later a car started close to the wall at the head of her bed. Just outside the house. Kent's car. He was leaving.

The frogs began peeping and bellowing again, a musical chorus that had sung her to sleep all her life. And although she had thought she would not sleep again that night, she slept in spite of herself. But she didn't know it until she woke up the next morning and smelled the bacon Mama was cooking.

She knew for certain then that Durk was home. Mama never cooked bacon unless he was home. They always ate oatmeal and toast, or biscuits and rice, when he was gone.

Jonie dressed and went into the kitchen to find her mother sad and quiet again, one eye swollen almost shut, her lips puffed and cut on one corner. Celia's eyes didn't meet hers.

Durk was drinking. For two days he hung around the house and they were afraid to move. When Drew had to go to the toilet he tried to slip silently against the wall and out of the living room, where their dad lay on the couch.

"Get back here!" Durk ordered in his coldest tone of voice, his hard eyes staring at Drew.

Celia said, "Durk, he has to use the toilet."

"I said get back here!"

Drew came back and sat down on the floor, his legs pressed hard together, his eyes never leaving the face of the big man who lay half reclining on the couch pillows.

Jonie saw the spreading wetness on Drew's jeans and prayed Durk wouldn't see. And for a long time he didn't. Then he saw, and he motioned for Drew to come to him and whipped him with his belt and called him a baby and sent him to his room.

Jonie was glad Drew was gone. At least he was safely out of Durk's sight, and if he wet his bed, Durk wouldn't know.

Between long silences he kept yelling at Mama.

"Just let me give you an inch and you take a goddamned mile. Here I thought I was being nice to you and the brats, bringing you a car so that you could go get your own goddamned groceries, and what do you do? You use it to run off to the police and get a court order against me! A court order! Well, let me tell you, girl, no cocksucker judge can tell me I have to stay away from my own house. I'll come home whenever I damned well please."

"Then we can leave," Celia said, surprising Jonie, because she'd hardly said a word all day. Even when Drew was being whipped she hadn't said much.

"You can goddamned well eat shit, too!" Durk roared, and then fell into a long string of obscenities Jonie tried not to hear.

For two days he was there, keeping them all where he could see them except for the time he sent Drew to his room.

Then he did something very strange. He went outside and came back with a box, and he held it out to Jonie and told her to open it. She shook her head. The room was so quiet. Her mother was there in the doorway, and when Drew came to stand silently near Blair, Durk didn't send him away.

"Open it," he said, and smiled at Jonie.

She dared shake her head again. She was afraid of what might be in the box.

"What have I raised?" Durk said in a strangely good-natured tone of voice as he opened the box himself, "A daughter who won't even open her present?"

She stared at the doll he took from the box.

She had thought he would always be there, this time, after he brought the doll. But suddenly he was gone again, sometime in the night. A week passed and he didn't come back. Her lovely doll stood on the dresser, smiling, smiling, the feathers in her hat moving in the breeze from the window. Durk was gone. But then they ran away again in the night, like the first time. *Why?* He was gone. Why was her mother so afraid?

Something tried to insert itself into Jonie's memory. In the swaying car where Celia was now quiet, no longer talking to Mel, where the boys slept in a kind of restless peace, Jonie struggled against the memory of the last night she had seen Durk.

She had a sense of a nightmare that had begun in the middle of the dark night, a nightmare of seeing Durk in her doorway.

He crossed the room to her bed, with only the light from the stars and the moon revealing him to her. He had come like a naked giant out of some horror movie to her bed.

She hadn't dared cry out. She sensed tonight that to let her mother know what was happening would end everything for all of them. Durk would kill Mama if she interfered.

Close your eyes and pretend he's not here, not hurting you, not bearing you down with his long, heavy, smooth body, his breath hot in your ear. His body like a snake's, only smoother, more revolting, wet and slimy, like the eel he had brought to the house once for her mother to cook.

She tried to stop the cry that bubbled from her when she felt the fiery pain between her legs. He was raping her, and there was no way she could stop him.

"Get off of her," Celia said, her voice loud but eerily calm and cold.

Jonie blinked against the sudden bright light in her room. Durk slowly slid from her, leaving his sweat and his stink, and Jonie saw Celia standing in the doorway. She was wearing her nightgown and was holding one of

Durk's shining black guns in her hand. A small one with a cylinder and a short barrel.

It was pointed straight at him.

Jonie turned over, pulling her clothes to cover her body, feeling as if she were dying, wishing she *could* die, wishing she had never been born. She covered her eyes with her hands and pressed her face into her pillow. Was this the night they all would die? Would Drew and Blair stay little boys forever in heaven? Would God let their dad into heaven, or would the devil be waiting? But no, Durk would not die. Only Mama, she, and the boys would die tonight. Durk would never allow Mama to take one of his guns and point it at him, he would never allow her to kill him.

They left Jonie's room, and it was suddenly dark again, the light turned off, the door closed.

Jonie didn't want to hear, but her senses seemed so aware they were like raw wounds. In the darkness of the night came the sounds of the swamp. The whippoorwills were loud to the north as if they were answering the calls of the bullfrogs in the water. Then she heard the frogs grow quiet, the way they always did when someone approached the water.

Then, long minutes later, it seemed, she heard the staccato sound of gunshots.

She lay still, as she always had when she heard the firing of one of the guns her dad owned. Lots of times he went into the pine woods to hunt, killing whatever there was to kill—birds, squirrels, dogs, sometimes, down at the edge of the swamp, when he couldn't sell them.

She lay still, wishing she could hear her mother. Flashing into her thoughts came a scene of horrible proportions: her dad, coming back alone to the house. Her mother dead, her body weighted with irons and thrown into the swamp where the body of Flint lay. She saw in that brief and terrible vision the bodies of many dogs, their flesh softened by the water and eaten by fish, their fur coated with small bugs, and on top of them all, her mother. She saw her brothers, taken from the house and thrown into the water, perhaps not killed first but left to drown. And she saw herself, trapped here in this room with him, not allowed to die after all.

A door opened, the squeak long and drawn-out, like a cry of pain.

Footsteps crossed the front porch and came down the hall to the bedrooms. They were light, but Jonie couldn't be sure they were her mother's.

Then Celia was in her doorway, a dim outline, like a ghost, and Jonie crossed the space between them, her arms out.

"Mommy," she cried, feeling her mother solid and whole, not a ghost, hugging her as if never to let her go, for that moment becoming a part of her once more. "Oh, Mommy."

"It's all right," Celia whispered against her forehead. "It's all right now, he won't be back. Are you all right? Did he hurt you?"

"No," Jonie lied, wanting to protect her mother from what had happened to her. If she never told, no one would ever know.

Celia hugged her, holding her for a long time, then she led her back to bed and tucked her in as if she were as young as Drew.

She must have slept, because the next she remembered she was seeing sunlight. The house was as quiet as if she were alone. Only the birds seemed to share this world with her. The night before was like a terrible dream only half remembered.

Jonie got up and ran to the kitchen, and there was her mother at the stove, stirring oatmeal. Celia looked at Jonie, smiled, and said, "You overslept, babe. Better get dressed now."

Durk didn't come back all that next week.

Jonie was sleeping again, seven nights after Durk had left the last time, when she woke with Celia pulling her up in bed.

"Hurry," she hissed in a whisper. "Hurry, we have to get out of here. Run to the car. Come on!"

So they had run away again in the middle of the night.

And Jonie knew now why she had been so surprised and so confused.

Now she remembered the night of the gunshots.

Celia killed Durk that night.

But Durk wasn't dead. He had known where they were all the time, and he had tried to catch them when he saw them leave the house. He had killed other people. Four people, maybe more, maybe some Mel hadn't heard about. He was out there in one of those cars whose lights were like eyes in the dark.

From the park bench she had seen him as he drove slowly along the street by the park. He should be dead.

But he wasn't.

Jonie knew, because she had seen him.

THE LOVELY FACE of her doll, lying in its bed of grass, settled in Jonie's mind. Moonlight highlighted the doll's forehead beneath the drooping feathers in its hat. She could see it so clearly, lying where she had left it, in the crushed grass at the back of the house. Her mother didn't know, but Jonie had never touched the doll after that day when he took it out of the box and put it into her hands. She could still hear the silence in the room. Drew and Blair stood back, watching. Their mother stood near them. Jonie's first feeling when she saw the doll was sharp, incredible delight. Her whole being went out to the doll, so lovely, so beautiful. The most beautiful thing she had ever seen in her life. No picture was ever so pretty. She had looked at so many pictures of dolls, wishing and wishing, even writing letters to Santa and begging, pleading—please bring me a doll with a pink dress and *a pink hat*. A doll with a ruffled dress, with lace, with little white shoes and stockings, a doll with a hat. Here, at last, was her doll. She even had lovely feathers in her hat.

She took it to her bedroom and stood it on her dresser.

She never touched it again.

When Celia put it into her hands the night they ran away Jonie thought of where it came from, and when they ran to the car she opened her hand and let the doll fall.

CHAPTER 23

"DADDY, please don't send me back."

Mel hugged Crescent to him. She was ten years old and had been visiting him on weekends and two weeks in the summer since she was five. At her mother's home she had a little half-brother two years old and now a new baby sister three months old. For the last two weeks Mel and Crescent had been vacationing. They had driven over five thousand miles, stopping off wherever she wanted to stop. They had started their vacation at Disney World, not far from home, and had gone from there over to the coast and north, taking in all the interesting places they could find. They had ridden roller coasters in five states, something Crescent loved.

It was her two weeks with him, and his two weeks with her, and he didn't want to let her go.

Her mother and Harley, with their two kids tucked into car seats in the back, had driven up in front of the house. Crescent's three suitcases sat in the hall by the open front door, ready to be carried out.

The look on Crescent's face broke his heart. With her eyes deep behind the overflowing tears she looked up at him. Her chin quivered, her lips quivered. Her plea was soft and low, and it hit Mel in the pit of his stomach and the roots of his heart.

"Don't make me go with them, Daddy. Let me stay with you."

"Sweetheart ... I would keep you if I could. The judge—"

"Daddy, go back to the judge. Beg him to let me live with you now."

He looked into her eyes, miserable.

Kyla, as curvy and lovely as she had always been, came smiling up the steps and across the stoop to the open door. The smile left her face when Crescent didn't even look at her.

"What's all this?" Kyla said. "Not even a hello for Mom?"

With his arm around Crescent's shoulder, and her face pressed against his shirt, Mel said, "Kyla, why don't you let her spend the summer with me?"

"The summer! With you working all week long? What would you do, go off and leave her alone?"

"We'd manage."

Kyla turned and motioned for Harley. He got out of the car and jogged around it and up to the house, a happy-go-lucky squareness on his shoulders.

"Hi there, Squirt, ready to go home?"

"There seems to be a problem," Kyla said, her face going darkly ugly in Mel's eyes. "Take her luggage to the car, why don't you, Harl?"

He picked up all three suitcases, tucking one under his arm, and went back to the car with them.

Kyla took hold of Crescent's arm. Crescent gave a little cry of anguish and jerked it away, wrapping both her arms around Mel's waist.

"What is this?" Kyla said angrily. "What are you trying to do, Mel, turn her against me? Crescent, listen, so you had a vacation, and so it can't be like that at home every day, but your home is with me, whether you like it or not. Now come on! I have an appointment I don't want to miss."

Crescent's face jerked toward her mother. "What kind of appointment?" she cried out, almost screaming. "Are you going away *again?*"

"What do you mean again? I go every Monday evening to choir practice, you know that!"

"And what am I supposed to do, stay with *him?*"

Kyla put her hands on her hips. "So that's what it is. You're turning her against Harl. I would have thought better of you than that, Mel."

Mel understood none of this change. Crescent had always grown sad when she had to go home, but this was the first time she had clung so hard to him.

"Let her stay," Mel pleaded. "Just for the rest of the summer." He hated having to beg to keep his own child, sometimes even to see her, to take her with him to a special family dinner.

"Oh yeah, sure. All right! I'll talk to Harley about it." She went stomping down the path.

Crescent watched her, loosening her hold around Mel. He had a feeling she was holding her breath. After a couple of minutes, while Kyla leaned in the door window and talked to Harley, Crescent sighed, long and slowly. Mel let out his own breath, not aware until then that he too had been holding it.

Kyla came back up the walk, her face contorted with anger. She stopped on the walk several feet from the house.

"Get in the car!"

"Can't I stay?"

"I said get in the car!" Kyla pointed her finger. "Now! And if you ever pull another trick like this I'll see to it that you don't come over here at all."

"Now listen here, Kyla, you make threats like that and we'll just take this custody thing back to court."

"Bullshit! You've been brainwashing her, and don't think we don't know. Harley feels terrible that you've turned Crescent against him. After all, he's raised her as long as you did!"

"Yeah, thanks to you!" Fury thundered in his chest. "Because you ran out on our marriage and stole Crescent! What you do is your business, but she's my kid!"

"I'm her mother! I gave birth to her!"

"Being her mother doesn't entitle you to her life! I'm her father, and she wants to stay with me!"

"Go to hell! Crescent get out there in that car! Just because you're not the baby anymore, you cry at every little thing."

Crescent went, her head down. At the car she looked back at Mel and he saw the most forlorn look he'd ever seen in his life. It reminded him of the expression on the faces of children he had seen in his work—abused, hurt in some way, sometimes horribly.

As that car drove away, Mel knew something had gone wrong in that family.

When he picked Crescent up the next Friday she was quiet. All weekend she seemed dreamy and distant, almost as if she'd been drugged. It prompted him to start questioning her.

"Nobody has given you anything, have they, Crescent?"

He had seen kids on the street as young as Crescent who thought it was cool to do drugs. He'd seen them half out of their heads with the drugs, dreamy, glassy-eyed, and so vulnerable to whatever creep happened around.

She shook her head. "You mean like crack and stuff?" she asked. "No, Daddy, I know better than to take anything like that. I don't mess around with stuff."

"Then what's wrong?"

"Did you go see about getting custody?"

He paused. "No, I didn't."

Tears filled her eyes. That look of anguish was there again. "Well, why not?" she demanded with a mixture of anger and something very like fear. "Why didn't you?"

"I just thought ..." What had he thought? He had worried about her all week and talked to her briefly each night on the phone to see how she was. He had really thought Kyla was right, and it was the vacation that had made her so anxious to stay with him. He told Crescent that.

"A vacation is not like retired life," he said, his longing to keep her with him a raw pain. "Sometimes we wish we could live like that forever, and it's just not possible."

"I know that! But what's that got to do with me living with you?"

"Crescent, what's wrong?"

She hung her head, wouldn't look at him or answer. He put his hand under her chin and lifted it. Though she kept turning her eyes away, finally she looked at him.

"Tell me," he said softly. Was it the new baby? Did she feel unwanted now? He wanted her to tell him in her own words.

"He said," she whispered, "no one would ever believe me. He said it would be his word against mine, and he's got a good name. He said he'd see to it that I never get to see you."

"Hey!" He shook her face gently. "Who are we talking about? Harley?"

"Yes, Daddy."

"What ..." Watch your language, he reminded himself just before the words slipped out. "What was he talking about? Your word against his?" A cold hard mass began to form in his stomach.

"He ..." She lowered her eyes again, and he recognized shame. "He does it to me, Daddy. When Mama's gone to choir practice, and even in the night when she's there. I don't think she cares, Daddy."

"Good God!"

The battles began. He refused to let Crescent go back. He took her to doctors and hired a lawyer to help him get custody. He charged rape and sexual abuse against her stepfather.

But the police came and got Crescent and took her back to them, and there was nothing Mel could do but continue to fight for her. The case of sexual abuse came to court and was dismissed. As Crescent had been threatened, it was her word against his, and although the doctors for Crescent testified that there was vaginal scarring and anal scarring, it could not be proved that it had been done by her stepfather.

For three years the battles continued. After two separate three-month suspensions for refusing to let Crescent go back with her mother, Mel clung to his job because he needed the money. His visits with Crescent were terminated by the court. He was influencing her against her stepfather, her mother, her family, the judge said. The child would be better off if she didn't see him at all.

And then came her thirteenth birthday.

They found her dead, locked in the bathroom. She had taken an overdose of tranquilizers she had stolen from her mother. In her hand was a note.

"I'm sorry, Daddy."

MEL'S HANDS gripped the steering wheel of the station wagon so hard his arms hurt.

He was still behind the truck, but it had pulled away, leaving them separated by a hundred yards or more. In his rethinking the last three years of Crescent's life he had forgotten what he was doing.

He looked toward Celia. There was no doubt she was asleep. Her head rested back against the seat, her face turned toward him. With parted lips she breathed deeply and evenly.

Mel turned and looked back toward the kids and saw that all were still, lying down, covered by their blankets.

Time and distance had passed, and he was driving into the outer lights of Omaha.

He sighed. He was tired and just wanted to reach the Mendel farm and crash for about eight hours in the comfortable bed they always provided for the driver.

Only thirty or forty miles more to go.

The clock on the dash told him it was 11:42. They should reach the farm by 12:30.

• • •

LORNE HAD GONE to bed every night at ten o'clock since Cora married him, except for a few wild Saturday nights in their younger days when he stayed up until eleven or midnight. He was up with the chickens, at the breaking of dawn or earlier. When the roosters in the henhouse began to crow at four in the morning, Lorne began to stir.

Cora was a night person. Sleep eluded her until midnight at the earliest, then she had to drag herself out of bed at five in the morning to cook breakfast for Lorne. She had learned to accept her hours and even to enjoy them. In the evening, after the television was turned off and Lorne had kissed her good night, she always drew a long sigh and settled back to read, Blue Bonnet on the braided rug beside her chair.

Those were peaceful hours, even on those nights when she was a little excited about a new family arriving. She never knew exactly when they would get to the farm. Sometimes they came in the darkest hours of the night. A group sleepy-eyed and tired. Cora loved taking them up to clean, safe bedrooms and closing the doors so they could rest in proper beds.

The last family to stop in was a man and his two children, a boy and a girl. The driver had been a man named Lowell. They were from the west, going east. The father of the children was thin and worried looking. Cora never learned the situation behind the flight and resettlement. She couldn't help her curiosity. It was rare that the fleeing family was headed by a man.

She lay back in her recliner, her novel open and lying flat on her stomach. On the floor Blue snored lightly. The clock on the mantel tick-tocked, a slow and easy rhythm. The clock had belonged to her grandmother, and she loved its sound. The newer clocks, like the grandfather clock in the entry hall, had am almost silent tick. Not at all comforting. A slow and lazy ticking was almost hypnotizing.

She closed her eyes. She had gone up earlier, as she always did, took her bath, and dressed in a robe. Although it was close to summer now, her long, warm robe felt good when the night grew late and cool.

Celia, she thought. Celia, Jonie, Blair, Drew. For awhile her child, her grandchildren. For a very short time her family. Then they would be gone, and they would have names different from the ones she would know them by, and she would never hear from them again.

But she would never forget them, as she had never forgotten anyone who had passed through her house.

She was getting sleepy. It was time to go upstairs.

She didn't move. The chair was so comfortable, it held her like a large cupped hand.

Blue Bonnet lifted her head, then gave a short, low bark and walked over to the window and stuck her nose into the center separation of the draperies. When the curtain was pushed back by the dog's head, Cora saw the car lights touching trees across the driveway, swinging round to the doors of the triple-car garage.

Cora got up and hurried to the kitchen door and turned on the back porch light, then went to meet them, as excited as if they really were her children and she hadn't seen them in months.

She was at once filled with a feeling, almost like a premonition, of completeness, of happiness and fulfillment. Celia and the children would stay here with her and Lorne in their big house on the farm. She and Lorne would adopt them, for after all, didn't they need heirs? The long trail would end here, for all of them, and peace would rein.

One thousand years of peace, as the Bible had promised.

Cora smiled at her own sudden vision of that passage in the Bible, she who wasn't a very religious person, who went to church only because it seemed the thing to do. But still her feeling remained. Their long trail would end here.

She would not have to face the rest of her life without her daughter and grandchildren.

CHAPTER 24

CORA HAD PICTURED them in an almost eerily correct way. Celia was like a girl herself, her rich brown hair softly and naturally curled to her shoulders, her eyes large, dark brown, her skin pale yet touched with ivory, as if she'd been out in the sun a lot.

Jonie was like Celia, except her hair was lighter and shorter. She was small for her age, Cora judged, light and slim, with a sweet smile that grabbed Cora's heartstrings.

The boys, asleep in the back of the station wagon, were round-faced babies still.

Cora hugged Celia first, then Jonie, who got sleepily out of the back seat of the car. The older of the two boys blinked awake and climbed over the back seat and out the open door.

Cora put her arms out for him. He hesitated, then lifted his arms to her. She lifted him out of the car and hugged him before she let him down.

"You must be Blair," she said. He nodded. "I'm Cora. I'd like you to call me Grandma. You're going to be staying with us, and I'm so glad. I hope you'll have lots of fun here."

He said nothing, but a small, bashful smile came over his face as he gazed up at her. He put his hand into hers.

The other child was still sound asleep, curled into a small knot in his blanket like a furled butterfly in its cocoon. Cora met Mel at the rear of the car and gave him a quick welcoming hug with one arm, Blair's hand warm in her other hand.

"I'm so glad to see you again, Mel. I'm delighted you brought Celia and the children to visit us. All the rooms are ready. You can take the baby right up and lay him in his bed."

"Good to see you, Cora." He pressed his cheek to hers briefly. The dog came up with wagging tail, and Mel reached down to her. "And how're you, Blue Bonnet? She's looking good. You must feed her a special diet, Cora, to keep her fur so rich looking. Some of your pies and fresh baked bread, I'll bet."

"Sometimes."

He opened the hatch and lifted the sleeping Drew into his arms. The little boy drooped over his shoulder, hardly stirring.

Cora joined Celia in lifting out what suitcases they could carry. "I could call Lorne to help," she offered.

"No, let him sleep," Mel said. "I'll come back and get whatever we need after I take Drew up to bed."

"You don't need much tonight. Pajamas, maybe. A robe. There are always spare robes in the bathroom. Would you like a snack before going to bed, or are you worn out and would rather just rest?"

"Just bed, thanks," Celia said, giving Cora a warm look of gratitude. "You must be worn out too, waiting up for us."

She had a girlish voice, and she spoke softly and meekly, as the women who passed through so often did.

"I always stay up quite late," Cora said. "The night can be a very peaceful time."

She saw Celia look out toward the darkness beneath the trees that made a windbreak around the sides and back of the yard. Beyond the trees lay the flat, distant horizon, Cora knew, but she understood that to Celia the world she was walking into might be an endless forest, the horizon cut off from view. Cora sensed that night and darkness were not comforts to Celia.

Cora waited until Celia and the children were upstairs and settled in their rooms before attempting to speak to Mel. He was on his way down to get the rest of the suitcases when she intercepted him, going down the stairs with the hem of her robe lifted at ankle height to prevent tripping.

"Norma's coming, Mel. She told me to be sure you waited for her. She wants to talk to you and Celia."

He stopped on the stairs so suddenly she almost ran into him. He looked back at her, their faces almost level even though she was one step above him.

"She wants to talk to Celia, especially, it seems. She said ..." Cora looked back up the stairway. "I think we should go on to the kitchen. It might be that Norma wouldn't want Celia or her children to hear this from anyone but her. She told me not to say anything to Celia."

He stared at her a moment longer, then he turned and went on down to the hallway.

The stairway rose from the hall that joined a front parlor, rarely used, and the rear of the house. The hall formed a T, with an outside door leading onto a small porch and to the driveway.

Instead of going out for the rest of the luggage, Mel went down the hall toward the kitchen.

"Did you offer me a cup of coffee, Cora?"

She smiled. "Sure, Mel."

She went ahead of him into the kitchen and turned the heat on beneath the old coffee pot. It had perked thousands of cups of coffee, the best coffee in the world, Mel had once told her, and even though she had a coffee maker Lorne had given her for her birthday a couple of years ago, it was hardly used.

He sat down at the table and leaned on it, his hands clasped together. Cora opened the cupboard and brought out the fresh cinnamon rolls she had baked during the day, put two on a plate, and put them into the microwave to heat. The smell of coffee grew stronger in the room, then the pot gave one *blurp* just before beginning a tattoo of *perks.* She turned off the heat.

"Norma called earlier tonight. She didn't say much except that something strange had come up and it was urgent that she talk to you both. And ..." She got a cup from the cabinet and poured rich, dark coffee into it. "I perked this a couple of hours ago, Mel. I hope it won't keep you awake."

"Something strange?" He took the cup of coffee gratefully.

"She said to tell you that Durk Nolan is dead."

"What!"

"That's all she said. Except she didn't feel she could talk to you about this over the telephone. So she's coming here, and she wants you to wait until she gets here. The death of this person—Nolan—changes everything, I suppose?"

"Only happens to be the guy we were supposed to be running from."

"Yes, she said he was Celia's husband. But she said there was something very strange going on."

His eyes narrowed and searched the wall beyond as if he might find answers printed there.

"Did Norma say how he died? Where? Or when?" Cora shook her head. "I wonder if there was a police shootout somewhere along the way."

"I have no idea how it happened."

Mel leaned back and let out a long sigh. "It certainly changes things all right. We can slow down, get our breaths. If you can put up with us a few days, I think I'll let Celia and the kids relax."

Cora felt a sudden, ecstatic rush of warmth gather within her, a rare touch of real happiness. Perhaps her feelings had been right and she could keep Celia and the children.

"You know we can. We'd love it."

"What time is Norma coming? Did she want me to pick her up at the airport?"

"Good Lord, no. After you driving night and day? She'd want you to go to bed and rest."

Cora set out pure cream from the refrigerator. She put the plate of cinnamon rolls in front of him and laid a fork and spoon on a napkin. She saw Mel staring at the wall, a frown between his shaggy eyebrows.

"How about a little cholesterol, Mel? To go with your caffeine. We have to sin a little now and then, don't we?" she joked, trying to take his worry away.

"She's flying, I suppose?" he said.

"Yes. Arriving on a 1:30 flight. She'll rent a car and drive out. She should be here by 2:30 or three. I'll wait up for her."

She sat in a chair across the table. Using the flat of her hand she smoothed a wrinkle from the tablecloth. The kitchen was warm and cozy, the blinds pulled against the dark, chilly night. Blue Bonnet had taken her place on the braided rug by Cora's recliner over near the heating stove. All the doors and windows were locked except the door out to the driveway. Waiting up would be a peaceful time, knowing that her family was close.

She felt her face redden with a blush, as if Mel could read her thoughts. As if he knew she had already made Celia and the children her own. The daughter she'd never had, the grandchildren she had so longed for. A private yearning expressed to no one. But Mel had begun to eat, his mind obviously within his own world.

He paused with a piece of cinnamon roll on his fork.

"This husband of Celia's," he began explaining. "She was divorcing him, had a court order to keep him away from her, but he must have gone back, or she was afraid he would. I usually don't talk about the family problems with the people I drive for, unless they want to. Some of the mothers, and kids, too, will talk, but most of them don't. Celia doesn't. Neither do her kids. Anyway, the getting away seemed to be urgent. Celia was afraid for her life and for the lives of her children."

Cora shook her head. "What a shame." Life with Lorne had not been very warm and close, but at least he had never been physically abusive to her, and she was thankful for that. "Well, they're safe with you, and safe here. A long ways from home now, I suppose."

"Yes, they're from one of the more remote areas of Florida. Not a long way from my own place in Georgia." He breathed deeply and took a sip of coffee. "They don't have to be afraid anymore, now that Nolan's dead. But I don't understand why Norma just didn't say to terminate the trip and come on home. I don't understand why she's coming here. If he's dead, what's the problem?"

"Are you going to tell Celia?"

"No, I think I'll let Norma handle it. There have been too many complications in this case, too much killing, too many tragedies."

"Killing?"

"Yes, he followed us. He killed four people along the way, we think. He evidently caught up with us in Kansas City. Jonie saw him. That's why we drove on tonight. There must have been a shootout with the police in Kansas City."

"Would Norma have known about that so soon?"

"So soon? What time did Norma call?"

"About eight."

"Eight!?" He stared at Cora. "And told you Nolan is dead? Then Jonie couldn't have seen him in Kansas City. It was after dark when we stopped."

"Maybe she just thought it was him."

"That's possible. She seemed scared half to death of the man. None of us saw the car she said he was driving. Fear could have put her father's face on someone else, I suppose."

"Well, you'll soon know all about it. Norma will be here in a few hours. You're tired, Mel. Why don't you go on to bed and forget about everything."

He put a hand up and rubbed his beard. Then he went to work on the cinnamon roll.

"You ought to be able to sell this recipe for a million dollars, Cora. I've eaten a lot of cinnamon rolls in a lot of places, but none like yours. There's substance to these. They're not a puff of air, like so many are."

As long as she lived she would be pleased by compliments on her baking. Mel was one of her most appreciative guests. How good it was to see him again.

"And all this gooey stuff on top."

He said it as a little boy would have, and she laughed. "That's brown sugar and butter. And the little hard things are pecans," she teased. She saw his mouth widen in a big grin.

The cinnamon roll was gone, and the coffee cup empty. Mel rose.

"You sure you don't want me to wait up for Norma?"

"I'm sure," she said. "Go on. Leave the rest of the things until tomorrow. Celia said they had all they needed for tonight."

"Yeah, good. Good night."

Mel came around the table, leaned down, and lightly kissed Cora's cheek. She felt the tickle of his beard and the warmth of his gesture. Despite herself, tears burned the backs of her eyelids. She turned her head quickly away so he wouldn't see. But he was going on, telling her good night again, yawning.

The kitchen door closed gently behind him.

Cora wiped her eyes. What was wrong with her? She didn't cry. She hadn't cried in so long she had almost forgotten how.

She got up, cleared the table, poured the last of the coffee into a cup to save for cooking, then rinsed the pot and filled it with fresh water and fresh coffee. She put it back onto the stove and turned the heat on beneath it.

She would let it start perking then turn it off. When Norma arrived, it would be ready to start again if she wanted coffee. It seemed strange that although Cora had been talking over the phone to Norma for ten years, she knew almost nothing about her. She didn't know her age, her tastes, nothing. But if she weren't a coffee drinker, she might be a milk drinker, and the refrigerator always held plenty of milk.

She looked at the wall clock. Almost 1:30. Almost time for Norma to arrive in Omaha. Another hour, two at the most, and she would be here, and Cora would meet for the first time a woman who had sent hundreds of families her way.

She went into the hall and to the side entry door. The porch light still burned, shining out upon the brown station wagon. It was dusty on the rear, and crusted with dried mud low on the sides. Cora turned off the light but continued to stand at the door, looking out through the glass. She clicked the lock into place. The windbreak trees gradually darkened against the lighter sky. She stood a moment longer, then remembered to turn the porch light back on for Norma.

She unlocked the door again, too, an open welcome to Norma. She went back down the hall, the porch light shining through the glass and lighting her way to the foot of the stairs. On the other side of the stairs Blue Bonnet sat in the hall waiting for her.

Cora went back into the kitchen, leaving the door open so she would hear Norma when she arrived.

MEL SAT on the side of the bed and pulled off his boots. He checked the guns and found them secure in their holsters. The barrel of the .38 had made a crease in the flesh of his right calf. He rubbed it.

It sounded like he wouldn't be needing either one of them, and he thought about taking them out of his boots and putting them into his suitcase.

Yet Norma's unprecedented decision to meet him and Celia here at the Mendel's disturbed him. Why wouldn't a phone call tomorrow be enough? Why did Norma feel she had to come all the way to Nebraska?

He frowned at the wall of the small bedroom, where tiny, feminine rosebuds and flowers melted together with their background colors to form a rainbow in his eyes. The dark frame of a painting appeared to frame Norma's face, and he struggled to read what was behind this unsettling development.

He decided to leave the guns in the holsters in his boots.

Without undressing he fell back across the bed and let himself sink into the soft mattress. As soon as she arrived he'd be ready to go talk to her.

Mel lifted one arm and drooped it across his eyes and drifted into a strange half-sleep. He saw Cora, slender as a teenager yet no gray in her hair, the freckles across her nose and cheeks untouched by makeup. He saw Celia beside her. They were like mother and daughter. Around them the children were running, happy, laughing, with Drew turning back to be lifted into Cora's arms and hugged. And Blair, wanting a hug too, his arms reaching up. He saw happiness.

Cora's face drew nearer and nearer, blocking out all others, with a background vague and darkening. She was staring intently upward, lines of sadness etched on her face. He heard no words, yet knew she was questioning God, pleading for recognition, for a sign of mercy.

Mel woke in a rush of anxiety. He took his arm off his face and stared at the ceiling, seeing nothing but the white paint and the center light fixture.

He turned over, his face covered by his pillow, and fell deeply asleep.

CHAPTER 25

THE CROWD in the airport terminal marched like ants in different directions, the atmosphere subdued at this late hour. At the car rental desk Norma chose a small Ford and went down to retrieve it.

The only advantage she could see in arriving in a strange city at almost two o'clock in the morning was the lack of traffic. At times only the lights seemed to be alive, with an occasional stray car or truck drifting along quiet streets. Sitting in her rented car with the doors locked, she studied her map. The Nebraska map resting open on the steering wheel showed county roads along which she had carefully inked the way to the Mendel farm.

She laid the map on the seat and started driving.

Once out of town she followed a two-lane highway that lay as straight as an arrow. Twenty miles west she turned right onto a gravel road that again ran straight as the fence posts beside it, north, and west again. She found the county road that on the map looked no more distinct than the thin, almost invisible vein in an infant's arm.

The road narrowed to one lane beyond a small village that had long ago closed for the night. Almost before she realized she was in a town she was out of it again. The town was marked on the map with a tiny dot and almost invisible letters, probably marked only because of the post office on the main street.

She drove past a convenience store with gas pumps, but most of the lights were out.

When she passed a crossroads she stopped the car and sat in the middle of the road checking her map again. She looked up. Off in all directions was the pale, indistinct line of the horizon set against a dark, star-studded sky.

Turn to the right at these crossroads, she read on her private map, a copy of which she gave to all the drivers who came to the Mendel farm. Follow the right road four miles, past four more crossroads, then go left two miles, then to the right again, and follow that road straight for eleven miles. The Mendel farm was the first lane to the right after a marked crossroads.

She started driving again, not worrying now about the one lane that seemed to have been made through the gravel. There was room to meet another car if both cars pulled close to the ditches on either side of the road.

Fences lined alfalfa fields, and dark blobs of resting cattle lay visible under the starlight like round boulders in the fields. On the western horizon a low line of clouds peeled away and revealed a big orange sinking moon. Its light lifted a bit of the black night from the landscape.

She drove into corn country, where beneath the moonlight the corn looked like a gentle sea that rippled and whispered beneath the constant surge of wind.

She turned the radio on, then turned it off. She didn't want to be distracted, she decided. Her hands held the steering wheel of the strange car with a tightness that made her arms ache.

Long before she reached the obstruction she saw it, a dark barrier in the road. She slowed. Her car lights eventually picked it up and revealed it to be a car.

It was parked precisely in the middle of the road, taking up the one track. If it had parked nearer the ditch, on either side, she could have squeezed around it. But as it sat, it blocked her way.

It was headed away from her, toward the north. Her car lights shined through it and showed, so far as she could tell, an empty car. She sat still, her foot on the brake, staring at it.

A couple of young lovers using the farm road for a lover's lane? Lying down in each other's arms? If so, why hadn't her lights brought them up?

Perhaps it was someone sleeping, or passed out on drugs or alcohol.

She pushed on the horn and eased her car closer to the rear of the other. She saw no rising heads, no surprised faces. She honked again.

Had the car stalled and its driver left it sitting there?

She looked back down the road behind her. There were crossroads every mile in this flat farmland. If she could turn around, she could go back to the corner section road and drive around the section and come out on the road again beyond the car.

But there wasn't room to turn around without risking getting a tire stuck in one of the ditches.

If she backed up, she'd have to back almost a mile.

She could go look in the car and see if the owner had left his keys. Yet something about the car put her off. Opening the door of an unknown car that had only the lights of her own car shining through it made her feel as if she were reaching into a dark space that might have creepy-crawlies or something worse. If she had her flashlight ... But it was in her suitcase, in the rear of the car. Why had she put it in the trunk?

She left the engine running and opened the door, then realized she'd have to have the key to open the trunk. She reached in and turned off the switch and pulled out the key.

What was the matter with her? She was too tired to think clearly. She hadn't slept at all on the plane. She hadn't even relaxed enough to rest.

She was out of the car, the key in her hand, when she stopped to wonder what good her flashlight was going to do. She looked again at the car blocking her way. It wasn't likely the driver had left the key in the car, even in this benign and peaceful country. The smartest thing was to get back into her own car and start backing the three-fourths of a mile to a turnaround place in the crossroads and simply detour around.

The lights of the rented Ford outlined the back of the other car, and it was then, as she started to get back into her car, that she really began to look at the rear end of the deserted automobile.

It was coated with dirt and old mud, so that at first its color did not register in her mind. Then when she saw it was blue, an eerie shiver slid over her.

What a strange irony, she thought. A car so much like the one Celia drove to the motel, the car stolen from the parking lot. It couldn't be the same car. Why would it be here on a country road in Nebraska? She stood still, listening to the sounds of rustling, of wind in the young corn growing in the fields across the ditches on both sides of the road. There still was no one visible in the car. Nothing had moved in answer to her honks.

She went closer to the parked car and peered down at the license plate. It was too coated with dried mud to read. It looked, she thought in dismay, as if someone had deliberately smeared mud on it.

With her fingers she cleaned away a portion of the dirt on the license plate, but long before she uncovered the *Fl* of *Florida,* she felt her legs turn weak with fear.

Good God!

Thoughts flashed without form through her mind, feelings of vulnerability, of the fool thing she had done by getting out of her car, of the incredibility of this car being on this road, blocking her way.

She whirled, the sound of gravel beneath a foot bringing fear as bitter as gall up into her throat.

He stood at the edge of the light beams looking at her. She saw his stature, more immense than ever, she saw his blond hair, the planes of his face, the narrow cruelty of his eyes. His shirt sleeves were rolled up to reveal bulging biceps. The neck of the shirt opened low on a hairless chest. But his neck, thick and corded, as wide as his head, was bandaged, and he held his head sideways, as if it were permanently drawn to one side.

He said nothing. But just as his car blocked her way on the road, his body blocked her way back to her car.

"Durk Nolan!" She began stepping sideways one step at a time, her left hand out towards the hood of her rented car.

"What are you doing here?" she asked, her voice a low cry of disbelief, of fear so strong she hardly knew she was saying a word. "You're ... You're —they told me you were dead."

He jabbed a finger at her suddenly as if he were stabbing with a knife. "No. You're dead. She's dead, the brats are dead. She tried to kill me. Me. But you ask her now if what I told her wasn't true. She can't kill me, and neither can you. And you have come to the end of the road, lady."

He took a step toward her.

"How did you find your way here?" Norma cried, still disbelieving. She must be hallucinating. The car blocking the road didn't exist. Durk Nolan's skeleton, flesh eaten away, had been found in the water near his home. Celia, they told her, had shot him.

Yet they were wrong.

She edged backward toward the curve in the fender. Why had she gotten out of the car? How could she have been so stupid? The key was in her hand. If she could get to the passenger door and get in, she could lock the doors, start the car, and back down the road. He had no weapons that she could see beyond his ham-like hands.

If she could get to the door of the car ... if she could distract him by talking ... she might have a chance.

"Whose body was found at your place?" she asked. "Someone your size was shot three times in the head and his body thrown into the water—"

He laughed, a loud, blunt sound. "So that's why you thought I was dead, eh? Well, she tried, but it didn't work."

"What do you mean? I don't understand." She inched backward, her hand sliding along the smooth fender. She cut her eyes sideways without turning her head. She was just a few feet from the right passenger door.

"I don't give a bitchin' damn, lady, whether you understand or not."

"How did you find your way here? You've been following them, haven't you? All the way, after all."

He took another step toward her.

The strangeness, the coincidence of him being on this road at this time struck her. As if he were waiting for her. As if he *knew* she would be coming this way. No one but Cora and Lorne knew she would be coming in tonight, and even they didn't know which road she would take. No one knew that but her.

Then it occurred to her that Mel must have driven in tonight, and Durk had become confused on the straight roads that bordered every section mile of farmland. At each corner four roads, all looking alike, went in four different directions. Durk had become lost. It was nothing more than an accident that she happened along the road on which he had stopped his car. A horrible coincidence. She had never believed in coincidences, yet here she was in one from which she might not escape.

"You're lost!" she cried.

He slapped the hood of the car so hard the entire car rattled. She jumped involuntarily and moved backward a step. She heard low curses, a string of obscenities, and knew she was right. Durk Nolan had tracked the two-tone brown station wagon to the flat plains of Nebraska and had lost it in the maze of roads.

"I'm going to kill you, lady, kill you slow. You're going to die for interfering in my life. Every one of you is going to die. Everyone but my girl, Jonie, and I'm taking her back with me. You see this?" He put up a hand and touched the greyish-white rag wrapped around his neck. In the brighter lights in which he now stood Norma could see a blackish wound on his lower right jaw. "She tried to kill me, the bitch I married. She *thought* she'd killed me. I would have caught up with her a long time before this if I'd wanted to. I want her to die slow, just like you. But tonight I'm going in there, and I'm going to end it for all of them. Starting with you." Low mutters of obscenities came from him, growls of rage.

She moved instinctively just before he lunged. She turned her back to him and ran, tried to run, around the fender of the car and to the door. She grabbed the door handle with both hands and in horrible dismay felt the keys slip from her hand. They fell into the darkness at her feet. She started to reach down, to search the gravel for the keys. Then she felt him behind her, smelled the odor of him, a dankness like the stale water in a swamp. In the second it had taken her to reach the door, he had reached her.

He grabbed her hair and flung her backward. She fell hard on the gravel edge of the road and slid head first into the ditch. A cold liquid covered her head and flooded her mouth. She choked, coughed, and swallowed, darkness surrounding her. The ditch was filled with water, but there was darkness within it, blessed darkness. She started crawling up the other side of the ditch, reaching for the dark rows of corn that stretched a mile across the field to the section road on the north side.

She felt something seize her ankle, but it didn't feel like a hand, it felt more like a tentacle—slippery, snakelike, tightening as she tried to pull away from it. She remembered what Celia said about her husband, about that horrible and incredible thing he had told her he actually was. *He's from out of the swamp, a creature with long writhing tentacles like a spider or octopus. Tentacles that strangle ... smother... kill.*

At this moment Norma could believe. In her terror-dazed mind she felt it, and believed it.

The tug on her ankle was slow and steady, pulling her back down into the water. She reached for the corn stalks and tried to pull herself up, out of the water, but the steady pull continued, and her hands slid down the steep bank with her fingers digging trenches in the soft dirt.

One of the icy cold tentacles slid around her neck and pulled her face into the water. Her lungs filled, expanded, and threatened to burst. She had to breathe. She tried to lift her head and found it weighted, pulled back into the mud by the tightening tentacle around her neck. He was drowning her, holding her face into the mud.

But he was lost. In the maze of roads he would not find Celia and the children tonight. When she didn't arrive at the farm by daylight Mel would know something had happened and would take Celia and the children and go on.

He had to. He must.

And then she thought of the car she had rented, of her suitcase in the trunk, of her purse on the seat with her false ID. Open on the seat was the map with the route traced in red ink. And in her purse a small notebook listed the names of the family in Wyoming and the destination in California.

She had grown careless.

She should have known. Nobody ... nothing ... could escape alive from Durk Nolan.

Celia had warned her.

CHAPTER 26

CORA FELT a kiss on her forehead. She opened her eyes, blinking. She hadn't meant to fall asleep, but she had, deeply. Lorne stood over her, dressed in a pair of the blue jeans and blue cotton shirts he wore for work. He smiled down at her. She was amazed, as always, at how bright Lorne could look when it was still dark outside.

"Didn't you go to bed at all last night?" he asked.

She sat forward, the back of her recliner going up with her. At her side Blue Bonnet got up and stretched and ambled sleepily toward the back door. Lorne let her out. Through the open door came a rush of cool morning air and the crow of roosters. The deep, strong voice of the granddaddy of them all led the chorus, with the piping squeaks of the young roosters who were just learning how to crow joining in. She saw that streaks of dawn were breaking in dim shades of grey across the backyard.

She blinked at the clock on the wall. Almost 5:30.

She jumped to her feet.

"Lorne!"

"Just sit back," he said. "I'll fix my own breakfast. I don't need you to get up every morning to make my coffee."

"Where's Norma? Didn't she get here?"

He looked out into the driveway. "Not unless she parked out front and is sleeping in her car."

Cora felt a terrible premonition. She hurried into the hall by the stairway and through the darkness there to the outer door. She looked out to see the brown station wagon still parked near the back of the house, but the rest of the long driveway out to the road was empty.

She stepped back into the house and closed the door. She left the porch light on, just in case Norma had been delayed and would be in later. She didn't really know Norma, she reminded herself. Norma might be the kind of person who changed plans easily if something more important came up, and then neglect to say anything about the change. Yet she still had the feeling that something was wrong.

She went back to the kitchen to find Lorne had turned the fire on under the coffee pot and was getting a bowl and cereal out of the cabinet.

"She isn't here," Cora said with a long sigh. "I hope she didn't have an accident."

"Don't worry. From what I've heard about Norma she can take care of herself."

"You're right. And a lot of other people, too," Cora added as she went to the sink to wash her hands. "Don't you want eggs and bacon? I thought you hated cold cereal."

"I'm thinking about my cholesterol. Decided to eat some of this fodder. I thought I heard you say it's about time I started thinking about how long I want to live."

"You've been listening too much," she said, trying to match his mood. She was only half joking. She believed in watching one's diet, yet her grandfather had lived to be ninety-six and had eaten eggs every morning. Lorne's father and mother were still alive, and still eating eggs and meat, fat meat, whenever they wanted. His mother baked the world's best beans, and over the top of the crock always floated crisp, oven-browned strips of bacon. Her own father was dead now, but he had died in a tractor accident, and her mother, eighty-three, was healthy. She walked two miles daily and spread pure, rich butter on her fresh-baked bread. Cora got out the milk and cream and silverware.

He sat down. The coffee was beginning to perk. "Why don't you go to bed and rest?" he asked. "You must have waited up all night."

"I slept in my chair."

"You'll have a bad back one of these days doing that."

"I don't sleep in the chair often. I'm worried about Norma. I waited up for her. She said she'd be here about 2:30 or three at the latest."

"She flew, didn't she? Maybe the plane went down."

"Oh, Lorne."

"You couldn't get me on an airplane."

"I know."

"I guess Mel and the family he's bringing got in all right?"

"Yes. Around midnight, a little later. I can't imagine why Norma hasn't arrived. She's almost three hours late. I don't believe she'd not have let me know if she changed her mind. Lorne—"

"Stop fussing and worrying. I have to get out to the field. Time to start cultivating. The sun'll be up soon."

Cora opened a can of dog food, took it out onto the back porch, and emptied it into Blue Bonnet's pan. The dog rose and came onto the porch, but instead of eating she raised her nose and sniffed the air. The hair on her spine stiffened, and her ears lifted, the ends flopping over like the flaps on small envelopes.

Cora watched her, an uneasy feeling creeping up her own spine. Then Blue Bonnet took off with a short bark toward the windbreak of trees at the back of the yard, going past the big red barn, the low, white chicken house. Chickens drifting blindly out into the grey light of dawn scattered, wings working uselessly to fly. The dog raced past them, uninterested. She went on into the trees, and a moment later showed up as a moving blur in the cornfield on the other side.

Blue Bonnet stopped, visible in the space beneath the limbs of the trees and the beginning of the corn.

Cora then saw three neighbor dogs, a big black dog and two smaller brown-and-white dogs. They all greeted one another with friendly sniffing and tail wagging.

"What is it?" Lorne asked.

Cora shivered and hugged her arms close to her as she turned away from the door.

"Nothing. Just the neighbor dogs."

Lorne got up from the table, leaving his dish. He went toward the washroom.

Cora said, "For a minute I thought something terrible might be out there, the way she took off."

"What kind of terrible thing could be out there?" Lorne laughed as water rushed from the faucet. He splashed handfuls of water on his face.

Cora went through the kitchen to the central hall and out to the side door. She stood on the stoop beneath the small roof and looked down the road.

The air was sharp and cool, but streaks of sunlight reached over the top of the three-story house and turned the tops of the western windbreak trees a rich golden green.

The driveway lay in shadow. On the road at the end of the lane a pickup went by. In the driveway not far from where she stood was Mel's station wagon, a bit dusty, looking as if it had come a long way. She had been hoping, she guessed, that Norma had driven in during the past ten minutes and had leaned her seat back and gone to sleep.

But there was no car other than Mel's, and beyond, parked beside the garage, Lorne's old red pickup.

Cora went back into the house to Lorne's office. She looked up the number of the major airport in Omaha and dialed.

When she got a connection she asked the woman at the airport, "Did the 1:30 flight arrive all right from Tallahassee?"

"Yes, it did."

"Was ..." Cora stopped. Would Norma have been using her own name? She knew that Mel always carried a false set of identification papers, and so did the families he moved. It was the same with all the other drivers. Norma was probably traveling incognito too.

She hung up the phone.

Maybe Mel would know what to do when he got up.

JEREMY BEYER HUMMED along with the singer on the radio. The roar of the tractor engine was muted by the cab of the tractor and the volume of the music. From inside the cab the big engine had a good, steady hum that Jeremy liked. She was a big piece of new machinery, sixty thousand dollars worth, pulling a cultivator that cleaned the young weeds from eight rows of corn at a time. He held the steering wheel steady, dividing his time between looking forward to see that he was staying between the rows and looking back to see that the many little cultivators were turning up the black soil and the weeds instead of the new corn.

He loved this time of *year,* when he could almost hear the corn growing. When he was a kid, and standing on this same section of land, he had sworn he could hear the corn grow. It whispered, rustling softly, the green blades stretching up, higher, higher, each minute of the night and day.

Because he had come from a small family he had been financially able to stay on the farm. He had gone away for four years of college, studying agriculture and farm management with incredible ease because he had grown up knowing most of the things that were in the textbooks. His grandparents still lived in the big white house partly hidden by the circling windbreak on the next section, six hundred and forty acres of land, and his parents lived in a similar arrangement on the section on which he now worked.

His own home was a modern, low, one-story ranch house. The windbreak on the north side of it wasn't much taller than the new corn that filled the fields. It was built a half mile from his mom and dad, on the north-south road called Beyer Lane. His wife was still a bride, and he had almost let the tractor drift into the long, straight rows of corn when he caught himself staring toward the house, trying to catch sight of her.

She was gorgeous, in his eyes the most beautiful woman who had ever lived. He had seen her in college, and for six months he admired her without asking her for a date. She was probably a city girl, he had figured, and would take off for faraway places to become a model, or go to Hollywood to become a star. And he didn't want to become involved with a girl who had that kind of ambition. He made no effort to meet her or even find out her name.

Then one day she came running across the campus to catch up with him. Her face was pink and flushed with the cold air of early winter.

"Hey," she said. "I was afraid you'd dropped out. I haven't seen you around this semester."

For a moment he couldn't even answer her. Then, with an awkwardness he'd never felt with any other girl, he asked, "Do we know each other?"

He could have kicked himself. His question had sounded downright smart-assed. Arrogant. Flippant. All the things he wasn't. What he had really meant was that he had been watching her but had no idea she had noticed him among all the other guys.

"No, we haven't really met, at least not in awhile," she said. "But don't you think it's about time?"

She put out her hand and he took it, finding it warm and soft, yet firm and strong, which surprised him. He imagined he felt small calluses, as if she had spent the summer working, gardening, maybe even herding a tractor.

"I'm Katherine Sparks. You don't remember me at all, do you?"

"Of course I do. You were on campus last year. I saw you around." *I looked for you, followed you sometimes.* But those were words he wouldn't be telling her until later.

She laughed. "That's what I thought. I mean, you don't remember me. Your ball team used to play my school. I even threw you a paper banner once, don't you remember?"

He had played football, and lots of girls had thrown him lots of stuff. For the life of him he could not remember having seen this lovely face before last year.

She laughed again. "You don't have to look so dismayed! My school was Northwest High, and your school was West Park, right?"

He nodded. West Park, yes. That meant she was from the same country town as he. His hand closed harder on hers.

"You mean you're not ... Omaha, or Lincoln?"

"Good Lord, no. I'm a farm girl, and I get so homesick I could start hitchhiking home. When I saw you I almost fell at your feet I was so glad to see someone from home. But you weren't friendly, and I thought maybe you were from somewhere else. I asked around and found out sure enough you were a hometown guy. Jeremy Beyer, right? Tell me I'm right!"

"You're right. I wish I'd known this last year."

"Why?"

"Look how much time we've wasted."

She slid her arm around his, and he put his hand on it and bent his elbow to hold her close.

"We've got the rest of our lives to make up for that wasted time," she said, giving him a half-serious smile. Later, when they were engaged to be married that July, after they both got their degrees, he accused her of having proposed to him that day.

"I did," she said. "The day I tossed you the banner at the game I told my girlfriend I was going to marry you. Ask her."

Jeremy straightened the front wheels of the tractor just as they were about to mash a couple of rows of corn and forced his mind back to his work.

How much better could life get? It was almost frightening sometimes, as if somewhere in the back of his mind he feared that life couldn't continue to be so good. They were going to have a baby. Son, or daughter? Neither of them had a preference.

The first grandchild in his family. His only other sibling, Christine, was still in high school. His grandparents had one great-grandchild from his uncle's side of the family, but they lived in California. So in a way, this child would be number one around here.

Life was good. Yet beneath his breath he prayed, God, keep it good. Take care of Katie and the baby. Keep them well.

He was approaching the end of the field, coming within a couple hundred yards of the south road, which stretched from section corner to section corner, a full mile, without house or barn on either side.

He squinted against the light reflecting off the hood of the tractor and stared. A car was parked in the middle of the road. It was blocking the way, as if it had died there and then been abandoned.

He knew the cars in the area, just as he knew the pets. Most of the farmers owned a section of land, so the homesteads were usually a mile apart, sometimes more when one family owned several sections or the owners lived in town, as sometimes happened.

He stood up in the tractor to get a better view.

The car was small, with the rounded bubble shape of a small Ford. It was not a local car.

He turned off the radio and steered steadily toward the end of the field, slowly coming closer to the car. When he reached the end he could see no one was in the car unless they were lying down.

He made the turn at the end of the corn rows and headed the tractor back in the other direction, then he shut it off.

He opened the cab door and leaped down to the ground.

There was no fence. His family didn't deal with livestock, and hadn't for many years. The three family cows were kept only for milk. They were more like pets them livestock, and had their own pasture up by his grandfather's barn. Fences around the cornfields were not needed. The land was cultivated right up to the ditches, and the grass there mowed when it became too high.

Jeremy approached the ditch in a fast walk and was preparing to leap over the ditch when he looked down.

In the muddy water a body lay, head submerged. Artificially colored blond hair floated to the surface of the water like a fan. The woman's legs sprawled awkwardly up the other side of the ditch, and both her hands reached up over her head toward the cornfield, the fingertips embedded in gashes in the black soil.

Jeremy uttered a cry and grasped her arms, pulling her up out of the water. But it was too late. When he turned her over onto her back he saw she was dead. Her face looked dark and bloated, her eyes wide open and staring up at the bright sky overhead. All the CPR in the world wouldn't bring her back.

He ran back to his tractor and reached for the CB mike with which he could contact Katie. When she answered he said, "Get help out here, Katie, along the south road. A woman is dead. I think she's been murdered." Then, wishing he had called his parents instead, to protect Katie from this shock, he asked, "Are you all right?"

"Of course I'm all right. I'm on the way to the phone. Over and out."

CHAPTER 27

I'M SORRY, Daddy ... Her hand held out to him folded small and close around the note in its palm. It reached out of the darkness of his unconsciousness, an isolated event occurring at the moment of waking. Seeing her hand reaching for him, and knowing the message it held, shocked him out of deep sleep, and he jerked up, trembling, with a cold layer of sweat coating his body.

Mel slumped, resting his forehead on his hands, his elbows on his knees. After several moments in which his heartbeat stabilized, he looked up. He was in this world now, not that. He could make up to Crescent, in part, by helping these children now in his care.

Bright sunlight spilled across his body, melting from the bed to the wall opposite, following each curve. Wind whined around the house, making weird little sounds in invisible holes at his window. He could hear the sound of tractors in the distance, and the cry of the birds that followed the upturning of soil and breakfasted on exposed worms and bugs.

He got up and stretched and looked out the window. The sun had risen high enough to shine over the top of the windbreak. In the bathroom next door to his room he heard the shower start. There were footsteps in the hall, and the sound of Cora's voice, with that special soft quality that people used with children.

It was a peaceful scene from his window. In the distance, visible between tall trees, he could see another farmhouse and barns surrounded by their windbreak of trees, but it was at least a mile away, rising almost like a blight on the flat horizon. He saw the earth for a moment in the way he used to imagine, when he was a kid fascinated by the mysteries of space, that an alien from another galaxy must view it. He saw it as a round ball covered with parasites, from the microscopic bacteria to the visible bugs, billions of which lived in every corner of the globe, on up to larger insects, then to animals. And then most noticeably, the animals that built shelters and scratched up the surface of the soil and made neat rows and planted seeds that would grow to maturity, which these odd animals who clothed themselves then harvested and ate. Once in the past Crescent amused him by saying, "My, quote, *angel's view,* unquote, of this puny little earth is unquotable. Or maybe my God's view. Who knows, Daddy, maybe God sent me here from some other galaxy to see what was going on and to report my opinions."

"And what are your opinions, Angel?" he had asked.

"You want to hear my opinions? Really? I think the ants and the bees that colonize are in better control than people are. I think there have to be rules. I think if there isn't a limit put on things like—like immorality—that people, allowed to be as bad as they want to be, will destroy us all. I'm not afraid of nuclear power destroying us, Daddy, I'm afraid of immorality."

He had been surprised that she had even considered such a subject as immorality. He should have been more surprised than he was; he should have drawn her out about it and asked what she was talking about. Immorality? That was all he had said. "Immorality, Angel?" He saw her frowning at the wall, her eyebrows brought low over her bright, dark eyes.

"Sure. Have you seen some of the new videos? They're filled with it. Disgusting language, all the time. Nobody can speak a sentence without putting in those words. Do you think they think it sounds smart, or what? And the things they do. It's like they never think of anything besides sex."

His surprise increased and edged uncomfortably toward embarrassment. Sex? She was ten years old. Barely. What did she know about sex? Her mother was supposed to talk to her about it, wasn't she? Take some of the mystery and fear out of it, and hopefully some of the curiosity. He felt discomfort thinking he might have to discuss it with her.

He said lamely, "Your mother lets you watch videos and movies like that?"

She looked down, and a moment later she was talking about school. He was glad enough to drop the subject.

And dear God, how many times had he wished he had drawn her out that day, before it was too late.

He watched a tractor, so far away it looked like a toy, moving slowly in a straight line across the field.

He heard the shower stopped, and turned to his suitcase and began getting out fresh clothing.

Norma would be downstairs, trying out Cora's great country breakfast, sitting with coffee, perhaps, and a variety of home-baked rolls. Mel checked his watch. It was after nine o'clock, late for him, but he felt more rested than he had since he started the trip. Having received the news that Durk Nolan was no longer a danger to Celia and the children was probably the reason he had slept so long.

He heard the bathroom door open and light footsteps passing down the hall. Another door closed. Celia, he guessed, dressing for the day. Or Jonie.

After showering and dressing he went down to the kitchen, where all three children were sitting quietly at the table. Blair smiled and patted a chair he'd been guarding.

"I saved it for you," he said.

"Thanks, pal."

A dab of blue jelly decorated Drew's upper lip. Mel ruffled his hair and took the chair beside Blair. He said good morning to Jonie, then he noticed the look on Cora's face. She seemed to be sending him some kind of message, a sober, serious stare of hazel eyes.

Norma.

Norma was missing.

Celia came to the table from the stove with a cup of coffee in her hands. She put it down in front of Mel.

"Cora has cooked a lot of good food," she said. "What do you want? Waffles? Eggs? Bacon?"

"Waffles and eggs, yes. Bacon, no." He watched Cora.

She said softly, "She never got here."

Mel stood up again. All faces stared at him. Celia stood with a second cup of coffee at another place laud for breakfast. She glanced from Cora to him.

"Did you call the airport?" he asked Cora.

"Yes. The plane arrived on time. I didn't ask if Norma was on board. I thought she might be traveling incognito."

"She might have, but she didn't have any reason to."

"I'll go call then, and ask."

Cora left the room. Mel sat down again. Across the table Celia slowly eased down into her chair. On her plate was a slice of toast, nothing more. As if she remembered suddenly, she got up, reached for Mel's plate, took it to the stove, and brought it back filled with eggs and waffles.

"Why was she coming here?" Celia asked slowly.

"I don't know exactly. She said something strange had come up." He looked at each of the three kids and wondered if he should say anything more in front of them.

"Something strange?" Celia cried in soft anguish, her features distorting. *"Like what?"*

Mel looked from one face to the other. In Jonie's face he saw a growing terror. Maybe, he thought, it would be better to tell them.

"She called Cora last night before we got here and said she was flying in because she wanted to talk to us. She said Durk Nolan is dead."

Celia's face did not change. And neither, he noticed, did Jonie's. The two boys looked from sister to mother uncertainly.

"He's ..." Mel hesitated, choosing his words carefully. "He's no danger to you now. Any of you. Norma was coming out, and wanted us to wait for her. I thought we'd stay a few days here on the farm before we head back home."

Celia's face whitened. Even her lips, naturally pale pink, grew white.

She went to the sink, drew some water into a glass, and took a sip.

Cora returned.

"No," she said. "There was no one on the plane named Norma Whiting."

Mel stirred cream into his coffee and sat thinking of the options open to him. Did he dare call Norma's home or office from the Mendel's? He was getting a sick feeling that something terrible had happened to her.

He got up.

"I'll go find a pay phone to make some calls and see if I can find out what happened. Celia," he added just before he went out the door, "try to relax. It's going to be okay. Enjoy Cora's company, and the farm."

DURK NOLAN IS DEAD.

He's no danger to you now.

Oh, God, if only that were true.

Celia walked along the edge of the cornfield. She didn't know exactly what time it was, and it didn't matter. Mel had left the house around ten that morning and still hadn't returned after lunch. Cora had suggested to Celia that she might like to go for a walk. She could see how restless she was, how she couldn't be still.

"I'll keep the kids entertained, Celia," Cora said as Celia paced the floor. Lunch was over, the laundry was done, clean clothes folded and put back into suitcases in the guest rooms upstairs. Celia had resisted the urge to bring them downstairs and set them all at the side entry door, where they could be quickly loaded as soon as Mel got back.

Durk Nolan is dead.

He's no danger to you now.

Celia sat down beneath a tree at the edge of the cornfield and stared off toward the distant horizon. It was so different here, but the line of trees at the end of the field became the line of trees at the swamp. They came closer to her, closer, and grew taller and thicker, and between them the surface of the still water of the swamp reflected the green world above. She was at home again, enclosed by the world she had lived in since she was sixteen.

The last night Durk came home was with her again, and her sense of well-being became the trap it had been that night. She knew she was entrapped in it as surely as a fly in a spider's web.

The children had gone to bed. It had been a good afternoon with Kent there. He was so different from Durk. She could feel the gentleness of this man's soul.

He seemed smaller that day than he had back at the shelter. When he came in the door he didn't have to duck his head the way Durk did. But she saw he was slightly stooped, his height disguised in the slump of his shoulders. There were no muscles on his arms. His shoulders lifted like featherless wings, all bone and gristle.

But he wore a smile and was nice to have around.

After the kids were asleep he sat with her on the screened porch, with the living room light behind them making a white track across the porch floor between her chair and his. They had brought out kitchen chairs, and he sat with his leaning on the back legs, his feet resting on the railing.

His voice was as slow and easy as his movements. He told her about Janice and her family, a black woman Celia had made friends with at the shelter. Jonie had played with Janice's second oldest daughter, close in the special friendship two eleven-year-old girls can have.

"They found her a part-time job at a laundry," Kent said, his slow voice soothing. The frogs serenaded them, made a background that was musical for Kent's voice. "They found her a house, too. I went over and cleaned up the yard, helped Janice and the kids. Her man's in jail for awhile, won't be botherin' anyone for awhile."

At that very moment Celia thought she heard a noise in the house, a noise that was too loud for one of the children to have made. She started to turn around, to look into the lighted living room, when the light abruptly went out.

She leaped to her feet, her hands against her mouth to stifle a cry. She had glimpsed the movement of something, an arm, a hand, maybe, in the doorway by the light switch in the moment before darkness. Not Jonie, not one of the boys.

In the sudden dark she heard the scrape of Kent's chair as he stood up. Her eyes had not adjusted to the dark when the gruff, low voice spoke.

"Don't move."

Durk! Durk's voice, deep-toned, angry. She could see him as dim light from stars and a new moon lessened the darkness on the porch. He was behind Kent. The two men made a double black bulk against the night beyond the screen of the porch.

"Hey, man," Kent said, "No harm done here. Just visiting."

In words that might have sounded calm and controlled to anyone else, but which Celia knew were filled with fury, his own cold rage, Durk ordered, "Get in the house, Celia."

A flashlight in Durk's hand came on, revealing Kent's back and the handgun Durk held against it. Celia hadn't moved. She was unable to move. The judge had ordered Durk never to come near her again, never to go near the home by the swamp, but she should have known Durk would ignore that warning.

"I said, go in the house, Celia."

"Don't," she said. "Let him go."

Durk laughed, a brief snorting sound of derision. "Don't worry. I'm not only going to let the bastard home-wrecker go, I'm going to help him. Out!"

He lifted his knee and rammed it into Kent's legs and Kent stumbled forward.

"Go into the bedroom, Celia," Durk ordered again. "And I mean now. Turn the lights on."

Celia's legs followed his orders, taking her without her own volition into the house and to the light switch. The glare of the single overhead bulb blinded her. She tried to see out the open living room door to the porch, to see what had happened there. She heard no sound, nothing. It was as if the two men had disappeared into oblivion.

He had told her to go into the bedroom. She was afraid not to obey. He was carrying a gun new to her. On the wall in the living room were his shotguns, his rifles, secured behind glass in a locked gun cabinet. She thought briefly of using a lamp to break the glass, of taking out one of the guns and using it to ... to ...

She was terrified of the guns. She didn't even know how to shoot one. She knew they had triggers, and that the trigger released the bullet, but that was all she knew.

She went into the bedroom and sat on the edge of the bed. Light from the living room spilled into the hall, and from there, dimly, through the open door into the bedroom.

Tense with fear she waited. What were they doing? What had Durk done? Where was Kent? His car was parked behind the house, close to the blue Oldsmobile she had come to think of as hers.

The frogs grew quiet. Celia's arms stiffened. Her shoulders ached and her ears throbbed with listening. Then a series of popping sounds pierced her brain. She cringed with each of them. One, two, three. Like firecrackers beneath a can. Like ... gunshots.

Only the frogs in more distant places of the swamp continued their piping. A bullfrog gargled deeply, far away. Celia waited, mouth dry, heart pounding slow and hard.

Then a car started. Kent's, not hers. It moved slowly away and the sound of it faded into the night. The frogs nearby began singing again, one, a dozen, hundreds. The night filled with their sound.

She didn't move. She was afraid to move.

A door closed. The back door. She stiffened. Durk had come back. She listened to his footsteps come through the kitchen, into the hall, and to the bedroom.

He came to the bed, put his hand on her neck and pushed her down.

"Don't ever try anything like that again, bitch woman. The next time, you won't live to turn the switch in the car, understand? You'll never drive away from me again."

His hand grasped her blouse at the neck and ripped it from her, but in the second before, she saw him slip the handgun under his pillow.

The rest of that night and the next day were dark blurs of hell in her memory. The next day, when they found their dad was home, the children were afraid to move. Celia rose sore and bruised from her bed and cooked breakfast in silence. Throughout the day she moved in silence. Durk had brought back a plastic bag filled with dirty jeans and shirts. He never wore socks or shorts or undershirts, and she was thankful she didn't have those to touch.

Jonie helped her with the laundry. They pulled the wringer washing machine out from the corner of the kitchen and filled it with hot water and washed his clothes. Together they hung them on the line to dry, neither of them talking. The two boys sat where Durk ordered them to sit in the living room, and when Drew wet his pants Celia prayed a silent, hopeless prayer that Durk would not see.

The smell of whiskey permeated the house. Durk's eyes had the glazed dullness of too much alcohol, but when he walked he walked steadily, and his eyes missed no movement.

Celia was thankful when dark came. She put the boys to bed and with a hand on their faces warned them in her silent gesture to keep quiet, stay in bed, don't move more than was necessary.

The night pulsed with the sounds of frogs. Once, as she lay stiff and untouched on the bed beside Durk, she thought she heard the dogs howling. Then she remembered the dogs were gone. Even Flint. Flint was gone a month now, maybe more. She was losing track of time.

She didn't sleep. Hours passed, and the sounds of the night diminished.

Then Durk moved. He eased out of bed, and she was awed that he was trying not to wake her. He cared what she thought?

In the faint light in the room, light of stars and moon that shone through the window, she saw his tall, muscular, pale body. Naked, he moved toward the door stealthily, and into the hall.

It struck her like a hammer blow to her chest. *He was going to Jonie.*

She sat up in bed, careful not to make a sound.

The floor creaked in the hall near Jonie's door. To her sharpened senses came the sound of movement, of bed-springs, of a settling, a rustling of clothing or bedding. The sound of a stifled cry, of threatening whispers.

Celia reached under Durk's pillow. Her fingers touched the cool, hard barrel of the gun.

She pulled it out from beneath the pillow and slid off the bed, her hands grasping the stock and both index fingers finding and settling steadily on the trigger.

She went down the hall to Jonie's room, and with her left hand she turned on the light.

He was on her, his white body as revolting as the body of a huge, slimy, bleached eel. With a stunned and disbelieving face he gaped at her.

She steadied the gun with both hands, and prayed uselessly that it was loaded.

"Get off her!"

Surprised at the calmness in her voice, she stared at Durk, feeling an odd power, a determination she had never been capable of before. She would not let him hurt Jonie.

"Get dressed," she ordered as Durk approached her, leaving Jonie turning in the bed, pressing her face into the protection of the pillow, pulling her gown down to cover her hips.

Celia moved aside in the hall, keeping the gun leveled at him. She didn't so much as blink. She felt her steadiness, her determination. This was it. This was the night Durk would die. As he had killed, she would kill him. As he had buried so many bodies, she would bury him.

"Be careful with that thing," Durk said, reaching out to take the gun.

She pulled back out of his reach and cocked it as she had seen him do.

He edged back, his eyes staring into the small hole in the barrel.

"You're crazy, woman," he said softly.

"Get dressed," she ordered again, and motioned with her head toward the bedroom.

She stood in the doorway while he pulled on jeans and shirt and shoes, his eyes all the while on the barrel of the gun. He at least had respect for that, and what it could do.

"You killed him, didn't you?" she said tonelessly as she motioned with her head for him to walk toward the screened porch.

For just a moment she saw the old sneer on his lips, but then, as she leveled the gun at his head, he turned and walked out of the house with her behind him.

"You know where to go," she said. "*Walk!*"

The moon dimly lighted the path through the weeds and grass. As they approached the swamp the frogs began closing down, as if they were watching and waiting. She could feel their eyes above the water, invisible bulges in the dark beneath the trees. The moon glimmered on the water between the big cypress tree and the grass, where it was deep and dark.

He turned and faced her.

She came closer, closer. How far would the bullet of a small handgun travel? She didn't dare only wound him. The first bullet had to be fatal.

Something within her revolted at her thoughts, so calm, so casual, as if she killed every night of the new moon. Then she saw again his white body crushing the life out of her child, and she stiffened her arms and aimed down the barrel of the gun, aligning it with his forehead.

He leaped suddenly toward her, his hand a weapon like a hatchet, and he struck her arms down just as the gun fired. The bullet went into the water, the mirror-like surface dimpling, with tiny waves moving out from the point of entry.

As suddenly as that, within the space of a breath, the gun was in his hands, and he was laughing that terrible laugh of victory.

"You white bitch. You think you can kill me? Even if you'd managed to get off that shot into my head, it wouldn't have done you any good. Even if you had buried me here, you know I'd still get you. You'd have to spend every night from now on waiting for me here, and you know it."

He lifted the gun and brought it down toward her head, and she put her arms up for what meager protection they would give. The barrel of the gun struck her arms and then her head, and she fell. His foot shoved at her, prodding, kicking. Curses rolled from his lips, and she knew then it was not he who would die this night. His kicks pushed her closer, closer to the water. With her hands she grabbed the grass, holding, clinging.

Her babies! Dear God, what would happen to her babies?

She heard the growl before she saw the black and shadowy movement in the water. It rose before her eyes, leaping from the swamp, its growl rattling in a throat that was supposed to be dead, dead a long month now.

Durk whirled and cried out. Celia recognized real fear in his voice as he faced the black phantom body of Flint.

The dog leaped, water dripping from his body. White fangs flashed in the moonlight, tearing at Durk's throat.

Durk screamed hoarsely and fell beneath the black body.

Celia saw Durk's white form roll away in an attempt to escape. She saw the gun in his hand, its barrel blending with the dark body of the dog that hovered over him.

"Flint!" she cried out. "Run, Flint!"

The gun fired, one shot after the other, several times. And Flint leaped away and was gone, a black, swift movement that she wasn't able to follow. The rattle of his chain faded.

Silence reined in the still, moonlit night.

Durk lay still on the ground, blood flowing from the wound in his neck.

Celia stood up. Her body felt as if she had crouched in the same position for hours. The past would never leave her. She seemed made up of pieces of memory, like a beehive filled with tiny larvae that would grow and develop into winged insects, to swarm around her forever.

She looked out over an unfamiliar landscape, flat and endless, filled with corn, and remembered she was in Nebraska. The sun was lowering over the trees to the west.

She stared until the sky blurred into streaks of rainbow colors.

She had buried Durk that night.

He was dead, yes, and yet ...

... he would never be dead.

She could only hope that across the next river, over the next hill, beyond the western mountains, she and her children would be safe at last. They had to keep going. They dare not stop.

CHAPTER 28

MEL SAT IN HIS CAR, his fingers tapping against the steering wheel. He was waiting for a phone call from Earl Bryant, one of his best connections in southwest Florida. Hours ago he had parked his car near the pay phone in the parking lot of a supermarket where he had made the phone calls to Norma's home and office.

From her office he had received an answer that did not surprise him. "No, sir, Miss Whiting is not here. She canceled her appointments for a few days. She'll be back on Monday. Could I take a message, please?"

At her home he had gotten Norma's message from her answering machine. "You have reached Norma," she said simply on the private line for all the drivers, contacts, and others in the Underground Railroad. "Please leave your code number and I'll get back to you."

He didn't leave any message at all. He said, "Norma, are you there?" and waited. If she were available he knew she would pick up the phone. They recognized each other's voices with no problem.

She didn't pick it up.

It was then he put through a call to Earl at his used car lot. "Get me all the information you can on Durk Nolan and call me back at this number." He gave Earl the number of the pay phone.

He dared leave only to get food for lunch. At a fast food place two blocks away he bought a baked potato loaded with cheese and broccoli, nachos with jalapeno peppers, and a large Coke. On his way out the door he was blocked for a moment by a woman who weighed probably three hundred pounds, and waiting for her to pass he decided to go back and get a dessert. The fried pies looked better than the packaged cake, so he bought the pie.

In the car the food helped to pass the time. At one o'clock he took a chance on tying up the phone to call Cora and tell her he was waiting for a phone call and would be back as soon as he could.

"Don't worry," she said. "We're doing okay. The kids are like a group of scared little chicks, but we're going to try to remedy that. I sent Celia for a walk, and the kids and I are going to go out and look at the baby chickens."

It was useless to ask, but he asked anyway, "Have you heard from Norma?"

"No, I haven't."

Back in his car, near enough to the phone to hear it ring, he waited. The radio played softly as he waited for news. The music continued past the hour of news time, and he switched to another station.

Cars entered and left the parking lot of the supermarket, women and sometimes men went in, stayed awhile, and came out with brown sacks carried by themselves or by sack boys. There wasn't much traffic here in this small farm town, and the parking lot looked almost empty in comparison to what he was used to.

Late in the afternoon he went back to the pay phone and called the local police.

"I'd like to know if there's been an accident. My wife didn't come home when she was supposed to, and I'm worried about her."

"What's your name?"

"Robertson," he said, muttering the first name that came to mind, keeping his voice slightly disguised in case he should meet this particular policeman. "Sam Robertson."

"And your wife?"

"Anne."

He was put on hold. In the background he heard the same noises he heard from any other police center. Phones ringing, voices overlapping. A dispatcher's drone distinguishable only by its peculiarly emotionless directions and instructions.

The voice came back. "When were you expecting your wife to come home?"

"Last night."

There was a pause. In the background the noises subsided, as if the policeman had put his hand over the phone. Then he said, "I'm sorry. You might come in and file a report."

Mel hung up. What had he expected? He had no idea what name Norma was traveling under. He dialed the Mendel number again to see if Cora might have heard from Norma. But there was no answer.

He went back to his car and sat tapping his fingers against the steering wheel.

A couple of teenage boys came by and used the phone for several minutes, sniggering together, their thumbs hooked in the pockets of their jeans. They took turns with the phone, talking forever, it seemed to Mel.

They finally left, and Mel drew a long sigh of relief. He put his head back on the headrest and closed his eyes and tried to think. How was he going to find out what had happened to Norma? He knew now it was serious. She must be incapable of communicating or she would have called Cora.

He was thinking about checking out the hospitals when at last the pay phone rang. He threw his door open and ran to it.

"Hello."

"Mel?"

"Right."

"Here's the info on Durk Nolan. Sorry it took me so long. I had to be sure. The man's body, or skeleton, was found in the water of the swamp near his house. There were three bullet holes in his skull. He'd been dead an undetermined time, because fish, turtles, and things like that, or something, had gotten to him and eaten a good part of his flesh. There was some hair left on his scalp, his back was pretty well left alone, but his fingertips were gone. So nix on fingerprints. The medical examiner figured he'd been dead ten days or so, maybe two weeks, maybe less."

"Are they positive it was Durk Nolan?"

"As positive as they could be. The guy had blond hair, pretty long, and he was the right size. Pretty much torn up. A gator had taken part of him away. One leg, both feet, part of one arm."

"Yeah," Mel said. "Okay, thanks, Earl."

"Sure. No problem. Where the hell are you anyway?"

"Nebraska."

"You don't happen to be running Celia Nolan, do you?"

"Why?"

"They're looking for her. Suspect, murder one."

"Okay."

He hung up the phone and used the rest of his change to call the one local hospital.

"Did you have an accident victim last night?"

"No, we didn't. Car accident, you mean?"

The voice was sweet and feminine. He pictured a young receptionist with a tiny engagement ring on her finger and a summer wedding planned.

She continued, "A man was brought in from a farm accident. He had broken his leg. Is that the one you mean?"

"No," Mel said, finding here an innocent and willing participant. She would probably have no idea there existed an underground network of people who helped abused families escape, people who came right through her area. She was not one of the cautious police, she was slightly bored with the lack of action and eager to talk. "I'm looking for a woman. About forty, with blond hair. She's about five-five and slender, maybe one hundred ten pounds. Something might have happened to her last night."

He heard an audible gasp, and felt in his bones that he had reached the right person to give him information without wanting to know who he was and why he was asking. She didn't even want his name.

"I'll bet you mean the murder victim! I don't know who she was, but she was found this morning out on one of the country roads. Could that be the lady you're looking for?"

Good God.

Not Norma. Not Norma who spent her time and energy helping people like Celia, Jonie, Blair, and Drew. Someone who would, and perhaps had, put her very life into helping others.

"What can you tell me about her?" he asked.

"All I know is what I heard when I came back to work after lunch. She was found in a ditch, drowned, face down. A homicide, they said, no doubt about that. She was driving a rented car from the Omaha airport. I don't know her name. Is that who you're looking for? Maybe you—"

He hung up. She was beginning to get curious about him now, and that wouldn't do. Where was Norma when she ran into trouble? How close to the Mendel farm? If Durk Nolan had been dead for ten days to two weeks, who was following Celia? Who was killing so many people who had tried to help her escape? Escape from whom?

He got into his car and sat a moment longer, trying to figure out his next move.

If Durk Nolan was dead, who the hell was killing off the people involved with helping Celia get away? The Merrows in Tennessee might have been a coincidence, but the death of Norma certainly wasn't.

And he had no doubt it was Norma.

It all fit too well. The car from the airport, a woman murdered on one of the farm roads ...

He became cognizant of a growing darkness around him. The sun had gone down. He wanted to go to the police station and try to find out something, but didn't dare expose Celia yet. Not until he understood more, at least. Not until they had bargaining power.

He started the car and drove over beneath one of the lights that had come on in the parking lot, its electrical glow competing with the last rays of a setting sun.

He took the notebook out of a secret little pocket beneath his seat and checked names. He was searching for contacts in the area northwest of Omaha. He found only the Mendels.

Lorne, he thought. Lorne Mendel could find out who the woman was and let him know. He had to be sure it was Norma, even though his heart said it was.

But no, neither Lorne nor Cora would be able to find out. They had never seen Norma. Not even a photograph, he was sure. And the name she had used would reveal nothing.

He drove back to the farm, watching all possible activity on all crossroads and seeing nothing. The landscape looked smooth and dark. He met few cars, few trucks this time of the evening.

When he reached the farm he parked his car near the side entrance door. Lights were on in the back of the house, a curtained glow beyond windows. The porch light gleamed from a yellow bug bulb, lighting the small, square porch and the three steps up to it.

The door was unlocked. He went in. The dog gave one woof and came into the hall to meet him.

Cora stood in the kitchen doorway, and he saw by her face that she was relieved to see him.

"I should have called again, I'm sorry," Mel said.

"It's all right. Come on in. I've put your plate into the microwave."

Lorne sat in a recliner near the heating stove. He got up when Mel entered and came to shake his hand. He was a man of medium size and coloring, his brown hair thinning and receding, giving the illusion of a high forehead. His hand was callused and hard. It had seemed to Mel that

Lorne tolerated the families who came through his house for Cora's sake. It was something she wanted to do, and he went along with it. But he didn't let it interfere with his work.

"The kids and Celia were tired," Cora said, arranging a place for Mel at the table. "They went to bed just a few minutes ago."

Mel looked at the clock and saw it was later than he had thought. Twenty minutes to nine.

"I don't need anything, Cora," he said.

"Don't be silly. Sit down and eat."

Lorne went back to his chair and picked up the newspaper again. The television droned a sitcom that no one seemed to be paying attention to.

"Did you see the evening news?" Mel asked.

"No," Cora said. "Lorne didn't come in until after dark. The news was off by then. And I didn't turn the TV on. What did you find out?"

"I found out that a woman driving a car rented at the Omaha airport was found murdered this morning on one of the farm roads. She'd been drowned in a ditch." Cora stood still, staring at him. Lorne put down his paper and swiveled his chair toward Mel.

"Which farm road?" Lorne asked.

"That's what I'd like to know. But I didn't know exactly how to find out." He went into the washroom off the kitchen, washed his hands and face, and came back to the table. "If I had gone to the police, we would have been exposed. A lot of people would be hurt, the Underground would be in jeopardy. Is there any way you can find out, Lorne?"

Lorne got up. "I'll be back. Wait for me."

Lorne went to the kitchen door, and Blue Bonnet got up and followed. Lorne made room for the dog, and the door closed behind them.

Cora poured two cups of coffee and sat down with one at the end of the table.

"What's going on, Mel?"

"I'm not sure, Cora. People are being killed, that's all I know. I want you to be very careful. Are you keeping doors and windows locked?"

"No," she said. "We've never had to. Of course, the front door is locked, and the windows haven't been unlocked. The weather isn't ..." She stopped, listening. Mel heard the sound of a motor start.

"Lorne's pickup," Cora said. "He'll find out."

Mel ate mostly to please Cora, to be polite, but the food that otherwise would have been delicious was like cotton in his mouth. He washed a few bites down with coffee. Cora stared at the wall with a worried frown.

"If her husband's dead," she said, "who's following ... who followed Norma?"

"I wish I knew. I think we have to get out of here, Cora, to protect them and to protect you."

"No!" she said with sudden passion and vehemence. "You're staying. They're safe upstairs."

She left the room suddenly and was back a moment later. "The side door is locked now. No one will be coming in. We'll wait for Lorne. He'll find out who the woman was and where she was. It will probably be on the news at ten. And there might be someone I could call ..."

Once more she left the room. He heard the murmur of her voice a few minutes later from Lorne's office.

Mel scraped his plate into the dog pan out on the porch. The porch light was on, but Blue Bonnet was nowhere in sight.

Feeling uncomfortably exposed on the porch, he stepped back into the kitchen to turn off the light.

He went outside and stood a moment, letting his eyes adjust to the dark. He saw the outline of the barn roof against the sky, a sharp black line against the star-studded expanse above. With one short whistle he called Blue Bonnet to him. She came from around the corner of the house, a dark blur of moving shadow.

He rubbed one of her ears, and she stuck her nose into his palm briefly, then she was gone again. He thought he could see her ears perked, as if she'd heard something. She ran a few yards out toward the back and stopped. Then she ran on again, silent, a shadow against the white chicken house. Mel followed her to the small white building where Cora's twenty white leghorn hens and half-dozen roosters were housed. He heard them shuffling on their perches, squawking to one another over space, then silence as they settled once more.

Mel looked back at the house. The pale glow from the curtained windows revealed only the outline of his car parked near the side door. Trees down the other side of the driveway gave way to the low, flat world of corn beyond the road.

There were no nightbirds here, no frogs crying in the dark. He heard the wind, singing in fine tones like angels, or demons in disguise, around the edges of the house and through the trees.

He circled the house, his eyes finally adjusted to the dark. On both sides were the trees, and beyond them the cornfields. At the back were the buildings, an acre of shade trees and open backyard, the chicken yard, the barnyard, and beyond that another line of windbreaker trees, and then the field, stretching almost a mile to the next road.

Blue Bonnet did not return. He waited for her on the porch, watching the shadows, until he heard Cora come back into the kitchen. When he went into the house Blue Bonnet was still gone. There was a warmth in the kitchen he felt was deceptive.

Cora was pouring more coffee into his cup and into hers. She sat down, scooped sugar into her cup, and stirred. He saw her swallow dryly. He watched the movement of her throat while she stirred the coffee. She didn't look up at him until she lifted the cup to her lips.

"Blue Bonnet is still outside," he said, needing at this moment an ordinary thought, something soothing and normal.

"That's okay," she said. "She never wanders away. She'll be back." She paused and swallowed her coffee. She looked tired, he saw. More tired than he'd ever seen her.

"Are you all right?"

"Well, I talked to a couple of people I know. Both of them had heard about the murder of the strange woman. We don't have that sort of thing around here much. One heard it on the news. She said the name of the woman was Clara Lansing, and she was driving a rented car. But she didn't know what road she was on, where she was going, or anything. I tried calling a few more places, but didn't find out anything more. A lot of rumors. Anyway, it wasn't a local woman. I guess it has to be Norma, doesn't it?"

"I'm afraid so."

"I've been thinking and thinking about what she told me on the phone. She said to tell you to wait, that something strange had come up. She said Durk Nolan was dead. She didn't say how or when. So I'm thinking maybe her being killed was just one of those strange and awful coincidences. Maybe some of those creeps that hang around the cities followed her and robbed her. Maybe it was something like that."

"Maybe," Mel said. But he knew it couldn't be that simple, that coincidental. The *something strange* Norma had spoken of probably would help explain it, but that information had died with her.

The ten o'clock news came on, and Mel and Cora went to stand in front of the television and watch.

The murdered woman was the lead story. Shown were police cars, the rented car, and the covered body of the woman as she was transferred on a stretcher to a waiting ambulance. The body had been discovered by a local farmer around ten in the morning.

"It is believed," the newsgirl said, "that the murdered woman was carrying false identification papers. Although her driver's license indicated her home was in Washington, D.C., she boarded a plane in Tallahassee, Florida and rented the car at the airport at 1:45 this morning. It is not known what she was doing on that particular road. If anyone has any information ..."

They had already told more than Mel expected to hear, but there was no more information, and Cora turned off the television. In the silence that followed came the sound of an automobile drawing nearer and turning at last into the driveway.

"Lorne," Cora said, and started toward the hall door.

Mel grabbed her arm and stopped her.

"Wait," he said, "If it's Lorne, he'll come on in."

"Yes, you're right."

They stood together in the kitchen, listening to the sound of tires on gravel and the silence that followed when the automobile stopped.

Wind whined beneath the eaves. Upstairs a board squeaked, a natural settling of the house ... or a furtive footstep on the floor ...

Then the wind quieted and the fine whistles and cries drifted away like a flight of dark birds passing over.

The silence grew heavier and thicker, like fog on a dark, still night.

CHAPTER 29

THEY HEARD footsteps on the back porch, walking without hesitation. Cora hurried to the kitchen door and turned on the porch light, opening the door with a quick gesture that indicated a vast release of anxiety.

Lorne came in, pushing past Cora without looking at her. Mel saw a fleeting look of disappointment and pleading on Cora's face, and for the first time in the years he had known Cora and Lorne saw that something wasn't right in what he had thought was a perfect marriage. But there was no time to dwell on that now.

Through the open door Mel could hear the barking of the dog. The barks were of the questioning nature, and reminded him of his own dogs when they thought something might be in the woods but they weren't sure. There would be a bark, a hesitation, another bark.

Lorne sat down at the table. He was wearing an alert, worried look. The overhead lights, suspended by a chain above the dining table, highlighted the deep lines that ran from his nose to his chin.

"Was it on the news?" he asked.

"Yes," Cora said. "A woman named Clara Lansing."

"It was a fake ID," Lorne said. "The police tried to reach her home in Washington, D.C., and no such person lived at that place. They don't know who she is. No relatives, no friends, no one knows her."

Cora gasped faintly in the silence that followed. "Are they going to bury her anyway? Doesn't she have family, Mel?"

Lorne said quickly, "You're assuming it's Norma. It may not be."

Mel's mind raced, trying to connect the ends of disjointed facts. He had little doubt the dead woman was Norma, but to be certain he would have to see her. Yet if he went in to identify her, he would be revealing to the police not only Celia but the existence of the Underground Railroad.

"Do they have any suspects?" Mel asked, a forlorn bit of hope remaining. Perhaps it was only a horrible coincidence. Some woman chased down by a psycho on a country road and murdered.

"None."

"Was she raped, anything like that?"

"Not that I could find out."

Cora asked, "Where was she, Lorne? How far away?"

"About eleven miles to the east, close to Drake Crossroads, on Beyer Road. She had passed a store a couple of miles back."

"Headed in this direction?" Mel asked.

"It seems that way."

"And somehow he caught up with her," Cora said, her voice low and faint. "She probably has a lot of enemies. She's helped a lot of families away from a lot of abusive circumstances."

Lorne was looking straight and steadily at Mel. "Celia's husband is dead, you say?"

"Yes, so we recently learned. And Celia is wanted for the murder of her husband." He felt as if he were betraying Celia and those three little kids to whom he was getting too attached, but he owed Cora and Lorne the truth.

"Oh, good God," Cora whispered.

Lorne leaned back in his chair with a motion of disgust or dismay and glanced around the room. But there was no way out. That was the way Mel felt, too.

"Like Norma said, something strange is going on. And I don't know what to do about it. I know this, as long as we're here, you people are in danger. I think the best thing is to take Celia and the kids and go."

"No!" Cora said.

Lorne twisted in his chair toward her. "Cora, the girl is wanted for murder! But there's not a jury in the world that would convict her if she was having enough problems with him that the Underground Railroad took her in. Don't they investigate their cases enough to know what they're doing, Mel?"

"You're right. Yes, they do. Norma had known Celia for quite a while, and knew she needed help. And you're right about no jury convicting her if ..."

If what she had made Norma believe was true.

He had no doubt Durk Nolan had been a cruel man, it was documented in too many places. But if he were dead, who was following them?

"Don't do anything tonight," Cora pleaded. "Let those poor babies sleep."

Lorne said, "I think you should call the police, Mel."

"Maybe you're right," Mel agreed.

"No, don't. Wait until tomorrow and let's talk to Celia."

Both Mel and Lorne looked at Cora and saw pleading in her eyes.

"They were so tired," she said. "They had such a big day, the little boys, Jonie and I. Celia took a long walk around the farm in the afternoon, and the children and I were so busy looking at baby chicks, at the kittens in the barn. They're such scared little children, and so good. And if Celia killed her husband, he deserved it."

"That's not the point, Cora," Lorne said. "Somebody is taking revenge for him, and if he knew where Norma was going, he might know where we live."

Mel had to agree. He thought of his own notebook of names, and the hidden map that traced thin lines to all points of the country, to all the shelters, the homes involved in the Underground. Railroad. If someone tore his car apart looking, they'd find it. Ordinarily they would have no idea what it meant. But if Norma had carried a map to the Mendel farm, and no doubt she had, the killer had almost certainly found it.

In the brief silence, the barking of the dog grew suddenly more noticeable. It was steadier now, more insistent that something strange, something unwelcome, had invaded her territory.

Lorne and Mel stood up at the same time.

"Do you have flashlights?" Mel asked.

"Yes." Lorne went toward the washroom, walking fast, and came back with two flashlights and a shotgun. "Let's go see what's out there."

Cora too now rose from her chair at the table. Her face had turned more pale, and tiny freckles stood out over her nose and cheeks.

"Lock the door," Mel said. "We'll be close."

They went out, leaving the porch light off, the flashlights off.

Lorne asked quietly, "Do you have a gun, Mel?"

"Yes."

Mel reached down, unsnapped the holster in his right boot, and removed the .38. No stun gun would help him feel safe in this darkness tonight.

"You go around that way, in the yard," Lorne suggested, and I'll go back toward the field where Blue Bonnet is barking. She might have spotted a badger, that's all."

Mel circled the house slowly, hearing back in the field the constant bark of the dog. He hadn't used his flashlight. He walked softly, trying to make no sound, alert to any sound made by a footstep. But the wind cried through the trees and around the buildings, drowning out more subtle sounds.

His eyes were adjusting to the dark. He looked for the shadowy bulk of a car parked in a place where it shouldn't have been but saw nothing. His own car was faintly visible in the glow beyond the draped window of the kitchen. Lorne's pickup was in the driveway beyond the station wagon, rather than in its usual spot at the end of the garage.

He went through a small door into the garage and turned on the flashlight. He saw one sedan, a grey Chrysler, and a collection of riding mowers, push mowers, rakes, pruners. He turned off his light and backed out, closing the door quietly.

He went out to the road, but the horizon was far away and straight as a board. The road was a pale, ghostly blur in the dark landscape, slightly lighter than its surroundings. There was no car within viewing distance.

He retraced his steps down the driveway and went on to the barn, feeling more at ease. The killer, he felt, had not reached the Mendel farm, unless he had parked on the section road beyond the field where Blue Bonnet was barking.

Mel went toward the field, the flashlight in his left hand, the gun in his right.

CELIA STOOD at the edge of the swamp looking into the black, mirrored surface of the water. Moonlight glistened across it, and something moved within, causing tiny ripples, an unsteadiness that broke the moonlight into lines. She stood cold and paralyzed with fear. She wanted to run away but knew she never could. She heard the distant sounds of death, the cry of a bird caught, the scream of a panther. The howl of dogs in terrible pain, echoing far away, somewhere in the blackness of the swamp where the moonlight couldn't penetrate.

The water at her feet bulged upward, the black, glassy surface rising in a round ball. Eyes stared at her, bulging from the black ball. Not frogs' eyes. Not even the eyes of a gator.

She tried to scream, to back away. It was not the water rising but *him*, coming toward her, the head with the bulging eyes attached to the creeping tentacles that slid swiftly through the grass toward her. Long, black, slimy tentacles.

She turned and ran, yet even as she ran she could see it rising from the swamp, rising onto its long tentacles. Like a man that had no body, nothing but a head and eyes, it came on arms and legs toward her over the grass, towering over her, its shadow falling across her even as she ran.

Celia woke, twisting in terror in her bed, cold yet wet, like the swamp she could not escape.

She heard the cry of the wind as she began to remember where she was. In a house in Nebraska, on a farm, with miles of flat fields reaching in all directions. She slept in a twin bed across a small room from Jonie. As she sat up, listening, she thought she heard Jonie breathing.

She had left the door open so she could hear the boys if they needed her in the night. Their room was next to hers and Jonie's, and she remembered that in it a window opened onto the roof of the back porch. And on that porch a trellis reached from the ground to the roof, a vine with white flowers twining from board to board.

She sat trembling, listening, knowing she was not by the swamp yet not able yet to pull herself completely out of the dream.

She could smell the fetid odors of the swamp. The stale water that scarcely moved, the green slime that grew within it, the mosses, the dead fish, the dead bodies of other creatures—of dogs and of Kent... and of Durk.

She could smell it, and knew at last in inexpressible horror that it was not in the dream.

It was here, in the house somewhere. In the hall, in the room, concealed in the darkness.

The darkness.

There had been a nightlight in the hall. When she went to bed, the nightlight had cast a soft glow along the hall and into the bedrooms. But there was no light now.

She could hear something that wasn't caused by the wind. Something slid along wood, coiling along the banister rising from below, coming up the stairs. A stealthy movement. A constant movement, like a snake, a hundred snakes, writhing along an uncarpeted floor.

Celia pushed her blanket back softly and put her feet onto the braided rug between her bed and Jonie's. She moved cautiously to the door and looked out into the hall.

It was on the stairs. The bulblike head was black against the darkness, a deeper globe of black in a house filled with shadow. She could see its movements, so slow at this moment, as if it saw her and hesitated, gloating, and she saw the sweep of its long tentacles as it reached toward the top of the stairs.

The silence in the house told her it had already found Cora and Lorne and Mel. Somewhere in the house it had found them, and it was coming for her and her children.

Her bare feet silent on the polished pine floor, she whirled back to the bed where Jonie slept and pulled her up. The girl came in silence, yielding to Celia's pull. With the slender arm firm in Celia's hand, they ran out into the hall and into the room where the boys slept.

She pulled the bedroom door shut, hearing its slam. Noise didn't matter now.

Drew cried out briefly, a cry of fear. Celia jerked his bed toward her, blocking the door with it.

"Get Blair up, Jonie," she ordered. "Open the window over the porch."

"Where're we going?" Blair demanded. "Where's Mel?"

"Mama ..." Drew cried.

"Hush! *Move!*"

She heard the window squeak open. In the darkness of Drew's bed she reached for him, her arm around his waist.

"Hang on, Drew. Climb down over the roof, Jonie. At the left end is a trellis. Climb down. Hurry! He's coming!"

Jonie said nothing. For a moment she and Blair were visible at the window, crawling through. Celia followed them, Drew in her arm, his arms around her neck.

"Mama," Drew wailed, "my teddy bear. I want my teddy bear!"

"Hush!"

She went through the window, scraping her back painfully to keep Drew close to her, to protect his head from the top of the window.

When she climbed out onto the sloping roof of the porch she saw Jonie going over the edge, Blair following.

She slipped and fell, the roof steeper than she had hoped it would be, but her hand clawed for a shingle and held, stopping their fall. Drew gasped in her ear, but didn't cry out.

She found the trellis and began to climb down, Drew clinging so hard to her neck she felt choked.

At the bottom Jonie and Blair waited. Still carrying Drew, Celia clasped Blair's hand.

"I don't want to leave my daddy," Blair sobbed, and she thought briefly, What a strange thing to say. Then the thought was lost in the urgency of getting away.

"Run," she said. "Down to the road. Run Jonie, Blair!"

They ran in the darkness of the driveway where the trees shadowed the road. Somewhere behind them, sounding far away, the dog barked steadily. But not at them.

They reached the road and Celia guided them west. She chose the west without thought, only instinct guiding her, because that was where they had been going. Somewhere west, where they would be safe.

CHAPTER 30

CORA LISTENED, her attention drawn back into the center of the house. The muffled barking of the dog ebbed and waned through the crying, whining wind. But somewhere within the house an unexpected sound came, a movement, almost felt rather than heard.

She had been standing at the kitchen door for so long, hours it seemed, watching out the glass in the door, watching for the flash of a light to indicate that Lorne and Mel were coming back into the house. Her attention was directed outside, not in. Then came the unexpected and startling noise from somewhere in the house, and she whirled.

She listened hard. It had been a footstep, a creak on the stairs. Not the step of a small bare foot, but the step of a man.

Frowning thoughtfully she went into the hall and looked up the stairs.

The light in the upstairs hallway had been turned off, and the darkness overhead seemed to loom down at her, filled with dangers that caused her skin to ice over and draw tight around her.

"Lorne?" she called out. Hearing the sound of her voice in the house she wished she could call it back.

No one answered her. Wind howled suddenly somewhere overhead, as if it had found an entry place unexpected and unfound before.

She started up the stairs, her hand sliding along the wall to the switch and turning the light on.

She stopped, staring upward.

The man stood at the top of the stairs. He was like a giant above her, as blond as the Swedish men who lived in the north, but with a cruel slit to his eyes that caught her as if she had been physically trapped.

He stood still, looking toward her. She noticed the way he was dressed, in tight blue jeans and a stained shirt open low on his chest. He wore a tiny gold earring, almost invisible, in his left ear. There was a dirty scarf or rag, once white, tied around his neck.

For a moment, during which she felt paralyzed with shock, she stood staring up at him.

Then she moved, whirling, thinking only of getting out of the house and going for Lorne and Mel. Celia and the children were upstairs, helpless, needing help.

Unless he had already found them.

She ran, her hand finding the newel post, using it to keep her balance. Behind her heavy steps thundered on the stairs.

She felt his hand clutch the back of her blouse and heard it rip. With the ripping of her blouse she tried to scream, one single cry, for Lorne.

Before she reached the kitchen door his hand closed around her neck. She felt herself being jerked back, as helpless as a rag doll. She tried to whirl, to use her hands against him, but she was choking. Pain radiated from her neck into her head and down into her chest. She couldn't breathe. She writhed helplessly in his hands, and the bright light of the kitchen faded away.

LORNE STOPPED, listening. He had gone out into the middle of the field, Blue Bonnet roaming several yards ahead of him all the way. At last aware that she was barking at something on the road beyond the field, or perhaps in the far reaches of the corn, he had turned back.

Blue Bonnet would come home soon. She had never been a wanderer. Her behavior worried him because it was so unusual. She obviously sensed something that didn't belong out there, but Lorne had to return to the house. He would take his pickup, he decided, and drive around the section. It just might be a strange car over there that caused Blue Bonnet's behavior.

He kept his flashlight off, going straight back to the house. He had reached the barn when he heard the scream.

It sounded far away, muffled, brief.

A scream choked off.

Cora!

Her cry stopped him, and then he was running as fast as he could, his feet pounding on the grass and along the walk to the kitchen door. He ran with his heart feeling as if it would burst.

Cora, he thought. Cora. *His Cora.*

He burst through the kitchen door. It bounced back against the wall and swung halfway closed again.

He tried to call her name, but his breath wheezed uselessly in his throat. His chest hurt, a sharp pain radiating from shoulder to shoulder. Panic seized him.

He went toward the open door into the hall and almost fell, his hand sliding along the wall beneath the staircase.

She lay on the floor, twisted, her head awry as if her neck had been broken.

"Cora ..." Dryness rasped in his throat in his attempt to call her name. He fell onto his knees and gathered her limp body up into his arms.

Her pale skin was livid, almost purple, and her open eyes bulged. He cradled her, rocking, weeping, trying to talk to her. He wanted to tell her about the surprise trip he had planned, the tickets he had purchased. For her birthday they were going to take off, leave the farm and animals in the care of his brother; they were taking a trip around the world. He was going to surprise her and get on an airplane, and fly with her to the West Coast, then to Hawaii, where they would spend a week on a cruise ship sailing around the islands. Then they were going on to Hong Kong. The whole world ... they were going to see the whole world. He had been planning this trip for five years, saving and planning.

He wanted to tell her now. The tickets were bought and the tour was ready to leave the first day of July.

He held her, and tears poured from his eyes. Then he remembered they now had an emergency number, and someone might be able to help.

He placed her gently on the floor and ran, half stumbling, toward the door to the office.

He never knew where the arm came from that encircled his neck. He didn't see or hear anyone.

One thought entered his mind as he felt the breath slowly choked from him. He was glad, glad he wouldn't have to face life without Cora. He yielded almost willingly to the pressure that was taking his life.

• • •

MEL STOOD NEAR THE BARN. His eyes had adjusted to the thin, dim light of the stars, and he saw the outline of buildings dark against their background.

The dog was still out in the field, perhaps even farther away. Her bark came steadily, blending with the cry of the wind through every crevice it could find, through every blade of corn and every tree.

He wanted to go out and see what she was concerned about. He had a growing feeling it might be a strange car. In the moments when she stopped barking he could almost see her with her nose to the ground, trying to find the footsteps that might be there somewhere in the field.

But he had to return to the house and tell Cora and make sure again she was taking precautions to keep the doors and windows locked. Also, he needed to find Lorne.

While he was still several yards from the house he saw the back door was standing open. Light from the kitchen made a bright, dwindling path across the open back porch and out onto the grass. No one stood in the doorway, or on the cement porch.

He stopped for a brief moment to assess the scene, then he was running, the gun in his right hand cocked and lifted.

He paused at the kitchen door to look from one end of the long room to the other. Cora was not there, nor Lorne. The room had an empty, deserted look, as if the owners had moved away, leaving everything behind. The mantel clock ticked hollowly. The window pane rattled with a fine, tinkling sound from a sudden gust of wind.

Walking quietly and cautiously, Mel crossed the kitchen to the hallway door.

The hall was lighted from somewhere above. Their bodies were in the shadows beneath the stairs, carefully placed side by side. Lorne and Cora.

A glance at them revealed they had been strangled. Strong hands around their throats. Neither of them had stood a chance. They looked as if they had scarcely struggled.

With his back flattened against the wall, Mel slid to the branch in the hall. The side door was still closed. The light was coming from the second floor hallway.

God.

It was a silent cry in his throat.

He went up the stairs, watching behind and above, moving along the wall. When he reached the second floor hallway he went past the master bedroom at the head of the stairs, past the bathroom and his own room.

He turned, keeping his gun leveled toward the dark rooms, and came at last to the room Celia and Jonie shared.

The door stood open. He moved slowly into it, sliding the flashlight into his pocket to free one hand, pushing the door wide. Light from the hall fixture showed him two empty beds, covers thrown back.

He moved quickly on to the boys' room. The door was closed, blocked by something that yielded when he shoved. He entered, pushing the door back.

Those beds, too, were empty.

He was turning to go back out into the hall when he noticed the open window. The curtains there blew inward with the wind, like banners flying. He looked out the window and saw the slope of the roof and the top of a trellis.

A surge of relief weakened him almost to the point of collapse. They had heard the killer, he hoped to God, and they had gone out the window.

They were somewhere out there. Possibly on the road.

He closed the bedroom door softly, crossed the bedroom in the dark, and slid through the window. He had to find them. He couldn't help Cora or Lorne, but he might be able to help Celia and the kids.

He climbed out onto the roof and crouched, listening for any sound, watching for movements below in the yard, trying to figure out what might have happened. He didn't think the killer had reached Celia and the kids. The blocked door indicated she must have heard him. Perhaps he was still in the house searching the rooms for her.

He climbed back through the window and moved quietly back to the hallway. He listened for the sound of a step, the sound of a breath, thinking of his own stupidity for not turning out the hall light. The killer had an advantage of darkened rooms and half-open doors onto the lighted hall.

He moved back toward the top of the stairs and the light switch, the solid stock of the revolver steady in his right hand, his thumb on the hammer, his finger lightly touching the trigger, ready to pull it in less than a breath. The killer was using his hands, which meant, Mel hoped, he was not carrying a gun.

With the hall darkened, Mel went to the master bedroom and turned on the light. The room was empty. He moved on to the next room, looking into the bathroom and the linen closet with a growing suspicion the house was empty. The killer had probably gone out the back door even before

Mel had returned to the backyard. Now he was somewhere out in the darkness with Celia and the kids.

He ran down the stairs, flashed his light briefly into the office, the front parlor, the dining room, then ran out of the house, leaving lights on, doors open.

He opened the car door on the passenger side and slid across to the steering wheel. He stuck the revolver barrel down between his legs, dug the car keys out of his pocket, and started the car. His one brief thought that the killer might have demobilized his car was dispelled in a long breath of thanksgiving as he felt the response of the engine.

He backed fast out of the driveway and into the road, the car roaring with speed, gravel flying from beneath the tires. In the road he turned on the lights. Instinct told him they would go west, not east. They would run from the direction they had come.

He had driven a hundred yards before it occurred to him that the lights would scare them. They would hide from car lights, from any light, from anyone coming after them. He turned off the lights and drove straight ahead, blinded for a minute by the sudden dark.

As he drove, starlight showed him the lighter color that was the road. He lowered the speed, slowing almost to a crawl so he could watch both sides of the road. The cornfield looked like a black sea under a starlighted sky. It smoothed away to distant horizons, its dim ripples lost.

How much time had passed since Celia and the children climbed out of the window and down the trellis? Only minutes, possibly. They couldn't have gotten to the end of the section road. He would drive around the section once, and if he didn't find them, he would head for the nearest police station.

NEEDLELIKE GRAVEL in the road pierced the bottoms of Blair's bare feet. Air trying to get in and out of his throat made his chest hurt. He ran, keeping up with the shadows of his mother and Jonie. His mother's shadow looked swollen, with two heads bobbing on the ground in front of Blair's flying feet. She was carrying Drew, he thought, because Drew was too short and fat to run very fast.

Where are we going? he wanted to scream at his mother, but his voice rasped in and out painfully, leaving no room for questions he wanted to ask. *Why are we leaving Mel?*

Why are we leaving my daddy Mel?

Tears tickled and burned his cheeks, and he flung up an arm to wipe them away.

"Hurry!" his mother gasped, and threw a look over her shoulder. "Jonie, get Blair. Get out of the road!"

Jonie whirled back and grabbed Blair's arm before he could throw it behind his back. He didn't have enough breath to voice an objection. Jonie jerked him toward the cornfield. Thin, sharp leaves sliced the tender part of his neck and made it sting. He saw a car light dance ahead of them as they ran into the field. Then suddenly it was gone again.

He found breath and yelled, "No! It's my daddy coming after us!" He bit his lip. Don't. Don't call him that out loud.

Nobody answered him. Didn't they know the sound of the car? It was Mel's station wagon. Didn't they know it was his daddy Mel?

Blair looked back just before someone pulled him down into the darkness of the whispering, stinging corn leaves. Jonie's hand clamped over his mouth. Blair struggled and tried to bite it, and Jonie squealed softly and let him go.

Blair stood up and ran back toward the road and the long brown station wagon that was about to pass them by and leave them behind. The car lights were out, and the car looked like a ghost. But he could see it.

His mother's voice followed him. "Blair! Come back!"

But Blair ran, into the road and in front of the car.

SUDDENLY IN THE road ahead of the car a small figure moved. Mel slammed on the brakes and jerked the car toward the ditch. He heard a soft thud and felt a sickening wrench in his stomach, fearing that he had killed one of the kids. From the cornfield to his left Celia and Jonie screamed.

Mel flung open his car door and started to get out, then a small ghostly figure materialized and leaped into his arms. It was Blair. His chest heaved as he gasped, and Mel thought he heard the words, *My Daddy,* but they were as soft as the whisper of the corn. Mel hugged him. Thank the Lord he wasn't hurt.

Mel turned on the car lights. Blair crawled over the seat into the back, then turned and grinned.

Celia came running to Mel, and to his utter surprise threw herself against him. For one brief moment he felt her tight hug and her teary face as she pressed it against his neck. Then she was pushing Drew and Jonie into the backseat of the car.

Their faces looked as white as the pajamas Jonie wore. Terrified, pale faces, eyes large and round. He had felt the cold sweat that bathed Blair, and had seen his willingness to throw himself into the path of a car in order to escape. A rage filled him. If it weren't for Celia, for Blair, Drew, and Jonie, he would go back to the farm and he would hunt for the bastard until he found him. And then he would kill him slowly, as he must have done his own victims—make him pay. He would never face a judge other than himself, and there would be no comfortable jail cell, no long years of appeals.

Whoever he was.

With everyone safely in the car, Mel locked the doors as he pushed the accelerator to the floor. Gravel spun again beneath the wheels. The road ahead was straight and wide, and he intended to follow it until he found a town, a county seat, and a sheriff's department.

He slowed at the intersection and looked carefully in all three directions. There were no stop signs on these country roads.

He looked back and saw the three heads of the children, alert, watchful. Celia, in the front passenger seat, huddled against the door, looking out. No one had spoken a word since Blair had stopped him.

He drove straight ahead. A few miles on he saw the lights of a town, and when he came to a paved road he followed it, though it turned right.

The town was small, as most of the towns in this area were, and nothing moved. Street lights shone down on silent streets, through trees that lined each street, into yards of darkened houses.

He slowed, found a town square, and saw a sign on a brick building that claimed it was the police station. He drove up to it and stopped the car.

It too looked as if it were closed. The double doors at the front were closed.

"What are you doing?" Celia cried in a hoarse whisper, leaning forward against the dash. "Why are you stopping here? Don't stop here! Please, Mel, don't stop here!"

"Celia, you need help."

"Please! Not here!"

Her hand suddenly and tightly clutched his arm.

"The police," he said, in an attempt to explain that her best chances now seemed to lie with them.

"No," she whispered, and he saw her face, tears gathering in her eyes. "You don't understand. Please Mel, don't leave us here."

"I wasn't going to leave you ..." The damned place was closed anyway.

He pulled the car away from the curb. Celia slumped in her seat. She looked so small and so helpless that Mel felt he wouldn't be able to turn her over to the police, not now, maybe not ever.

He looked back and saw the children were still sitting up. He needed to talk to Celia, but he didn't want the children to hear. Yet how was he going to avoid it?

"Lie down, kids," he said. "Cover up, go to sleep. We're heading west."

He drove around the square and found the highway again. In the back the kids had obeyed him instantly, their heads disappearing into the darkness of the car.

He drove in silence for the next hour, finding the interstate west and joining the long-haul trucks that moved continually along the highway.

"Celia," he said softly, wondering if she had gone to sleep, hoping she had. If she were sleeping he could talk to her another time.

She moved and looked toward him. He saw her large eyes wide open, her tapered pale face framed by her dark hair and the blanket held to her chin.

He said, "You know you're wanted by the police, don't you?"

"What for?" she cried.

He knew then that her fear of being left with the police wasn't what he had thought it was. She wasn't afraid of being arrested for the murder of her husband.

"Murder," he said.

"Of Durk?" she asked, her voice holding an almost humorous sound of disbelief.

"Yes. His body was found in the swamp. What was left of it. Evidently the gators and fish had pretty much eaten it."

She turned her face away, looking straight ahead.

Mel tried to keep his eyes on both her and the traffic. He wanted to see the expression on her face, if he could. Only in that way did he feel he might understand. She was not very communicative. She hadn't opened up to him at all, in view of the recent discoveries, and he wanted to know if that was because she had murdered her husband and was using the Underground Railroad as an escape from the law rather than from her husband.

She seemed aware of his attempt to read her expression, and turned her face toward the window. He could now see only the curve of her cheek.

Mel said, "There were three bullets holes in his skull."

To his surprise, Celia's face jerked toward him. Her eyes were large and round. As she stared at him a frown settled between her brows.

"Bullets?"

"You knew all the time that Nolan was dead, didn't you, Celia?" Don't be taken in, he warned himself, by that look of innocent surprise on her face. She was probably a killer. And there were a lot of things that didn't make sense. He had to find out what she knew.

She continued to stare frowning at him, then she looked away without answering.

Mel said, keeping his voice low and gentle, "I know you were badly abused by your husband, and so were your kids, or Norma would not have tried to help you. But you haven't been telling us the truth, Celia. I want to know what the hell is going on."

She swallowed with difficulty. A surge of protective sympathy gripped him, causing him an emotional pain he thought he would never feel for anyone after Crescent's death. He forced it back and waited. But Celia said nothing.

Mel went on, "Durk Nolan was shot three times in the head, and his body weighted with junk iron and pushed into the swamp. It happened a week or two before we started this trip. But somebody is following us and killing everyone who has tried to help you or who gets in his way in his search for you. So who the hell is it, Celia?"

Two large tears rolled down her cheeks. She lifted her left hand and wiped them away.

"I'm sorry," she whispered. "I didn't think ... I thought he only wanted to kill me and my kids."

"Who? Who the hell are you talking about?"

"You just wouldn't understand," she said. "Nobody ... could ever understand. I tried to tell Norma, but I think she only thought I was crazy."

"You know I'm going to have to turn you over to the police. I don't want to, but you'll have to explain all this, Celia."

"No! *No!*" For just a moment she clutched his arm, then she released him and pulled the blanket tightly up beneath her chin. Her voice was muffled. "I didn't shoot Durk. I was going to. He had come back after the court told him to stay away. Kent had come to see us, just visiting, that was all. And Durk held a gun on him and made him walk down to the swamp. I heard shots. I knew he killed Kent and then drove Kent's car into the woods or the swamp. It must have been Kent's body they found."

"Kent?" Mel was shocked at the sense of relief that surged through him. Celia had not killed her husband. He wanted desperately to believe her.

"Yes. Kent was the handyman from the shelter where we stayed. But then Durk wouldn't leave, and we had no way to let anyone know he was there. He stayed two days, and in the night he went to Jonie's room and ... hurt her. So I took his gun from beneath the pillow and made him go down to the swamp. I was going to shoot him, but he knocked the gun out of my hands. He was going to kill me, but Flint came back. It's true I rolled Durk's body into the swamp. It's there. But I didn't kill him. Flint did."

She looked at him and must have read the confusion that was suddenly muddling his brain. It had been simple, just for a moment, when a mysterious Kent was the murder victim. But now ...

"Flint was my dog," she explained softly. "A large black Doberman. Before we first ran away and went to the shelter, Flint attacked Durk because he threw Drew against the wall, so Durk killed Flint. Then the night I was going to shoot Durk, and he knocked the gun out of my hands, Flint leaped up out of the swamp. He killed Durk. Tore his neck open. Durk shot at him, but bullets couldn't hurt Flint anymore. He was already dead."

"A dead dog, Celia?"

"See? You don't believe me. I knew you wouldn't."

"I can see that you were tricked, Celia. Nolan is not dead. He's been following us, killing whoever—"

"Yes, he's following. And he killed the Merrows, Norma, and the Mendels, and maybe others. And I'm so sorry. If I had known, I ... I would have left my kids in a safe place and gone back. It's me he wants." Mel heard a tone in her voice he didn't like. An acceptance of her fate, a giving in to a killer husband.

"Well, he's not getting you, Celia. Not as long as I'm alive. It was a guy named Kent whose body was found. And Nolan is the killer. Somehow he has managed to track us, at least as far as the Mendels. I understand now."

"No, you don't understand," she said. "Durk *the man* is dead. It's the *other* Durk that's after us. He doesn't need a map to find me."

Her voice was almost a whisper, a part of the sound of the tires on the pavement, of the air leaking in shrill whistles around the windows of the car.

The other Durk ... ?

CHAPTER 31

THE LANDSCAPE CHANGED in western Nebraska, from cornfields to sandhills covered with grass and spotted here and there with cattle grazing. In Wyoming the landscape changed again. The breaking of day revealed a far-reaching wildness. Tall, thin buttes on outwardly uninhabited, eroded land could have been the tombstones of ancient gods and goddesses. But Mel knew it was not uninhabited. The broad valleys contained large ranches, and it was to one of those they were going.

Wyoming. The feeling of the West had begun in western Nebraska, in the sandhills. The highway seemed less inhabited, as did the land stretching away to the northwest, leading them at last, he prayed, to safety.

The children in the back were still. Occasionally he looked over his shoulder and saw small round bodies beneath blankets. Celia lay as still, but he had a hunch she hadn't slept much. Her face was turned away from him; perhaps she was staring out the window, or, if the angels accompanied them, maybe she did sleep.

A sick feeling stayed with him, dragging his thoughts back to Cora, to Lorne. Back to the Merrows in Tennessee. He hadn't known the Merrows quite as well nor for as long as he had Cora and Lorne, but his heart ached for Robin's loss, for all that had been taken out of her life. He wished he could at least have acknowledged the passing of her parents. When he was free, perhaps he could do something for her, though nothing would make up for the loss.

As for Cora, he knew her face would stay before him like a picture for the rest of his life—the pretty, freckled face, freckled just enough to make her look like a sixteen-year-old just out of the sun. She had loved the children so much, it was a pity she'd never had a houseful of her own. She should now be enjoying several grandchildren, coming for those big Sunday dinners she liked to cook, staying over the weekend, playing with the current new batch of kittens in the barn or feeding the young chicks fresh corn rolled straight off the cob. He could still see her sitting in the midst of her hens, roosters, bantams on an upturned rusty old bucket with a small pile of field corn between her feet, rolling off the hard kernels one by one. The chickens had feeders, always filled, but the corn, straight out of Cora's hand, was a daily treat not only for the chickens but for Cora.

"It's so peaceful there," she had told Mel once, a sad look on her face as she gazed past him. "Out in the backyard, feeding corn to the chickens. They have such happy voices." She glanced at him, smiling. "I'd never allow anyone to kill one of my chickens for the pot. Not one of my chickens. They're like pets. Each hen or rooster has a personality of its own. Just like we do. Lorne calls it a *chickenality.*"

Mel wanted to remember her that way, sitting on the bucket, peeling corn kernels off for the chicks with their special chickenalities. And Lorne, out on his tractor where he wanted to be. Would he have said different tractors have different tractoralities? Each different in its own way, even though it was a piece of machinery? Yes, Lorne was like that.

Mel tried to think ahead, of reaching California and safety. Of getting to the Cooper ranch in Wyoming, where Celia and the kids would be safe while he slept for a few needed hours. Or would they?

The sun rose higher and warmed the car. He was aware of Blair sitting up in the back, and of the gas gauge pushing against the red mark.

Jonie stirred and sat up.

"Good morning," Mel said, and they answered him, voices low and timid. Would their shyness ever leave them, or would they be socially crippled for life because of their early years? "We're going to pull off here in a minute. We're close to Laramie, Wyoming, and just a few miles from the ranch."

"Did he follow us?" Jonie asked at Mel's shoulder. Her voice was soft and shy, as if she wanted only him to hear.

"No. Of that I'm positive. There has been nobody behind us, only a few trucks."

He spotted an exit down into a small shopping center grouped around a gas station and a truck stop. He slowed and drifted into the busy everyday activities at the shopping center. He pulled the car up to one of the gas pumps and turned off the switch.

Celia sat up.

"Take the kids and dress them," he said, tucking money into Celia's hand. "I'll wait here. We can eat out at the ranch. But bring a bag of package foods that can be eaten in the car if we have to."

"Thanks." She looked at the money and folded it tightly into her hand like a child afraid of losing it.

Celia got out of the car, the kids following her. Mel watched as they crossed the parking lot toward the discount store. None of the cars parked near was occupied.

He filled the car with gas, checked the oil and tires, and found them holding up well. In the convenience store he bought several boxes of granola bars for emergencies, and filled up two one-gallon thermoses with ice water.

Lorne's hired man would have gone to the house hours ago to see why Lorne hadn't shown up in the field. He would have found the open back door and the bodies of Cora and Lorne. The police were there now, probably, trying to understand what had happened.

And they would find in the small guest rooms upstairs the suitcases and clothes of Celia, the children, and himself. And Celia's purse would be there, with her false identification, and Mel suddenly wondered if she had written down her destination on something she carried in her purse. If she had, they could not go on to Alturas.

When he returned to the car they were back in their places. The boys wore new jeans and pullover knit shirts. Jonie and Celia wore cotton slacks and blouses. Celia put her hand out to give him back the rest of his money. He closed his fist over her hand and pressed.

"Put it in your pocket."

You might need it, he thought. If something happens to me, you'll at least have a few dollars. But he didn't want to tell her that. He had a feeling it was more than she could stand to hear at this time.

He started the engine, pressed the lock button, and drove to the highway out of town toward the ranch.

"Celia," he said when they had left town and were on the almost deserted two-lane highway out toward the ranch, "What kind of information did you have in your purse?"

"None," she said. "Norma gave me a new driver's license with my new name. She told me the names the kids would have when we reach there. That's all."

"What state was the driver's license issued in, Florida?"

"Yes."

Mel breathed a soft sigh. *Thank God.* "Then we're okay," he said. "You can still go on to Alturas. The police will have found your false ID by now, but it won't matter. You can get another one in Alturas. But I think you really should consider going to the police for help. You and the kids might be safer with them until your husband is caught."

She shook her head and said nothing.

"Well, kids," Mel said, trying to brighten his voice. "Here we are."

"Where?" Blair asked.

Mel laughed a little. He understood Blair's consternation. The narrow road led off into the hilly, treeless land, winding out of sight between two buttes with flat, rocky tops.

"It's the ranch. See the arch there and the sign."

It had come into view when they rounded a bend in the road. A *C* surrounded by an *0*. The brand for the Cooper ranch.

"Cooper ranch," Mel said. "See, they brand their cattle with a *C* and *0*."

"Is that what that is?" Blair asked.

"Yes."

Drew said, "I could see that."

"You couldn't either. Not till Mel told us," Blair answered almost huffily, and Mel thought in sad amusement that it was the first time he had heard even a suggestion of a quarrel among the children.

"I could use a nap," Mel said. "Mr. Cooper will probably take all of you horseback riding this afternoon. He used to run a dude ranch. Our next stop, by the way, is at a real dude ranch in Nevada, and the next stretch will take you on to your new home."

The road curled around another butte, then sloped downward into a valley. Not far away were the horse barns, the corrals, and the ranch house. A weathered board fence stretched around it all.

It had a deserted look that brought a feeling of dread up into Mel's chest. His hands tightened on the wheel instinctively. His eyes searched the treeless area surrounding the ranch house for some signs of activity.

Nothing moved. In a corral behind the barn nearest to the house a saddled horse stood with one leg resting, his head down.

Usually Tom or Thomas Junior would be out somewhere in sight. There were no women living here anymore. Thomas Junior's wife had died years ago, leaving him with two small children, whom he had reared with Granddad's help. Both children were grown now and away at college.

Today the ranch looked completely deserted except for the one horse. A pickup sat behind the house, near the steps up to an open porch. It came into view for a moment when the road curved up close to the fence, but Granddad Cooper, a usually familiar sight coming out the back door to greet guests, was not there.

Mel drove through the gate and along the road. The tires were almost soundless on the packed dirt of the narrow road.

Celia had tensed. He could see from the corner of his eyes that she had leaned forward slightly.

"Mel ..."

He didn't answer. He eased the car slowly along the road by the ranch house, past tumbleweeds that had gathered against the board fence. There was no smoke from a chimney today, no one coming out of the kitchen door, no one near the barn.

The body came in view when the car reached the end of the long porch at the back. A man lay face down, his arms spread wide, his fingers clawed into the ground.

Mel pushed on the brakes just long enough to see that it was Tom Cooper, senior. Granddad, he had wanted to be called by all the children who came by. *Granddad,* who wore his cowboy garbs the way he had fifty years ago, high-heeled boots, tight-legged dungarees, Western shirts, a wide leather belt with his name and his ranch brand in white on the back.

Toward the house Mel saw another body, probably Thomas, lying on the porch.

"Mel!" Celia cried in a rasping whisper. "He's here! He's waiting. Don't go in there." Her hand clutched his arm, holding him as he opened the door, preparing to get out.

He drew back, pulling his leg back into the car, drawing the door shut again. He hadn't turned off the engine. He jerked the steering wheel to the right and narrowly missed the fence as he swung the car around and headed back toward the road.

The bastard! The heartless, humanless killer had reached the ranch ahead of them, and probably lay in wait somewhere in the house or behind a barn or a butte. How had he known? How had he known Celia would be coming to the Cooper ranch?

Norma, he thought. Norma had been carrying the information. Durk Nolan, alive and following, no doubt had the names of all the stops on the way to Alturas.

He gunned the engine. Behind him dust fogged, hiding the house, the landscape of a valley horse ranch.

He said nothing until he reached the highway. Then, pulling out onto the two-lane deserted road, he turned left, away from Laramie, away from the interstate west.

He had a clear field ahead and behind. The road went straight southeast, angling off through a treeless, hilly land. He pushed the accelerator to the floor and held it on seventy until he caught sight of a pickup pulling onto the road from a ranch off to the right. He slowed slightly, then pulled around it and went on, looking sharply at the man.

Not blond, not large, not young middle-aged as Nolan had been described to him, but a whiskered old rancher driving thirty miles an hour to somewhere.

"He has all the information," Mel finally said. "He must have found it on Norma."

Celia said nothing. He glanced over and saw her right hand gripping the armrest. She stared straight down the road. She cast no glance back as he would have expected. He remembered what she had said earlier, when the children were sleeping. He doesn't need a map to find me.

Durk the man is dead. It's the other that's after us.

An eeriness seemed to be riding with them, almost like a ghost hovering over their shoulders. If he was ever going to believe in that kind of thing, this would be the time. That the man had tracked them so successfully was uncanny. But Mel didn't believe in nightmares coming to life, or dead dogs rising to kill.

Celia was right, he didn't understand. He knew only that he had to get them somewhere safe, leave them, and then go hunt for Nolan. Alone. Find him and stop him.

Jonie asked, "Where are we going then?"

"South. Back to my place. He doesn't know where that is. Not even Norma knew where it is."

Jonie was silent a moment, then she said timidly, "I thought you said he was dead."

"The police made a mistake," Mel answered. She was leaning forward, her chin propped closely behind his shoulder. He reached back and gave her a pat on top of the head. "Don't worry, Jonie. I won't let him hurt any of you."

The tires made fine-pitched whistling sounds on the pavement, and wind pierced one window in shrill cries through tiny cracks and openings that only the wind could have found.

He said, "We'll stop in a motel for the night and rest." Mel slowed to the speed limit, following highways leading southeast. His travelings had made him acquainted with the country he crossed now. He knew the routes he would take—limited access interstates through Colorado, Kansas, Oklahoma, Arkansas, and down across the corner of Mississippi, through Alabama, and home to Georgia.

He knew of a motel hidden by trees on the bank of a creek in Oklahoma that they could reach by dark with steady driving. They would stop there and wait.

CHAPTER 32

THEY WERE EXHAUSTED, Mel knew, and he wished he could cradle them all in his arms forever, hold them, comfort them, and help them live in peace. They had been damned good kids. Not a word of complaint. Drew had waited so long for a bathroom that he had almost wet his pants before Mel found a rest stop and pulled into it and helped the little boy out of the back window of the wagon.

He hadn't rushed them. After taking Drew and Blair into the restrooms and seeing to it they were alone and safe, he left again to stand outside the door.

He watched the road, and he saw what he was looking for. A dusty, dirty blue Oldsmobile went by, but it stayed just enough out of sight behind other cars that Mel could not see the driver. He had no doubt it was Nolan, though, obsessed in his hatred and his irrational anger at a woman who dared defy him. The car slowed as if to exit into the rest stop, then accelerated and sped by. Somewhere along the road Durk Nolan would pull off and let them pass.

How he had gotten this far with a car that must have been described to police puzzled Mel. Then, so tired he knew he wasn't thinking straight, he thought again. Who would have described it? Not Norma. It was part of an illegal system that changed the serial numbers on cars to be resold.

He was no longer sure of anything. As heat waves shimmered over the four-lane highway he no longer was sure he had even seen a blue Oldsmobile.

From the secret compartment he took one of the amphetamine pills he saved for emergencies, and washed it down with water from the thermos. As he waited for Celia and the kids he sipped icy water from a cup and found himself reaching into his shirt pocket, where he no longer carried cigarettes. He stared at the pay phone until it blurred, considering whether to call the police and describe the Oldsmobile and have them pick up Nolan. But he knew from his own experience how the police had to work with tied hands so much of the time, how criminals brought in had to be released almost immediately, their rights violated by incarceration. Gall rose bitter in his throat at the thought of crimes and criminals unpunished. And always before him was the face of his daughter, his precious Crescent, lying dead, her hand clenched around the note. *I'm sorry Daddy.* And the stepfather responsible for her suicide living untouched, raising a family of children. He was a model father, the court had declared. The stepdaughter had lied.

No, he wanted to meet Nolan and end it his way.

As they drove on they ate granola bars and potato chips for lunch and for supper, and drank fruit juices from small cans. Dark fell. The landscape had changed again. They were in green farmland once more, with creeks, and trees growing along the edges of the water. The country roads curved gently from farm to farm, small town to small town.

The motel was half hidden in the trees on the bank of a small, fresh-voiced creek. He remembered lying on a hard bed with the window open listening to the trickle of water over tree roots that had been washed clean, over a few stones and rocks uncovered by the water.

It was fully dark when he signed into the motel. He got two adjoining rooms at the far end, where they would have the most privacy.

He unlocked the doors between the rooms.

"Don't open either door," he told Celia when he left them in the room. "I'll be right there, beyond that door, but don't open it unless you have to. If you hear anything there, keep it shut. But don't run, Celia. Wait for me."

He left her standing just inside the door, her large, tired, questioning eyes looking at him. The kids were behind her. As he pulled the door shut he saw Jonie reach for the television knob to turn it on. Good. Maybe it would keep them occupied until they all fell asleep.

He waited on the narrow cement walk in front of the half-dozen motel units until he heard the click of the lock.

From the secret compartment beneath the driver's seat he removed a silencer, and in the shadowed privacy beside the station wagon he fitted it onto the .38. No other occupants had checked in near their rooms, and he prayed it stayed that way. He wanted to avoid attracting attention from anyone but Nolan.

He entered his own room and inspected it briefly. It had no pretensions to being anything other than a place to shower, sleep, watch a little TV, whatever. The bathroom fixtures were clean, and the towels were white and utilitarian, though worn. There was no window in the bathroom, but there was one at the back of the room.

This he unlocked and slid open a couple of inches to make it easy for entry. He let the short, flowered drapery fall back across it.

He went outside. The motel office sat adjacent to the line of motel rooms, which stretched away behind it along the edge of the shallow creek. There was a small forest of trees along the creek and beyond the road. The road itself made a circle into the trees near the last room in the motel. Four other cars sat parked in various places along the road, at their numbered spots. The neon light on the sign at the front of the office glowed a steady *Vacancy*, the No darkened.

The night was silent. They had left the interstate a couple of miles behind, and the noise of traffic was too far away to hear.

He slipped the .38 beneath his belt. From his car he took a flashlight, but didn't turn it on. He went casually down the walk toward the dark grove of trees at the end, where the road made a neat little circle through the trees. But at the last unit he turned toward the creek instead. He wanted to check out the approach to the back of the motel where Celia and the children were staying, and the open window of his own room.

The land sloped sharply down toward the creek, and he stood for a moment listening to the gentle ripple of water on its way to a small river, then a large river, probably the Mississippi, and from there on into the Gulf.

THE ROOM WAS dark except for the light from the television. Celia had quickly cleaned up both boys and put them into bed, and Jonie lay on her stomach watching the moving figures on the lighted TV screen.

Did she dare leave them to take her own shower? Yes, she thought. Mel was next door, just beyond the closed but unlocked door that separated his room from theirs.

She listened at the door briefly, motioning for Jonie to mute the TV. In the silence she heard movement in the room, a single footstep on the floor, the whisper of something else, perhaps the bedclothes. Or maybe Mel was undressing for his own shower.

With a sense of security that she didn't often feel, Celia went back to the small bathroom.

"Can I turn it up now?" Jonie asked.

"Shhh," Celia cautioned from old habit, then nodded.

She closed the bathroom door and began removing her clothes. She laid them carefully over the sink. She might rinse her underwear later, so it would be ready to wear tomorrow night. She had brought only two sets of panties each for herself and Jonie, only one set of outer clothes. For the boys she had bought three pairs of undershorts, simply because they came three in a package. They would have to wear their outer things until ... until ...

She could not plan ahead. She was totally dependent on Mel, and she was sorry, because he didn't deserve all the problems they had brought onto him. But she had no money, nothing. Only a house that she hoped she would never have to see again.

She couldn't take her kids back there. She knew he would be waiting. And he would devour them, slowly and horribly. Now completely reptilian, a thing of the night, he had even less of the quality that might have made him human.

She turned on the shower, let it warm, and stepped into it. The water cascaded down over her head and she turned her face up into it. The sound of the water became her world, closing out for a time the grief, the fear.

"Can we watch?" Blair asked, and Jonie saw they were sitting on the foot of their bed.

"Only if you lie down."

"But we can't see."

"Sure you can." Jonie plumped the thin pillows and adjusted them beneath the heads of the boys. "There. Is that okay?"

"Okay," Drew said. He looked tired. His eyes weren't staying open very well, and Jonie knew he would be asleep soon.

She pulled the sheet up beneath the chins of the boys and kissed them. She was sad they weren't going on to their new home in the mountains in northern California. In Mel's car, before today, back when she had thought they had really gotten away, she had looked at some of the brochures

Norma had put in the suitcase about the area where they would be living. There were tall pine trees, almost like the trees back home, only those trees grew on mountain sides. And there were trails to walk, and huge rocks called boulders to climb on. It would have been nice.

She sat on the foot of the bed she would share with her mother, and with the remote control device in her hand turned the TV low. Over the sound of the voices on the new Elvis show she heard the shower running.

Elvis was singing, and for a moment Jonie became a part of the crowd in the nightclub where Elvis sang, and she was grownup enough to dance, to move with the rhythm of his music.

She saw the door to Mel's room open, but it was a moment before she looked up. Behind her, from the boys in the bed against the wall, came a soft, almost inaudible cry. And it was then Jonie saw it was not Mel who had entered their room.

She stared upward, seeing his head duck as he came through the door as he always had. Moving toward her, his shoulders for a moment blocking the door, his eyes narrowed in those cold slits that meant pain. Terror blocked her movements, froze her voice. Like a craw-dad she backed on her hands and knees as far away as she could.

Durk closed the door into the other room so softly it hardly made a sound.

Then he came toward her, walking between the beds, the narrow space hardly wide enough for him.

CELIA WASHED HER HAIR, allowing herself the luxury of feeling only the warmth of the water, the cleansing rush of it down her body. But she had taken time enough.

When she shut off the shower she heard a noise, a muffled cry. She was so finely attuned to any sound her children made when they were out of her sight that she felt herself stiffen instinctively. She listened and heard nothing more except the sound of voices and music on the television.

Was it only her imagination?

Then abruptly there was movement in the room outside the shower, a sound of stifled cries, of stumbling steps, of scuffling bodies.

She jerked open the bathroom door, her naked body streaming water onto the floor, her hair down in her face, blinding her before she swept it back.

She stared in horror, unable to accept what she saw.

Durk, tall and strong, was standing between the beds, his arm around Jonie's shoulders, his broad hand clasped around her throat. His blond hair caught the TV light and flared above his large, square face. His narrowed, ice blue eyes seemed to reflect fire. His fingers dug into the soft flesh of Jonie's throat as he forced her head back. His eyes stared into Celia's.

Like stone she stood, unable to believe he had not died that night at the swamp. A bandage on his neck, only partly covering a wound, was all that kept her from madness. *It had happened.*

Jonie's eyes bulged, her mouth worked in silence, opening, closing, as she struggled to swallow. The boys were on the bed against the wall, huddled together, staring at their father.

Celia cried out and ran toward him, her hands as clawed as the hand he had on Jonie's neck. She reached for his face, bringing her fingernails down over his cheeks, and felt that he was flesh after all, human. But she wasn't fooled. His flesh was cold and slimy and evil.

MEL WALKED along the creek bank behind the two end rooms of the motel. His own room was darkened, and it was there he wanted Nolan to enter, there where the window was cracked and ready to be pushed aside.

He moved in the darkness along the back of the buildings, near enough to the wall to touch it. On his right the creek gurgled like a happy baby safe in its crib. Down at the end of the motel a car drove in from the highway, its lights outlining for just a flash the window where the soft lights from Celia's room shone through the curtain.

In that brief illumination he saw also the window in his own room, the window that should have been open only two inches.

Now it had been pushed wide, and part of the curtain had been pulled to hang outside against the wall. At that moment he heard a muffled cry in the room occupied by Celia and the kids.

With a single movement he used the flashlight back-handed against Celia's window, shattering the glass, the sound joining with the tinkling of water in the creek.

CELIA'S MIND registered the bursting of the window at the back of the room, but her eyes remained riveted to the reddened furrows in Durk's face. He released Jonie and threw her aside as if she hadn't been his target at all. His eyes narrowed in hatred but looked beyond Celia.

"*Get back, Celia!*" ordered a voice from behind her.

It was Mel. Mel, thank God!

Jonie had fallen to the floor. Celia reached for her and dragged her aside.

The two men met at the foot of the bed and seemed to blend into a blur of bodies. Then Celia heard a muffled *pop, pop, pop.*

The bodies separated slowly, and one of the bodies fell heavily. A hand reaching for support pulled the blanket off the bed behind her.

But Celia was holding Jonie, searching her face for a sign of life. Jonie began to cough. Moisture, tinged pink, appeared at the corner of her mouth, and Celia wiped it away, unable to see Jonie's face through the heavy rush of her own tears of thankfulness.

They could never get away from him, but if it would save her children, she would go back.

She heard the boys crying. It seemed the only sound in the room now. Then she felt a touch on her bare shoulder, and the touch reminded her she was naked and wet from the shower. She looked up.

Mel was looking down at her, his face as blurred in her vision as was Jonie's and the boys'. Then she turned her tear-filled eyes to search the room.

She stared, her vision clearing.

A long body lay on the floor at the foot of the beds, legs spread, feet splayed wide apart.

Celia stood up slowly and went to look down at him.

Durk lay with his open eyes staring upward. They seemed to look straight up at her, the way they had on the edge of the swamp. Blood soaked the front of his shirt, easing slowly out into the material like a flooding river. He was not moving.

"He's dead, Celia," Mel said. "You'll never have to be afraid of him again. He's dead."

Celia stared down. Blood came out of his mouth in a sudden rush, as if he were mocking her. It died away in a reddish black trickle into the dirty bandage around his thick neck. In the corner of the room the boys whimpered. Behind her Mel comforted Jonie. She heard their sounds as she had heard them all their lives—small, frightened animals crying in the corners of the barn, searching for escape. No matter how many times Durk died, it would never be enough.

She remembered herself and thought she should cover her nakedness. Yet she couldn't move. He was dead, but he had been dead before. Mel didn't understand.

She was trembling suddenly, and so weak she couldn't stand. She reached back for the bed and collapsed upon it.

CHAPTER 33

"Are you all right?" Mel asked, bringing the blanket up from the floor and pulling it over Celia's hunched body. He swore to himself. He had come so close to not being in time. He had almost failed Celia and the kids —and himself. Durk must have been waiting behind the motel when he cracked his own window. Instead of setting a trap, Mel had made Celia and the children easy prey.

Celia nodded and rose shakily to her feet.

"Can you get dressed?"

She nodded again.

"We have to get out of here," Mel said. "I'm sorry, but it's back into the car."

After a moment's hesitation, in which she stared down into the shadowy recess where the body lay at the foot of the bed, Celia walked around Durk's spread feet and into the bathroom. Jonie was already across the bed, scrambling toward the door, her hand against her throat. Mel stopped her, took her hand down, and quickly examined her throat. It was bruised, but it would heal.

He gave her a quick hug. "Go on out to the station wagon." He gave her the keys. "Unlock the door; get in." He motioned for the boys and they came, as Jonie had, across the beds. Neither of them looked at the man on the floor. They ran, following Jonie.

Celia came out of the bathroom wearing slacks and shirt, her hair still dripping down her back. She grabbed up the sack that held what few clothes they had and hurried out. Just beyond the door she stopped and looked back.

Mel saw raw, unleashed terror on her face as she looked at her husband, then she turned away, and he heard the car door close softly.

With the .38 in his hand again Mel bent over the body. The man looked enormous on the floor. His hands were twice the size of ordinary hands. He could understand how easily the man strangled his victims. If he had wanted Jonie dead, he could have killed her in the brief time his hand was at her throat.

Mel used his left hand to feel for a pulse in the man's neck, his temple, his wrist. The three bullet holes were directly into the heart. The man was dead, no question about it.

He saw no reason for the terror that had been in Celia's face. It was as if she expected him to rise, to take vengeance on her beyond anything she had experienced before.

With a towel, he wiped fingerprints off the doorknobs, obliterating all evidence of their identities.

The motel manager wouldn't find the body until tomorrow around noon. That gave them several hours.

In the station wagon he removed the silencer from the gun and stuck it into the compartment beneath the seat. He put the gun back into the holster in his boot, took another amphetamine pill from the small package beneath his seat, and washed it down with water from the thermos. The boys were in their places in the back, each with a blanket pulled up to their chins. Jonie sat huddled in the back seat.

Mel gave Celia the towel.

"Maybe the manager won't miss one towel," he said, trying to make his voice light, and failing. Celia said nothing, but she used the towel to dry her hair partially.

Silence filled the car, broken only by the sound of the tires on the pavement as Mel drove back to the interstate and onto the southbound lane.

He sensed when they slept. It was as if he could feel a lessening of the tension. As if he knew within himself their relaxation, their sinking into the oblivion of sleep.

Mel needed sleep too, but first he had to get them far away from the motel.

Then he would find a bus station and send them home.

The motel manager would find the stranger in the rooms that had been rented to a man named Clyde Gorman and his family. The manager hadn't asked how many were staying, or even if there were kids. All he would have when he called the police tomorrow would be a name that couldn't be traced and a license plate number that didn't exist. Mel didn't know if Durk carried any identification, but he doubted very much that he did. However, the blue Oldsmobile would be parked nearby. Eventually it would be traced back to Celia. But by that time she would be at home, and with her husband's body found dead in an Oklahoma motel, she would be cleared of any implication in his death. Also, by then they would have discovered that the body in the swamp belonged to another man.

He was not worried that she would be in trouble.

She stirred beside him and sat up.

"Where are we going?" she asked, her voice only slightly above a whisper.

"Home."

He was aware of an unrelenting tension in her body, a tightening of her reflexes, a scrunching down into herself. He was suddenly and painfully reminded of Crescent the last time he had sent her back to her mother and stepfather. She had tightened into herself, as if to pull a hard crust of protection around her. And still she had been so vulnerable. There was nothing she could do to protect herself.

Only in death had she found true protection. In death she went into the custody of God. Her earthly father had failed her.

But with Celia, Jonie, Blair, and Drew it was different. The man who had harmed them was dead.

Mel had killed before, once, and had suffered from it. A drug dealer, who had turned out to be only nineteen years old, had chosen to shoot it out with him. Then he'd had regrets. This time there was only relief.

"You're safe, Celia," Mel said, keeping his voice down. He wanted the kids to sleep, and sleep soundly. Sleep had restorative powers that nothing else had. "He's dead."

He saw from the corner of his eye the slight shake of her head. He felt it was not meant for him.

"I saw to it myself, Celia. He was dead, shot three times through the heart. His body was growing cold the last time I touched him. You and the kids can go home safely. You're free to sell the place, do whatever you want. We'll tell the police what happened, and that the body they found belonged to another man. You won't have to worry anymore. Not about your husband."

She whispered, "He was cold because he has no warmth. There's no blood in that body. He's not dead. Not the way you think. He'll come back. He'll always come back." She was hunched down into the seat, the blanket pulled up tightly beneath her chin. Her legs were drawn up. She was as folded into herself as she could manage. She stared straight ahead, her eyes only slightly higher than the dash.

Mel felt a strange chill at her words. His heart went out to this woman who was half crazed by the husband who continued to torment her even in death.

In the east a streak of morning light was showing, like a rainbow after a storm, in hues of rose and blue. The sleepiness he had felt a few miles back had dissipated, leaving him feeling open-eyed and steady. They had passed through Oklahoma City hours ago and were on Interstate 40 near Little Rock, Arkansas. A peculiar and beautiful form of cedar tree grew along the banks at the side of the road. It was the only place in the country that he had seen a tree so perfectly sculptured. He pointed them out to Celia, but she only glanced at them.

With her face still turned away from him she said, "I have to tell you, Mel. I've never told anyone but Norma. And I don't think she believed me." She suddenly looked at him, held him steadily with her eyes, as if it would help her to communicate what she had to say. "The nightmare Drew had. When he said a big octopus was climbing into his window ... ? I don't know when he saw it, but he must have. Maybe the night I took them away, the night I went back to Norma for help. Because it came up out of the swamp. I was standing there watching the water, because I knew, I *knew* he would do as he had said he would. He would rise from the dead, he would turn into this creature ... this ... *thing*."

Mel glanced at her, looking for madness in her eyes. He had seen madness in the eyes of the insane, the inward-reaching of their vision. He had seen the crazed look of people strung-out on drugs, they too having chosen insanity over reality. But the look in Celia's eyes was different. It was the look of terror.

"It'll be okay, Celia. It's over now. You can go home now."

"Please don't take us back there," she pleaded. "Please. He'll rise again from the swamp. Like an octopus or a spider, enlarged a hundred times, a thousand times. I saw it, that last night at home. That was what we were running from. *It was that.*"

"Celia, you were in a state of panic. What you saw could have been shadows, anything. The limbs of trees, maybe. Snakes, maybe, climbing a tree, tangling together, dropping—"

"No! Listen! It came after me, on land. It followed the car. Its shadow covered the car even as I was driving away. It uses its tentacles to strangle its victims. During the day it hides in murky water, where it won't be seen. It was in that Tennessee pond, and came out in the night and was coming into the house for us. Drew must have seen it."

"Good God, Celia! Drew had a nightmare, that's all. That's all it was. A goddamned nightmare!"

"No! It was more than that. He could never have made that up in all his life. I would never have told any of my children about that. It was there in Tennessee. In Nebraska ... I heard it on the stairs. That slithering sound, that reaching of those arms, those feelers. When you hear that sound you never forget it, Mel. I knew that it had gotten Cora and Lorne, and I even thought it had gotten you. There wasn't anything for me to do but get my kids out of that window and down to the ground and try to get away. Don't you see?"

Large tears filled her eyes and rolled down her cheeks. She lifted the blanket and wept into it.

"Celia," Mel said as if he were talking to a child. "The killer is a man. Just a man, a deadly one, but a man. He has followed us every step of the way, deliberately killing everyone who gave you sanctuary. You saw him yourself. Durk. A flesh-and-blood man."

She turned her face away. "You don't believe me." He said nothing. He opened his mouth and tried to bring out words of comfort. Yet he said, "It's important that you see the truth. More important than you might ever know." Good God, what was wrong with her?

"I should have known you wouldn't believe me. Norma didn't either."

"Has he traumatized you so much?" He shifted in the seat, feeling a slight cramp in the calf of his right leg. The .38 felt like it was pressing a permanent hole in his flesh. "Where did you ever get that idea in the first place? From him? When he brought you, a sixteen-year-old kid, to his place, he told you he could change into that slimy thing from the swamp, didn't he?"

"Yes," she whispered, looking out the window toward the cedar trees.

"Don't you see what he was trying to do?"

She glanced back at him. "Sure, I know. I thought so too in the beginning. But then ... that night he came back to the house, I was going to kill him myself. I made him walk down to the swamp. I used his own gun, and I was going to kill him and put his body into the swamp. But he jerked the gun out of my hand. Then, from the water, Flint came. I saw him in the dark, as real as before he died. He attacked Durk. It was Flint who killed him. He ripped his throat out, tore the jugular vein. He bled to death, and I pushed his body into the swamp."

Mel frowned, thinking of the body he had seen on the floor in the motel, remembering the dirty rag around his throat. But at the edge of the rag had been a sign of torn flesh, as of a wound not quite healed. *Something* had attacked him. But he could no more accept a phantom dog than he could a phantom octopus, spider, eel, or whatever from the swamp. It must have been another dog, one that Celia had only thought was Flint.

Celia said, "Durk's blood was all over the ground that night. I stood there watching. The moon was shining. His body got cold then, too. And I went to the barn and got weights and tied them to him and pushed him into the swamp. Every night I went down there to make sure he was still in the swamp. Only I couldn't see anything because the water was so dark."

He said nothing. Let her talk. Try to understand how she thought, whether she might be a danger to her own kids.

"Then, on the seventh night, I went to the swamp, just as I had every night, and this long, black, tentacle coiled around my ankle. I got away and ran, but it came after me. Just as he said it would." Her voice had grown more hushed. When she glanced back toward the sleeping kids he understood. She didn't want them to hear.

She turned her face away and was silent. Mel drove, both hands on the wheel. His arms began to ache, and it occurred to him that he was clutching the wheel so tightly the strain was working up into his shoulders. He made an effort to relax.

"The kids would have seen it then, Celia," Mel suggested, sorrow in his voice. What had he expected they could do for Celia? Just move her and wipe away all past terrors?

"They didn't see anything. I took them out the back door. I made them get down in the car and stay down. When I drove away it had caught up with us. But the kids didn't see it. I drove away. I guess it stayed in the woods, I don't know. During the day it would hide, you see, in whatever body of water it could find. Like the pond at the Merrows' or the irrigation ditches at the Mendels'."

He drove in silence, wondering what to do. He couldn't just dump them off at home with Celia in her condition.

He had to try to make her see she was plagued by fear, that she suffered from delusions.

"Then who, Celia, was that man in the motel? The man in your room, fighting you? The man I killed?"

After a long pause she said, "Durk."

"Don't you see, Celia? You thought he was dead. I'm sure he must have been attacked by one of the dogs. Maybe one had gotten loose and had gone wild. And you probably put his body into the swamp—"

"I did!"

"And he let you think he was dead. But he untied himself and got out. He would have no problem swimming beneath the water, would he?"

She finally admitted, "No."

"He got out and he watched you, night and day. And finally, you alone there with the kids, thinking of that monster he had put into your mind, you thought you saw it. Maybe he was dressed in a wet suit or something. Anyway, he wasn't dead. He managed to follow you every step of the way. He got ahead of us in Wyoming deliberately, probably got the information from Norma. Don't you see?"

"I can see how it might seem that way."

"Celia, if you ... if we had taken the time to look around the motel, we would have found your car. I saw it myself when we were at the rest stop before we stopped in the motel. It went by, I was sure it was him. I figured he would find us at the motel. My only mistake was I thought he'd wait later than he did. I didn't intend for him to get into your room."

He drove in silence for awhile. Traffic was picking up. Little Rock would soon be behind them, and Memphis wasn't far away. Then, across the top corner of Mississippi, down through Alabama, and home in the southwest corner of Georgia. Lord, he'd never been so glad to be headed home.

"Mel," Celia said, "please don't make me go home." No, he thought. He would have to take her somewhere else. With help, a mental hospital somewhere. Maybe she'd only have to stay a few months. Meantime, the kids could stay with him.

It was about time he took leave from the Underground. Now that

Norma was gone, he'd drop out too. The kids needed a place to stay, a chance to go to school. Someplace safe while they waited for their mother.

"We'll go to my home," he promised her. "I have ten acres, and some ducks and a couple of dogs. The house has only two bedrooms, but we'll manage. I can put a bunk bed or a trundle bed in my room for the boys." When Celia buried her face in her blanket and began to sob in silence, he reached over and put his hand gently on the back of her head.

"It's okay, Celia. We'll figure it out somehow."

CHAPTER 34

Mel was beginning to feel as if he had never slept. Even though he had taken a ten-minute nap in the afternoon somewhere in Alabama while Celia and the kids did a little more shopping, he felt now as if once he hit his bed he'd never be able to get out of it.

They had crossed the Georgia state line close to an hour ago, and the gates of his driveway were just ahead. The clock on the dash read 12:42 am, and he had been driving in silence for the past two hours, the kids asleep in the back, Celia asleep in her blanket against the passenger door. Once she had turned and put her head on his arm, then, as if shocked awake, she lifted her head, stared at him wild-eyed for just a couple of seconds, sighed, closed her eyes, and moved back to the corner by the door.

He began to try to figure out where to bed them down. The spare room had twin beds, and that was good. Celia could have one, Jonie the other. One of the boys could share his double bed, and the other could have a bed on the couch. They would sleep and rest a couple of days before he took them in to talk to the police. Then, he hoped, the police could find a doctor for Celia. Meanwhile the kids could be put in his custody until Celia was able to take care of them.

He slowed. The two-lane strip of blacktop he'd been driving on for fifteen minutes had no traffic at all. Pine forest lined each side of the road, breaking only occasionally for a house or driveway. He had passed his neighbor's house a half mile back. There were no lights on in it, but that wasn't surprising. Elvin was an early-to-bed, early-to-rise person.

The gate to his place stood open, and he drove onto the narrow lane through the trees. Pine needles softened the tracks of the road and almost totally silenced the movement of the car.

Celia sat up suddenly.

He saw her looking down the road ahead where the car lights revealed the tree trunks and the winding lane.

"Where are we?" she cried suddenly, alarm in her voice.

"Home," he said.

"Oh no, oh, God, you promised!" She twisted and reached for the door handle. He grabbed her just before she opened it.

"What are you doing?" he demanded. "I told you I was taking you to my home. This is it."

She sat back in the seat, still staring ahead. Then she said, "But it looks, it looks just like the driveway to ... to ..."

Then he understood. Pine forest. It was the pines. Any track through a grove of pine trees would look like almost any other. Sometimes, as in the western mountains, the trees would be taller, larger through the trunk, but still there was a similarity.

"We're almost there. Just a few yards more. See."

The cleared area around his house was almost as dark as the piney woods that surrounded it. What starlight penetrated the open acreage dimmed under the streaks of bright light from the car, creating deep darknesses in the contrasts.

"I have a couple of dogs that always come to meet me ..."

He drove the curving lane from the edge of the pines toward the house. His lights picked up the cedar posts of his front porch and the two doghouses at the side of the house. But there were no dogs coming to meet him, bounding happily down the lane, their barks filling the air.

Where were they?

He eased the car to a stop with the lights still outlining the front porch and the doghouses. Puzzled, he shut off the engine but left the lights burning.

"Their names are ..." *Cress and Butch.* Cress, named after Crescent, because she would have liked that. Butch ...

The dark length of something that didn't belong there became visible. It lay on the ground near the steps of the porch, and Mel stared. The edge of the car lights picked up the dark, torn flesh, the broken body...

He flung himself out of the car and ran, passing through the beams of car lights. He stopped. With his back to the bright lights he now saw Cress. She was lying on the other side of the doghouses, limp, her head thrown back at an awkward angle. He could see the other thing now, the torn and bloody thing by the front steps.

Butch.

He stumbled toward Butch, because he was more in the light. He put one hand down to touch the torn, ripped body of the dog, and felt the flesh still warm. Blood was still oozing from the wounds on Butch's belly.

He straightened, aware of the easy target he made in the lights of the car. He was blinded by the lights, unable to see what in the hell had attacked and killed his dogs just minutes ago.

He ran back to the car and leaned in for a second, reaching at the same time for the flashlight and the gun in his right boot.

"Keep the doors locked!" With his left hand he used a knuckle to press the car lights off. "Don't move out of this car! Whatever you do, don't get out! If I'm not back here in five minutes or less, you start the car and get out of here. Do you hear me? Get out of here if I'm not back in five minutes!"

He had a last glimpse of her white face before the dome light went off as he pushed the lock button and slammed the door shut.

In the dark, blinded by its depth and intensity, he hesitated a moment. Then he pushed the button of the flashlight and followed its beam to the front door of his house.

He tested it and found it still locked. He backed away from the door, swinging the light in an arc around the front yard, taking in the station wagon, seeing for a second Celia's face, and behind her, Jonie's. Both of them were like pale masks behind the closed windows of the car.

Then he swung the light beam onto the body of Cress for just an instant, and saw she had been torn and mutilated too, as Butch had been.

The silence struck him. The shock of finding his dogs killed so viciously, so recently, thundered away, settling in his heart, and he could hear the unusual silence beyond the pounding of his heart.

This time of year when he came home he expected to hear not only the barking of his dogs but the singing of frogs from the ponds, the calling of whippoorwills, of mockingbirds, of jarflies and katydids.

But it was as silent as the coldest winter night.

Whatever had killed his dogs was here. The creatures of the night knew it and were silent, drawn with wariness to keep their silence, to hide within it.

There seemed to be nothing in the front yard except the car, parked twenty-five feet from the porch. The flashlight beam reached the edge of the pond, but he saw no ducks squatting in their feathers at its edge. Had they too been killed?

He headed around the house toward the back door, shining the light out toward the sheds behind the house, into the trees, toward the path over to Elvin Cross's place. The back door was still locked, and he tucked the flashlight into the crook of his arm while he dug out his keys and opened the door. He needed more than the revolver. He needed his shotgun, and it was in a locked gun case in his bedroom.

CELIA SAT STILL, afraid to move, chilled to the marrow of her bones with terror. She was aware that Jonie had awakened, but she prayed the boys were still asleep. She watched the darkness take over as Mel disappeared somewhere behind the house.

She turned her head slowly to see her surroundings, trying to define the black world in which grey shapes were forming.

Starlight created vague, dim light at the front of the house and across the smooth lawn, leaving deep darkness behind the house and in the trees beyond the yard. The front yard sloped gently to a flattened area several yards from the trees, and she stared at that level place, that mirrored surface. A flash of lightning came from somewhere beyond the trees to the west, followed by a low rumble of thunder, and in the greater light she saw the water.

She stared at it, a terrible, hollow feeling in her heart.

Something had killed the dogs. It was waiting for them here, beneath the deceptive surface of the pond. The pond might be a connection to a swamp, dark among the trees, reaching to a distant shore, an ocean with unplumbed depths, like the swamp at her own home, less than a hundred miles away. A swamp perhaps that connected in some way to the swamp near her house. *His* house, never hers. His home.

She twisted in the car seat and looked back at Jonie. Her face was a pale, white blur, suspended in the darkness of the car. Another low flash of lightning made Jonie's face seem hollow-eyed, already dead, the skull containing only the dark halo of hair, the deep sockets where once her bright eyes had been.

"Get down," Celia said in a low, hushed voice. "Lie down and cover yourself with a blanket. I'll be back soon."

"Mama, don't go," Jonie cried in whispered anguish.

"I have to. But I'll be back."

No, she wouldn't be back. It wanted her, and if it had her, perhaps it would leave Jonie, Blair, and Drew alone. Maybe it would be satiated and leave Mel with the children. They needed him.

She opened the door and slid out, then pushed the lock button.

"On no conditions get out of the car," she said. "Unlock it for nothing and no one except Mel."

The pale face stared at her, and then disappeared in silent obedience as Jonie settled down in the seat.

Celia closed the door.

Lights came on in the house and on the porch, streaming out into the yard, turning the short grass a greenish-black. The air felt sultry and heavy, the silence so complete it seemed to buzz in her ears, a soft, insistent sound of silence.

Lightning lit the western sky in a jagged strip, going rapidly one way and then changing course and shooting toward the ground. It seemed close, casting an eerie white light for just an instant over the landscape, touching the treetops and the glassy surface of the pond. The rumble of thunder came belatedly, farther away than the lightning had seemed.

But the surface of the pond was not smooth, Celia saw. One portion of it, out in the center, was stirring. As the swamp water had stirred when something moved just beneath it, the pond water moved.

She stood halfway between the car and the sloping bank. The light from the porch ended several yards back, yet its residue seemed to pass by her and reflect off the pond surface, so that in the darkness where she stood she could see the movement of the water in a straight line from the center toward her.

She couldn't move. She had intended to go forward to the pond, to wade into it and offer herself. But she couldn't move. She was filled with terror. Her heart beat slowly and heavily, vibrating through her veins, shaking her body.

She longed to lift her head, as a dog would have, and howl toward the heavens. *Let it be over. Leave us alone. Stop tormenting us.*

But she recognized her cowardice, her willingness to yield and yet her failure to yield entirely to his command. Her fear had not helped to liberate her. Her hatred had not harmed him, only herself.

She saw it rising from the water, saw its mockery of her, saw the incredible size of it, the black and terrible slime, the round head-body, the long tentacles on which it walked and with which it fed itself. It came toward her to torture her and keep her as its prey. It rose from the water, huge and hideous, and its snake-like feelers reached toward her, coming through the grass with the slithering sound that had caused her to awaken countless nights in the past in nightmare. That slithering sound that preceded his coming home, his suddenly showing up in her bedroom door in the figure of a man laughing at her cringing.

She heard a scream, and then another and another, but it was not coming from her. She recognized the cries of her children and knew they saw it. In a sudden and bright flash of lightning she saw it above her and felt the cold, tight, slithering reach of the tentacles closing around her body, her arms, her legs, her throat. The closing was slow and deliberate, as deliberate as its waiting had been, for its prey had to be warm and alive and struggling.

She had not intended to struggle, to give Durk that satisfaction, but instinct took over and she began to writhe and to fight.

Flint. Flint, help me!

Her fingers clawed at the slippery skin of the tentacles, and she felt it give beneath her fingernails and moisture from it rush out into her palms. She twisted and turned and sought to release herself as she had only partly released herself from the nightmare of its existence.

Then, as if she were standing aside watching, she saw the long, sleek, black body of the dog. It rushed out from the trees, and its growl was deep and distant, mingling with the moan of the thunder. She saw Flint leap and saw his jaws open, the fangs long, white, and sharp flashing in the dark as they sank into the head of the thing from the swamp. She felt the release of its tentacles one by one, and she fell and rolled toward the water of the pond. She pulled herself up at the edge of the water and swayed there on hands and knees, unable to rise.

In front of her the dog fought the Other. Writhing tentacles blended in blackness with the snarling, whipping body of the dog. The white fangs were like flashes of ghosts in a world always without light.

Celia began to crawl away toward the car, toward her children.

MEL WAS OPENING his gun case in the bedroom when he heard the scream of the children. Their voices sounded muffled, at first only a part of the thunder. He struggled with the key in the lock of the gun case, unable to turn it. In his hurry he had jammed it. With no time to lose, he kicked the glass front of the case. Shards of glass sprinkled down onto the floor, catching the light like diamonds. He jerked down the shotgun. From the box of shells he grabbed a handful and ran out. The gun was loaded, always, and ready to fire.

On the front porch he paused, finding himself blinded by the porch light. The area beyond the light was dark and impenetrable for that first moment.

He ran down the steps.

Lightning flashed, and in its brief light he saw the station wagon, frightened faces pressed against the glass, and behind it, pulling herself up at the rear bumper, Celia. He saw her clothing muddied and torn, and her face a sharp white, colorless. Then darkness fell over it all.

The sounds came from near the pond. He recognized the snarling fight of a dog and something else that fought in silence. It was only a sound in the grass as the rolling bodies moved back toward the water.

Jerking his flashlight from his belt, he pushed the on button and directed the light toward whatever it was fighting near the pond.

He saw the lightning-quick body of a large dog, and saw too the reflection of its eyes, red as fiery orbs, for just a second. And then, as he drew closer, adjusting the shotgun against his shoulder, the flashlight held in his left hand on top of the barrel, he stopped, staring.

Disbelief washed over him, leaving him cold and frozen in horror.

Black tentacles from an octopus-like creature larger than any he had ever seen writhed with the body of the dog. But the dog was winning, and the round head-like body rolled beneath it, as if searching for the water in an attempt to escape.

He found his hands trembling on the flashlight, and the shotgun wavering. He steadied it, aiming at the thing beneath the dog, waiting for a shot.

For just an instant the dog leaped back, and Mel fired.

The dog stopped in mid-leap, and then there was silence. The black body with the tentacles coiled upon itself, then lay still.

Mel went toward it slowly, his light shining on it, outlining a mangled horror that made him feel he had somehow entered a nightmare made by another mind he could never understand.

The thing on the ground was torn apart, more from the fangs of the dog than from his shotgun shell. Moisture oozed from its broken tentacles and from its round body. The lidless eyes stared toward a sky that lighted it coldly and from a great distance.

In the silence Mel heard the sound of a chain. He swung the beam of the light toward the sound and saw the large dog trotting away into the pines. It stopped and looked back at Mel and Celia, wagged its tail once, and disappeared. As if the darkness in the forest of pines had swallowed him, he was gone. An eerie howl marked his passing.

Mel turned away from the thing on the ground. Celia was standing halfway between him and the station wagon. The children were quiet.

Mel went toward them. When he reached Celia he put his arm around her waist and led her back to the car.

With the lights still burning in the house, the doors open, Mel helped Celia into the car. He went around to the driver's side and got in.

As he drove away he thought of telling her again, You're safe now. Now. At last. Whatever it was is dead.

But like her, like the children who crouched in silence behind them, he said nothing. No words, it seemed now, were adequate to explain what he still found too incredible to believe. He had seen it lying there, mangled and torn. Killed more by a phantom dog than by the real pellets from a shotgun shell.

Fantasy had met fantasy, and one had destroyed the other.

And yet, how could it be fantasy when he had seen it?

CHAPTER 35

MEL GOT out of his station wagon and stood looking around. The bodies of his dogs were still lying where they had been two nights ago when he had thought he was bringing Celia and the children to a safe place, to his own house and land.

In the bright sunlight flies were beginning to swarm over the bodies, large greenflies. Black and red ants, too, all sizes, had found them. Battles raged over the bodies.

On the pond a few of the ducks swam, keeping to the opposite bank, away from the thing on the near shore. When they saw him they came swimming, their voices loud and insistent, as if telling him of the horror they had seen. But in the middle of the pond they stopped, treading water, their cries filled with trepidation.

Mel went to the house, where the lights still burned, and walked through, turning them out. He went out the back to the shed and got the shovel.

In the soft soil of the piney woods floor he dug a wide grave. Then he took two blankets from the house and one by one he wrapped the bodies of the dogs and carried them back to the grave and laid them safely within. He shoveled dirt over their blanket-wrapped bodies. When he finished tears blurred his eyes.

He reached up and wiped them away. The dogs had been his companions for a long time. If he hadn't seen them again, horribly torn apart, he wouldn't have believed that it had happened. When he drove again down his lane it had been easy for him to think that he had entered a nightmare for awhile, and that now he was waking from it. But the deaths were real.

Carrying the shovel he went around the house and down to the edge of the pond.

It was still lying there, black and torn, its body ripped apart and spread over a ten-foot-square area, its tentacles like pieces of a huge black lizard's tail that could, if not destroyed, regenerate. Torn as it was, it seemed much smaller than it had in the dark two nights ago. It could have been a mutant octopus out of the mysterious depths of the ocean.

With the shovel he dug a hole near the edge of the water, and using the shovel as a rake began to scrape the pieces into the hole.

He noticed an oddity. No insects crawled on it. No flies hovered upon it. It was as if it actually didn't exist, even now, in the natural world.

He thought of Celia and the kids. He had left them at the shelter. They had gone to the police and explained the death of Durk Nolan at the motel in Oklahoma. The police now knew Nolan was the murderer of the Merrows in Tennessee and the Mendels in Nebraska. They knew he had probably killed Norma and the trucker and the girl in the motel in Georgia. Norma Whiting's body was being shipped home to her family.

Celia had explained to them that her husband had shot Kent, whose last name she didn't know, and it was his skeleton they had found in the swamp.

Mel had thought about talking to someone about the thing killed by the dog at the edge of his pond, but he hadn't.

He stood leaning on his shovel for long minutes after the ground was smooth again over the buried carcass. The ducks, braver now, swam toward him.

They wanted feed.

Carrying the shovel, he went back toward the shed and the feed sack.

How empty and lonely it seemed here now.

"I can never go back to my house," Celia had said to him. "Not back there. It's not really my home. It could never be."

He had left her and the kids standing by the sidewalk leading up to the front door of the shelter, where they would be staying until a house in town could be found for them. He had left them, and yet still he carried with him the sight of their faces.

He could still see Blair, who had settled into a special place in his heart. Blair had started to cry when Mel drove away. He covered his face with his hands and turned his back, standing apart from the other three. Mel's heart felt as if it were breaking all over again.

And now he faced something he had not consciously recognized before.

He was lonely without them.

He loved them one and all.

A sound came from the pines, a rattle of a chain and a movement. He looked, his eyes searching the shadows beneath the trees.

The large black Doberman pinscher stood several yards back into the woods. When Mel spotted the dog, he saw the tail wag. And then the dog was gone again, drifting away into the woods, blending with the shadows there.

But Mel had a sudden feeling it would always be there, just beyond touch. It was as if the dog had come home.

Mel took a bucket of grain and carried it back to the duck feeder at the pond.

Birds were singing again today, reaching into his heart and warming it.

And he knew he was going to hurry back to the shelter and bring Celia and the kids home with him.

OTHER RUBY JEAN NOVELS

1974 The House that Samael Built
1974 Seventh All Hallows' Eve
1974 House at River's Bend
1975 The Girl Who Didn't Die
1978 Child of Satan's House
1978 Satan's Sister
1978 Dark Angel
1982 Hear the Children Cry
1982 Such a Good Baby
1983 The Lake
1983 MaMa
1985 Home Sweet Home
1985 Best Friends
1986 Wait and See
1987 Annabelle
1987 Chain Letter
1988 Smoke
1988 House of Illusions
1988 Jump Rope
1989 Pendulum
1989 Death Stone

OTHER RUBY JEAN NOVELS

1990 Vampire Child
1990 Lost and Found
1990 Victoria
1991 Celia
1991 Baby Dolly
1992 The Reckoning
1993 The Living Evil
1994 The Haunting
1995 Night Thunder
Pending Bear Hollow Charlie
Pending Cry of the Soul
Pending Pride of Bella Terra
Pending Animal Backtalk

www.ingramcontent.com/pod-product-compliance
Lightning Source LLC
Chambersburg PA
CBHW020258030826
48979CB00026B/1393/J

* 9 7 8 1 9 5 1 5 8 0 5 0 6 *